Nemo James was born in Camberwell, London in 1952.
He spent 30 years as a professional musician.
Just a few seconds is his first book.

Reviews for *Just A Few Seconds*

I cannot believe it. Crack of dawn and I spent all night turning the pages of 'Just A Few Seconds. 4.12am? Says it all really. A riveting read. A tantalizing cocktail of pathos, drama, suspense, philosophy and humour.
Barrie Tracey – Received Lifetime Achievement Award for services to journalism.

I am not an avid reader of autobiographies but every now and again there is one that comes along and takes you by surprise, one that you don't expect to be as good a read as it is. One such book is Just A Few Seconds. ***Thoroughly recommended*** *and a pleasure to read*
Anthony Lund, Allbooks Review

He is an engaging story teller, and his writing skilfully blends humor and pathos. I Loved the book
Joseph Yurt, ReaderViews.com

I was entertained from the very first page up to the last sentence. I truly enjoyed this book
Valentina, Carabosse's Library

I just finished reading your book and I must tell you how much I have enjoyed it to the point that I felt sorry I was done with it. I really love your sense of humor.
Guillermo Bettocchi PHD – United Nations High Commissioner

"His writing is intelligent, reflecting a deep desire to express his experiences. And his ability to bring to life the daily living of a struggling musician is utterly captivating."
Norm Goldman – Bookpleasures.com

Captivating. Written with an ironic and witty sense of humor. highly recommend.
Douglas R. Cobb – www.bestsellersworld.com

For photographs supporting this book and details of Nemo's music, videos and other news go to www.nemojames.com

Just a Few Seconds

Nemo James

First Printed in February 2011

Nemo James
www.nemojames.com

ISBN 978-0-9567986-0-2
5

Published by
Derek Newark Publishing
Tupina 16
20207 Mlini
Dubrovnik, Croatia
www.dereknewark.com

To Federika

Chapters

1
The End

For whom the bell tolls. A phrase I was familiar with for most of my life but like most phrases, I never stopped to think about what it actually meant. For all I knew it could have referred to the happy church bells of a wedding or the welcome sound in a boxing ring telling you to take a break before receiving further bashing around the head. Maybe the depressing ring of teacher's bell telling you that playtime is over or the pretentious sound of a bicycle bell ordering you to get out the way. It wasn't until my first summer in Croatia that I heard the slow unavoidable sound of the local church bell tolling that I discovered that it usually means someone in the parish has died. From that day on it was hard for me to escape the vision of us all standing in line waiting for the bell to toll for us. Today it is finally my turn.

It's been a good life. Except for Eurovision of course. That was shit. It wasn't the song contest itself I had a problem with and I have to admit I never missed it once I no longer played guitar for a living, it was that every freelance musician in the country lived in fear of another *Congratulations* coming along, not to mention the songs of Abba, Brotherhood of Man and Bucks Fizz. They are great songs but having to play them three times a night for most of your working life it was not surprising so many of my colleagues turned to booze or even suicide.

I wonder how many people will turn out for my funeral? I remember the time there was a queue a 100 metres long which was unheard of in such a tiny village as Mlini. That funeral was for one of the sons of the village who was killed by a drunk driver. I wonder if I get a bigger turnout than him? What am I doing! I spent my whole life competing and here I am doing it in the afterlife. What is wrong with me? This is a new beginning so I must make the most of it. I must learn from my mistakes and move forward. No more competing.

Yes, it's been quite a journey. I failed in nearly everything I did and yet always loved life and ended up enjoying the kind of success that the rich and famous only dream about. All that effort and hard work and yet it was nothing more than blind luck that brought about my success. No amount of talent or hard work can replace luck.

I must say it's a nice day for it. The smell of orange blossom made sweeter by the knowledge that I won't have to pick up the fallen fruit from our garden. The sound of the sea gently kissing the pebbled beach that is slowly emptying as the tourists go back to their hotel to prepare for dinner. How lucky I was to spend my last years here amongst the kindest and most honest people I ever knew. I will miss it all but it's about time I started a new adventure.

The bell is still tolling.

I wonder.

I'm sure I am getting more tolls than usual.

2
A Criminal Fraternity

We all have patterns in our lives that repeat themselves constantly. One of my main patterns became evident when I was only five years old. I was seated in class when the teacher asked each of us to stand up and describe our parents' wedding day. No problem with that. Each child gave the usual account of white dresses, bridesmaids, flowers and wedding cakes.

"And you Derek. How was your parents' wedding day?"

I shot to my feet. It wasn't often I was asked a question I knew the answer to.

"My mum and dad were married in Italy. It was very hot. The priest needed a shave. The church was very big and my mum wore a parachute."

The teacher looked confused even before I continued with my final, shocking revelation:

"After the wedding a policeman took my dad to prison."

She took a few seconds to regain her composure and said:

"I'm sure that can't be right Derek."

I was devastated. At last I had given an answer I knew was correct but no one believed me. Life can be tough for a five year old.

"Honest Miss! That's what happened!"

She moved quickly on to the next child. I felt cheated and couldn't understand why teacher hadn't believed me so that night I told my parents about the incident. My father, who was one of the most honourable men that ever lived, was mortified at the thought of the whole school talking about poor young Derek coming from a criminal fraternity. What I said was true but far from being something to be ashamed of, my father's imprisonment turned out to be one of his greatest moments.

My parents met in Milan where my father was stationed at the end of World War 2. He fell in love with a local girl and they wanted to marry as soon as possible. The British Army was happy to allow its soldiers to marry but permission was being withheld in his regiment by a power hungry captain as every soldier that married and returned to England was one less under his command and he couldn't stand to see his empire crumbling. Totally out of character my father went ahead and married without permission. They were married in a beautiful church in Milan not far from the El Duomo and my mother being a gifted dressmaker made her wedding dress out of an old silk parachute. At the tender age of five it was inconceivable to me that anyone could make a real wedding dress out of a parachute so I naturally assumed that all she had done was cut a hole in the top and worn it over her head like a poncho. As for the priest needing a shave, it was the only thing my father remembered about the ceremony so I figured it must be important. My father was not the most romantic of men.

Shortly after the ceremony finished and photos were taken the Military Police arrived and took my father to prison where he shared a cell with two murderers. When the company commander found out what had happened he was livid and ordered a full inquiry with the outcome being that all the men were free to marry. The hated captain was disgraced and my father became a hero. Until that day in class I honestly believed it was normal that at the end of every wedding the bridegroom was taken to prison. So there you have the main pattern of my life… *nothing* was ever simple for me.

Another incident was in secondary school whilst seated at my first French lesson. Every other year my family drove to Italy to visit our relatives and one problem we always had was getting through France at a time when no one spoke English. My father never understood that French was a different language to Italian or maybe it was just a matter of waving your hands in a different way. It was always my mother who was pushed out the car to ask for directions so I was overjoyed that I was going to learn French. I spent the whole of the first lesson daydreaming about our next trip through France when I would be the family saviour. We would go into restaurants and I would call the waiter over and order in fluent French while my family sat back and watched with amazement and pride. My second lesson took me daydreaming through little French towns, talking and laughing with the locals and bargaining for cheese at market stalls. After three months of this I was devastated one day when the boy next to me stood up in class and spoke a whole sentence in French. I didn't understand a single word and realised it was too late for me to catch up on all that my daydreaming had caused me to miss. During the remainder of my French lessons I returned to my old dreams of being the first man to captain England in football, cricket and fishing.

And there you have the second main pattern of my life; I would forever be at the mercy of my dreams. It is a shame however that dreamers are generally looked down on by society and that there is only one word for two different kinds of dreamer. There are passive dreamers who sit on their backsides and do very little to follow those dreams and there are active dreamers who devote their entire life to following their dreams and if they succeed we all benefit from their perseverance. There is no doubt that during my French lessons I was a passive dreamer but no one reading my story can disagree with my claim to later becoming an active dreamer.

3
Hard Times

I was born in Peckham, South London in 1952 and christened Derek Newark. To be honest, our house was actually in Camberwell but most people have never heard of Camberwell and Peckham sounds much more fun. To be fair, we were so close to the border that a fart at the end of our street in Camberwell could be smelt in Peckham just a few yards away, a claim my mates and I put to the test whenever physically possible.

My exam results were a constant mystery to my parents and teachers as I alternated between top of the class and the bottom. If I was interested in a subject my marks were good unless I sat next to a girl I fancied in which case they were bad. I loved sport and represented my comprehensive school in every team possible, not always because I was good at them but because it was a small school so for the less popular sports anyone able to run in a straight line without falling over was selected. One year our sports master entered a boxing team into the London schoolboy championships and as always I volunteered. I had never even worn boxing gloves let alone boxed so I don't know why the probability of me being bashed around the head for five minutes never occurred to me. I was able to look after myself in the school playground but fighting a trained boxer was much harder than standing up to the school bully. I was only a few seconds into the first round when I was attacked by what felt like a swarm of flying rhinos. The referee stopped the bout after deciding that my spinning around in circles didn't constitute an ability to defend myself. It was a humiliating experience but it only made me determined to learn how to box. I joined a club and became quite a good boxer although I lacked the killer instinct and always felt the need to apologise to my opponent after hitting him.

My favourite sport was cricket and not only did I captain the school team but I also played regularly for London and the occasional game for the South of England. I wanted to become a professional cricketer but every time I mentioned it to someone they laughed so I put the idea out of my head. Every week during winter I went to the Crystal Palace Recreation Centre with my friend John where we were coached by professionals. One day a group of us were sitting in the cafe after practice and the usual subject came up:

"What are you going to do when you leave school?" asked John.

"I'm going to be an electrician," I said.

The only thing that had led me to this momentous decision was I had recently fixed our front door bell and my father was so impressed that he thought I should do it as a career.

"How about you?" I asked John.

"I'm going to be a professional cricketer."

We all fell about laughing and sneered as people do when hearing about the dreams of others, especially when their own have been abandoned. He was a quiet, sensitive boy who was hurt by our mockery. It was many years after we lost touch that I heard the news on the radio:

"On his 36th birthday John Embury has been selected to captain England in the forthcoming Test Series."

At that time he was regarded as the best spin bowler in the world. Maybe I would never have made it as a professional cricketer but that was the last time I let anyone talk me out of a dream.

My biggest passion was fishing. It all started on a family holiday in Devon when my father saw me fishing with a metal coat hanger for a hook and a whole crust of bread as bait. My parents always encouraged me in my many interests and although my father knew nothing about fishing he had a shrewd idea that I wouldn't catch much with a coat hanger so he bought me a little hand line and showed me how to find limpets to use as bait. I sat happily on the rocks for hours without catching anything until I pulled up my line to find a load of seaweed tangled around the hook. As I cleared away the seaweed I screamed with terror when a fish suddenly appeared. No child has ever been as proud of anything as I was of that fish even if it was no bigger than my eight year old hand. When we returned to our tent I refused to carry anything but my fish and swaggered through the campsite like I had a freshly hunted stag on my shoulder.

Fishing when you live in the middle of London is not the easiest sport to pursue. A regular weekend excursion for me in the winter was to go on Saturday morning to the Serpentine Lake in Hyde Park where I caught small roach to use as bait for pike. I returned on a crowded bus with all my fishing gear and a bucket containing several live fish that caused great amusement amongst my fellow passengers. The next day I woke at 5.00 a.m. and gathered a large collection of baggage which included my bucket of fish. After a long walk to the main road there was a 30 minute bus ride to Waterloo Station. From there I had a 45 minute train journey to Hersham in Surrey ending with a three mile walk to a small lake where I sat in the freezing cold until the end of the day when I repeated the process in reverse. One glorious day I actually caught a pike.

Camping played a major role in my childhood and we went every weekend during the summer. I have fond memories of us all playing cards or shove halfpenny by the light of a gas lamp. We had a large, heavy duty tent that was left up the whole summer at Walton Camp Site in Surrey and we used to go there every weekend without fail. The camp had a good social committee that organised events every weekend for the many enthusiastic and friendly campers. There was bingo, barn dances, cricket and football matches, sports tournaments, talent competitions and whatever else came into the minds of the imaginative organisers. Best of all was the River Mole that ran alongside the campsite meaning that fishing was only a few yards away.

One year at the beginning of the summer school holidays we were packing up at the end of a particularly brilliant weekend's camping and I was thoroughly miserable at the thought of going home.

"Can I stay here? I asked, not expecting for a minute my parents would agree to their thirteen year old son staying at the camp site by himself but they made the mistake of hesitating before saying no. I seized on that hesitation like a dog with a bone and pleaded with them to let me stay.

"What will you do all week? You'll soon get fed up with fishing and none of your friends will be here for company. I can't come and pick you up in the middle of the week," said my father.

I assured them I would be alright so reluctantly they agreed and gave me money for food and the train fare home if I got too homesick or lonely. I ended up staying for the whole six week summer holiday every year until I left school. It was paradise. I fished all day and often all night as well. I had no wristwatch and with all the night fishing I was doing my built-in time clock went haywire. On one occasion I woke up and an hour later became alarmed when the sun starting to set and for a while I was convinced it was the end of the world. It was the night fishing I enjoyed most when I sat in blissful silence with a flask of tea and a sandwich. There would be wild life all around me and it wasn't unusual to see the slice of bread I was using for bait walking off into a bush dragged by something small and furry. Far from missing the company of friends I found I loved the solitude and the only time I was ever scared was when a pigeon got into my tent while I was sleeping and was flapping around like something from a horror movie.

My mother gave me ten shillings (50p) a week to spend on food but half of that went on bait and fishing tackle. My tent was legendary for its untidiness and one person suggested I charged people to look inside. I went for weeks without washing or brushing my teeth although my food hygiene wasn't too bad as nothing I bought ever saw a plate but went straight from the can or wrapper into my mouth. Although I loved the solitude I was happy to see my family and friends arrive for the weekends. Years later my parents would have been arrested for giving their child the kind of freedom I had but although there were risks I have wonderful memories of that time and never had any doubt that the experience was invaluable.

I had a happy childhood except for suffering from chronic hornyness that I developed at a very early age. I had a permanent erection from the age of seven until my first steady girlfriend at 16. It wasn't just that I was looking for a shag (although I wouldn't have turned one down), I actually longed for love and romance for as long as I can remember. The worst time was at mass every Sunday when with nothing to occupy my mind all I could think about was sex and the knowledge that I couldn't have a quick one off the wrist for at least an hour. It didn't help that my mother was a dressmaker and often had customers come to the house for fittings. As we only had one small room where the family ate and watched television her customers would change right there in front of me. I was traumatised on one occasion when a bride and three bridesmaids stripped to their underwear and started trying on dresses. I must have looked so young and innocent pretending to watch television that it never occurred to them that I would have shagged the four of them senseless given half a chance as long as one of them was prepared to give me instructions.

I also matured physically a lot younger than most kids and I was the first in my year to need a shave. Unfortunately my mother hated seeing her little boy growing into a man so she wouldn't let me shave. I was also the last kid in our year to wear long trousers so I had to suffer the indignity of strutting around the playground with short trousers and a moustache.

4
The No Talent Contest

I always wildly overestimated my ability and although at times it resulted in me half killing myself with overwork and causing me a great deal of heartache, at the end of every lost battle I came away stronger and more determined to attack my next limitation. It was one of my most absurd overestimations that led me to a life in the music business. Walton Camp Site was holding a talent contest one August Bank Holiday so me and three mates decided to form a pop group and enter. The first two days we spent discussing what we would call ourselves and what our image would be. After a lot of arguing during which time we almost broke up without playing a single note we finally agreed on a name.

"That's decided then. We'll call ourselves The City Gents and our image will be to dress up in pin stripped suits and bowler hats," said Pete, our self appointed leader.

"Yeah brilliant. That's never been done before. We can't fail with an image like that."

We all agreed enthusiastically although I could see a snag.

"Has anyone got a pin stripped suit and bowler hat?" I asked despite knowing the answer. Everyone shook their head.

"That doesn't matter, we can wear our normal clothes for now and then buy suits when we get a record deal," said Pete.

We took it for granted that record deals were handed out automatically to any group of kids that formed a band.

"Les has got a guitar so he can be the guitarist. I will play drums and Chris will be on bass. What about you Derek?" asked Pete.

"I'll be the singer," I said. How hard could that be?

"Everyone must bring their instruments next Friday so we can start practising on Saturday morning. We only need one song for the contest so it gives us a whole day to rehearse. Now let's go to the Cannon to celebrate," said Les.

The Cannon was our local pub despite being two miles away and we had never had any trouble getting served there from the age of 14. I hated beer but I wasn't going to be the first of my mates to admit it.

The day of the contest came and there was still no sign of Les or his guitar and Pete's drum kit turned out to be one snare drum with one drum stick. We were starting to worry that we wouldn't be ready in time.

"We can at least decide on a song for the contest so we can start rehearsing the minute Les gets here. What songs can you sing Derek?" asked Pete.

"How about *Wild Thing*?" I asked.

It was an obvious choice as it was the kind of song where if you forgot the words you could make up your own without anyone noticing. As the hours passed with still no sign of Les we became anxious as stardom slipped away from us. He did eventually turn up halfway through the talent contest but it was too late. It was a disaster but we consoled ourselves with a bottle of cider in the band tent while we rubbished the other contestants who were nowhere near as good as we would have been.

The next morning Les bought his guitar over to my tent and showed me how to play the intro from the Rolling Stones classic, *Satisfaction.* Someone else taught me the chords for a 12 bar blues and that was it, I was totally hooked. I was afraid that Les might want his guitar back so I snuck off into a deserted field where I spent the rest of the day practising. Handing back the guitar at the end of the weekend was like handing over my right arm but fortunately it was the end of the summer holidays so the entire journey home was spent plotting ways to liberate the guitar that my brother Denis owned but never played. He never let me borrow it in the past because fair enough I would probably have used it as a cricket bat. It took three days of me being a complete pain in the arse until he finally agreed to sell it to me. A friend taught me the chords to the *House of the Rising Sun* and I stayed up practising it until my fingers were so sore there were tears in my eyes. My mother as always encouraged my new hobby.

"If you like playing guitar so much why don't you go to lessons?" she asked.

I jumped at the chance despite the only evening class she could find me was a five mile, one handed bike ride away (the other hand carried my guitar). I never missed a class and always nagged my teacher to give me extra homework. My teacher, John Denton was one of the few people I ever knew who was able to explain a difficult subject in a simple way. Not being academic I never thought I would be able to read music but he taught me in one lesson, something my music teacher at school hadn't managed in five years.

Playing guitar took over my whole life and even sport took a back seat. Despite the non appearance of The City Gents at the talent contest we did manage to meet up during the week in Islington and rehearsed the old classic *Hang on Sloopy* several hundred times. By then my guitar playing had improved so much that there was no question that I would play lead guitar which was just as well because I was a lousy singer. Despite the fact we never played a single gig and only knew one song we still had a fan club with nine members that had meetings and collected subscriptions. How easy it is to impress young girls. We were keen but living in different parts of London made rehearsing difficult so we drifted apart.

I was desperate to join a band and well past the stage of sitting around talking about it. I wanted to rehearse regularly and fulfil my greatest ambition of playing live to a real audience. I discovered a friend of mine had a drum kit so we skipped school most days and went to his flat to practice. We still went to school for lunch every day and it was one of the dinner ladies that told us her son's band had just split and he wanted to form a new one and that led me to my first real pop group: The Flare, so called because of our flared trousers. I don't know why we thought flares would make us stand out considering the entire country was wearing them at the time.

In June 1968 when I was sixteen we played our first gig, a wedding. I stood nervously and ecstatic on stage while we waited for the singer to open the curtains.

"Ok John. We're ready."

As he pulled the rope the curtains opened and there was a huge round of applause from the audience as I started with the Shadows instrumental *Apache.* Half way through I was mortified when everything went deathly quiet. We looked at each other wondering what had happened before discovering that John had got so excited he had tripped over the mains cable and pulled the plug out of its socket. He replaced the plug quickly and we started from the beginning but my confidence had taken a knock so I made several mistakes. Despite the setback, the evening was a great success and we all went back to my house for a post gig discussion which lasted until breakfast time. Not only did I have the best night of my life I also earned £5 which was ten times my weekly pocket money.

We only did two more gigs before breaking up when Tom the drummer decided the annual Lambretta run to Brighton was more important than doing a gig so we had to turn it down. It was inconceivable to me that the band was just a hobby to the others so I decided it was time to find other musicians who were as serious about music as I was.

5
The Disappearing Backside

I left school when I was 16 with two CSE's which we were told was equivalent to GCE's except no one told the employers that. At that time it was possible to leave school without a single exam and still have your pick of careers. I found a job as an apprentice electrician and my first assignment was at the massive Barbican Centre development in London. It was not surprising the development went so far over budget considering that in the three months I was there I hardly saw anyone doing a stroke of work. The site was so big it was impossible to supervise so most of the time workmen sat around talking or playing cards. We even developed a game of cricket using a half brick as a ball with a small plank of wood as a bat and had organised matches between the different trades. After three months I was transferred to a building site in Stoke Newington where I finally had to do some work. It was the middle of a very cold winter with heavy snowfalls and I only had a light summer jacket as every spare penny I had went towards a new guitar. There were no electric drills then so my entire day was spent hitting a raw plug tool with a hammer so it could take 20 minutes to make one hole. My firm started sending me to a technical college one day a week where I had great difficulty adjusting from a freezing cold building site to a hot stuffy classroom. It didn't help that I had so little sleep as I practised guitar every night until the early hours. I found it impossible to keep awake during lessons so I started skipping classes thinking it would be the same as school where no one seemed to care. A few weeks later I was sacked for skipping classes.

Being out of work didn't bother me as there were plenty of jobs available and all I could think about was becoming a professional guitarist. It wasn't long before a friend of mine got me a job as a solicitor's clerk in the firm where he worked. I accepted it without having a clue what I would be doing as the only thing I cared about was that the salary was twice as much as my previous job and I got to spend most of the day in a nice warm office.

With a steady income and a lovely new guitar I advertised in a local music shop and found myself a five piece band, The Earthquake. Our first gig was at the Streatham Ice Rink where a different band used to play every Saturday night. We weren't ready for the gig but it was too good an opportunity to turn down as some really good bands played there. When the big night came we carried our equipment through the back door of the venue feeling like superstars. We were only on stage a few minutes when we found out why it was so easy to get a gig in such a prestigious place. I was in the middle of a guitar solo when it felt like someone had tipped a bucket of icy slush on top of me. I stood there with water dripping from my long hair and as I looked out onto the ice rink I saw a group of skaters laughing. A few minutes later I looked up to see someone gathering speed and then stop suddenly in front of us spraying me with slush again. I played on like nothing had happened and tried to concentrate on my solo but Ron our drummer was always ready for a punch up. He slammed his drumsticks down and was just about to get down from the stage when we pointed out that a sheet of ice was not the easiest place to fight, especially when your enemy was wearing skates. Ron wasn't a hard man but he had the eyes of a psychopath that made people think twice about tackling him. I don't know whether it was Ron's eyes or that the skaters got bored but there were no more slush attacks for the rest of the night. The gig was a great success and we got everyone singing along with the number one hit at that time, *Hey Jude.* On the way home we were in a state of euphoria as it sank home that we were a real semi-pro band with a future. We didn't care about fame and fortune but were happy getting paid for doing something we loved and if we got to shag lots of girls as well then that was a bonus.

My whole life was taken over by the band and the dream that one day we would turn professional. Paul, our manager got us one or two gigs a week and while the money was good it never began to cover what we paid out on equipment and repairs to our tired old psychedelic van. My party piece during a gig was to imitate my hero Jimi Hendrix by playing the guitar behind my head while Kenny Chappell our singer put his head between my legs and lifted me onto his shoulders. Whilst Jimi Hendrix was able to play just as well behind his head, the noise I made in this position was truly awful but the audience loved it. Our biggest claim to fame was when we were a support act for Joe Cocker while his smash hit *With A Little Help From My Friends* was in the charts. His backing group was The Greaseband but whoever designed the poster mistakenly worded it, "Joe Cocker and the Earthquake" so people thought we were his backing group instead of just an unknown band booked to play a few songs before he came on. We put the poster in the back window of our van and drove proudly around London as if we really were Joe Cocker's backing band. Sometimes people saw the poster and approached us.

"*Oy.* Where's Joe Cocker then?"

"He's stoned in the back and doesn't want to be disturbed. You can have our autographs if you want."

That was the only time we ever signed autographs.

With all the rehearsing and dedication we had a good sound but there was nothing special about us. Our hopes were raised when we won a talent contest at Brixton Town Hall but apart from a good write up in the local press nothing ever came from it. Our biggest problem was that none of us could write songs. I tried so hard and really felt I had it in me but the only thing I came up with was a couple of weak folk songs with pathetic lyrics.

My job as a solicitor's clerk mainly involved photocopying huge quantities of documents or taking writs to the courts to be stamped. When there was nothing for me to do I taught myself to touch type in the hope that exercising my fingers would help my guitar playing. My life was a mixture of great joy when I was playing in the band and misery when I was at work. When I walked away from the office on Friday nights with the whole weekend in front of me I thought I was in heaven. My employers were happy with my work but unhappy about my shoulder length hair which was much longer than when I was first interviewed. I was supposed to get a wage rise at the end of my first year so when it failed to materialise I approached one of the partners about it.

"We are very happy with your work and will give you a raise if you are prepared to have your hair cut shorter," he told me.

It was bad enough that they owned my life during the day but to dictate my appearance as well was more than I could take so I handed in my notice. The stupid thing was I never really liked having long hair as it was always getting in my eyes. It irritated me so much that at home I often wore my mum's hair clips until the day I forgot to take them out when I answered the door to my mates. It is amazing how often we enslave ourselves in order to establish our freedom.

The same afternoon I went to an employment agency and was offered a job as a barrister's clerk in the Inner Temple earning 50% more than before. I was glad of the extra money as I needed a new amplifier but the job was even more boring than the previous one. It was a chambers that specialised in taxation and as every year there were several million new tax laws published I used to spend most of my time replacing the old laws with the new ones in loose leaf binders. I also had to go running around after the barristers like I was a servant carrying their briefcases to court or even just a set of pencils on one occasion.

There was one breath of fresh air when Led Zeppelin came into the office to sort out some tax problems.

"What is Led Zeppelin?" asked my boss. I felt great pity for him.

"Only one of the best bands in the world," I said.

I never got to see them but I did see two large, scruffy arses disappearing into a barrister's office.

6
Don't Look Up

Nothing seemed to be happening with The Earthquake so I started to lose heart. I was desperate to turn professional and knew it was never going to happen with them so I looked around for another band. The Melody Maker music paper was the bible for musicians with pages full of bands looking for musicians and vice versa. After answering an advert I went for an audition for a professional rock band called Jasper. It was held in a pub in North London and when I arrived there must have been 20 guitarists waiting for their chance to prove themselves. The existing members of Jasper all had long hair, were very scruffy and I loved them. Their music was loud and overpowering and I couldn't wait for my chance to play with them though it was daunting having to perform in front of my competitors who were busy making judgements. At last it was my turn. The lead singer counted us in and as I joined in I had the feeling of riding in a juggernaut crushing everything in our path. It was the first time I'd been able to let loose and play so loudly and I feel like the music was taking over my whole body. When the previous guitarists were playing the band stopped them after only a few bars but in my case we continued until the end of the song which gave me great encouragement. As I went back to my seat the singer and bass player came over to speak to me.

"That was great man. We'll call you over the next couple of days to let you know."

I was disappointed they didn't offer me the job there and then but realised that would be unfair on the guitarists that hadn't auditioned yet. I never had any doubt that the job was mine and my dream of being a professional musician was finally going to come true. I spent a restless night deciding what was the best way to hand in my notice at work and how I should celebrate the occasion. I stayed home the next few nights to wait for a call from Jasper but there was none. Being convinced that there must be something wrong with my phone I called them and was relieved to find that they remembered me.

"Hi man. Yeah we've still got a few more people to see. We'll give you a call over the next couple of days to let you know."

I waited in every night for a week but never heard from them again. It was the start of my love-hate relationship with the telephone and my first experience of *don't call us, we'll call you.*

The problem with answering adverts in the Melody Maker was that musicians had to queue up and play in front of dozens of competitors cramming years of practice into a one minute demonstration. I decided to place an advert of my own in the hope that I could turn the tables so the bands would be calling me and I could do the choosing. I had dozens of calls but mostly from bands similar to The Earthquake who had nothing concrete to offer whereas I wanted a band that had enough work for me to turn professional. I was getting a little despondent when one day a caller asked:

"Would you be interested in playing country music?"

His tone of voice was almost apologetic. Country music was looked down on from a great height by serious musicians of all other genres and I was just about to say no when he added:

"We are going on a three month tour of American army bases in Germany. We leave in two weeks so we need someone urgently."

Suddenly country music didn't sound so bad.

"What's the money?" I asked.

"£30 a week."

I couldn't believe it. As a barrister's clerk I was taking home £11 a week so I was being offered the chance to treble my wage and turn professional overnight. I went to an audition and was happy to find that I was the only guitarist there. The band was called Nashville Skyline which was a good name at the time as people thought they were well known when in fact they were getting confused with a Bob Dylan album of the same name. They offered me the job and my journey home was a mixture of elation and confusion. I had finally found what I had been looking for but would playing country music be bad for my career? The next day I handed in my notice and it was the only day I ever looked forward to going into work.

"We'll be sorry to see you go," said the head clerk, "I wish you luck but if things don't work out we'll hold your job open until the autumn if you want to return."

I was touched but irritated that he should consider the possibility that my success in the music business could be anything but assured. A week later I walked away from that office for the last time feeling like I had just won the lottery. The next morning I woke up in the knowledge that from then on any work I did would be for my own benefit and not my bosses. At last I was a professional musician.

I started rehearsing with Nashville Skyline and was surprised to find that I quite enjoyed playing country music and hadn't realised how much scope there was for guitarists to play solos. There were two weeks of rehearsals planned before going on tour and as a tryout we took a weekend gig in a Northampton night club. Before going on stage we were told we had to play some background music for the cabaret artist. I didn't think anything more about it until a woman appeared a few feet in front of me and started taking off her clothes bringing a whole new meaning to the phrase *ringside seat*. It was a surreal experience supporting a stripper for the first time. While she was stripping I played a long guitar solo thinking what on earth was the point as who was going to be listening to me while a woman was getting naked in front of me. Purely for research purposes I looked up to see what all the fuss was about and was surprised to see a woman painfully past her strip-by date. I returned to my guitar solo but made the fatal mistake of looking up just as the naked stripper bent over to take her bow. It took me weeks to erase the image from my mind and put me off sex for several hours.

It was hard work learning so many songs in such a short period of time but I was getting there and the band seemed happy with me. My intention was to stay with them for a year or two and then get back to the more serious business of rock and blues where I was sure my future lay. It was three days to go before our departure for Germany and I was counting the hours with great excitement when there was a phone call from Mike, the leader of Nashville Skyline. It was short and brutal:

"I'm sorry but our original guitarist wants to come back and as he already knows our repertoire we have decided to take him back."

I was stunned.

"But I thought you were happy with me?"

"We are and I know you won't have any trouble finding another band. It's just that you still have a lot more songs to learn and we don't have enough time left to rehearse."

"You know I've left my job to go on this tour?" I said, leaving out the bit about the job still being there if I wanted it.

"I'm sorry but that's what we've decided."

There was no point in arguing so I slammed the phone down. Like the lover who has been jilted and is sure he will never find love again, I was sure I would never find another band and was devastated. One minute I was living my dream of being a professional musician and the next I was looking at the prospect of going back to my day job with my tail between my legs. I had a long chat with my dad.

"What do you think I should do?" I asked, sure he would advise me to go back to the kind of job that he would have killed for.

"Why not try it out for six months and see if you can make a living from music. If not, I'm sure you won't have any trouble finding another job. We can lend you money to get started if you need it."

I was so surprised and touched that I struggled to hold back a little tear.

"I would like to try and make a go of it. From the moment I first picked up a guitar I knew this was what I wanted to do."

"That's why you have to give it a try; otherwise you'll spend the rest of your life wondering what might have been."

The next day I drove to the centre of London to put another advert in the Melody Maker and despite my devastating setback I was full of hope.

7
Walking Sticks At Dawn

My next advert was even more successful than the previous one with calls from all kinds of bands. A lot of them were just forming and although some sounded promising the most important thing for me was to start earning money and the only sure way I could do that was by playing country music. I started working with a Scottish duo led by a singer called Hugo McGill. Frank was the other half of the duo and although it was Hugo that found all the gigs Frank felt for no particular reason that he should be the leader. They argued about everything and it was not uncommon for them to break out into a fist fight during a performance. We worked in Irish pubs playing Irish and Country music and had some great nights when we took several encores. It wasn't long before we were working four or five nights a week and it seemed like I was earning a fortune. After closing time at most gigs everyone went to a room around the back and started the serious drinking. I would have preferred to go home as the dense cigarette smoke made my eyes sting badly but as we all travelled in the van together I had to stay with them. There were some magical moments though when one of the elders would stand and sing haunting Irish songs without musical accompaniment and even the hardest men had tears in their eyes.

I enjoyed working with Hugo McGill but the constant bickering got to me so I put another advert in the Melody Maker. By that time I was becoming quite competent at self promotion and one of my more elaborate adverts caught the eye of a singer known as Welsh George. He was the lead singer in a band that had a six night residency in a well known pub in Leytonstone called The Green Man. They weren't really looking for a guitarist but after being impressed by my advert George thought I might be a good addition to the band. He suggested I sat in with them one night in the hope that the pub owner would take me on permanently. They were a four piece band led by the blind organist Peter London, a talented musician and singer but a miserable sod who decided he didn't like me even before I started playing. Welsh George was a tall, one legged man (not counting the wooden one) of about fifty who on more than one occasion threatened to wrap his walking stick around Peter London's neck. I think half the regulars at the pub only went in the hope of seeing a punch up between a blind man and a one legged man. They played all kinds of music and I had a lot of trouble keeping up with them as I didn't know the chords to most of the songs. I was out of my depth but I made it clear how much I wanted the job and would work hard to learn their repertoire. We finished the last song and I was putting away my guitar when I heard the dreaded words from Peter London:

"Thanks Derek. We'll give you a call and let you know."

The drummer nodded in approval. Welsh George went over to talk to them and after waving his walking stick around Peter's head a few times an agreement seemed to have been reached which George kindly relayed to me.

"We will give you a week's trial to see how it goes. I will get the owner of the pub to come and see you play next Sunday lunchtime. If you can impress him you'll get the job regardless of what those two think."

I was thrilled at having the chance to play with such experienced musicians even if it was only for one week. Sunday came and the pub owner was there to watch me play but as I was never much of a showman I knew it was unlikely that I would impress him. George sang a few ballads and then announced:

"Now we're going to feature our brilliant new guitarist Derek Newark in the Deep Purple song *Black Night.*"

We launched into it full throttle with Peter singing brilliantly as always. My big guitar solo came and something came over me that was completely out of character. I was getting completely carried away with my solo and oblivious to the pub owner watching me when I grabbed the microphone stand and started rubbing it up and down the guitar strings making the most horrible noise imaginable. The audience started applauding and after a big finale with some more horrible guitar noises they went mad. The pub owner walked straight over and offered me the job at an incredible £35 a week.

It was a relief to know that the Green Man was a secure job as the band had been resident there for two years. I felt so secure I even started considering where to go on my summer holiday and what pension plan I should consider. I hadn't yet learnt that security is an illusion. I was only there two months when we were told the owner wanted a change of bands so we were given a week's notice. I was disappointed to leave such a good job but was beginning to get a taste for change and it seemed that all it took for me to start a new life was an advert in the Melody Maker. I looked forward with great expectation for Thursdays when my adverts brought in a fresh crop of possibilities.

For the next couple of months I played freelance for different bands but it was always Irish or country music. It was good experience and my ear for music was developing while I sat in with different bands playing songs I didn't know. One pleasant surprise came when Mike from Nashville Skyline called me after their early return from Germany.

"It was a disaster. Our guitarist was really homesick and spent most of the time crying. We had to cut the tour short and come home. Would you be interested in coming back to us?"

Call me a bitch but it was music to my ears.

"Thanks for the offer Mike but I've got too much work on to consider going away."

There was a good circuit of country music pubs in London with the main venue being The Nashville Rooms in Kensington where they had live country music every night of the week. It was compered by an American called Tex Withers also known as "The Hammersmith Hillbilly" and what an amazing character he was. He was four feet tall with a hunchback and always wore cowboy clothes with matching gun holster. He told me in his thick American accent that he used to live in a tent in the woods with his horse and of course I sucked it all in. In my defence I wasn't the only person to believe him and some swore blind it was true although no one ever actually saw the horse. There were plenty of other characters who dressed up as cowboys and strutted around the place, accountant by day and gunslinger by night. I was resident there every Friday with a good little band called *Country Pie* and it was the first time I had to talk to the audience and announce each song. It looked so easy when other people did it but I had the greatest difficulty and spent more time mumbling to my shoes than talking to the audience.

I was so hooked on Melody Maker adverts that I left one running every week whether I needed work or not. It was only six months since I turned pro and already I was earning a good living and had played with dozens of different bands although most of them played the same songs. The trouble was I didn't want to be playing country music all my life and was still hungry for a broader experience. My guitar playing was improving rapidly but like all young musicians I wanted to be rich and famous and that was never going to happen with country music in England. My next gig was to take me in the opposite direction of fame and fortune but it did offer a new adventure.

8
Abroad Experience

It was a cold February morning in 1971 when I had the phone call.

"Are you interested in working abroad?" a man asked.

The thought had never occurred to me so it took me by surprise.

"Where?"

"We have a three month gig in Malta and need a guitarist urgently. It's £35 a week with free food and accommodation."

Ten minutes later I was on the road to Southampton to audition for a job with a three piece band in their forties playing pops and standards, not quite the stuff legends are made of but I was excited at the prospect of working abroad.

"We will be playing in a restaurant and as people will be dancing we need a young guitarist to liven things up a bit," they told me on my arrival.

The George Meadows Band were great guys and we all got on well but even to my inexperienced ears I could tell they were not good musicians. It wasn't difficult passing the audition and after a celebratory cup of tea we started rehearsing right away as it was only a week before we were due to fly out.

As our departure date grew closer I became anxious that something was going to go wrong. Apart from the German tour I had already been let down on several other occasions so every time the phone rang I was sure it was bad news. It wasn't until I had cancelled all my gigs and upset most of my contacts that I realised how vulnerable I was. If the Malta job did fall through I would have to start all over again.

On the day of our departure my father drove me through the deserted London streets at 5 a.m. to Heathrow Airport where I met the other guys. It was the first time I had ever flown and although I wasn't scared I still said a few "Our Fathers" dug up from what was left of my Catholic upbringing. Once we were above the clouds I relaxed and settled down to my first in-flight meal. Everything went well until we started our descent and hit some turbulence. Mike (the drummer) assured me it was normal when flying through clouds so I didn't think anything more about it. Forty five minutes later we were still in thick cloud with the turbulence getting worse and flashes of lighting all around us. The air hostess made an announcement:

"Ladies and Gentlemen. If you are wondering why we haven't landed yet it is because the captain was not happy with our first two approaches so we are circling around to try again."

This of course meant nothing to me but as Mike had been in the RAF he was able to translate.

"When the pilot approaches the runway he has to be 100% confident that he is at the right angle and speed before he decides to land. With this kind of weather the plane might get pushed off course so if he is not happy with the approach he ascends, makes a big circle and then tries again. Don't worry, six approaches was my record."

Because it was my first flight I assumed all this was normal so wasn't at all scared although I did wish I hadn't finished off Mike's meal as well as my own. Thankfully I had no idea that the turbulence was far from normal and it turned out to be the worst flight I ever experienced in a lifetime of travel. On the next approach the captain landed the plane and it wasn't until we were safely on the ground that the air hostess allowed her fear to show.

"That was the worst flight I have ever been on. The captain told me we were struck by lightning twice," she said.

Our agent was at the airport to meet us.

"You couldn't have picked a worse day to arrive. They said on the radio this is the worst storm in Malta for over thirty years," he said.

The five of us squeezed into his tiny Mini and drove along roads that looked more like rivers until we reached a new restaurant in St. Julian's Bay called The Tigullio. Our accommodation was a small concrete block hastily built on the flat restaurant roof. The good thing about being young and from a humble background was that I didn't know any better so our little cell block looked fine to me. On the rare occasion it rained there was an inch of water on the floor but we found that more amusing than irritating.

The next day we woke early and went for a walk along the sea front to Sliema. When we had left England it was a miserable freezing cold February morning so I was surprised to see people in Malta walking around in light shirts on what seemed like a lovely summer's day. Everyone spoke English and they even used the same currency as in England which was still pounds, shillings and pence. That evening the management gave us a good welcome and the chef prepared a special meal for us. It was the first time I had ever eaten in a posh restaurant and I decided that was the life for me. We played that night and although there was no chance of us winning any awards the customers were happy enough and we managed to keep them dancing most of the time. Everything was perfect until the end of the first week when I had my first experience of one of the scourges of the music business: *The Agent.*

We were dealing with a small local agent who was asked by The Tigullio to supply an English band. All the agent did was phone another agent in England and thereby made 10% of our entire three month salary for making a couple of phone calls and picking us up at the airport. The English agent also took 10% for doing even less. It was not uncommon for agents to pass gigs around amongst themselves three or four times leaving the band with 50% or less of what the venue was paying. As if that wasn't enough our Maltese agent wanted to take it one step further.

George was in town at a meeting with the management so there was just the three of us at the Tigullio. The agent turned up with our first week's salary and was very pleasant and chatty.

"Everyone is very pleased with the band and I'm sure I can find you something else when this contract has finished."

We were flattered and happy at the prospect of more work in the future.

"By the way, I am going to England for a couple of months at the end of the week so as I won't be around I will be taking my three month's commission today."

The other two had always left business to George so they just shrugged their shoulders to indicate they had no objection. It put me in an awkward situation. I was 20 years younger than both of them so the idea of me taking control seemed ridiculous but I was sure the agent was pulling a fast one.

"I'm sorry but I don't think that's right. We don't get paid in advance so I don't see why you should."

He looked patronisingly at me and turned to Mike and Ray.

"You guys are more experienced. I'm sure you don't mind do you? It's perfectly normal."

They both shrugged their shoulders. The agent waffled on about how immature and unreasonable I was being and was getting into his car to drive off when I took the keys from the ignition and put them in my pocket.

"We are going to wait until George returns," I said in a manner that made it difficult for him to patronise me any more. He reluctantly agreed and although it was a relief that things didn't get violent I was worried I had gone too far. Maybe this kind of thing was normal practice but it just didn't seem right to me. Maybe we would lose our job because of my actions. I looked at Mike and Ray hoping for support but they just stood there shrugging their shoulders. Fortunately it wasn't long before George appeared and I explained the situation to him.

"Is that true?" he asked the agent.

George being far less patient than me only allowed a few seconds of pathetic whinging from the agent before grabbing him by the throat and holding him against the wall.

"Are you going to give me our wages or shall I take them?"

The money was handed over immediately less his commission for that week. I gave the agent his car keys and as soon as he was safely out of striking distance he turned and shouted:

"You are all fired. I'm going to see the manager and make sure you are on the next plane out of here."

I was heartbroken at the thought of being sent home but George said not to worry and that I had done the right thing. He went back to the owner's office and we spent an agonising hour wondering if we still had a job. When George returned he was smiling all over his face.

"Don't worry lads. The owner just laughed when I told him what happened. He said if the little weasel turns up at his office he will have him thrown out the second floor window. They'll keep his commission until he returns from England and won't use him again."

That may well be the only time in history when musicians have won a battle against an agent.

Another great thing about Malta was that there was a shortage of young men. It was the Maltese culture that as soon as most men were old enough they worked overseas while the girls stayed at home to help their mothers. After a brief period of blissful promiscuity I settled down with Anna. She was from a very respectable family so her mother was mortified to discover her daughter was going out with a long haired, scruffy musician but being accustomed to parental disapproval I didn't lose any sleep over it.

Some people wake up one morning to find out that without any effort they have the most wonderful singing voice and although I can't complain about the gifts I was given at birth, singing or showmanship was definitely not one of them. I had never sung in public and although I was confident as a guitarist I was still very introverted on stage. I didn't particularly want to sing but knew it would be good for my career and Malta was a good place to start. George was having to do most of the singing so he was happy to go along with anything that took some of the pressure off him. My first few attempts at singing were abysmal but I slowly improved to the point where customers stopped putting cheese in their ears.

Halfway through the second month we all came down with a surprise attack of homesickness. England was going through the worst postal strike in history so apart from a short phone call I hadn't heard from my parents for weeks. The strike ended after seven weeks and although post started to arrive it only made us more homesick. I began to get bored with the music we were playing and longed to get stuck into some heavy rock solos but in our sophisticated restaurant it would have been unthinkable.

At last the day came for us to go home and although I couldn't wait to leave it was difficult saying goodbye to Anna. In a moment of madness I asked her if she wanted to get engaged and she said yes. The next day I was stunned when she started talking about saving for the wedding. The two words I feared most in life, "wedding" and "saving" and she used them both in the same sentence. Who said anything about getting married? I don’t know if it was just me and my circle of friends but getting engaged had nothing to do with getting married. It was just something you did if you had been going out for a while and wanted to go to the next level. For those who didn’t even want to commit to buying a ring there was another level: "unofficially engaged." Although I hated the thought of never seeing Anna again there was no way I wanted to marry her so for the last few days I did my best to avoid the subject. We promised to write to each other regularly and she talked about coming to England to see me but we both knew her mother would never allow it.

The band was going straight on to a summer season at a holiday camp on the south coast but being a job for a trio there was no place for me. I would have loved to spend the summer working in a holiday camp but knew in order to improve I had to find much better musicians to work with so I was happy with the situation.

It was a beautiful spring day in May when we arrived at Heathrow airport where my family was waiting to greet me. I'd had a great time but was happy to be home and was sure it would be a long time before I got the urge to travel again.

9
The Asylum Creeper

Back at the Melody Maker office the receptionist greeted me like an old friend. With the whole summer before me I felt sure I would get a residency in a holiday camp or hotel. Since turning professional there had been a steady improvement in my ability, my income and the quality of gigs so I was beginning to take progress for granted. Thursday came and I was surprised at how few answers I had to my advert. I wasn't too worried as many of the calls in the past were from time wasters so I made the wording of my adverts more selective in the hope of getting fewer but better quality calls. I did get a couple of calls from bands needing a guitarist for the summer season and even a cruise but they needed someone who could sight read music. I could read music and could work out what it was I had to play but sight reading meant playing a guitar part from beginning to end without ever having seen it before. I was determined to learn how to sight read and practised every day but it didn't come naturally to me. My slow progress was disheartening but there was never any thought of giving up.

I found a few gigs here and there but nothing regular so my savings from the job in Malta rapidly dwindled. What surprised me was how much I missed Malta. I had been so desperate to get away and yet I was starting to feel the same desperation to go back again. I went down to the holiday camp in Portsmouth where the George Meadows band was playing and was shocked at how shabby the place was compared to The Tigullio.

"This is a shithole" was the first thing I said to them. They laughed and nodded their heads in agreement.

"This is one of the posher camps," said Ray.

"I can't believe I am saying this but I really miss Malta. Is there any chance of being asked back there?" I asked George.

"No chance. I made enquiries but business has been better using a local band which is much cheaper."

To make matters worse Anna's letters were becoming more scarce and I hadn't heard from her for a month so during an attack of loneliness one day I called her. Her voice sounded weak.

"Why haven't you written?" I asked.

"I have been in hospital."

"What's wrong?" There was a long pause.

"I lost our baby."

I was stunned as the revelation that I was going to be a father and then not going to be a father in the space of a few seconds slowly sank in.

"Are you alright?" I asked.

"Yes I'm fine but I must go now. If my mother finds out I'm speaking to you she'll kill me. I'll write soon."

I waited anxiously for Anna's letter but all I ever received was this scribbled note from her mother:

"God has punished Anna for her wickedness. She is a liar and you are not the only man she was sleeping with. Anna will have to marry someone from her own class instead of a low fellow like you."

So her daughter was a wicked lying slut who was too good for me? It always surprised me how people with an inflated view of their own superiority often have such inferior powers of logic. I never heard from Anna or her mother again. What the truth was I will never know but there was no doubt Anna did stretch the truth at times.

The summer passed quickly and although I was getting enough gigs to get by I was starting to lose some of my enthusiasm. The only bright spot was meeting the beautiful Linda. She was working in a mental hospital until starting a teacher's training course in the autumn. She was the first well educated girl that I ever went out with and she was astonished to learn that I had never read a book in my life. She gave me a book of poems which fitted in well with my passion for daydreaming and I was surprised by how much I enjoyed it.

Linda was very patronising which was no problem for me as I was unaware of it at the time. We had a strange relationship as we were complete opposites but we still respected each other's opinion and got on well. One day I went to see her at the mental hospital where she worked. We were sitting on a bench in the grounds when a short, fat, hairy woman in her thirties stood in front of me and after a few minutes of intense staring threw her arms around me.

"My boyfriend has got long hair just like you," she said.

I smiled and said a few words to humour her but her grip on my neck was getting tighter as she started screaming:

"I love you. I love you. Please take me with you. I can't live without you."

Linda managed to disentangle us and calm the woman down but she still spent the next hour staring at me from behind a tree. That night Linda smuggled me into her room where we had sex until the early hours with her groaning mingling with that of the clinically insane. It was around 4 a.m. when I left her room to make my way across the unlit grounds to my car.

"You might see some patients walking around but don't worry, they are harmless," said Linda.

I had no idea whether she was joking or not but I walked towards the exit as quickly as I could without the indignity of running. It was pitch black and the only thing I could see was devil-like shadows lurking behind every tree. What if someone from security saw me and thought I was an escaped patient? I would be put in a strait jacket or maybe locked in a room with the woman who attacked me that afternoon. It was such a relief to arrive at the large metal gates at the entrance.

By the end of the summer I still had no regular work so I decided it was time to stop messing around and look for a good rock band. Every week I received calls from aspiring bands that sounded brilliant on the phone but after travelling half way across London to meet them I would find them to be timewasters. I did get a call from one unknown band that had heard me playing at one of the rare blues gigs I did a few weeks earlier. I arranged to meet them and intended to go but having already seen several bands that week I couldn't face another wasted journey so I didn't turn up. They phoned back the next day and a few times after that, always leaving messages with my brother Dennis. One day I found a large angry note from Dennis who was pissed off with me for not returning the calls:

"Phone Peter Gabriel From Genesis.
I'm not taking any more messages from him!"

Peter who? Never heard of him. Genesis? Don't tell me: yet another band that had some great material and were going to make it big. I had just gone through a period when I had heard the same story from a dozen unknown bands that turned out to be hopeless and I was fed up with it. I never did return that phone call.

The annoying thing about that near miss was the number of bands I did go to see just because they had been well known in the past. I rushed to meet them in the hope of instant fame but soon found out that fame and fortune didn't always go together. Love Affair was a famous band from the sixties so when they called I got excited and expected to find them rehearsing in a plush studio instead of the bass player's bedroom where we met. All they were offering was a tour of England for £30 a week each, less expenses. There were also a lot of calls from musicians who had left famous bands and were looking to start one of their own. Some of them were really weird like the drummer who said he had been working for the Eric Clapton band Delaney and Bonnie. I went to see him at an exclusive private housing estate in Surrey. I parked my rusty old Austin A40 outside a magnificent mansion and was shown into a room where large patio doors looked out onto what was either a very large garden or a small park. I spent an hour listening to this nut job telling me about how many famous people he knew while he shot at birds with an air rifle. I never took my guitar out of its case and he never gave me the slightest idea as to why I was there.

Some famous bands advertised for musicians in the Melody Maker but the auditions were horrendous. The bigger the band, the more people turned up for the audition, many of whom knew they had no chance of getting the job but went just so they could say they had played with a famous band. Supertramp for example were looking for a guitarist and I went for an audition. I waited in a tiny room packed wall to wall with guitarists waiting their turn, each of them trying to impress the others with all the well known bands they had played with. The George Meadows quartet was not high on the list of names worth dropping so I kept my mouth shut. Give me a dentist's waiting room any time over a roomful of bullshitting musicians. My turn came and I was taken to a rehearsal studio where Supertramp were waiting and someone plugged my guitar into an amplifier.

"OK, play something," I was told.

"What shall I play?"

"Anything you want. We just want to get an idea of what you are into."

I had no idea what they were looking for in a guitarist so I launched into a solo like a sprinter trying to beat a world record without warming up first.

Ten seconds later they stopped playing.

"Thanks a lot. We'll let you know."

I was beginning to lose hope of ever finding a band when late one night I had the call I had been waiting for and ten minutes later I was on my way to the audition.

10
Cheeserat & Gorilla

Going from a terraced house in Peckham to that lovely private estate in Esher it was hardly surprising I was impressed and wanted some of that for myself. I figured that anyone who lived in such luxury must have enough money to make success inevitable. Several people were waiting for me at the front door looking excited. After the usual introductions we went into the garage to jam for a while and after a few rounds of long, self indulgent solos everyone was happy so we returned to the house to talk business. The band's name, Cheeserat and Gorilla was made up from the nicknames of the two leaders. Lenny was Cheeserat and his nickname described his appearance perfectly. He was short, thin and pasty with long blond hair that he constantly flicked over his shoulder. Stuart, alias Gorilla, didn't seem to have much in common with gorillas except perhaps at mealtimes. The two of them had grown up together and were best of friends. There was also Simon on drums, Sue the girl singer and some friends of the band.

"So what do you think then? Do you want to join us?" asked Lenny.

"I'm definitely interested. What do you have planned?"

"We're going to rehearse every day in a studio in Esher and learn all the usual pop rubbish so we can get a residency and earn some money. Then we'll start writing our own material and with all the contacts we've got there will be no problem getting a record deal. What do you think?"

All I heard were the words *record deal.* They weren't really the kind of band I was looking for but they were the best I'd found so I told myself it was now or never.

"OK I'm in."

We all shook hands on it and Lenny looked slyly at Stuart.

"Shall we tell him?" said Lenny.

"Yeah. I'm sure we can trust him," said Stuart.

"Tell me what?" I asked. The strange look in their eyes had me worried.

"Our master plan. It's going to make us famous so you have to promise to keep it to yourself. We don't want anyone stealing our idea."

"OK. I promise."

I could see they didn't trust me but Lenny was desperate to demonstrate his promotional genius.

"As soon as the band is ready we are going to hire a big barn in the middle of nowhere and put on our own concert making sure there's plenty of press and record company people there. During the concert we're going to do loads of disgusting things."

"Like what?" I asked.

"For example, in the middle of a song Stuart is going to puke up on stage and I'm going to get on my knees and eat it."

I was horrified.

"You're going to eat his puke?" I asked, wishing I hadn't stopped for Kentucky Fried Chicken on the way to the audition. Stuart continued enthusiastically:

"It won't be real puke. A few minutes earlier I'll put some potato salad in my mouth so that's what Lenny will really be eating."

He paused for a minute to look for signs of admiration on my face and after failing to find any continued with other equally disgusting exploits until he paused for his grand finale:

"Just as we build up for our big finish," another pause for effect.... "we're going to set fire to the barn. With all the press there we'll be instantly famous."

He seemed to be serious.

"You don't think the fire officer might disapprove of you burning people alive?"

"Don't worry. The front door will be open so everyone can get out. No one will get hurt."

I suppose at that point I should have guessed there was something not quite right with Cheeserat and Gorilla. I knew they would never carry out such a ridiculous plan and I really wanted to commit myself to a band so I just smiled and went along with it. As it turned out, apart from the bit about burning people alive the other disgusting ideas were not so stupid after all, just ahead of their time. A few years later the punk scene came along and that kind of behaviour became a licence to print money.

We parted company in high spirits and arranged to meet for rehearsals five days a week until we were ready to audition for a residency. I could still do freelance gigs at night and rehearse during the daytime and while Lenny and Stuart weren't happy about me doing gigs they could hardly object on the grounds of jealousy. Rehearsals went well and we started to develop a good tight sound. For the first time since my days with The Earthquake I was a part of something and it felt good. We did an audition for Mecca Entertainments, one of the biggest agents in the country and passed the audition easily. They offered us a six night residency on the south coast with good money but I was irritated to find that Lenny and Stuart weren't so enthusiastic about the offer and told the agent they wanted a few days to think about it. The next day Lenny called.

"We've had an offer to do a tour of the American army bases in Germany. I've had a chat to the others and they all want to do it."

"What's the point of driving all over Germany doing one night stands and ending up with less money that if we do a residency in England?" I asked.

He gave me a couple of reasons but neither of them made any sense. It seemed ridiculous to me but I reminded myself that I was in a band now so I had to go along with the majority decision. A few days later we all went along to see the agent for details of the tour.

"You will get £30 a week each for up to six nights a week working in American military bases all over Germany."

"What about hotels and other expenses?" I asked.

"You'll have to pay for those yourselves but there are plenty of cheap hotels in Germany."

"But I thought everything was more expensive in Germany?"

Lenny and Stuart were getting irritated with my questions.

"Some things are more expensive but the hotels are cheap enough" said the agent before quickly changing the subject.

"Our office in Germany will send me 20% of your salary which I will put directly in your bank accounts. It's something to do with their tax laws."

Alarm bells started ringing. That was like asking a fox to look after your chickens. It was a terrible deal but I was the only one in the band that recognised it and when I tried to raise my concerns I was just sneered at.

The next few days were very difficult as I didn't know what to do. I didn't want anything to do with the German tour but I had invested a lot of time and effort in the band and didn't want to throw it all away. A few days later Lenny phoned.

"The offer has been confirmed. We leave for Germany next week."

"I'm sorry but I don't want to go. We are going to be working really hard and end up with nothing. It's ridiculous when we have a much better offer here in England."

"Come on, it will be fun and if you don't go, none of us can."

He was holding a gun to my head so I said reluctantly:

"OK, if both Sue and Simon definitely want to go then I suppose I've got no choice but if either of them says no you can count me out."

I knew Sue wasn't keen on going so I felt pretty safe. Half an hour later Lenny called back.

"They both want to go so that's settled. I have to go now and start getting things organised."

Once I'd put the phone down I felt relieved that the decision had been taken out of my hands and even a twinge of excitement about a new adventure.

I cancelled all my freelance gigs and upset my contacts yet again so there was no turning back. I said my goodbyes to Linda who was due to start her teacher training course shortly. We swore to write to each other but with both of us starting new lives we knew it was a good time to end our relationship. I met a lot of girls during my early years as a musician but none that had such a profound effect on me as Linda. I suppose she was the first woman I'd ever had an intelligent conversation with. She made me realise that even though I had left school without any real exams maybe I wasn't so stupid after all.

Why is it that we so often allow circumstances to force us into making decisions that we know are really stupid? Maybe because it's the stupid things we do that makes life more interesting rather than the clever things. If I had done the clever thing and not gone to Germany with Cheeserat and Gorilla I wouldn't be able to tell you about the tour from hell.

11
The Tour From Hell

We were due to catch the last ferry from Dover and they were already two hours late picking me up when I started to get anxious and cursed myself for not having the courage to turn the tour down. When they finally arrived I was determined to put my foot down.

"We are never going to make the ferry now so we might as well leave tomorrow morning," I said firmly.

The next thing I knew I was sitting in the back of the van driving recklessly towards Dover. The van belonged to Martin, a friend of Stuart's who had agreed to come along for the fun of it and a little pocket money. Miraculously we arrived just as the ship's ramp was about to go up. Once on the boat I can't deny feeling a little excited about the prospect of travel and adventure. The crossing was smooth and it was a beautiful autumn night. I went on deck where I could see the moon reflecting on the looking glass sea and my spirits soared. Linda had filled my head with romantic visions of foreign travel and managed to make German autobahns sound like Amazonian backwaters. I strolled around the deck happy to be alone while the others were getting pissed at the bar. Everything was going to be alright and maybe I had made the right decision after all. At the end of the three month tour the band would sound really tight and we could return to England to start working on our first album.

After driving through Belgium we stopped at a small service station for breakfast and I have to say that Stuart could be very amusing. He had the German diners in stitches as he read the contents of the incomprehensible menu out loud. Most of us played safe by pointing to anything that looked like a sausage but Stuart was determined to be more adventurous and ordered a Strammer Max. He was devastated when nothing more exotic than ham and eggs on toast was put in front of him. That night we checked into a hotel in Wiesbaden and made our way to the nearest bar where we talked endlessly about our plans. Life was great. Our band was great. The beer was great. Germany was great but most of all .... being pissed was great.

The next day we met the German agent who gave us contracts to sign. Lenny and Stuart could never take anything seriously and filling in forms was no exception. They put in as many silly answers as they could and while some of them were undeniably funny the agent wasn't amused and it got us off to a bad start. We were also given a list of dates for the first week starting at an army camp near Karlsruhe that night. We arrived in plenty of time to set up our equipment and as we went through our sound check we were surprised to see soldiers walking in and separating themselves into blacks on one side and whites on the other. The black soldiers demanded we played soul music and the whites demanded Country and Western but luckily we could play both so managed to keep them all happy. They were all great guys and there was a never ending supply of free drinks sent up to us. When we finished playing for the night we stayed on to drink and play pool taking care to divide our time between the white and black tables. There was an amazing array of characters and they all seemed to have a natural ability to entertain.

"*Agh* man. I don't want to spend another winter in this damn shithole. I'm telling you, last year the snow was so deep it was asshole deep to a tall giraffe," one man told me.

When the bar eventually closed they insisted we continued drinking in their barracks. It was strictly against regulations but as long as we kept quiet and hid our van behind a wall then no one would ever know. I was concerned about sneaking a girl singer into a building full of horny soldiers but I was sick of playing the cautious old man and decided if Sue wasn't worried then why should I be.

As soon as we entered the barracks I was taken aback by the overpowering smell of marijuana. We were offered a wide variety of dope and it seemed like everyone was either pissed or stoned. Most of the soldiers we spoke to had been conscripted and forced into a world they hated with the possibility of being sent to Vietnam always hanging over them. I was never into recreational drugs, not through any moral high mindedness but simply because they terrified me. I always had an irrational fear that if I took one drag on a reefer I would be instantly transformed into a homeless drug addict. The others in the band indulged themselves to some degree while Lenny and Stuart were like kids in a sweet shop.

We had a great time playing pool and being entertained by the servicemen which was ironic considering we were being paid to entertain them. At 4 a.m. I was shattered and so asked if there was anywhere I could get some sleep.

"No sweat man. You can take my bed. I'll show you where it is," one man told me.

"What about you. Where are you going to sleep?"

"Oh man, I had me so much speed I ain't going to sleep for a week."

"Didn't you say you were off to play war games tomorrow and will be driving a tank?"

"That's right."

"Won't all those pills you're popping and the lack of sleep affect your judgement?"

"Hell yeah but we're all so fucked up out there nobody knows what's going down anyway." His friends laughed and agreed.

"Whatever happens just make sure you're all off the base by 7 a.m. and that no one sees you. If anyone finds out you stayed here the night we're all going to be swimming in shit for a week."

"Don't worry" said Lenny, "We won't be sleeping tonight so we'll call you in plenty of time."

I was led to a large room full of metal beds.

"That's mine. You take that one," I was told.

I threw myself on the bed fully clothed and the next thing I knew I was being shaken by someone trying to revive me from a deep sleep.

"Wake up man. You've got to go," a stranger was ordering me.

"What time is it?" I asked.

"8 a.m. You should be long gone."

Everyone was waiting for me by the van. Lenny and Stuart had smirks on their faces and had obviously been up to something.

"Get in. We've got to get out of here quickly," said Lenny.

As we drove through the camp I was amazed to see every army vehicle in sight was covered in bright yellow Cheeserat and Gorilla stickers reducing the cream of American military weaponry to a mobile advertising campaign for our band.

We made our way in high spirits to our next gig at an army base in Mannheim. At a service station we met more American servicemen and Stuart entertained them with his favourite party trick. He walked around the tables collecting the dregs from cups and glasses and emptied them into his own glass of coke. He then added the contents of an ashtray, some ketchup, gravy, salt and mustard and anything else he found laying around. If there had been some dog shit in the restaurant I have no doubt that would also have gone into his cocktail. Standing on his chair in the middle of the restaurant he swallowed the whole lot in one gulp, cigarette butts and all. Sometimes after his performance he had to run to the toilet to throw up and other times he didn't but either way it was all the same to him.

Things started to go wrong when the van broke down twenty miles from the army base. We phoned our agent who arranged for someone from the army base to rescue us and after waiting an hour in the cold a big Cadillac arrived driven by the chauffeur of one of the army big knobs. He connected a tow rope and we all got in the Cadillac except for Martin who was needed to steer the van. Our journey was along narrow country lanes and I noticed the speedometer dial passing the 60 mph mark. From the safety and comfort of the Cadillac it was hysterical to see the look on Martin's face as he tried desperately to steer the van and stop it from crashing into the back of us every time we slowed down for a bend in the road. Our driver was obviously irritated at having been ordered to leave the bar and wanted to get back to his drink as soon as possible regardless of what damage was caused. Miraculously we arrived at the army base without a crash and even our driver had to join in the laughter when we saw Martin step down from the van in a state of shock with his shirt wet with sweat.

We were over an hour late starting and the audience made it obvious they were not happy about it. It turned out to be a reasonable night but being a club for officers and their families it was very formal and without any of the chaotic fun of the night before. There was certainly no chance of being asked to stay behind for a drink after the show. While we were playing one of the army mechanics fixed our van so at the end of the night we were able to drive away and find ourselves a cheap hotel. Lenny and Stuart slept in the van and came to our room the next morning to get cleaned up which was what they were intending to do for the entire length of the tour.

Next morning was bright and sunny but the temperature had dropped sharply. It was a relief to find the van started first time and seemed to be running well so we made our way to the next venue. Halfway through the afternoon we were growing tired of the never ending autobahns so pulled off to take a more scenic route for the last 70 miles of our journey. We were in the middle of nowhere when the van ground to a halt. We had no idea where the nearest phone was and even if we found one we were too far away from the army base to be rescued again. Lenny and Stuart hitched a lift to the nearest town but being unable to get a lift back they had to walk for miles.

"There were no garages open so we'll have to wait until morning," said Lenny on their return.

"But what about the gig?" I asked.

"We don't have to worry about that. The agent has sacked us."

We were all stunned.

"Just because we've broken down. That could happen to anyone!" said Sue.

"It's not just that," said Lenny sheepishly, "apparently some stupid general in Karlsruhe saw our stickers on the tanks and found out we'd spent the night on the base. There's going to be a Court Martial over it."

Despite the cold we sat in a circle on the grass verge and prepared for a band meeting. I felt nothing but relief that the whole thing was over so we could go home but Lenny had other ideas.

"We're here now so I say we stay and find some gigs in Germany."

I was horrified. It never occurred to me that anyone would want to stay there without work.

"What are we going to do for money? We were expecting to get paid at the end of the week so we're all broke," I said.

"Martin's dad gave him £200 in traveller's cheques for emergencies. We can use that until the gigs start coming in," said Lenny.

"Don't worry, there's plenty of work out here for good British bands. I say we stay," said Stuart.

We put it to a vote and although I wanted to go home I didn't want to be the only person voting against staying so it was unanimous. I did feel bad about using Martin's dad's money to bankroll the band as I knew he couldn't afford to lose it.

It was a long, cold night and as I lay there tired and hungry on the metal van floor I thought of Linda's warm body and her soft dreamy voice. Then I thought of my mum's cooking and my cosy bed and all the other wonderful things that I took for granted.

12
Pissing on the Dance Floor

Early next morning Stuart and Lenny hitched a lift into town and it wasn't long before they returned with a tow truck that took us back to a garage. The fault was soon traced to a blocked carburettor and we were back on the road in no time. It always surprised me how the tiniest piece of crap in the wrong place can cause so much trouble. It was nearly 24 hours since we had eaten so the first priority was to get some lunch and discuss what our next step would be. With our stomachs full the world seemed a much brighter place and with high spirits we decided to drive to the nearest city and look for an agent. The nearest city was Reutlingen and when we reached the centre Stuart opened the window and shouted to a pretty young girl who was preparing to cross the road in front of us.

"*Oy! Fraulein! Kommenze here.*"

It was only meant as a joke but to our surprise the girl came over and talked to us in perfect English.

"Are you a band?" she asked enthusiastically.

"Yeah. We've just arrived. We're looking for a place to stay and some gigs," said Lenny.

"I have friends who manage a club for young people. Maybe you can stay there," she said.

I don't know if it was out of kindness or because she was lusting after the good looking Simon sitting by the window but she jumped into the van and led us to salvation.

"That sounds great. If they let us stay there we can play for free," said Stuart.

She introduced herself as Sandra and then directed us to the youth club where her friends were getting the hall ready for a folk concert that night. Everyone was very friendly and when we told them our situation they were happy to let us stay. There was a large hall with a door on one side leading to a room with some lumpy old leather couches just long enough to sleep on as long as I lay on my back with my legs hanging over the arm of the couch. There weren't enough couches for everyone so Lenny and Stuart slept on the wooden floor in the hall as comfort never seemed to bother them. The next day Sandra came to see us.

"I have found the name of an agent who might be able to get you some gigs," she said.

Lenny phoned the agent who offered us three nights in a large night club fifty miles away. We couldn't believe our luck. When we had finished congratulating ourselves I asked Lenny:

"How much are we getting paid?"

"I don't know."

"You mean you accepted a gig without asking how much we'll get paid for it?"

"We haven't got much bargaining power have we? Whatever we get it will be better than nothing."

He was right of course but I was horrified that our leaders did business in this way.

Once we settled into our new home things didn't seem so bad. We had our own en suite rehearsal studio with unlimited time on our hands to write and rehearse our own songs. That night a few of our new German friends took us out for some beers and we returned full of enthusiasm and vowed to get up bright and early next morning to start working on our first album.

It was midday before we were all awake so we didn't set up our gear until after lunch. From the day we first formed we never doubted that given the opportunity we would be able to write some great songs and now we had that opportunity. We started the session with some improvisation just to get warmed up but an hour later that was as far as we got. You would think that with five musicians in a room one of them could come up with some tiny shred of an idea but we had nothing. We abandoned the session and went to the local *Bierkeller* to find inspiration but all we found was sore heads from drinking on empty stomachs. For the rest of the week it was the same boring ritual every day. We sat down to write a song, one of us played a riff and then everyone joined in for an hour or two while we took turns to play the same meaningless improvised solo that we played the day before. It was in the middle of one of those jam sessions that it finally dawned on me that we were nothing more than an average band only capable of playing other people's songs and that the whole episode was a waste of time. I put my guitar away while they were still playing and went for a walk without anyone noticing I was gone. I wanted to go home there and then but thought I should at least wait to see the outcome of the gig.

By the time we arrived at the venue we only had a few Deutsche Marks between us and had eaten very little for days. By now it was much too cold to sleep in the van so we had the extra expense of hotel rooms. It was a large night club and we had to share the evening with a disco. A lot of the songs we learnt for the army bases were unsuitable for the gig so we supplemented our repertoire by playing long improvised solos at every possible opportunity. During our first break the barman asked us if we wanted a drink and we all accepted eagerly thinking what a nice guy the manager must be. Drinks kept coming up all night even when we didn't order them and as the barman never asked for money we assumed they were free like they had been on the army bases. The first couple of sets went quite well and people seemed to like us but as the improvised solos grew longer and more self indulgent the air grew heavy with boredom. On Saturday the weather turned bad so I wasn't even able to take a walk around town during the day to relieve the monotony. The boredom and hunger made us all irritable with each other. The only food we could afford was a coffee and a plate of chips at a mobile van and even that was restricted to once a day. By Sunday afternoon I needed to get away from the constant bickering so I went for a walk despite the dismal weather. I was thoroughly miserable and had never felt so hungry in my life. It was dark, the air was cold and there was a thick drizzle that kept everyone indoors. I was so different from the others in the band and I couldn't understand why on earth I had joined them let alone gone abroad with them. I had always been so serious about music while they treated it simply as an excuse for not doing a day job. Just as I was feeling at my lowest I found myself standing outside a railway station in front of a grubby little window. Suddenly I heard a choir of angels singing around a burning bush and it dawned on me the man behind the glass could sell me a ticket to freedom.

"How much to London?" I asked.

He didn't speak English but recognising the word *London* he wrote down a figure and showed it to me. It was much less than I had expected. I had no idea how much I would be paid for that weekend but it had to be at least enough for my train fare home. I returned to the club feeling like a huge weight had been lifted from my shoulders.

"Where have you been then?" asked Stuart.

"For a walk."

"He's been to get something to eat," said Lenny sneering heavily.

"Yeah I bet he's got some money stashed away and is keeping it to himself while we're all starving," said Stuart.

The simple act of going for a walk alone had distanced me even further from the band. At the end of the night Lenny went to get our wages and when he returned it was obvious something was wrong.

"Bad news?" asked Sue despite knowing the answer.

"You could say that. He only paid us 500 marks for the three nights."

It was a fraction of what we were expecting.

"That's 80 marks each. It's still better than nothing." said Stuart.

"It gets worse. He gave me a bill for all the drinks we've had," said Lenny.

"But no one said anything about paying for drinks. Half of them we didn't even ask for!" we all shouted in unison.

"Well they weren't free and the bill came to nearly 350 marks. That leaves us with 25 marks each."

That amounted to about £3. We had been well and truly ripped off and there wasn't a thing we could do about it.

"The bastards can't do that. Fuck it. I say we wreck the place." said Stuart.

None of us were keen on that idea if for no other reason than there were still some mean looking bouncers hanging around. Stuart got some satisfaction from pissing on the dance floor but considering it was the cleaner that would have to clean it up it was a pretty futile act of revenge.

As soon as we got back to Reutlingen I called my parents to ask them to send me the train fare home. Two days later the money was in my hand and I practically ran back to the club to tell everyone I was leaving that night by train. I was expecting a big argument but was surprised to find little reaction to my announcement. Lenny gave me the surprising news.

"While you've been out we've been talking. Sue and Simon also want to leave which is ok with us but we've just been offered a gig as support band for Warm Dust in a big concert hall. If you just stay for that gig we will drive the three of you to Ostend the next day. Stuart and I are going to stay here and form a band with local musicians."

I didn't know what to say. I was all set to go home that night but there I was yet again feeling obligated to stay. I didn't trust Lenny for a second but Simon and Sue confirmed that they were just as keen to go home as I was. I had heard of Warm Dust from their excellent reviews in the Melody Maker and it would be good to do a gig in a real concert hall.

"When is the gig?" I asked.

"Next Tuesday."

That was five days away.

"And you'll take us to Ostend the next day?"

"Yeah I promise."

"OK I'll stay but I'm telling you there is no way I will stay a minute longer."

Guessing that I probably wasn't eating properly my father had sent a little more than I asked for so I went straight to the nearest Wienerwald for a slap up chicken dinner, not exactly the Ritz but it was one of the most memorable meals of my life.

The next few days passed slowly and I spent as little time at the club as possible. As the end drew near the atmosphere in the band improved and for the first time we really started talking to each other.

"Why did you want to go to Germany when we had such a good job offer in England?" I asked one day when I was alone with Sue and Simon.

"I didn't want to go," said Simon indignantly.

"Neither did I," said Sue.

"But Lenny told me you were both keen to do the tour?" I said.

"And they said the same about you!"

There was nothing we could do but laugh.

"So why do you think Lenny was so keen to leave England?" I asked.

"Because he bought that Hammond organ with a bank loan using his aunt as a guarantor. He hasn't made a single payment so if he had stayed in England they would have repossessed the organ," said Sue.

"Why didn't his parents lend him the money or act as guarantors? They must be loaded," I asked.

"They knew Lenny would never pay it back so they refused."

"So the loan company will demand the money from his aunt?" I asked.

"That's right. Lenny was boasting how they are threatening to repossess her house if she doesn't pay the loan back in full."

So the whole disastrous episode all came about because Lenny didn't want to lose his Hammond organ.

The night of the concert arrived and the atmosphere in the hall was electric with the audience standing and packed together like sardines. We did our set and although I loved playing to such a large audience I was acutely aware of how average we were and that people were not there to see us. The audience clapped politely and we proceeded to remove our gear from the stage. Everyone was waiting patiently for Warm Dust to appear and when they did there was an eruption of applause. From their first song to their last I was mesmerised. Not only were they great musicians but their music was brilliant and I couldn't understand why they weren't world famous. Never was I more aware of the futility of what I had been doing with Cheeserat and Gorilla.

After the concert both bands were in the street loading the vans. Lenny and Stuart having been completely outclassed on stage felt the need to make some kind of an impression on the friendly and unpretentious members of Warm Dust. They were busy keeping us all amused with their usual party tricks when they introduced one we hadn't seen yet. Stuart turned to Paul Carrack, their lead singer:

"Do you want to see him piss on my face?"

Thinking he was joking everyone egged him on. The next thing we knew Stuart lay down in the middle of the street and gave the cue to Lenny:

"OK I'm ready."

Lenny whipped out his cock and started pissing all over Stuart and judging by the amount of piss he had in him it must have been planned. There were groans of disgust mingled with embarrassed laughter which only encouraged Stuart.

"Be careful. You're missing my mouth. Don't waste it!" shouted Stuart.

After Lenny pissed himself dry Stuart got up expecting a round of applause but only received an embarrassed silence. Not being one to give up easily he then announced:

"Do you want to see him shit on me?"

We all groaned and tried to talk him out of it but he lay on his back again with Lenny's bare arse towering above him.

"Come on Lenny. What's the matter with you?" shouted Stuart in disappointment.

"I'm trying but I can't."

Try as he could Lenny was unable to come up with the goods but there was no doubt if it were not for his uncooperative bowels they would have gone through with it. Everything went quiet after that and both bands went on their way. The mood in the van on our journey back was sombre and the stench of piss from Stuart's clothes was overpowering. In trying to impress everyone our leaders had only succeeded in demoralising us even more.

ON OUR LEFT: We have *Warm Dust.* **Achievements:** World class band, great music and a huge following all over Europe.

ON OUR RIGHT: We have *Cheeserat & Gorilla.* **Achievements:** Keyboard player pisses on the bass player's face.

What a joke we were.

The next morning we set out early for the long drive to Ostend. At the port we found a large four wheeled trolley and filled it with our equipment. We struggled to push it up the steep ramp onto the ship while a queue of cars waited impatiently behind us. At Dover we had to push the trolley for what seemed like miles from the ship to the port exit where we offloaded our equipment onto the pavement wondering how on earth we were going to get it all home. I could have easily gone by train but that would have meant leaving the other two stranded with all their gear. The only solution was to hire a car and as I was the only one with a driving licence it was down to me to take the risk. I wasn't old enough to hire a car so I had to lie about my age and pray I didn't have an accident.

That night when I sat down to eat with my family I felt like I had woken from a bad dream. The experience of Cheeserat and Gorilla with all the arguing, hunger and frustration was now in the past and I would never make the same mistake again.

13
Rug Ed Customers

After telling my parents about my gruesome adventure they half expected me to give up the music business but there was nothing further from my mind. That afternoon I drove to Fleet Street to put another advert in the Melody Maker and looked forward to another throw of the dice. It was like a lottery where I won nearly every time and got to choose from a number of mystery prizes although admittedly my last throw had got me a booby prize. With all that behind me I now had the luxury of putting it all down to experience.

I soon had a call from a band playing in a night club off Regent Street called The Stork Club. All the band members were much older than me and played mainly standards that I had never heard before; wonderful songs like: *Misty, Stardust, Around Midnight* and *When Sunny Gets Blue*. It was the first time I had played with such good musicians and the first time I had felt so inadequate. It was a live audition meaning I sat in with them to see if I fitted in. I tried to keep up with them as best I could and whilst it was a thrill to play with them I never expected to get the job. I was expecting to be asked to leave after the first few songs but they were very patient and encouraged me in every way they could. During a break I let them know how much I enjoyed playing with them and how I would love to learn more about the music they played and to my surprise they had already decided to offer me the job.

I stayed for the rest of the night during which time I had the unnerving experience of backing the famous jazz singer Salina Jones. It was the first time I had ever heard a real jazz singer live let alone play guitar for one and I was blown away by her extraordinary voice. Although I had kept up with my reading practice I was still far from being a sight reader. Trying to keep my place amongst the mass of dots and squiggles on the sheet of music was like trying to hang onto a bolting horse. I was lost 80% of the time and didn't have the experience to find my way back. During the next break I looked at the sheet music that the pianist had played from and wondered how it was humanly possible to play it so perfectly at first sight.

At £40 a week the money was good but the working hours were tough being seven days a week from 10 p.m. until 2 a.m. and on top of that I had to spend most of the day practising my reading but it was exactly the kind of job I wanted. It was like being well paid to go to music college except I would have never learnt as much at music college. After such a roller coaster start to my career it was a relief to find out that the band had been at the Club for three years so hopefully the job would be there for as long as I wanted it. The next night we started playing before any customers had arrived so I was able to take a closer look around. The first thing I noticed was that it was full of gorgeous single women. I thought I had hit the motherload.

"Wow. Why are there so many women here?" I asked. The others smiled.

"You don't want to get involved with any of those," I was advised.

Despite being a famous night club in its day it was now little more than a high class brothel. Customers were shown a selection of girls seated at the back of the club and asked to pick one. The head waiter would click his fingers at the chosen girl and then show them to a table where the customer was encouraged to spend as much as possible on food and drink. They often disappeared for a while and then later the girl would return alone to offer her services again.

Whenever possible the girls discreetly made fools of their clients aided by the dim lighting. One girl spent ages with her arm around a customer discreetly adjusting his wig. The drunker he got, the more she moved his wig until it was almost touching his eyebrows. Whenever possible she caught our attention making it impossible for us to sing and laugh at the same time. When Salina Jones came on to do her show she made the mistake of looking at wig-man halfway through her song and got the giggles so ended up having to leave the stage. The bass player jumped to the microphone quickly and announced:

"Sorry about that ladies and gentlemen. Salina has something stuck in her throat. She has just gone to get a rug of water.... sorry, I meant a jug of water."

At that point the drummer lost control and also had to leave the stage but even though he was in the band room he was laughing so much we had to play really loudly to drown him out.

After five weeks at the Stork Club I had paid off all my debts and even had a little saved when the management decided they wanted a change of band and gave us a week's notice. Three years they had that job and it only took five weeks with me for them to lose it. I was beginning to wonder if I was jinxed.

It always amazed me how the tiniest, most insignificant actions like walking into a room or turning our heads a few inches can turn our lives upside down. I was spending a boring evening at home watching a boring television program when the phone rang. I always had a special relationship with the seven steps that led down from our lounge to the dining room. It was not just that they taught me the proper way to fall at an early age but they also led to where we kept the phone which had now become the centre of my world. I had picked up that phone a thousand times before but on that particular occasion it not only changed my life but the lives of people I met in the years to come.

14
A Concrete Overcoat

It was the beginning of January and I was feeling down having only had a few replies to my advert that week when I answered the phone to a man who spoke with a strong foreign accent.

"My name is Renato Sambo. I am in England for a few days to look for a guitar player for my band. Would you like to work in Switzerland?"

As soon as he said his surname was Sambo I was sure it was someone taking the piss and was close to slamming the phone down but decided to go through the motions.

"How long is the contract for?" I asked.

"This contract is for two months but there will be other contracts after that. Can you come and meet me so we can talk properly."

"What's the money?" I asked.

"It depends on the job. Come and see me. I'm staying in Knightsbridge. Do you know where that is?" Yeah right and I was Frank Zappa staying at the Jupiter Savoy.

"I'm sorry but there's no point in me coming to see you if the money is no good. Tell me how much you're offering and I'll tell you if it's worth us meeting."

He mumbled something but still avoided my question so to get rid of him I agreed to meet and pretended to write down his address. Even if it was genuine the memory of the Cheeserat and Gorilla tour was still fresh in my mind and the thought of going overseas again made me nervous. Later that night I had a call from a well known band called East of Eden who told me they were looking for a new guitarist and someone had recommended me. I had seen them in concert shortly after their single *Jig a Jig* made the top ten and was very impressed. They were an excellent band playing just the kind of music I liked so I was looking forward to meet them.

The next afternoon, to my embarrassment I had another call from Renato Sambo. I was taken by surprise as in the past if I didn't turn up for an audition they got the message and never called back.

"What happened to you? I waited here all night. Couldn't you find the address?" he asked.

"I'm sorry. I couldn't get my car started. I would have called you but I lost your phone number."

It was a pathetic excuse but all I could think of on the spur of the moment.

"Can you come and see me now? I'll pay for a taxi if you like. I need someone urgently."

He sounded so nice I found it difficult to say no.

"OK I'll be there within the hour. My car is alright now so there's no need for a taxi. Give me your address and phone number again."

I took his details and put the phone down cursing myself for not having the courage to tell him I wasn't interested. I couldn't let him down again so I begrudgingly made my way to Knightsbridge. I only took an old acoustic guitar with me as I didn't want to take my heavy amplifier and electric guitar for what I was sure was either a hoax or a waste of time. The Knightsbridge address I was given turned out to be the house of Renato's girlfriend, Caroline Hepworth whose family owned Hepworth Tailoring, a major chain of clothes shops. Caroline answered the door and showed me into what was either a large dining room or a small museum. It was full of antique furniture and various other expensive looking ornaments.

"This is Renato Sambo and this is Pete who plays saxophone. I will leave you to discuss business," said Caroline.

We sat at the end of an enormous dining table and after no more than a minute of small talk Pete and I were taken aback when Renato offered us the job.

"Don't you want to hear us play?" I asked.

"There is no need. I'm sure you both play very well."

I liked him but the unprofessional way he did business made me more suspicious than ever. He continued:

"We have just returned from a successful six months in Japan and now I want to add a guitarist and saxophone to my band. I like English musicians so I have come to London to find some."

"So tell us more about this gig in Switzerland then," I said.

"It is in Gstaad. Have you heard of it?"

Pete and I shook our heads. Renato looked surprised and a little deflated.

"It's a very famous skiing village. A lot of famous people go there. Even your Royal Family."

We both shrugged our shoulders.

"We are playing at the Palace Hotel where we have played every winter season for the last nine years. It is a fantastic place and I know you will love it. Plenty of pretty girls."

"So what is the money?" I asked. There had to be a catch. Maybe he was expecting us to pay him.

"It is always different, depending on the job."

Yet again he avoided telling me how much he was offering and I was starting to lose patience.

"But what will you be paying us for this job in Switzerland. I'm sorry but I'm not going anywhere unless I know exactly how much I will be paid."

At last Renato got the message and took a notepad and pen from his pocket and made some quick calculations.

"I will pay you £60 a week."

Pete and I looked at each other in disbelief.

"What about food and accommodation," I asked.

"That is all included and there is no tax to pay. I will also pay your fare to Switzerland."

I tried to look cool but it wasn't easy. I even looked around the room for a hidden camera. The average salary for a residency in England was around £30 a week.

"So what do you think? Do you want to join my band?" asked Renato.

"OK. I'm in," I said.

"And me," said Pete.

"Fantastic. I will leave for Switzerland tomorrow and I want you to come out next Monday. We don't have much time to practice."

He took out a wad of notes from his pocket and gave us far more money than we needed for our fare.

"We don't need all this," I said, hoping to impress him with my honesty.

"It's a long journey and you need to eat on the way. You won't let me down will you? You are definitely coming?"

"Don't worry we'll be there," we both said at the same time.

We shook hands on it and over some weird tasting tea and biscuits we started talking like old friends. Renato was one of the warmest and most charming men I ever met. He was 39 years old and was a mixture of Italian and Lebanese. He had a round face that was permanently smiling and was dressed immaculately. He told us about all the things he had done and the places he had been to and it was a joy to listen to him. The more he told us about Gstaad, the better it sounded and I couldn't wait to get there.

"Will we be able to ski?" I asked enthusiastically.

"No. It is in our contract that we can't ski. The hotel is worried that you might have an accident and won't be able to work."

I wasn't disappointed as in the circles I moved skiing was only for the rich so I never expected to go myself. We made the final arrangements and shook hands warmly as we said goodbye. Pete and I stood on the pavement outside and started laughing.

"What do you make of that then?" asked Pete.

"Don't ask me. It all seems too good to be true and he never even asked us to play for him. It's all so weird."

We agreed that we would go in my car and I would make the travel arrangements. Driving home I should have been overjoyed about the job but there was something niggling me. It just didn't seem to make sense. You speak to a complete stranger for ten minutes and not knowing the first thing about you he asked you to drive halfway across Europe to play in his band. The thought of getting stuck in a foreign country with no money again horrified me but he had given us more than enough for the fare so what was the risk? My imagination started running wild. Renato was an Italian mystery man with lots of money. It had to be something to do with the Mafia. Maybe if we weren't good enough musicians we would find ourselves wearing concrete overcoats and taking a one way cruise to the bottom of the sea.

To make my uncertainty worse there was still the audition for East of Eden that evening. I had waited so long for a break and now there were two at the same time. Even though I had accepted the job with Renato I went to the audition just to see what it was all about and so drove halfway across London to the flat where the band lived. It was a large Victorian house with steps leading up to a forbidding black door with a row of doorbells on the side wall. From the pavement I looked up at the door and stood there motionless. Inside that house was a famous rock band playing the kind of music I liked and I had been recommended to them so there was every chance of passing the audition. What a life changing crossroads that was. I was normally very decisive but on that occasion I stood glued to the spot for fifteen minutes wondering what to do. Without any conscious decision I found myself walking back to my car as if my legs were tired of waiting and had made up my mind for me. East of Eden dropped out of sight and were never heard of again.

Over the next few days every time the phone rang I was dreading it was Renato telling me the whole thing was off. At last the time came for me to leave and I was just saying goodbye to everyone when the phone rang. It was Renato.

"There is a problem with the chalet. Can you wait a few more days before coming out?"

All the disappointments of my past came flooding back and I couldn't control my irritation. He wasn't cancelling the gig but it felt like he was going in that direction.

"I have booked the ferry tickets and my car is packed. I was just about to leave. This is very inconvenient."

Renato realised how annoyed I was and said calmly.

"Don't worry. I'll sort something out. Leave now as planned and I'll see you tomorrow night."

I was taken aback. One minute I was sure the whole thing was off and the next I was on my way. I felt more insecure than ever but at least I wasn't just sitting at home in limbo.

It was 8 p.m. when I picked Pete up and we set out on the 700 mile drive to Gstaad in my old Austin A40. I had recently put in a new engine so I felt confident that it would get us there but there was no heater and I could see the road through a rusty hole in the driver's door. My dear old dad always used to say that every car has a safe driving limit and you knew when you had reached that limit when the cheeks of your arse start to quiver. With that old car the AQL (Arse Quivering Limit) was 50 mph so it was a long, slow drive through Belgium and Germany. We entered Switzerland at Basel and at that time there was no motorway to bypass it so we stopped at a lovely old restaurant overlooking the Rhine and had an excellent meal. I wonder how many special moments like that I lost due to the convenience of motorways. I can't recall a single memorable service station meal.

A few hours later we started our ascent to Gstaad. It was very dark and very quiet and our excitement grew as the odd patch of snow started to appear by the side of the road. Slowly we drove along the winding roads feeling like we were entering a Walt Disney movie. At the top of a hill a few kilometres past Schönreid I just had to stop and catch my breath as we got out and looked down at the lights of Gstaad. There was absolute silence. The air was crystal clear and everything sparkled. We drove the last few miles slowly to the centre of Gstaad and stopped outside the Hotel Olden where we had been told to meet. As soon as we got out the car we looked up and there at the top of a steep hill was the fairy tale building of The Palace Hotel. During the daytime this building is spectacular but at night, when it is brightly lit from all angles it is just breathtaking. We went to the Hotel Olden reception.

"We have come to see Renato Sambo," said Pete.

"He is at the Palace Hotel at the moment but he has left instructions for you to check in and he will pick you up tomorrow at midday."

We were shown to a small double bedroom where for the first time I enjoyed the luxury of a continental quilt and wondered why on earth we didn't use them in England. Despite my tiredness I lay on the bed for ages trying to get to sleep. There was something very special about Gstaad and I couldn't wait to find out what it was.

15
Beware of the Nuts

When we finally woke next morning I went over to the window. The scene outside was extraordinary. There had been a heavy snowfall during the night and everything was covered with a thick blanket of glistening snow. There wasn't a cloud in the sky and the streets were packed with people wearing fur coats and colourful ski suits. What surprised me most was the holiday atmosphere you would expect to find at a Mediterranean summer resort. Pete came to the window and we couldn't help but laugh at the number of people hobbling past on crutches making the high street look like an après-battle scene from *Gone with the Wind.* It wasn't surprising that our employers didn't want us to ski.

We had a couple of hours to kill before meeting Renato so after the luxury of my first ever room service breakfast we went for a stroll along the high street. There were small designer shops on each side of the road and the people that went in and out seemed to be glowing with affluence. We passed *Chez Esta*, a café in the middle of the village and even at that off-peak hour it was packed. As I absorbed the atmosphere I felt an excitement that I hadn't felt since childhood. At the end of the village was an open air ice skating rink with banked seating where parents were watching their children enjoying themselves. Strauss was blaring out of the loudspeakers while skaters glided skilfully on the ice or not so skilfully hung onto the side rails for dear life. The place was swarming with beautiful people and strange looking characters that looked like they had stepped off a film set. One man was wearing a huge Stetson hat and hairy snow boots that went up to his knees, another man wore a black cape over his shoulders like Count Dracula. There was an abundance of fur coats worn by men and women and posers in designer ski suits who had no intention of ever going near a ski slope. Next to the ice rink was Charlie's Bar where we sat at an outside table. I ordered a coffee and became confused when the waitress asked me what kind of coffee I wanted as I had no idea there was more than one kind. Pete came to the rescue.

"I'll have a cappuccino," he said.

"I'll have one as well please," I said to save complications. I really wanted a coffee but a Cappuccino would have to do. A few minutes later she brought us two cups with mountains of cream on top and wonder of wonders .... a little wrapped chocolate on the saucer. I closed my eyes and was surprised how hot the sun felt on my face. I was scared to open my eyes in case I woke up. We returned to the hotel where we found Renato standing proudly beside his brand new Ford Mustang. We followed him on the five mile drive to the small village of Launen where he had hired a chalet for us to stay while we were rehearsing. The roads were still covered in snow from the previous night's fall but I had bought some chains in England so driving was not only safe but great fun. The scenery was amazing but as we turned one bend in particular we were greeted by a spectacular mountain range that spread out over the entire landscape. Inside the chalet we were introduced to the rest of the band who were waiting eagerly to meet us. We set up our gear quickly and after a quick jam session that confirmed that Pete and I could actually play our instruments we sat at a table and got to know each other.

The band was called The Renato Sambo Orchestra. It sounds very grand but most bands were referred to as orchestras on the continent regardless of size or instrumentation. Including Renato there were seven in the band and I was at least ten years younger than any of them. They all spoke fluent English. Renato was very famous in Gstaad and loved by everyone. Having spent a lifetime making rich and influential friends he was acknowledged as one of the top jet set singers in Europe. His greatest talent was his charm and the ability to socialise at any level. If you knew him, you liked him; it was as simple as that. He was a true professional, always dressing immaculately and whilst not expecting us to meet his high standards he insisted that we were always smart on stage. He knew exactly what his audience wanted and fed them great dollops of old romantic French and Italian songs at every opportunity. He was divorced and the only time I ever saw him sad was when he spoke of his daughter who was growing up without him.

I had to share a room with Pete which was not easy as he could be very moody so I had to walk on eggshells all the time. Dennis was on drums. He was a straight-laced Englishman who had lived in Italy for many years and spoke Italian like a native. He had been the leader of a band called *I Quatri Santi* that was very famous in Italy in the sixties. Mario the bass player was Italian and had typical Latin looks. He had a fixation about his bottom and was incapable of walking past a full length mirror without checking that the lines of his trousers fitted snugly around his arse. He had the uncontrollable habit that many Latin macho men had at that time of rubbing his crotch whilst talking to people. His favourite phrase was "all women are bitches" and he regarded them as nothing more than walking vaginas. Being afraid that he might be thought of as a mere mortal he would at every opportunity make the following profound announcement:

"I ave fucked women all over ze world. Ask any of zem and zey tell you I am ze best."

He said this with the pleading look of a child who has said something that is true but that no one believes. As a bass player he was not great but he did have a wonderful voice and it was strange that despite singing being the one thing he was unquestionably good at it was the only thing he never boasted about. The most annoying thing about him was that despite being such an arsehole and stitching me up on many occasions I still couldn't help but like him.

Paolo the trumpet player was also Italian. He was Mario's best friend and although very similar in character didn't have the bitter streak that Mario had. He had rejoined the band recently having left the year before to get married. His German wife was from a very wealthy family and she had insisted on him giving up music and going into the family business. Soon after they had a daughter and although Paulo adored his wife and child he was thoroughly miserable doing a 9 to 5 job and managed to talk his wife into letting him go back to music. Finally there was Gianni our musical director, a brilliant Hammond organist and musical arranger. He was light years ahead of us all musically and being a kind and patient man I was able to learn a lot from him. He was very overweight and not having much luck with women he took refuge in music. The band had been with Renato for several years and thought the world of him. It took a while for me to get used to the volatile Italian way and I was concerned the first time I saw them explode into a terrible argument over the dinner table until I discovered they were only arguing over whether a Ferrari Dino was a better car than a Porsche 911.

Pete and I moved into the chalet with the rest of the band and settled down to a week's rehearsal before starting the gig. At night we went to the Hotel Olden where Renato had arranged for us to have dinner. We were given the full set menu which included food I had never even heard of like asparagus, artichoke, croissant, rösti, fondue, raclette, Coupe Denmark, sorbet, the list was endless. Every meal was an adventure and there was nothing I didn't like. Until then an Angus Steak House was the height of luxury for me. I had never even drunk wine before and soon acquired a taste for it.

After dinner we played Yatzee and at times the noise from the excitable Italians was horrendous. Every time someone was happy with the dice they had thrown they shouted "CAZZONE!" at the tops of their voices. This is not strictly speaking Yatzee terminology but the Italian word for *big prick*. I don't know why they chose that particular word other than the fact it was a subject never far from their minds. In contrast, the three English musicians who played in the restaurant and were seated at another table got their kicks from moaning about the Italians.

At last the big day came for us to start work at The Greengo, a small, plush night club decorated entirely in green velvet with large silver mushroom shaped objects covering the ceiling. The club was usually empty when we started playing at 10 p.m. but it soon filled up until it was transformed into a film set with famous people everywhere you looked. Over the next few weeks the clientele included David Niven, Bridget Bardot, The Kennedys, Roman Polanski, Peter Sellers, Tom Jones, Elizabeth Taylor and countless other celebrities.

Renato seemed to know everyone personally and one night he whispered to me while we were on stage:

"Look, Gunter Sachs has just walked in."

"Who?"

"Gunter Sachs. Don't tell me you've never heard of him?"

I shrugged my shoulders.

"What does he do?" I asked. Renato looked at me with pity.

"He's a playboy."

I had heard of playboys but didn't know it was something people did for a living so I remained puzzled. After that Renato gave up on pointing people out to me. At the end of the first week we moved into a chalet that was provided for us by the Palace Hotel. We started eating at the Palace where we were treated like royalty and served five course meals with food even better than the Hotel Olden. Renato rented a whole chalet to himself where his neighbours were Peter Sellers and Yehudi Menuhin.

Having got rehearsals out of the way we had more time for socialising and that was when I discovered the village was swarming with horny young girls from the local finishing schools. Most of them were American and I didn't know if it was their culture or the fact that there was a shortage of young men in the village but I was surprised at how forward they were. It must have been the best ever time and place to be young. Every girl I met was on the pill and sex before marriage was practically compulsory. VD and other nasty sexual impediments were easily cured and not usually caught as long as you were reasonably careful although Mario frequently boasted he had caught the clap 35 times and had his own parking place at the clinic.

I had friends from all different walks of life and it was unthinkable that we would one day go our separate ways based mainly on wealth. As a teenager my old Austin A40 with the steering wheel on the wrong side was a novelty to my rich friends. They argued over who travelled in my car with me rather than in their friends' sports cars. It was so funny to see a row of parked cars which included Ferraris, Porsches and Lamborghinis and there in the middle was my little old banger. If I had been ten years older the same car would have given me the social standing of a leper with halitosis.

For the first few weeks I went crazy and slept with every girl I could. They were mostly from rich or famous families who had sent their daughters to finishing schools. I did have one special relationship with a girl called Jenny Thaxton, the daughter of Lloyd Thaxton who was a big celebrity in America. Jenny had a generous allowance from her mother so she was free to do whatever she wanted and having spent the previous year at a finishing school in Gstaad she decided to spend the winter season there. Jenny was 17, petite and stunning. She had long golden hair like the kind you see in hair commercials and luckily for me she hated the flash men that tried to impress her with money and fast cars. She was also bullshit proof which meant she was safe from the predatory Mario and his type of whom there was an abundant supply in the village.

In England my friends had regarded me as a man of the world but there in Gstaad and especially with Jenny I felt very naive. Jenny was two years younger than me and yet it was she who first opened my eyes to sex. I had never had any complaints so I thought in common with most men that I must be a good lover. She was the first girl I ever met who had no inhibitions about sex and told me exactly what she wanted although I did wish at times she did it with a little more subtlety. I was young and romantic so I found it hard to deal with when walking through the snow on a beautiful moonlit night she would say:

"Come on let's hurry back, I'm desperate for a fuck."

We became very close but saw each other as nothing more than really good mates that shagged each other to sleep every other night.

My inexperience was often a source of amusement to the rest of the band. On one occasion a crowd of us were sitting around a table in the Greengo with some nibbles in front of us. One plate contained some weird looking grapes and next to it was a plate of small nuts. I didn't like the look of the grapes so I stuffed a handful of nuts into my mouth taking care to act as *cool* as everyone around me. The nuts were disgusting and when I conceded that they were too tough for me to break with my teeth I discretely spat them out into my serviette. I would have got away with it if it hadn't been for Mario shouting:

"Hey look! Derek az just tried to eat ze olive stones!"

How was I to know that the grapes were olives and the nuts were the stones people had spat out? I had never seen an olive until that day. On another occasion I was invited to a birthday dinner for an Arabic princess. It was held in the fine dining restaurant at the Palace Hotel and our enormous table was full of some of the richest and most powerful men in the world. Everything was incredibly posh and there were waiters hovering everywhere. If I took a sip of wine a waiter came along and replenished my glass. When I dropped my knife a waiter appeared from nowhere to replace it with another. I was sure if I had farted a waiter would have came and sprayed my arse with cologne though I refrained from putting it to the test. That was the night I discovered that when squeezing a lemon onto your fish you must put your hand over the lemon to avoid spraying everyone within a ten yard radius.

Not being allowed to ski didn't bother me as there were so many other great things to do. I could go from bar to bar playing Yatzee, take day trips to the lovely city of Montreux or eat cheese in Gruyere. There was also Bern, Geneva, Lausanne, Zurich, so many fantastic places to visit and for the first time in my life I had real money to spend.

Gstaad was such a small village that you could walk from one end to the other in a couple of minutes and yet it took an hour sometimes as I stopped to talk to friends along the way. Après ski was best when there was standing room only in all the cafés and bars. There were many bands in that region but The Renato Sambo Orchestra was *the* band. It wasn't unusual for us to be sitting in a café trying to impress some girls when someone would recognise us from the Greengo and send over a bottle of champagne in appreciation of our music.

We were allowed to use the indoor swimming pool at the Palace so after a hard day of touring the cafés I spent a couple of hours sunbathing under the solarium lamps and watched the snow fall only inches from the large patio window. Sometimes I saw deer foraging for food amongst the nearby pine trees. A quick swim, a shower and it was time to get ready for a fantastic meal, all of which cost me nothing. It was paradise and for the first time since turning professional I had a secure job. Renato's band had been working constantly for many years and as he was very happy with me there was no reason to doubt that I wouldn't be with him for many years to come. I was never going to become rich and famous working for him but I was living the life of the rich and famous so what did it matter. Without realising it my great love for music had been pushed to the background.

As we came to the end of our contract I became restless but wasn't worried as I had no doubt that all of Renato's gigs would be as good as Gstaad and life would be one long party with the occasional break for holidays. We were booked to play in Sweden in May and Mario only had to hear the word *Stockholm* and he would turn into one of those dolls where you pull a string to hear the same message repeated over and over.

"Zere are beautiful women everywhere you look and you can fuck as many as you want. I fuck five or six every day and because I fuck zem so good zey come back every day and beg for more."

Even Gianni had found love in Stockholm the previous year and his eyes misted over every time we talked about the magic city. Yes, Gstaad had been fantastic but I was young and eager for new adventure.

By the middle of March Gstaad started to empty and it was time to leave for a two week gig at the Hilton Hotel in Dusseldorf. Jenny wanted to come with me and although I wasn't keen on the idea she had a way of always getting what she wanted. As we drove through the village we must have stopped ten times to say goodbye to friends that were passing.

It is impossible to exaggerate the profound effect that season in Gstaad had on me. Until then I never realised that such a lifestyle existed and I wanted to be a part of it. I loved the warmth and affection that the Italians openly displayed. I loved the food and the service. I loved how cosmopolitan the village was and how everyone mixed regardless of race, income or class. I loved the music, the girls, and the wine. I loved my new life but most of all, I loved the idea that I would never have to go back to working in pubs, and working men's clubs.

16
The Inconceivable Conceived

After a long drive to the Dusseldorf Hilton we set up our equipment and were shown to our hotel, the sight of which made my spirits sink. My room was dark and shabby and had a neon sign outside our window which flashed 24 hours a day. Jenny loved it.

"It's so much more fun than those boring old suites at the Hilton my dad takes us to," she told me.

The gig was in a restaurant so most of the time we played boring background music. I was glad Jenny had come with me as with nothing else to do we spent most of the time having sex or playing pool, sometimes combining the two.

Two weeks later we arrived in Geneva for a two week contract at the Club 69. I dropped Jenny off at the station where we said an emotional farewell before she took a train to Gstaad. She had changed her mind about shabby little hotel rooms and was looking forward to getting back to her cosy little bedsit. We were both ready to part but it was difficult saying goodbye. I soon cheered up when I found a lovely little hotel next to the lake and was ready for action. I had been with the same girl for nearly two months and I was ready to take the women of Geneva by storm.

Club 69 was a sleazy night club upstairs with a strip club downstairs. The head waiter drove a Lamborghini so I suspected it offered a lot more than drinks and music. Time passed slowly and I didn't meet any girls all the time I was there. It was frustrating having to listen to the band talking in Italian all the time without having a clue what was going on so I started to learn Italian. My day was split between practising guitar and studying Italian and while I knew it was all very good for me it was also very boring and the constant rain prevented me from even going for a walk. I was very lonely as the only women I met were at the Club 69 and they terrified me. We finished in Geneva at 2 a.m. one morning and had to start at the Park Café in Wiesbaden the same afternoon. Once again we stayed in a cheap hotel and to make matters worse I had to share a room with Pete again so I soon missed being lonely. Everything since Gstaad had been a big disappointment but we would soon be in Stockholm where I was assured it would be one long shagfest.

After two weeks in Wiesbaden I started out at 2 a.m. on the 800 mile drive to Stockholm. At Kiel in Northern Germany we took the ferry to Gothenburg and it wasn't until then that I realised what a rip-off off the English cross channel services were. It was cheaper to travel on an overnight luxury ship from Germany to Sweden, complete with cabin, disco and a smorgasbord breakfast than to travel on the tatty old cross channel ferries that only lasted an hour and a half. It was a long and tedious drive but I was full of hope and excitement with no doubt it was going to be a great gig and make up for the boredom of the last few weeks.

I arrived in a deserted Stockholm at 5 a.m. and the first thing I saw was a beautiful young couple walking stark naked along the pavement carrying their clothes in their hands. This was my kinda town! The second thing I saw was a condom machine next to a large poster that had a drawing of a penis with fluid dripping into a puddle; talk about killing the mood. I booked into a hotel and slept until lunch-time. When I returned to my car I found it had been broken into. My electric guitar was safe as I always took it with me but a window was broken and my acoustic guitar had been stolen.

We had to find our own accommodation so I went to an agency who offered me a room in an apartment with a family. The family spoke English but never invited me for a drink and a chat and seemed to disappear whenever I was around. How weird it was living in the same house as people I never saw. We were playing in an exclusive restaurant at the back of the Stockholm Opera House. They didn't feed us so the closest I got to sampling their food was when I grabbed a handful of chips from the kitchen when no one was looking. Stockholm turned out to be nothing like I expected as I found the people to be cold and unfriendly and the city sterile and soulless. During the two months we were there we all had our cars broken into at least once while Gianni whose pride and joy was his new Alpha Romeo had his car broken into and damaged four times. Someone put sugar in Renato's Mustang which cost him a fortune to have pumped out and repaired. It was inconceivable that Renato had upset anyone so it must have been out of sheer envy.

My dissatisfaction grew each day and I started to feel very homesick. I was sick of the music we played and longed to get stuck into something heavier. Everything irritated me and where Mario's behaviour had before been just annoying it was now driving me crazy. One night I did what would have been inconceivable just a few weeks before; I handed in my notice. I was taken aback at how upset Renato was.

"I was half expecting it. You haven't looked very happy for a while. Is it because of Mario?" he asked.

"What makes you say that?"

"I know how irritating he can be. Many of my musicians have left because of him in the past."

"So why do you keep him on?"

"I have sacked him many times but then he phones to say how sorry he is and swears he will change and I always take him back."

"It's not just Mario, it's also the music we are playing. I need to play more rock and blues."

For Renato, music was purely a means of making money and enjoying a good lifestyle. The idea that someone should leave a well paid job just because they didn't like the music they were playing was inconceivable to him.

"If that's what you really want then I wish you luck but I'll be very sorry to lose you," he said with great warmth as we shook hands and said goodnight.

That last month in Stockholm was truly awful although I only had myself to blame. Knowing that I was returning to England with no work I wanted to save every penny I could. Since joining Renato's band I thought I would always have a good wage coming in so I had been reckless with money and hadn't saved a penny. Food was very expensive in Sweden so I bought as little as I could but boredom on an empty stomach made me feel even more depressed. To pass the time I started to read for the first time in my life and having no idea what books to buy I went for the authors my father had often talked about like Somerset Maugham, Ernest Hemingway, George Orwell and my favourite, Emile Zola. I became obsessed with going home to England and the more I thought about it the more depressed I became about Stockholm. The only thing that took my mind off my homesickness was reading so I read for hours at a time which made me even more reclusive. It was early June and there is practically no darkness in Stockholm at that time of year so when we finished work at 2 a.m. the sun was already shining brightly. My curtains were very thin so as I found it difficult to sleep I started to read and got so engrossed in my book that it would be 9 or 10 a.m. before I fell asleep. What with my body clock going haywire and the hunger I started to hallucinate and at times found myself merging with characters from the book I was reading. For most books it didn't matter too much but I started reading *The Shoes of the Fisherman* and became convinced I was the Pope.

The day finally came for me to leave and I said goodbye to the guys in the band without the slightest regret. After six months of being away I returned to England believing it to be the best country in the world. Stupid as it sounds I was even looking forward to playing in smoky pubs again.

17
Back to the Future

Back in England I was surprised at that lack of response to my advert although I did do some gigs for the bandleader Don Lang. He became well known in the sixties when he was featured regularly on a television program call Six Five Special. It was a twelve piece band with an excellent brass section which was a thrill to play with. It was the first job I ever did where I had to sight read music and although I had practised my reading a lot since leaving Gstaad it was still a struggle for me to keep up. We backed some well known cabaret artists like Matt Monroe, Vince Hill and Peter Gordeno which was all good experience for me. Unfortunately Don had difficulty in finding regular work for such a big band so the gigs were few and far between.

The summer dragged on and I was getting nowhere when disaster struck: there was a strike in Fleet Street which meant that the Melody Maker was not being published. I hadn't realised until then how dependant I was on my adverts and my experience and ability meant nothing without them. The strike dragged on and I didn't have a single gig in my diary. To make matters worse my dear old Austin A40 broke down for the last time and had to be replaced. Things were looking pretty grim when the phone rang and I was surprised to hear Renato Sambo's voice again.

"Do you want to come back to work for me. I am getting rid of Mario."

How good it was to hear his voice and all the bad memories of Stockholm disappeared.

"Yes I would love to. Where will we be working?" I asked without caring whether Mario was leaving or not.

"We have a one month contract in Gothenburg and then a month in Zurich."

"Will we be going back to Gstaad for the winter?" I asked.

"Yes of course. Can you find me a bass player and arrange for him to join us in Sweden? He can practice with us in Gothenburg and start when we get to Zurich."

"No problem. I know just the man."

Once again in the space of a few seconds a phone call had turned my life upside down. The next day I went along to see Kevin, a bass player I had worked with several times and I knew would be perfect for the job. After telling him about my experience in Gstaad I think he would have done the job for nothing.

"The only thing is you have to be able to read music which I know you are a bit weak on. You've got three weeks before joining us so you had better practice as much as you can," I said.

"Don't worry I will. There is plenty of incentive with an opportunity like this."

I arrived in the German port of Kiel with less than a £1 in my pocket and a few drops of petrol in the tank. It is amazing the risks we take when we are young without even realising it. I don't know what I would have done if I had broken down on the way and it was long before credit cards came on the scene. Everyone in the band was pleased to see me and we had a good night in the disco on the ferry crossing to Gothenburg. I had been concerned that there might be bad feeling between Mario and I considering I was helping to replace him but he was on his best behaviour and very friendly towards me. Although it was good to be returning to regular employment and new adventures I was worried about playing in Sweden again and afraid that the Ghosts of Stockholm Past would come back to haunt me. I hadn't yet learnt that our opinion of a place is mainly influenced by our personal circumstances rather than the place itself and as I met a gorgeous girl in Gothenburg I thought it was a wonderful city.

It was one of the few gigs we did where we had a night off and it was on one of those nights that we were flown to Paris to do a private party for the Aga Khan.

"You have heard of the Aga Khan," asked Renato determined to educate me in jet set hierarchy.

"Yes of course. He is an evil warlord," I said.

Renato looked puzzled.

"I think you're getting mixed up with Genghis Khan" said Pete.

"So who is Aga Khan then?" I asked.

"A very rich Arab famous for giving away horses," said Pete.

We were picked up at Orly airport by a stretched limousine driven by a chauffeur who thought he was driving a turbo charged tank so even the speed loving Italians were in fear of their lives. We each had our own room at the Hilton hotel with a view of the Eiffel Tower just a few blocks away. How drastically my life changed in those days. One week a penniless musician and the next my own room at the Paris Hilton.

The party was at a restaurant in the centre of Paris and Renato seemed to know the Aga Khan as well as most of the guests. For the same money he could have employed any famous band in France but he had insisted on having his old friend Renato. If only I had picked up just a fraction of Renato's social skills my life would have been so much easier.

Back in Gothenburg I was surprised at what little concern Mario was showing at his impending unemployment.

"Mario does know he is being replaced doesn't he?" I asked Renato.

"Yes of course. Why do you ask?"

"He doesn't seem very bothered about it. Kevin will be arriving tomorrow and I am concerned that you might have changed your mind about Mario."

"Don't worry it's definite this time. He caused a lot of trouble during the summer in Munich."

The next morning Renato and I went to pick up Kevin from the port where he was arriving by ferry from England. We watched the boat dock and were surprised at how long it was taking for Kevin to appear. An hour later we were approached by a policeman.

"Are you waiting for Kevin Davies?" he asked.

"Yes," said Renato.

"We are keeping him here. Come back tomorrow," said the policeman aggressively.

"What is the problem? Are you ...." and before Renato had a chance to finish his sentence the policeman left without a word. Kevin was the last person in the world to get into trouble with the police so I was mystified. The next morning we returned to the port and had to wait over an hour before anyone spoke to us.

"Come with me," said an official as he led us to an interview room.

"Mr Davies arrived in Sweden with a single ticket, with very little money and no work permit. Is he going to work for you in Sweden?" asked the policeman in a voice which implied we were under suspicion of murder.

"He is going to work for me when we go to Switzerland in two weeks. He has come to Sweden only to practice with us," said Renato.

"Will you be giving him money while he is here?"

"No nothing. He will just get a room and food."

The policeman went away and came back half an hour later with Kevin by his side.

"You can take Mr Davies with you but if we find out he is working here you will both be arrested and deported."

We were happy to leave the port but angry at having been spoken to like we were criminals. Kevin was badly shaken as he explained what had happened.

"It was hell. They strip searched me and put me in a cell for the night. All I've had to eat is one sandwich since yesterday lunchtime."

Renato felt bad for Kevin so took us out for a slap-up lunch. We started rehearsing that afternoon but it soon became obvious that Kevin's reading was no better than the last time I had worked with him.

"I thought you were going to practice your reading?" I asked.

"I wanted to but I've been so busy."

"But you said you had no work?"

"I had to do some jobs for my mum and then there were some problems with my car."

It was all crap of course. I realised he was one of the many musicians who turn professional not for the love of music but for the love of not getting up in the morning. Although Kevin was a much better bass player than Mario it was taking him too long to learn our repertoire so Renato had to send him home and give Mario yet another reprieve. I suspected Renato never had any intention of sacking Mario and just brought Kevin out to give Mario a scare. I felt very bad for Kevin but he took the news well knowing it was his own fault as it was his reading that had let him down. That night we put his amplifier in my car and parked in the secure underground car park beneath our apartment building. We rose early the next morning to drive to the port only to find that my car had been broken into and Kevin's amplifier was gone. You had to feel sorry for the man. It was the first time he had ever worked overseas and his experience was to be arrested, strip searched, starved, sacked and then had half his equipment stolen. I never heard from Kevin again and often wonder if maybe his boat was hit by a meteorite on the way home.

The most memorable thing about the Mascot Club in Zurich was The Jolly Ville Motel where we stayed and which seemed at first sight to be incredibly good value for money. We all had our own room with a colour TV, nice bathroom and even a vibrating bed. It was only at night that I discovered why it was so cheap. All the walls were paper thin to the extent that you could hear someone brushing their teeth from two rooms away. Mario and Paolo loved the hotel as it gave them a chance to demonstrate their sexual prowess in public. The snag was they weren't the only macho men staying at the hotel so every night there was a cacophony of moaning as both men and women competed for the title of best lover with the prize going to the couple who made the most noise.

Before starting our season in Gstaad we had to do a private gig for Lord Rothschild at his Château in Paris. We set up our equipment in a hall that was obviously designed to stage theatrical productions. There was a large, kidney shaped stage at one end and several small boxes high up where people could view the stage. There was an army of staff rushing around getting everything ready for the party and spectacular flower arrangements everywhere I looked. It wasn't until the guests started arriving that I realised it was a fancy dress party but not like any I had seen before. Fortunes must have been spent on costumes and as I turned one corner I had a shock when I bumped into a woman with two heads, one on top of the other, each one being identical. She must have had the second head made especially so it was a perfect replica of her own.

18
Going Downhill

I drove up the winding mountain road that leads to Gstaad as slowly as I could to relish every minute of the journey. After setting up our equipment we were taken to our accommodation which was in a staff block rather than our own chalet but we were happy enough. I soon slipped back into my old routine which was even more idyllic than the year before as I already knew my way around.

Halfway through the season the atmosphere in the band seemed to decline rapidly for no reason. There were constant arguments which were mostly in Italian so I had no idea what they were about but there was no doubt Mario had a lot to do with it. It came to a head one day when Mario enticed a young girl into his bedroom knowing it was the girlfriend of one of Renato's best friends. There was no doubt that she led him on but equally no doubt that she refused to have sex with him which is when things got nasty. Her boyfriend found out about it and being one of the richest men in Gstaad he could have stopped Renato from ever working there again but he accepted Renato's assurance that Mario would be sacked as soon as the season was over. That night Mario stormed into the band room in a foul temper and gave us his side of the story.

"Zat fucking bitch. She come to my room because she want me to fuck her and Zen she change her mind. I say ezer you do it wiz ze mouse or we fuck. I not young boy you can do with ze hand. Zen she start to scream so I srow er out. She iz going to be sorry she mess with me. I am going to make it that she beg me to fuck er and iz going to be so good she never wants any ozer man. Zen when she wants me to fuck her again I say no."

Mario truly believed that the greatest punishment he could inflict on a woman was to not have sex with her a second time.

I was getting bored with hanging around the cafés all day so when Paolo suggested we tried skiing I jumped at the chance. He had discovered that it wasn't the hotel management that didn't allow us to ski but Renato and with things in the band being so unsettled we knew he wouldn't say anything. We hired skis and boots and made our way to the slopes with the thought of having lessons never crossing our minds. How I ever survived that first afternoon I will never know and needless to say we didn't have any health insurance. Our attempts at skiing involved getting as far up the T-bar as we could before falling off; pointing ourselves across the slope; skiing as far as possible across the mountain before crashing; laying on our backs while we swung our legs in the air so they faced the opposite direction and then repeating the same process in reverse. A really good run was when we managed to stop without crashing but we still had to lay on our backs and swing our skis around to face the other direction.

That night at work I had to constantly switch the weight from my leg with the badly twisted knee to my leg with the three inch gash caused by Paolo's ski when he crashed into me. When we finished work I hobbled back to my room and as I lay on my bed hardly sleeping due to multiple pains I vowed to never go skiing again. That resolution lasted until lunchtime the next day when I was back on skis again despite the fact I could hardly walk. I had a major breakthrough that afternoon when I discovered a technique known as "stopping" which avoided the need to crash every time I wanted to turn. I found that if I leant my body to one side and turned up the hill I slowed down until I came to a stop. After that I was hooked and skied every afternoon without fail but finished in plenty of time for après ski and relaxation under the sun lamps by the hotel swimming pool. Throughout the season I hoped that Jenny would turn up and cursed myself for not keeping her address but there was no sign of her. She loved skiing and we would have had such a good time together.

I went to many wonderful places in my life but the only time I was ever sad to leave a place was that winter season in Gstaad. For the rest of my days every time I smelt a log fire burning it filled me with exquisite memories of that magical time.

In early spring we left Gstaad for a one month contract at the Munich Hilton and it was there that the band fell apart. Gianni accepted an offer from a well known Italian singer. Mario definitely had to leave at the end of the Munich gig due to the incident in Gstaad. Denis had agreed to join the trio that worked in one of the other bars at the Hilton. Paolo was going to settle down with his wife in Germany after his father in law bribed him with a Porsche. Pete had been away for over a year and was ready for a change so that only left me and I was very restless as the music we played was driving me crazy. During a four hour night I was lucky to get two or three guitar solos and the rest of the time I was just strumming chords to old ballads. I also wanted to start singing again but Renato was not keen on the idea as my voice was still very weak. I loved the lifestyle that went with working with Renato but I was worried that if I stayed with him I was digging a rut for myself. Renato must have suspected that I was thinking of leaving when he called me to his room.

"I have just accepted a job in Greece. Would you like to come with me?" he asked.

"But who will be in the band? Everyone is leaving."

"We start in Athens at the beginning of June. I will find some new musicians and we can start rehearsing in Gstaad in May." The very mention of Gstaad was enough to swing it for me.

"What about Mario? Is he definitely leaving this time?"

"I don't have a choice. If my friend finds out Mario is still with me I will never work in Gstaad again."

"If I stay will you let me sing and play more guitar solos? It's driving me crazy just playing rhythm guitar all night."

"Of course. With Mario and Paolo gone I will need someone to help me with the singing. I'll even let you play some Santana."

He knew how much I loved Santana so it was an offer I couldn't refuse.

"OK. I'll stay."

I went to stay with some friends in Cannes and returned to a deserted Gstaad for three weeks rehearsal with the new musicians. Renato kept his word about letting me sing as long as I did my own musical arrangements which I was happy to do for the experience. The new band had none of the passion of the old one but we got on well together and Renato was happy to substitute passion for peace. One welcome addition was an American called Bill who wasn't a member of the band but managed to attach himself to us in the way that American travellers have a knack of doing. Renato agreed to let him drive the van to Greece in return for board and lodging while we were there. I never had many male friends in my life as I always preferred the company of women but Bill was the exception. We got on like a house on fire and spent most our time laughing and making fun of each other's culture. He was a natural entertainer so when we played Yatzee in the cafés it wasn't long before we had an audience and a queue of people wanting to join in.

By the end of May we finished rehearsals and set off on the long drive through Italy to the port of Brindisi. The 24 hour ferry trip was amazing as we sat by the swimming pool and watched thousands of small islands pass by. Athens had always sounded so exotic to me that I was half expecting to see men walking around in togas and carrying scrolls so it was a bit disappointing to find a noisy city which looked like many others. I rented an apartment with Sandro, the new keyboard player. It was the ideal bachelor pad except for the six lane dual carriageway only yards from my bed but what it lacked in peace it made up for in convenience as the beach was just the other side of that road. The most important thing for me was that apart from a large army of Hezbollah trained mosquitoes I had a room of my own. We were playing in a restaurant in the grounds of a horse racing course and although we were booked to play for five hours a night there were times when we only played for a couple of hours as business was bad.

Our ground floor apartment was not only opposite the beach but more importantly it was next to a bus stop. Every evening Bill and I sat on the balcony with a few beers and a loud game of Yatzee until some girls stopped to wait for a bus. Bill was definitely not what you would call a charmer but he never failed to bring back girls from that bus stop to join us for a drink.

It was a great summer but unfortunately halfway through our four month contract we were told that business was so bad they were terminating it without notice. In that situation musicians are faced with the choice of demanding the contract is honoured in which case the agent will never book them again or just accepting it. Unlike some of the other guys in the band who had families and really needed the money I wasn't that bothered. I had enough to get by for a while and knew it wouldn't be long before Renato found us another gig.

Bill and I thought we would make the return journey more interesting by travelling overland through Greece and Yugoslavia. We went to Constitution Square in the middle of Athens and sat at table with a piece of paper in front of us which said "Dubrovnik". Bill wanted to include the words "chicks only" but after I pointed out it might scare off some girls we came to a compromise whereby if any men approached us he promptly told them to fuck off. We were soon approached by two American girls who agreed to join us and share the petrol, one of them in the van with Bill and the other with me.

I was used to driving long distances with little sleep but it was usually on motorways where I put my brain on autopilot and drove effortlessly. That journey was much tougher as most of it was on little more than country lanes. The first afternoon driving through Greece was unbearably hot and I was constantly dehydrated. Driving through southern Yugoslavia we became so tired we parked near some haystacks to get some sleep. It was in the middle of nowhere so feeling vulnerable we both loaded our spear guns and slept on our backs with the guns by our sides. It was a pretty stupid idea as there was far more chance of shooting ourselves than a possible axe murderer. We must have looked such a sight: four strangers fast asleep up against a haystack in the middle of the countryside armed with spear guns. When we awoke there was a crowd of children standing around looking at us like we were Martians.

Halfway through Yugoslavia it started to rain making the roads very slippery and we saw a surprising number of accidents. It was late at night and I was very tired when I braked just before a bend and instead of the car turning it just continued sliding towards the edge of a cliff. The instinct for anyone going into a skid for the first time is to slam their foot on the brake and keep it there but after two seasons of driving in snow in Gstaad I was in the habit of pumping the brakes which on that occasion undoubtedly saved my life.

"What's wrong?" said my passenger after me struggling to control the car had woken her up.

"I just went into a bit of a skid. Nothing to worry about."

She never knew how close she came to death that night.

After a few days in the wonderful city of Dubrovnik we all parted company and I returned home to England. A few days later I had a call from Renato.

"We have a gig in Venice tomorrow night. Your flight tickets are waiting for you at the British Airways desk at Heathrow Airport."

The next evening I was sitting in the restaurant of the Luna Hotel Baglioni, one of the best hotels in Venice listening to a gondolier singing in the distance with a voice that wouldn't have been out of place at *La Scala*. The gig was for Count Volpi, a rich Italian aristocrat in what from the outside looked like a derelict building but from the inside was a magnificent palace. After setting up our equipment we went out onto a balcony where we saw a long procession of gondolas making their way slowly to a drop off point just beneath us. Glamorous couples stepped onto a red carpet that led to the Count's palace. It was just like a fairy tale.

The palace soon filled up and everywhere I looked there were faces of the rich and famous which included Grace Kelly and Sophia Loren. I had done several very lavish gigs with Renato but nothing on that scale. One woman wore a pair of sandals made entirely of diamonds with handbag to match. During my time with Renato I had often eaten in top class restaurants but the food I saw and tasted at that party was on an entirely different level. The clothes, the flowers, the decorations, the furniture and ornaments, the servants in their immaculate uniforms, everything was amazing. We played until six in the morning without a break but with the money we were paid and the way we were treated none of us complained. The next day we met Renato and after paying us double what we had expected he said:

"The Count was so pleased with us he said you can stay for a couple more days in the hotel if you want. All your food and drinks will be paid for."

I was surprised to find that I was the only one of us to take up the offer as they all had other commitments but nothing would have prevented me from making the most of an opportunity like that. In the afternoon there was a big regatta with hundreds of magnificently decorated vessels gliding along the main waterways while music was being played on every street corner. After dinner I sat in St. Mark's Square and listened to a small orchestra playing Mozart's *Elvira Madigan* while I drank a

Bacardi and Coke that cost the same as a meal for two in England but it was worth every penny. How I loved the life I led with Renato and I realised for the first time that I wanted to stay with him for good. I just had to learn to accept the rough with the smooth and if there were gigs or places I didn't like I had to learn how to make the most of them instead of complaining and feeling sorry for myself. My ambition was no longer fame and fortune but contentment and there is no greater goal in life.

19
The Waiting Game

Back in England I waited eagerly for Renato's call to take me to my next adventure but after two weeks passed with no word from him I started to feel restless. There was no point in looking for gigs in England when I could be called away at any minute but apart from that I couldn't bear the thought of going back to work in pubs and clubs. A month passed and I was running out of money and patience so I phoned Renato.

"What's happening? It's been a month now and I have to find work quickly."

"Don't worry. I should have something soon. I'll call you when I know for certain."

He sounded very positive but as the next definite gig wasn't until Gstaad in December I decided to put an advert in the Melody Maker as insurance. I soon had an offer from an American country singer called Tom Passmore who was touring the American military bases in Germany. I told him I didn't know how long I would be available for but he needed someone urgently so was happy for me to work for him even if only for a few weeks. It was convenient for me as Tom paid my fare to Germany and I could go straight onto Renato when he found a gig.

Tom Passmore was a colourful American character from the Deep South who spoke fluent German having lived in Germany for the past three years with his wife and children. There was also a bass player and drummer who were active servicemen and played in the band in their spare time. Considering we rarely got home from a gig before 4 or 5 a.m. I don't know how they managed to function. I rented a nice little apartment on the outskirts of Kaiserslautern. We worked three or four nights a week and although I enjoyed the gigs the travelling was horrendous as we frequently drove two or three hundred miles to a gig and returned straight afterwards. When we weren't working I made futile attempts to teach myself German and an equally futile attempt at writing songs. I was bored and lonely but it didn't matter because Renato would call at any minute to rescue me. The worst that could happen was I would have to wait another two months before starting in Gstaad.

Winter was setting in and the interminable drives to gigs were taking their toll on me. I was also having trouble getting my wages from Tom so if it hadn't been for the chance of working with Renato I would have gone back to England. Another month passed with still no word from him so I called again. There was no answer. I called him repeatedly for a week until Renato's mother finally answered.

"Hi. This is Renato's guitarist. I am having trouble contacting Renato. Can you tell me where he is?" I asked.

"He is working in Sardinia with his new band."

I was devastated. It took me two days of detective work and expensive phone calls to find out that Renato had been offered a job in Sardinia but it wasn't paid enough to include a guitarist so he went without bothering to tell me I wasn't needed. The next day I packed my car and went to Tom's house to collect the money he owed me. His wife showed me into the living room where he was sleeping full length on a couch with his back to me looking remarkably like the cartoon character Andy Capp. I called his name a few times and he ignored me a few times so I left in disgust knowing that I had worked the last two weeks for nothing.

It rained non-stop during the long drive back to the England and the road works seemed to go on forever. At first I was angry at having been treated so badly by Renato but I was determined to be positive about it. If I had stayed with him life would have been sweet but I would never have become the kind of guitarist I wanted to be. It was time to return to my old path.

20
Cruising Crazy

It was a cold and miserable autumn day when I made my way to the Melody Maker office with my tail between my legs. With an advert in place the next step was to start taking songwriting more seriously. I always knew I had it in me to be a good songwriter but every time I tried the only thing I created was frustration. Finally I managed to drag a few songs out of me and bought a tape recorder to make some demos. With the help of a hammer and nails I managed to transform a few scraps of wood into a table that Chippendale himself would have been proud of. My first bedsit recording studio was in business.

I had six songs ready to record and got to work on them but it was not easy as my tape recorder was so basic I needed to get from beginning to the end of a song without a mistake. With better equipment it is easy to go back and correct mistakes and also add to what you have already recorded. I played my demos to a few friends and they were impressed so it was time to submit them to the big boys. I looked in the Yellow Pages and selected six record companies at random who were to be given first refusal of my songs. I was concerned that I might get offers from two or more companies at the same time and they would get pissed off being in competition but I would cross that bridge when I came to it. I stood next to the post box with demos in hand thinking how exciting it was that any one of those packages could lead me to rock stardom. It was a Tuesday morning and during the short walk home I calculated that the earliest I could expect an offer of a recording contract would be Friday.

That night I could hardly sleep I was so excited. With any luck the record company would give me an advance so I could concentrate on writing more songs rather than wasting my time playing in pubs. I lay in bed working out how much advance I needed in order to live comfortably while I was recording my first album. I took it for granted the record company would want me to put a band together and promote the album with a tour so I started creating the Melody Maker advert in my head: "Drummer and bass player wanted for major new recording contract and world tour."

Friday came and went and there was no sign of record companies hammering on my door. Every morning I waited eagerly for the post and every morning there was nothing. By the end of the fourth week I'd had two replies with standard rejection letters and nothing from the remaining four. It took a while for me to accept that the songs were rubbish. The tunes were weak and like so many songwriters with no talent for lyrics I wrote a few obscure lines and pretended to myself they had hidden meanings. Amazingly some people liked the songs and even found hidden meanings of their own but they certainly weren't any that I had intended. It was a great disappointment but I convinced myself it was a minor setback and there was no doubt in my mind that I would get there in the end.

My next job was at a five night residency split between the Tottenham Royal and The Empire Ballroom in Leicester Square working for the bandleader Ronnie Smith. Few people outside the music business will be aware that the person with the least musical ability is usually the bandleader and Ronnie Smith was no exception. He was unable to do even the simplest musical arrangement so despite my lack of experience he paid me extra to do them. I had no idea what I was doing but as the band was so bad no one was any the wiser. I was happy to be doing a lot of the singing so although my voice was still very weak it was improving. In the past I had always been the youngest and most inexperienced member of the band but for the first time I was musical director and enjoyed being a big fish in a tiny puddle. It was during a break at the Tottenham Royal that I decided to go for a coffee not knowing that it was another trivial decision that would change my life and the life of a young girl waiting to be served at the coffee counter.

Julia was 21 (the same age as me) with long frizzy brown hair that she hated but everyone else loved. She gave me her number and the next day we spent hours on the phone talking about nothing. I discovered that after leaving school her father had pushed her into a job as a trainee health inspector but with the prospect of yet more years of intense studying she handed in her notice and started a secretarial course. She didn't want to be a secretary either but at least it was a profession where there was never any shortage of work. On our first date we went to see *Jesus Christ Superstar* at the Palace Theatre and with the last of my savings had a meal at a lovely little Italian restaurant opposite the theatre. Everything was perfect and by the end of the evening we were in love. Having spent so long travelling and without being able to establish a relationship it was not surprising I was so keen to jump into one with Julia.

After growing tired of Ronnie Smith demanding we work extra nights without getting paid I left and joined a band called Joseph's Colours. The bandleader, Johnny Joseph was a kind and honourable man but unfortunately he insisted on playing drums badly with the band instead of waving his arms around and pretending to conduct like other bandleaders. We played three nights a week in a large dance hall in Croydon and every Sunday at the famous Café de Paris in Leicester Square. Every minute at the Café de Paris was purgatory for me and to make matters worse we had to play for the afternoon tea dance as well as at night. We played mainly old dance standards and sing-alongs and as it was the trumpet player and saxophonist that got all the solos I had nothing to do but strum chords for hours on end. The only thing that broke the monotony was watching the gigolos at work. One woman who came regularly was so old she could hardly walk let alone dance. She would stand in the middle of the dance floor and tremble in time to the music while a beautiful young man danced gracefully around her with undying love written all over his faces.

In late spring we were offered a five month contract to work on the QE2. I had several friends who loved working on cruise ships so it was with great excitement I set out on my first voyage which was a tour of the Caribbean via New York. It wasn't long before my excitement was replaced by an overwhelming desire to die as the weather turned bad and seasickness consumed my entire body. It came as a surprise to me as I had never suffered from travel sickness before despite being in some pretty rough seas. The experienced sailors amongst us assured me it would take three days to get my sea legs and after that I would be OK and sure enough, after the third morning I never felt sick again.

All the musicians on the ship had to share a cabin with someone and at first I thought I had drawn the short straw when I was told to share with the bass player Colin Johnson whom I had never met before. He looked like he had been living rough for the last six months but he turned out to be a kind and well natured man and certainly the ideal cabin mate. He had a permanently dazed look with a repertoire of silly but infectious expressions like *yamaholla* and *skidalalambo* that spread around the ship until everyone was saying them. When he walked into a room people started laughing in anticipation of what he would do next as even the simple act of making a cup of tea could leave the band room kitchen area looking like a war zone. He never told jokes or made any conscious effort to be funny; he just *was* funny in a natural way.

"Every time you work the boats you lose a shitload of brain cells. I've done five world cruises and dozens of shorter ones so all my brain cells left me years ago," he told me on many occasions.

It was reassuring to be sharing with someone who knew the ropes aboard ship. We were given the same class of cabin as the passengers but they were the most basic cabins available at the bottom of the ship. There were two beds with just enough room to walk between and a small toilet and shower. We had no porthole so on waking up after a late night we often had no idea whether it was day or night. Within minutes of us occupying our cabin Colin got to work with what he said were the *essentials* of life on the boats. He tied a washing line across the full length of the cabin and as he had brought a lot of dirty washing with him it was soon in use. He disconnected the cabin speaker so we wouldn't be bothered with fire drills. He tied a piece of string to an old key and taped the string to the wall so the key was free to move around.

"What's that for?" I asked.

"That will tell us which way the boat is moving, whether it's side to side or up and down," he said with great authority.

"What difference does it make to us which way the boat is moving?"

"Don't know. I saw someone do it once and thought it was really cool."

After he had finished settling in he lay on his bed and went to sleep despite being 11 a.m.

"Sleeping sickness is a big problem on the boats. You mustn't fight it," he was constantly telling me.

Our first day was the only time any of Colin's clothes were in his cupboard as after that they were either on his washing line or on him. They became part of the fixtures until one day I looked up and noticed his torn underpants which were hanging just a few feet from my head.

"I've just realised. Those bloody underpants of yours have been there for three weeks! Why don't you put them away?"

"Yeah but I like them *really* dry," he said. It was impossible to get angry with Colin.

We ate in a corner of the main dining room and chose from the same menu as the customers. We could have caviar, smoked salmon, fillet steak and anything else in between. Unfortunately waiters usually hate serving musicians and resent them being treated better than other members of staff. This meant we often had to wait a long time to be served by grumpy waiters. After a few weeks some of us were so fed up with the lavish menu three times a day that we ended up eating baked beans on toast in the crew's mess but we were then resented by the crew who said we should be eating in the restaurant.

After the Caribbean cruise all we did was go backwards and forwards to New York for a few weeks so it became very monotonous. The crossing was five days and we were only in New York for twelve hours so it meant 10 days at sea with only a few hours on land to break it up. Crossing the Atlantic even in the middle of summer can be very grim so walking on deck is an ordeal. It was a bad time to be on the QE2. The grand days of cruising on ships like the Queen Mary were over and there was not enough competition amongst cruise liners for them to make any effort to keep customers happy. There was a cinema but they only changed the films every couple of weeks. The health and fitness facilities consisted of a tiny room with one weight lifting machine which couldn't be used because it was next to the infirmary and made too much noise. There was a small indoor swimming pool with no seating around the outside and I never once saw it being used. I spent most of my time playing table tennis but had trouble finding good partners as musicians are not generally known for their sporting ability and it was not the easiest sport to play when the boat was moving around a lot. On the rare occasions when the weather was good enough to go on deck the wind created by the boat's movement was so cool that I had to look for a sheltered spot and sit under a blanket. If that wasn't enough to put you off, the sun loungers were often covered with soot from the ship's funnels.

Working on a cruise ship affects people in different ways. A few weeks into our contract and the personality of some of the musicians started to change. Two of them stayed in their cabin most of the time drinking and listening to music. When they did surface they were very aggressive and blew up at the smallest thing. It got so bad that one of them had to be replaced the next time we returned to port. The Scottish trumpet player who was belligerent at the best of times was beginning to show psychopath tendencies and wanted to fight everyone. One of the saxophone players despite having a fiancée at home was making his way through the limitless supply of gay crew members much to the distress of his very straight cabin mate.

There was a brilliant pianist called Pete Lee who worked in a jazz trio in the nightclub and it was he that warned me about the perils of working on a ship.

"I was on the QE2 a couple of years ago and had a breakdown. They stopped me diving into an empty swimming pool from the first deck and I had to spend the rest of the voyage in the infirmary drugged up to the eyeballs."

He was full of similar stories of musicians who spent too long on cruise ships and I started to be concerned for my own sanity. The only thing that kept me going was that every time we returned to Southampton I drove home to London even if it was only for a few hours. It was on one of those home visits that my mother passed on a surprise message.

"Renato called. Phone him urgently."

All I could think of was how sick I was of the QE2 and how I would do anything to go back to the life I had with Renato. I phoned him immediately. How good it was to hear his voice again.

"Do you want to come back and work for me?" he asked.

No mention was made of him letting me down before and I didn't care.

"Yes I'd love to. When do you want me?"

"I'm not sure yet. When will you be home next?"

"In ten days."

"OK. Call me then and I'll have some news for you."

I put the phone down and started dancing around the room with joy until our Labrador thought it was a game and started biting my ankles.

Working for Renato wasn't going to be easy as I now had Julia to consider. I loved her and didn't want to lose her but there was no way I was going to turn down an offer from Renato. I could start working with him and then when I was settled Julia could join me. I had talked to her endlessly about my travels with Renato and as she also loved travelling it was the ideal situation. In Gstaad we would have a fantastic time skiing every day although I put to the back of my mind the other gigs where she would have to spend most of her time sitting in a shabby hotel room.

The next voyage was more frustrating than ever with the thought of Renato and Gstaad making me even more discontented. As soon as we docked at Southampton I ran to the nearest phone box and called Renato. There was no answer. I phoned constantly the whole time we were in port but there was still no answer. It was with a heavy heart that I rejoined the ship knowing it would be another ten days before I could contact Renato again. Ten days later the same thing happened and I felt even more frustrated. After that I called Renato every time we got to port and even tried from New York but there was never any answer.

Back on board ship life was more difficult than ever and I even found myself drinking too much which is something I had never done before. I told John I wanted to finish my contract two months early and he was very understanding. You either love or hate working on the ships and I met several musicians who spent most of their lives on them. For some it is a refuge from an unhappy home and for others it is the perfect solution to bad debts or a fear of responsibility. Some loved the cheap booze available 24 hours a day and some became institutionalised with a fear of living in the real world again. As for me, I was too attached to my brain cells to ever consider working on a ship again.

21
Suspicious Packages

It was the middle of August 1974, a time of year when there wasn't much work around so I was happy to get the offer of a five night residency at the Hammersmith Palais with an excellent band called The Sands of Time. They had a minor hit the year before with a song called *Down by the River.* It was a good gig but the hours were unusually long with us being at the venue for six hours a night. At the end of our one hour sets the stage revolved and the Ken Macintosh Big Band took over during our breaks. Disco music was really taking off so there was an incessant BOOM BOOM BOOM from the bass drum most of the night that continued inside my head until lunchtime the next day.

The disco era was the start of a revolution in music that took musicians unaware and was to result in the decimation of live music in dance halls all over the country. Until then it was normal for bands to stop playing after every song and the audience would stop dancing and applaud so there was an interaction between band and audience. When disco started, drummers were instructed to keep the beat going between songs so there was no break in the dancing. It seemed like a good idea at the time and was certainly what dancers wanted but without realising it we were destroying our relationship with the audience. There was no longer an opportunity to applaud and show appreciation of our music. At that time nearly every city in the country had two or three dance halls with two resident bands meaning around 16 musicians were employed all of which were replaced by one DJ. It wasn't just that discos were cheaper; youngsters simply preferred them to live bands. We played every Sunday night at the Ilford Palais where the audience was very young. During our set no one danced and everyone sat around looking as miserable as sin. The minute we stopped playing and the disco started they all packed onto the dance floor and started enjoying themselves. I knew it wasn't us as it was the best band I ever worked with, it was just that the kids seemed to be more comfortable with a DJ. A war between discos and musicians had started and we didn't even know it.

It was not the only war that was going on at that time, the level of violence at the Palais was appalling. Every night fights erupted which we could see clearly from the stage and at times looked like a scene from a Wild West film with chairs and bottles flying everywhere. It seemed to be an unwritten law that if anyone was badly hurt they dragged themselves onto the stage where they would be left alone to recover. It is usually best for a band to continue playing when there is trouble so we often played with injured bodies scattered all over the stage.

It was also the time of the infamous IRA bombing campaign that included the atrocities in pubs in Birmingham and Guildford. Everyone was told to be especially vigilant and look out for suspicious packages but every night we had to play with dozens of handbags and packages left on the stage only yards from us.

I enjoyed the gig and we got on well together as a band. We already had record company interest so we just needed to find the right song and there was every chance of another record deal. I had plenty of guitar solos to play and was even getting a small following of guitar enthusiasts coming to watch me. Julia and I had been together for over a year and were very happy so we started looking for a flat so we could move in together. It sounded so easy when we made the decision but it was a terrible time to find rented accommodation. We frequently turned up to view run down, overpriced flats with queues of people waiting outside prepared to pay anything to move in. To our surprise we found it was cheaper to pay the mortgage on a house than the rent on a flat so we put down a deposit on a small terraced house in Edmonton. On the day we exchanged contracts I asked Julia to marry me and she accepted.

Disaster struck a week before the wedding. One night at the Hammersmith Palais I returned from a break and went to pick up my guitar when to my horror I found both my guitar and its case had disappeared. Someone must have calmly walked out the front entrance carrying it in full view of several security guards. It is a devastating blow for a musician to lose their beloved instrument and it didn't help when the policeman investigating the case implied that I had stolen it myself as an insurance scam.

On 1st March 1975 Julia and I were married. We had no money for a honeymoon and I couldn't even afford to lose a night's wages so I worked on our wedding night which neither of us minded. An announcement was made and we were presented with a bottle of champagne on stage while the packed dance hall shared in our happiness with a big round of applause.

What a magical moment it was to walk through the front door of my own house for the first time even if it was just a tiny terraced property. As I looked around the empty rooms it was hard to believe that we could decorate or change anything we wanted without asking anyone's permission. For me the best thing was the garden as the house where I grew up only had a tiny concrete back yard. The idea of growing my own food really appealed to me and much to the dismay of our elderly neighbours I transformed what was a pretty little flower garden into a vegetable farm.

Two weeks after my guitar was stolen we returned from a break to find the bass player's rare Fender guitar suffered the same fate. Tom had kept his guitar case in the bandroom as a precaution but the thief had just walked out the front door with the guitar under his arm and still no one stopped him. A week later the drummer had his cymbals stolen. A few days after that Tom walked into the bandroom one night and dropped the bombshell:

"I've got bad news. We've got the sack. Apparently having our gear stolen is causing the company too much trouble."

"But I thought they told you we were one of the best bands on the circuit?" said Val the singer.

"That's right but it's easier to sack us than to sort out their security," said Tom.

It was a bitter blow and couldn't have come at a worse time as unlike the previous occasions when I was out of work I now had a mortgage and all the other bills that go with it. I needed a residency and not just the occasional gig which I had been able to get by on in the past. Tom tried hard to find us another residency but it was hopeless as it was Mecca that employed most of the bands like us and we had been blacklisted because of the trouble we caused them in having our gear stolen.

By now my sight reading was quite good so I was able to get gigs with big bands but although they were well paid they were awful. We would meet the coach in London at around 3 p.m. and the band would be driven two or three hundred miles to the gig. We set up our gear and played two long sets of mainly old sing-alongs that could be played by any first year guitar student. At the end of the night we packed our gear onto the coach and drove back to London arriving at around 5 a.m. By the time I got home, slept and had lunch it was nearly time to meet the coach for the next gig. Some musicians loved that kind of life as you get paid to have a night out with the boys and drink as much as you want but for me it was hell.

Julia had a good job but we were still struggling to pay the bills. I left an advert in the Melody Maker running every week but very little came from it. The one consolation was that it was the glorious summer of 1975 and I woke up every morning to the sight of my vegetables thriving in the constant sunshine.

I was getting quite despondent when the surprise phone call came:

"This is Bob Adams calling from Johannesburg. You sent me a tape a few weeks ago?"

I had no idea what he was talking about but then remembered a friend of mine suggested I send him a tape as he was often looking for British musicians.

"Oh yes. I had forgotten all about that."

"I'm very impressed with the tape. Are you still interested in coming to live in South Africa?"

"Yes definitely," I said with growing excitement.

"I have a six night residency at the Carlton Hotel and judging by your tape I think you would fit in perfectly."

"What's the money?" I asked.

"It's £70 a week and you will have no trouble getting session work which you can do during the daytime so you will be able to earn a lot more."

£70 a week was already a lot more than I earned at the Hammersmith Palais and the thought that I might finally get some recording session work made it exactly the kind of job I was looking for.

"Will you pay my fare?"

"No you will have to pay that yourself."

This was a big drawback as not only would we have to borrow money for the plane fare but having the employer pay travel expenses is one of the few safeguards a musician has when working abroad. It shows the employer is serious and if something goes wrong at least you only lose money for the gigs you have turned down. I was nervous but the chance of earning a lot of money with the excitement of travelling to a new country was worth taking the risk.

"Ok. I accept."

"Excellent. I'll send you all the details by post today and I'd like you to come out as soon as possible."

One minute I was sitting at home wondering how I was going to pay the mortgage and the next I was preparing to emigrate. What a brilliant way to live. I phoned Julia straight away.

"What do you think of your job?" I asked.

"You know what I think of it. I hate it. Why?"

"I want you to put the phone down, walk straight into your boss's office and hand in your notice."

"Don't tempt me," she said laughing.

"Don't argue. Just go and do it."

"What's going on?"

I left a long pause before saying:

"We are going to emigrate to South Africa." She screamed.

My first job was to go to the library to learn more about this mysterious place we were emigrating to. I didn't have a clue where Johannesburg was or even South Africa for that matter so I was a bit disappointed to discover that it wasn't by the sea. A few days later I received a very professional letter from Bob Adams that detailed the gig and living conditions. I would arrive on a tourist's visa and then apply for temporary residence from there.

We didn’t know what to do about the house. If we rented it there were ridiculous laws that made it almost impossible to get the tenants out when we returned. If we left it empty there was another ridiculous law saying that squatters could move in and it would be equally difficult to remove them so either way we were stuffed. We decided to leave it empty which just goes to show why it was so difficult to find rented accommodation at that time.

On the morning of our departure we were at Julia’s parents’ house waiting to be driven to the airport when I noticed the newspaper headlines: "South Africa. The greatest threat to peace in the world today." I knew nothing about South Africa or politics in general so I asked my father in law what the headline meant.

"Don't worry. It's just the press being sensationalist."

I was sure he was right but it was still a headline I would rather not have seen on that particular day.

22
Scrap Metal Man

On September 1st 1975 Bob Adams picked us up at Johannesburg airport and drove us to his house for lunch. It was a fabulous detached house built on a hill so there were three separate levels. The second level had a large swimming pool with a small thatched building at one end which was the changing rooms. Being the first day of spring and a public holiday there were several guests for lunch and everyone made us feel welcome.

Before emigrating to South Africa in the sixties Bob Adams had played saxophone for many of the leading bands of the day including Geraldo and Jack Parnell. His claim to fame was the raunchy saxophone solo in Frankie Vaughan's *Green Door.* When he first arrived in Johannesburg in the sixties the white music scene was practically non-existent but with the help of Bob's experience and good business skills he soon got things moving. He organised tours of musicals, singers and pop groups and became the top concert promoter in the country. For the past two years he had been resident at the Three Ships restaurant in the Carlton Hotel and I don't know if it was due to the music or the food but it was so popular that tables were booked solid for two weeks in advance. The band was a trio and now he wanted to add a guitarist which is where I came in.

"You're going to love it here and trust me it won't be long before you have more session work than you can handle," said Bob.

A session musician is someone who is called into a studio and asked to play on a recording. Usually they need to be able to sight read any piece of music and play most styles well, as studio time is very expensive so there is no opportunity to practice your part. Sometimes they only have to play a simple backing that requires very little expertise but other times they may have to read a complicated piece of music that would take a lesser musician days to learn. Apart from the prestige of being a session musician it was also well paid. Unfortunately being good doesn't assure you of session work as like most professions you need to be in with the right people. In England I knew no one and as the competition for session work was fierce I hadn't even got on the bottom rung of the session ladder but maybe in South Africa I would be given a chance.

"Apart from studio work, television has only just started here so they are going to be desperate for good musicians. There is only one guitarist in Johannesburg who can read music at the moment." said Bob.

After lunch he took us to the hotel where we would be staying until we found a flat. It was in the middle of Hillbrow and although our room was an anticlimax after the luxury of Bob's house it was better than I had expected. That night Bob booked us a table at the Three Ships so we could see the band working. It was the first time Julia had eaten in a five star restaurant and she was beaming with pleasure while everyone spoiled us. We returned to our hotel full of hope for the future.

The next day we started rehearsing Bob's large repertoire and the years of practising my sight reading finally paid off when I had no trouble playing any of his music. Apart from playing in the quartet I also did two solo sets on classical guitar while the rest of the band took their break. Although I knew some classical guitar pieces I had never made a serious study of it so found the solo sets hard going at first but I practised for hours every day and quickly improved. I was surprised how much more demanding it was than electric guitar and happy to find that the increased demand on technique improved my playing in general. The only snag was that Bob didn't want anyone in the band to sing which was a shame as during the last year with The Sands of Time I had done a lot of singing and was starting to feel comfortable with my voice.

We both loved our new lives but Julia was getting restless and wanted a job. Bob had a word with the hotel and was surprised to find they were looking for someone to help the restaurant manager and the position was hers if she wanted it. Her work involved showing people to their tables and selling cigars and although it was a dead end job that required no qualifications it was the first job she ever enjoyed.

I had only been in Johannesburg a few days when Bob phoned me early one morning:

"A friend of mine has just called in a big panic. He is conducting the orchestra at the Sari Music Awards tonight and his guitarist has dropped out. He asked me if you could do it."

"Yes of course. How does he know about me?" I asked.

"Word gets around fast here. Under normal circumstances I would have to say no because I need you at the restaurant but as this is a special event and it will be a good opportunity for you to get your foot in the door you can do it this time."

When I arrived at the concert hall that night the place was buzzing with excitement. The Sari awards was an annual event for the music industry and for the first time it was going to be broadcast live. It was the first television show I ever did so I didn’t know what to expect but I could still recognise chaos when I saw it. For one part of the show a whole section of the orchestra couldn’t be heard because the microphones had been kicked over accidently when the musicians went to their seats. During the evening I was introduced to several record and radio producers who were eager to take my number which was in sharp contrast to England where record producers were more likely to accept a phial of anthrax from me than my business card.

A few days later one of the top radio producers, Bez Martin phoned to say his guitarist hadn't turned up so could I rush there to take his place. From there the sessions snowballed and it wasn't long before I was booked most days. With everything going so smoothly I wondered if just for once there were not going to be any setbacks but I should have known that the patterns of our lives never change.

Bob Adams turned up at our hotel one day to give us the bad news.

"We've got a big problem. I've just had the leader of the Musicians' Union on the phone. He told me you can't get a work permit without his permission and he has refused it." Julia and I were devastated.

"Didn't you know about this before you brought us out here?" I said angrily.

"This is not like England. They make the laws up as they go along. Don't worry. I have arranged for us to meet him now to discuss it."

We walked the few blocks to the Musicians Union head office while Bob explained the situation.

"It's nothing like the Musicians Union in England. It's run by one man who conned the government into thinking he represents musicians and then persuaded them not to allow foreign musicians to work here unless he gives permission."

"But there are so few musicians in South Africa how can he make a living out of being head of the union?"

"He doesn't. His main job is a scrap metal dealer and he is also an agent."

"An agent who is head of the union? That's like putting Count Dracula in charge of a blood bank." Bob laughed and agreed.

"It could only happen in South Africa," he said.

We walked into a small office and behind a desk sat a fat, middle aged man glowing with arrogance.

"So what is the problem with Derek working here?" asked Bob.

"I would have thought that was obvious. There's not enough work for the musicians that are already here so why import more?"

"Because the only musicians that can't find work here are those that aren't any good. If you were a musician yourself you would know that," said Bob, struggling to control his temper.

"That's not true. We have plenty of good musicians here."

"I have been looking for a guitarist for The Three Ships for months. Only two people came to audition and neither of them could read music well enough. Derek played all my arrangements first time and without a mistake. Speak to any producer and they'll all tell you they are desperate for a good versatile guitarist, especially now television has started," said Bob.

The union leader looked completely disinterested and replied:

"Leave it with me. I'll have a think about it."

Walking back to the hotel Bob tried to reassure me.

"Don't worry. There's no way he's going to get away with this."

Over the next few days Bob Adams got every producer in town to phone the Musicians' Union leader to complain so he had little choice but to let me stay although he made it a condition that Bob handed over the booking of the cabaret acts for the Top of the Carlton night club to him. Ironically my problem with the union turned out to be good promotion as it put me in the limelight and from then onwards I was booked solidly.

Working in the same restaurant as Julia was convenient as we could travel to work together but she was a very jealous woman so it was not easy for her watching me work in a restaurant full of attractive wine waitresses. Although I never noticed it Julia swore the waitresses flirted with me to wind her up. One night after a silent drive home she launched into an attack.

"You and Dawn were staring at each other all night. You're having an affair with her aren't you!"

She was completely wrong and most of the time I was so wrapped up in what I was playing I wouldn't have noticed a pink elephant doing a cha cha in front of me.

"I am not having an affair with anyone. If you look at me when I'm playing you'll see I stare straight out in front of me."

She accepted what I said but still had her doubts. The next night I made a conscious effort to look away every time Dawn came near me. After another silent drive home Julia went on the attack again.

"You were deliberately avoiding looking at Dawn tonight, that means you *must* be having an affair with her." I couldn't win.

After three months of living in a hotel room we had paid off all our debts and bought a car so we could look for an apartment. We found a great little flat in Northcliff, a little suburb about 10 miles from the centre of Johannesburg. It was a large, two storey complex called Villa Barcelona built in a Spanish style. It had a swimming pool, tennis courts, restaurant, shops and barbecue and it was just like living in a holiday village.

Television had only just started in South Africa and although a huge amount of money had been invested in equipment the South Africans insisted on doing most of the work themselves rather than using experienced professionals from overseas. This led to all kinds of fiascos including inexperienced cameramen with the most expensive equipment crashing into each other in the middle of a show. Sometimes we turned up for a TV session only to find they hadn't even started building the set so we spent the day being paid to sit in the café.

My favourite SABC (South African Broadcasting Corporation) cock up happened during a weekly variety program called *Sing* which was hosted by the talented British entertainer Peter Elliot. At the end of the show the producer always asked the audience to wait a few minutes while they checked the recording was ok. After a long wait the embarrassed producer came out and told the audience:

"I am sorry ladies and gentlemen but there has been a technical problem with the recording so we will have to do the whole show again."

We repeated the show with all the same routines while the audience did their best to laugh at the jokes they had heard only half an hour earlier. The technical problem turned out to be not so technical after all: someone had forgotten to press the record button. This could not normally happen as programs were monitored in another part of the building but on that occasion whoever was supposed to be monitoring it was watching rugby on another channel.

The entire Johannesburg music scene was built on a few dozen musicians. That was great for us as it meant lots of work but it became farcical during a weekly music program called *Sounds Live Velvet* which was supposed to feature different local bands every week. Most of the time it was the same band but with the name changed depending on whose turn it was to play bandleader that week. It didn't really matter what was on television as hardly anyone watched it anyway. Televisions were incredibly expensive and there was only four hours of broadcasting a night of which two were in Afrikaans despite the fact that half the TV owning population couldn't understand a word of it. The quality of the Afrikaans programs made locally was terrible and I didn't know a single Afrikaans speaking person that watched them. They did broadcast some foreign imports like the brilliant BBC documentary series *The World at War* which was very successful but it only made the local productions look even worse.

I earned a good reputation and was sometimes featured on television programs. I was even asked by the head of SABC to record a jazz album for the radio so I was able to do my own arrangements and slip in a few of my own compositions. It was the first time I had my own band and control over what we played and I loved every second of it.

In The Three Ships we played a lot of jazz and I was getting plenty of solos. Bob regularly added new and sometimes difficult arrangements to our repertoire and I got to the stage where I could sight read almost any piece of music put in front of me. I began to develop a love for classical guitar and practised for hours every day so my solo sets at night improved rapidly and some people came to the restaurant just to hear me play. For a while we had a pianist called Dave Simpson playing with us at the Three Ships. Before emigrating to South Africa in the sixties Dave played with the Ted Heath Orchestra. He was one of the best musicians I have ever worked with and other pianists often ate at the restaurant just to hear him play which for a musician is the ultimate accolade. Dave had been a child prodigy so his parents doing what they thought was best for their son forced him to practice every day for hours when all he wanted to do was go out and play with his friends. We assume that people who have an extraordinary talent for something always enjoy using that talent but certainly in Dave's case that was not true. One night in the middle of a brilliant piano solo he slammed the piano lid down, stood up and announced to us:

"Playing the fucking piano has ruined my life."

He stormed out of the restaurant and went home. It came as a big shock to me. Here was a man who was the kind of musician I had always aspired to be and yet he clearly despised what he was doing.

It was during that period that another disillusion hit home hard. Every night the pianist played a short solo set while the rest of the band took a break in the bar where the music was piped through. When it was Dave Simpson playing we sat in the corner and listened to him with admiration while nearly every other person in the restaurant ignored him. When Dave was not available he was replaced by an elderly pianist called Ronnie Monroe who had been very popular on South African radio many years earlier. One night when Ronnie was doing his solo spot we returned from our break while he was playing Scott Joplin's *The Entertainer* with the kind of sensitivity you would expect from Mike Tyson but what he lacked in skill he made up for in volume. When he finished the piece the audience erupted with applause. I realised for the first time that there was a big difference between music and entertainment and that audiences will always appreciate a good entertainer more than a good musician. The problem for me was that I was not a good entertainer and when I was concentrating on my playing I looked as miserable as sin. Some people have a natural smile on their face whereas I had a natural look of boredom. It was so bad that I was in the middle of a guitar solo on one TV program when the producer stood in front of me (out of shot) with a piece of paper saying "smile" on it. I smiled; he was happy; my solo went down the pan.

Having been so short of work in England I found it hard to turn sessions down so there were times when I worked in the studios all day and at The Three Ships all night. The money was rolling in and for the first time Julia and I were able to splash out on a few luxuries. Life was great and it was difficult to imagine what could possibly go wrong.

23
Suite Beginnings

We were only in Johannesburg for nine months when restlessness set in. The work I was doing was no longer challenging and although my playing and reading had improved dramatically I was rarely given the chance to use those skills. I often worked with big radio orchestras where not only were my parts very easy to play but I was so far in the background no one could hear me anyway. When I did get any time off it was usually on a Sunday when everything was closed for religious reasons.

Having reached the top of the session ladder I needed a new goal in my life so I returned to songwriting with great enthusiasm. I was still hopeless at writing lyrics so I asked Julia to try and write some and although hers weren't great they were still better than mine. The only market for music in South Africa was for pop so I started by writing and recording six pop songs. With new demos recorded on a good quality tape recorder I was very hopeful as I had plenty of record company contacts from working in studios. I had been so successful as a musician in South Africa that I assumed success in songwriting was inevitable. The first record company welcomed me into their offices and seemed to be looking forward to hearing my songs but that look changed to surprise when they heard how bad they were. I wasn't too disappointed and told myself it would take time for me to develop as a songwriter, I just had to persevere and be patient.

As lyrics were such a problem for me I thought I'd try writing instrumental music and that's when everything clicked into place and I really started to enjoy composing. I was full of ideas but fell into the trap that many serious musicians do in thinking that music has to be complicated to be good. I spent weeks writing and recording my first piece which was a long classical rock instrumental called (don't laugh) *Pavan for a Dead Chicken.* I was pleased with it without realising it was a guitarist's showpiece rather than a properly structured composition. I took my new demo to a couple of record companies who clearly thought I was insane.

"You've got no chance of getting anywhere with this kind of music in South Africa. You'll have to try England or the States," they said.

I started to develop a passion for composing but was getting frustrated at having to spend so much time doing session work and at the restaurant instead of writing my own music. Every spare second I had was spent writing and I became a workaholic to the extent where I was composing music while I ate lunch. Sometimes when I felt it was getting too much for me I forced myself to spend the afternoon by the pool with Julia but all the time I lay there tunes came into my head and I felt the need to go back to the flat to write them down. My obsession got so bad that I started to feel ill and so decided to lock my tape recorder in a cupboard and force myself to take it easy. After a couple of months I felt better so resumed my writing and found myself drifting into a classical/rock style that I found very exciting. I played my new compositions to more record companies and whilst their reaction was encouraging they once again told me there was no market in South Africa for it. If I was going to have any success as a composer I knew I had return to England.

By the end of our first year boredom and frustration set in and I knew there was nothing more for me in South Africa. I talked it over with Julia and whilst she was not as keen as I was to leave she did recognise there was no future for either of us there so we agreed to return to England in April which gave us enough time to save some money and avoid the English winter.

One day some friends came to visit us with the most perfect baby I had ever seen. It spent the whole day laughing and entertaining us and by the time they left we had decided we wanted one of our own. With any luck we could turn up at the airport and give our parents the surprise of their lives. That night we got to work and bingo, we hit the bull's eye first time. We were both ecstatic and went around telling everyone as if we were the first couple ever to have a baby. A few weeks later Julia had a miscarriage. It was a bitter disappointment for both of us but we were still young and there was still plenty of time to start a family.

My composing was gathering momentum and I was working on a full scale classical rock piece called *Francesca Suite* that I intended to make a professional demo of as soon as I returned to England. I knew how difficult it was to get a record deal for instrumental music but the great success of Mike Oldfield's *Tubular Bells* gave me encouragement.

Two months before our departure Julia and I were laying in bed when I asked her:

"Do you still love me?"

It was just one of those stupid things that lovers say expecting a little hug and a reply of "of course I do, silly" but this time she didn't answer.

"Why do you say that?" she asked.

Something was not right. I remained silent and waited for her to continue.

"Have you heard something?" she asked.

I sensed impending disaster and felt as if my insides were going to explode. I had no idea what she was talking but went along with her.

"Maybe."

"What did you hear?"

I said nothing and felt like I was standing on the edge of a cliff. After a long silence she continued:

"You know about me and Robert then?"

All I knew was that Robert was a waiter at the restaurant.

"I have no idea what you're talking about but I think it's about time you told me what's going on."

Her concern turned to confusion but it was obvious she wanted to get something off her chest.

"You know it's been very quiet recently?" she said.

"Yes."

"I've been spending a lot of time chatting to Robert in the linen room and I suppose we've become very attracted to each other."

I felt an invisible blow to my stomach far greater than any inflicted on me in the boxing ring. As the realisation of what had happened sank in I began to feel very angry.

"You mean while I've been sitting on stage you were only a few yards away having an affair."

"It's not an affair. I feel terrible about it but I swear nothing has happened."

"What do you mean nothing has happened?"

"I haven't slept with him or anything like that. It's just that we've been talking and getting to know each other and now he says he wants me to stay here with him when you go back to England."

"You're going to leave me?" I asked in disbelief.

"I don't know. I'm so confused."

The next few days were terrible but as I started to evaluate our relationship I found my anger turning to guilt as I realised I hadn't given our marriage a lot of thought. I had taken it for granted that I was a good husband and that we were both happy with each other. I began to realise that I had often been an intolerant bully and felt ashamed of myself. I thought of the times I had made her cry and instead of having the humanity to reach out and comfort her I had stormed off to work leaving her alone with her misery. There had been times when we had argued and I told myself I would be better off without her but now there was a real chance of that happening I was heartbroken. We started talking as equals for the first time and she was surprised at the change in me. We talked for hours but like most couples on the verge of breaking up we just went around in circles. If she had told me she definitely wanted to leave then I would at least have known where I stood but she didn't know what she wanted. I couldn't go on with the uncertainty so I pretended I was resigned to us separating. In the beginning she was relieved but then she became disturbed.

"You seem to have accepted things now?" she said with concern.

"I don't have much choice do I? I can't force you to stay with me. Besides, I must admit there is someone at the hotel that I am attracted to and I wouldn't mind getting to know her better."

She became hysterical.

"What. How could you? I thought you loved me? Who is she? How long have you fancied her?"

She threw her arms around me and cried like a baby. From that moment her affair paled into insignificance and her only concern was that she might lose me to another woman.

"Who is she? You have to tell me. I know, it's Sue isn't it?"

She kept going through all the possible contenders and I kept refusing to tell her who it was because I didn't know myself.

"Why should you care? You're the one who wants to leave me," I said.

"I was just being stupid. I don't want to leave you. I don't know what came over me."

From that moment on she never gave Robert another thought.

Since Julia's miscarriage she still had some occasional bleeding and a general feeling that something was wrong. She went to the doctor a few times but he told her it was just an infection and sent her away with some pills. A few days before we were due to leave Johannesburg we moved out of our flat and into a room at the Carlton Hotel. The morning before we were due to fly home we went to a mine dance about fifty miles from Johannesburg. It was held in a large open air arena in the grounds of one of the many mines and each tribe that lived and worked there had their own speciality. Some tribes sang, some danced and some made the most wonderful music from crude, home made instruments. We had been there once before and I found it to be the most spectacular entertainment I ever saw so I wanted to see it again.

It wasn't until we took our seats in the arena that Julia started to deteriorate quickly and halfway through the show she felt so bad I helped her to the manager's office where she lay on the floor. She looked terrible and deathly white.

"Can you call an ambulance," I said to a man who appeared to be in charge.

"There's no point. This is a black area, it will take ages for an ambulance to get here from a white hospital. The mine dance will be finished soon so the best thing is to wait and go back with the coach," he said.

I had no idea if it was serious or not but now Julia was out of the sun she felt much better so we agreed to wait. The journey back to the Carlton seemed to take forever and Julia was in a lot of pain. From the coach I took her in a wheelchair to our room and called a doctor who came quickly. I went through her recent history explaining the miscarriage and how she had been bleeding for the last month. He looked puzzled and asked:

"Is she normally this pale?"

"No. She spends a lot of time in the sun so usually has a good tan."

"I am worried about her colour. I think it is best to admit her to hospital as a precaution."

An ambulance soon arrived and took her to the hospital while I was told to stay at the hotel. A few hours later I went to visit her and was shocked to see her looking paler than ever. Nobody had a clue what was wrong with her but they didn't seem too worried. That night I returned to the hotel and was just dropping off to sleep when the phone rang.

"This is Doctor Philips from the General Hospital. I'm afraid your wife's condition has become serious so we have decided to operate."

"What's wrong with her?"

"We don't know yet. She appears to be bleeding internally and the safest thing is to open her up and find out what's going on."

"I'll be there right away."

"No it would be much better if you stay where you are and I promise I'll call you as soon as we have any news."

I put the phone down and sat in a daze. What on earth was wrong? I knew it could be serious but it never occurred to me she might die. I lay on the bed staring at the ceiling for hours and was surprised at what a strange collection of thoughts were going through my mind ranging from the mundane to the exact words I would use if I had to tell Julia's parents that her daughter had died. A few hours later the phone rang.

"This is Doctor Philips again. Your wife is alright and is back from theatre. She had an ectopic pregnancy. Do you know what that is?"

"I have no idea."

"She conceived but instead of the baby growing in her womb it grew in one of her fallopian tubes. The tube burst and that was what caused the internal bleeding. We tied it up and now she will make a quick recovery."

"Can I come and see her?" I asked.

"No she will be asleep until morning. It's best you wait until then."

The next morning I went to see her and was shocked to see how ill she looked but at least the colour had returned to her face. I spent the whole day with her during which time she seemed to improve by the hour. At one point a doctor pulled me to one side to have a word.

"Julia is very lucky. Everyone had gone home last night and I was just about to go myself when I had this niggling feeling that something wasn't right about her condition. I thought I'd do one last test and it wasn't until then that I found out she was bleeding internally. If we had left it until the morning she probably wouldn't have survived."

"She will make a full recovery won't she?"

"Yes there's no question of that but during the operation I noticed that the other fallopian tube is in a bad condition so it is very unlikely she will be able to have children."

At first the news had little affect on me as I was just happy that Julia was alive but later that night I felt a terrible sadness when it finally sank home that we would never have children of our own. We never knew whether the ectopic pregnancy was from her miscarriage and that they hadn't performed the D&C properly or whether she had conceived a second time.

The most recurring pattern of my life that nothing ever came easily to me sadly also affected Julia. Most couples decide to have a baby, they do the business and nine months later out pops a baby. Not me. Julia and I decide to have a baby and the next thing we knew we were stranded in a South African mine with Julia at death's door. When considering marriage it is wise to look at your partner's life patterns before going through with it because you can be sure that good or bad you will be sharing them.

Julia recovered quickly and a week later we to returned to England. South Africa was a great experience for us but we were both relieved to be back in our little terraced house. It felt like we had not so much left South Africa as escaped from it.

24
The Winning Ticket

It was great to be home. I had been worried that Julia would miss South Africa but she hadn't realised how much she had missed her family until she saw them all again. We lost a lot of money on the flight tickets we had to cancel due to some microscopic print in our travel insurance but we still had a reasonable amount saved so neither of us had to rush out and find work straight away. Before leaving South Africa I had finished writing *Francesca Suite* and was looking forward to record a demo of it. I wanted to make an album in five movements with a line up of electric string quartet, guitar, bass and drums. It would be a crossover between classical and rock music and although a few bands like Deep Purple had made classical rock albums I felt they hadn't succeeded in fusing the two styles together. Most of the time it was a rock band playing for one section and then an orchestra taking over for a while so it wasn't so much a fusion as two styles taking turns to play. I couldn't afford to book a string quartet so I made a demo of two of the movements with guitar, bass and drums and hoped that the record company would have enough imagination to see what I wanted to do.

I spent a week recording the demo and was delighted with the result. I sent copies to six record and publishing companies feeling more hopeful than ever as for the first time I really believed in my music and I had a good demo recorded in a professional studio. A week later I got the call that I had been dreaming of since I first picked up a guitar nine years earlier.

"My name is Denis Sinnot and I'm the general manager of Orange Music Publishing. You sent me a demo called *Francesca Suite*?"

"Yes that's right."

"I've just been playing it and I'm very impressed. I really think I can do something with this. Can you come to my office to discuss it?"

"Yes of course. When were you thinking of?"

"Tomorrow at three?"

"OK. See you then."

After all the years of rejection someone was finally interested in my work and I was going to see them to discuss a deal. Not one second passed for the rest of that day when I didn't think about that phone call and what could come from it.

It was a long night. I love day dreaming but at night when I am trying to sleep I find it is exhausting. One minute I saw myself stepping onto a stage to accept a platinum album and the next I was at the Royal Albert Hall with a full orchestra. I even rehearsed what I would say on chat shows and Melody Maker interviews. I resolved never to let fame change me and that I would always sign autographs when asked.

The next day I was on the London underground looking at normal people going about their normal lives and feeling terribly sorry for them. They had no idea that they were in the same carriage as someone who was going to sign a record deal and become a rock star. The most exciting prospect was that I would get a big advance which meant I could devote all my time to my own music and not have to go begging for gigs any more. If the advance was big enough we could rent a nice little villa in Spain for three months where I could complete *Francesca Suite* in the sun.

I stood outside a gloomy old building in Denmark Street and saw a small plaque on the wall saying "Orange Music Publishing." I made my way up the creaky wooden stairs feeling like I was entering a Dickens novel and half expected to see John Jarndyce standing at the top. I pushed opened a gloomy old door and walked into a gloomy old office where Denis Sinnot was seated at a gloomy old desk.

"Hi. You must be Derek?" he said rising from his desk to shake hands.

"I was listening to your tape again last night. It's brilliant. Did you play all the guitar parts yourself?"

"Yes, everything."

"Very impressive. Have you approached anyone else with it?"

"I sent out six tapes last week but you're the first to get back to me."

"I am confident that I can do something with it but I have to be honest, it's not easy getting record deals for instrumental music. I'd like to offer you a contract where you sign the publishing rights over to me for three months. If I can't get a record deal within the three months then the rights revert to you. It's a standard arrangement."

"Will there be any advance?" I asked. He smiled.

"The only artists getting advances these days are those that don't need them."

"What do you mean?"

"If a composer is successful and generates a lot of royalties I know I'll get at least some of the advance back but if I can't get you a record deal the music is worthless to me. You can try other publishers if you like but they will all tell you the same thing."

"What do you think the chances are of getting me a record deal then?"

"I have some contacts who I know will be very interested. I can't promise anything but I have a good feeling about this. Take a copy of the contract away with you and have a think about it."

I had joined the Composer's Guild a few weeks earlier and as their office was just around the corner I took the contract to them to look over.

"Yes, everything looks in order," I was told after someone took a brief look at it.

"Do you think the terms are alright? This is my first publishing contract so I have no idea what to expect."

"It's difficult to get any kind of contract these days, especially for instrumental music. You don't have much bargaining power so I would grab it with both hands if I were you."

I signed it and went back to Orange Music before making my way home wondering how I ought to feel. I had just signed my first publishing deal so surely that was good? But all I really had was the vague possibility of a record deal. I felt like I had won first prize in a major raffle only to find that the prize was a ticket for another raffle. I hadn't realised that publishers were no more than agents who promote your songs rather than your act. Being published doesn't mean a thing unless your music is being played and your music won't be played unless it is recorded and released. It is the record companies that take the risk which is why they are so nervous about investing in unknown artists.

As there was no prospect of a record deal I had to start the depressing job of finding work. It was so much easier in the days of the Melody Maker when I just sat at home and answered the phone but the kind of work I was looking for now I would never get from an advert. I had been advised by a friend that now I could sight read so well I would be better off establishing myself as a freelance musician rather than looking for a residency. In the beginning it would be hard making contacts and finding work but in the long run it would be more secure and better paid. It made sense but in order to find work I had to forget I was a musician and become a salesman which for me was hell. I took a deep breath and phoned all the numbers I was given by friends and was surprised to find that it wasn't long before I had enough freelance gigs to get started.

I waited patiently for a call from Orange Music but it never came. At the end of the three months contract I phoned Dennis Sinnot to ask what the situation was.

"Sorry. I played it to lots of people. They thought it was great but nobody wants to take a chance on it. Record companies are only interested in disco or punk music these days."

"I suppose it would be different if I were well known?"

"Of course. Even if you had played with a well known band it would help. The copyright reverts to you but I'll keep trying and get back to you if something turns up."

I was right back to square one but I really believed in *Francesca Suite* and was encouraged by the enthusiasm that not only Orange Publishing had shown but almost everyone I played it to. I just had to persevere. Tubular Bells was turned down by dozens of record companies until Richard Branson took a chance and made it into one of the biggest selling albums of all time.

I made twenty copies of my demo and sent them to every record company and publisher I could find an address for but most of them were returned with standard rejection letters. A couple of companies took the trouble to write back and say they liked it but didn't think there was a market for it. The head of A&R for the major publishing company Dick James Music phoned to say he loved it and I signed a publishing contract with them but after another three months and still no interest from record companies the publishing rights reverted back to me again.

I never lost faith in *Francesca Suite* and it occurred to me that the reason I couldn't get record company interest was because they didn't have the imagination to hear what the demo would sound like with an electric string quartet. I knew they would be nervous about paying out a lot of money in recording costs so the only solution was to complete all five movements of the suite, get a band together and record it myself.

I spent months composing and arranging until I ended up with a pile of sheet music a foot high. I managed to put together a string quartet that included two members from the London Symphony Orchestra and with the brilliant Les Cirkel on drums and equally brilliant Melt Kingston on bass I was in business. I had a great bunch of musicians who liked the music so much that they agreed to do it for a share of the possible royalties rather than session fees which I could never have afforded.

During rehearsals it was so funny to see the straight laced classical musicians getting excited as they played along with a rock drummer for the first time. The sound was exactly how I had envisaged it and I was certain that if we ever got the opportunity to play live concerts we would be a great success. It was hell organising rehearsals as everyone was so busy but after several weeks we were ready to record so all I needed was the money to pay for a studio. Fortunately I had just discovered a wonderful new invention, a plastic card that you took to a bank and in exchange for your signature they gave you money. Somewhere in the back of my mind I knew the money had to be returned but that was no problem as I could pay it back with the advance I got from the record company.

I put down the basic recording with the other musicians but as it was mainly guitar based music there were still weeks of guitar tracks to record. I got a good rate from the studio by working through the night which I found very gruelling but I eventually came away with a master recording that was everything I hoped it would be. At last I had something tangible to offer record companies and they wouldn't have the expense of putting me in a studio as I was offering them a finished product.

I spent the next month playing my album to everyone that would listen to it but whilst I had some excellent feedback I still couldn't get a record company to commit themselves. A few months passed and I had almost given up hope when I had a call from the head of A&R for EMI Music Publishing, Harold Franz.

"Listen darling. Someone gave me a copy of *Francesca Suite* and I think it's fabulous. Are the publishing rights still available?"

"Yes they are."

"Then come and see me as soon as possible. I am sure I can do something with it."

That afternoon I walked into the plush EMI offices in Tottenham Court Road and introduced myself to Harold Franz. He was a lovely man who although happily married (to a woman) always addressed me as *darling*. His job mainly involved taking people to lunch and getting them pissed in the hope of signing deals. I signed the same kind of contract as I had done before but this time Harold seemed certain he could secure a record deal and I couldn't see how I could fail with EMI behind me. Three months past and a distraught Harold Franz called me.

"I'm sorry darling. I have played it to everyone I know. They all love it but no one is prepared to go with it. I really don't understand it."

"But if you are EMI publishing can't you just tell EMI records to give me a record deal?"

"I'm afraid it doesn't work like that darling. We work independently. If you managed to get a deal with EMI Records they would insist we published it but it doesn't work the other way around."

"It all seems so unfair."

"I know darling but don't give up hope. The publishing rights revert back to you but I promise I'll keep trying."

In total I had six publishing deals for *Francesca Suite* but they all came to nothing. If everyone had told me it was a load of rubbish it would have been easier to accept as I could have put it down to experience and started work on something new but with everyone telling me how good it was I didn't know what more I could do. I put everything I had into something I truly believed in and all I got for my trouble was a pile of useless publishing contracts and a debt that would take years to repay. The next time you hear someone saying if you believe in something enough and are prepared to work hard for it you will always succeed, tell them from me they are talking out their arse.

25
Forgetting My Name

It was in May 1978 while I was still recording *Francesca Suite* that we moved to a bigger house. We couldn't afford it but the property was being sold by the council at well below the market value so we had to go for it. It was a detached house with an enormous garden in a beautiful tree lined avenue in Oakwood, Enfield. The local council had requisitioned it after the war and the reason it was such a bargain was because it was in the middle of a housing boom and the council moved so slowly that from the time of being valued to the time it was up for sale it had already risen considerably in value. For this working class lad from Peckham it was a dream come true.

Buying the house put us seriously in debt but when contracts were completed it was already worth 30% more than we paid for it so we knew we had done the right thing. It was sold without carpets, curtains or even light bulbs and although at first we were just happy to have such a beautiful place to live it wasn't long before we felt the need of the luxury of carpets and a table to eat from. Fortunately we had our magic credit cards so we used them to buy just enough to make it more habitable. The debts started to mount up and although Julia was working and I was getting a lot of freelance gigs it still wasn't enough to cope with the mounting debt. Out of desperation I put an advert in the Melody Maker and was surprised to get the offer of the perfect residency. It was in a Japanese nightclub just off Regent Street called Club Yumi. It must have been the only residency in the country with Saturday nights off and if a well paid freelance gig came in during the week I could put someone in to cover for me at the club.

Club Yumi catered for wealthy Japanese and Korean businessmen who paid an hourly rate to sit with an attractive hostess and buy food and drink at exorbitant prices. Although it appeared to be another knocking shop like The Stork Club, any girl found offering *other services* to the customers was sacked on the spot. One of the perks of working at the Yumi was sharing a dark corner with the hostesses during our breaks and as we split the evening with a Japanese solo singer our breaks were a wonderful 45 minutes long.

One of our duties was to back the many customers who wanted to sing. Most of them were so drunk they hardly made it to the stage and nearly every song they chose involved heartbreak, tragic death or a mixture of the two. They started singing at normal speed but gradually got slower and more morbid until on some occasions when emotion and alcohol overpowered them they ground to a halt and had to be guided back to their table. Their favourite song was the old Irish favourite *Danny Boy*, which appears to be a story about a woman who will probably die while her beloved is away and looks forward to him walking over her grave; that was one of their more cheerful songs.

Apart from the Yumi I was getting a lot of freelance gigs. There was a thriving scene for bands doing private functions in the big hotels but it was ruthlessly exploited by agents one of whom used to drive to work in a Rolls Royce. The chain of rake offs started with a hotel banqueting manager who would be asked to supply a band for a function. He would use whichever agent offered him the biggest kickback, the agent took a huge slice of that fee for doing little more than making a couple of phone calls and then paid the bandleader his fee which was a fraction of what the client was being charged. Finally the bandleader took his share and paid his musicians the basic rate as laid down by the Musician's Union. We never knew how much money changed hands but we did discover by accident one night when the client was charged £3000 for a well known danceband. The 12 musicians received £60 each, the bandleader took £1200 and the agent creamed off the remaining £1000 for himself and as if that wasn't enough he also charged the client for meals for the musicians which we never got. Considering the agent might have had 10 bands working for him that night it gives you an idea of the kind of money he was making for doing practically nothing. Only a few weeks earlier we had heard the same agent and bandleader complaining that musicians were "pricing themselves out of the market."

A couple of years passed by with me getting plenty of work but I no longer enjoyed playing music and saw it purely as a way of making a living. Even my marriage was getting stale as Julia and I hardly saw each other with me working most nights and her worked during the day.

Marie was one of the hostesses at the Yumi. She was French and extremely sexy. Every head in the club turned when she walked past so I could hardly believe it when she showed an interest in me. I have read surveys that tell of the high percentage of married people who are unfaithful but those figures include those who don't have any choice. An unattractive man who works as a lavatory attendant must in all honesty put his fidelity down to fate and not willpower and his inclusion in a fidelity survey would distort the result. I want to see a survey of men who remained faithful after a sexy woman showed interest in them. If I did have any pangs of conscience about starting an affair it faded when I remembered how Julia had responded to temptation in South Africa. I knew she had said nothing happened but I was always very doubtful.

It was on one of the rare Saturdays when I wasn't working that I took Marie to a hotel where we made love for the first time. As we approached the reception desk I tried to act cool and was doing alright until

I had to fill in the registration card. I had booked the room in the name of David Cooper, an old friend of mine but when I came to sign I used my own name out of habit. The girl smirked as she leant forward and whispered to me:

"Excuse me sir but I think your name is David Cooper."

I was carrying my guitar at the time as I was supposed to be doing a gig and didn't want to leave it in the car.

"Sorry about that. Dave Cooper is my stage name."

I was hoping that my guitar would give some credence to my pathetic excuse but judging by the look on her face it didn't. I hated the deception and never realised how much lying went into an illicit love affair. What surprised me was having been falsely accused of being unfaithful so many times in the past, now that I really was guilty Julia never said a thing. How much harder it is to defend yourself when you're innocent because you are not prepared for interrogation whereas with a real affair you have the benefit of preparing your alibis.

For the first few months I loved being with Marie and spent as much time as possible with her but although an illicit affair can be very exciting it can also be very tiring. Marie lived in West London so to see her during the daytime meant spending hours in the London traffic. I finished playing at 2 a.m. so meeting her after work meant not getting home until 4 or 5 a.m. which left me shattered the next day. I knew I still loved Julia and the life we had built together so I started seeing less of Marie and was relieved to find our affair fizzling out without any serious drama.

Everything returned to normal and after a fruitful winter with me working every night for the three months leading up to Christmas I finally managed to clear our debts so the fear of losing our lovely house was no longer hanging over us. Maybe we would have spent the rest of our lives living there had we not been struck down by a terrible addiction that was to drain us of all our money and change the course of our lives dramatically. Be warned, addiction can strike anyone at any time.

26
Sky's The Limit

It all started when Julia wanted to take up a sport and dragged me screaming to the public squash courts. I had always played ball sports so picked up squash very quickly but although Julia was a brilliant athlete she was hopeless with a ball so I found it very boring. That might have been the end of it had the council not closed the courts for a month to be renovated. We were returning from the Enfield cinema to our car one day when we stopped outside the entrance to the North Middlesex Squash Club. Julia was missing her weekly game so she suggested we went in just to have a look around. Who would have thought that walking through that door would lead to yet another major turning point in my life.

We were surprised when the receptionist told us there was no waiting list and the annual subscription was quite reasonable. We joined there and then and went home to get our kit. Looking through the large windows at the people playing squash below I couldn't believe how good they were compared to people I had seen playing at the public courts. After Julia and I finished our game I noticed someone practising by themselves and asked if I could play him. He agreed and despite me only winning the odd pity point and being completely thrashed I loved every minute of it. I spent the first three weeks getting stuffed by every man, woman and child I played but defeat only made me more determined so I improved quickly. What I liked most about the club were the league tables and I became obsessed with them. Unlike the music business it was not who I knew that determined my position in the leagues but how well I played. We also loved the social side of the club and when we weren't playing squash we were chatting with friends or looking through the large glass windows at the people playing in the court below. Squash took over our lives and waged war on our bank account. Most people played twice a week at most so court fees didn't amount to much but as we both played at least twice a day the fees became considerable and that's without the cost of squash racquets (which we broke regularly) drinks and clothing. We knew we couldn't go on spending like that but the idea of even moderating our addiction was unthinkable. From the first time I picked up a guitar music was the most important thing in my life but now it was relegated to third position behind squash and doing up our house and garden. The more disillusioned I became with the music business the more I sought refuge in squash. I improved so quickly that I went from the bottom of the league tables to the top of the ladder without losing a match.

With my career in such a deep rut I needed to return to composing but having failed several attempts at resurrecting interest in *Francesca Suite* I had to try something else. Record companies were only interested in punk and disco and as I couldn't see myself as a punk musician I thought I'd have a go at disco. I wrote four songs and went into a studio with some friends who did the session as a favour to me.

My first call was to Harold Franz at EMI Publishing who was keen to hear my latest compositions. I popped my cassette into his player confident that he would like them and he sat expressionless until the last song finished.

"Sorry darling. There's nothing there I can help you with," he said.

"What about the second song, *Funky Kinda Lady*?"

"It's a hell of an arrangement and it's definitely the most commercial but it's not for EMI. I think you should stick to what you do best which is instrumental music."

He offered me a drink from his well stocked desk draw but I declined.

"I was disappointed not to get a deal for *Francesca Suite.* It's still one of my favourite pieces of music," he said.

It was meant to console me but it just made me feel more frustrated than ever. I was determined to get a deal for my new songs so I sent out dozens of copies to record and publishing companies but they were all rejected. Eventually I admitted to myself that the songs were nothing special and as usual my lyrics were rubbish. I had made the classic mistake of compensating for mediocre songs with a good production. Despite my return to Rejection City I still had an overpowering feeling that I was meant to be a songwriter. I wrote another ten songs and made demos of them in a friend's home studio. I changed my name to *Warren Street* and sent out more demos; a new name, new songs but the same old rejection letters. I was beginning to wonder if anyone actually listened to the tapes so I started to mark them to see if they had been played or not. The result was that out of 20 tapes, 5 of them received no reply, 10 were rejected without being listened to and 5 were listened to but only up to the first or second track.

Despite a high joint income our debts grew steadily while we compensated for the jobs we hated by spending money. We constantly borrowed from one credit card to pay the minimum payment on another and when we went over our limit the only response from the credit card companies was to increase our limit. We tried to budget but the only cutback that would have made any significant difference would have been to stop playing squash but how could we do that when it was the most important thing in our lives?

In December of 1979 I had a phone call that could finally lead to the big break I was long overdue, it was from Harold Franz.

"Can you come round to see me right away darling. Something has come up that I know will interest you."

Harold was never one for empty promises and I could tell by his voice it was something big. Within minutes I was out the front door and on my way to his office. The receptionist was expecting me and took me straight into Harold's office.

"The BBC are producing a new television series called *Great Rail Journeys of the World* and they are looking for a soundtrack with guitar in it so I immediately thought of you."

"That sounds fantastic. Tell me more about it."

"It's a weekly series that is going to be a big hit and sell worldwide. If this comes off you will make a fortune and it will establish you as a composer."

I was so excited I nearly burst into tears.

"Have they heard my music?"

"Yes darling. I played them *Francesca Suite* and they loved it."

"So why can't they use sections from that?"

"They want something written especially for the program. Something that gives the feeling of riding on a train."

"That will be no problem. I'll give them exactly what they want."

"I'm sure you will. We need a demo of four pieces about two minutes long and we need them by the end of next week. We'll pay for a studio and session musicians."

I hurried home with my head full of ideas. This was my big chance. I was being asked by a major publisher to write music for a major BBC documentary series.

I was never so happy as when I was composing music for that programme. I spent every spare minute I had and even cancelled all my squash games. I wrote seven compositions and chose the best four to take into the studios. It was a tough day's recording as I had to overdub lots of guitar parts but I was delighted with the result. The next day I returned to a very anxious Harold Franz with my demos. It was an important publishing deal that he wanted almost as much as I did. Harold sat nervously in his chair as I played him the pieces. I could tell straight away he liked them and when the last piece finished he came from behind his desk to shake my hand warmly.

"They are fantastic darling. Just what I wanted. Wait there. I want to play it to someone else."

I thought I would explode with excitement. Harold returned with several colleagues and played my music again. Everyone nodded their heads approvingly and came to congratulate me.

"It's not definite yet darling. I have to play it to Mike Harding at the BBC this afternoon but I am sure he's going to love it," said Harold.

I floated home on a blissful daydream and later that afternoon Harold phoned.

"Mike Harding loved it. There's just one more hurdle and we are home and dry. The producer of the program has the final say and he lives in Manchester so I have to send the tape to him. Don't worry. I'm sure he'll like the demo as much as everyone else."

The next few days were agony. On the one hand there was a lot of money and my dream of making a living as a composer and on the other was a mountain of debt and a future of boring gigs. I was just on my way to the squash club to make up for the games I had missed when Harold rang.

"I'm sorry darling. It's bad news. The producer liked it but he wants to use music from Sky's latest album as he's a friend of John Williams. Apparently there was a big argument about it but the producer always gets the final say."

For a horrible moment I thought I was going to start crying.

"That is such a blow. I thought I'd finally cracked it."

"So did I. If it hadn't been Christmas I would have travelled to Manchester to take the producer out to lunch and get him pissed like I normally do."

Harold was the kindest man I ever met in the music industry and I think he was as upset as I was. How thin the line is between success and failure. All my hopes, dreams and years of effort shot down by one man. I had done everything that was asked of me as a composer and it still wasn't enough.

A year later *Great Rail Journeys of the World* was shown on television and as predicted became an enormous success. Since then it has been shown all over the world and repeated many times. The day after it was first broadcast I read a review of the program in one of the national newspapers and the headline read "SKY REALLY IS THE LIMIT." The reviewer said the program was brilliant but was let down by the soundtrack.

Any remaining enjoyment I had for playing music drained right out of me. To make matters worse I was doing a lot of gigs for a bandleader called Chris Allen and for extra money I acted as his roadie as well as his guitarist. It made sense that if I had to go to a gig I might as well take the band's gear and get paid for doing two jobs at the same time but it made me dislike gigging even more. I drove for two or three hours, set up the band's equipment, performed all night and at 2.a.m. packed the gear in my car and drove home again. I did it in an effort to reduce our debts but by now they were so big whatever I earned just went into a bottomless pit.

The irony was that a lot of the work I was doing was exactly what I had once dreamt of. I was backing famous artists like Cliff Richard, Tom Jones, Petula Clark and dozens of well known comedians and cabaret artists but playing a simple song for a famous singer is no less boring than playing it for an unknown one. The only place I felt challenged was at the squash club where I spent every afternoon. Julia went there straight from work and after she played her two games I took her home and went to work myself. Apart from weekends the only time we ever saw each other was at the squash club.

Our one consolation was that the property market had risen so much that our house was worth twice what we had paid for it. It didn't make us any less in debt but it did mean that overall we were worth a lot more than we owed. We tried looking for a smaller house so we could take some of the profit and pay off our debts but it was too depressing looking at houses that were nowhere near as nice as ours. One day I heard a financial expert on the radio advising people who owed a lot of money on credit cards to get one bank loan to pay them all off. It was the answer to our prayers. I calculated that with a £8000 loan over four years we could manage the repayments comfortably and eventually be debt free. I went to see my bank manager and explained that although it was a big loan we had no children and both had good salaries so there would be no problem making the repayments. There was also £28,000 equity in our house that we were happy to use as collateral. It seemed such a perfect solution with no risk to the bank that it never occurred to me they would turn us down.

"I'm sorry Mr Newark but there is no way we can lend you money just to pay off your debts. The problem seems to me that you are not able to live within your means."

He was so arrogant and unhelpful that it was one of the few times I ever lost my temper in public. The last thing I remember was shouting "we *can* live within our means" as I stormed out of his office.

Things were looking very grim when I answered the phone and instantly recognised a voice from the past.

"Hello Derek. This is Renato Sambo."

27
Living Within Our Means

Hearing Renato's voice caused a chain reaction of flashbacks to race through my mind and I started to tingle with excitement. It was nearly eight years since I last heard from Renato and I knew there was only one reason he would be phoning me now.

"Would you like to come back and work for me?" he asked.

"Where?"

"We are in San St Moritz until the middle of May. After that we go to the Munich Hilton and then Japan."

"I am definitely interested but I am married now so I'll have to talk it over with my wife. I'll call you back tomorrow and let you know."

For so many years I dreamt about the wonderful times I had with Renato not realising it was actually my youth that I was really yearning for. It was the best time of my life and during the last few difficult years it hurt to think those days were gone forever. Now there was a chance of going back to it but it wasn't so easy any more to go abroad at the drop of a hat. I had a wife and a lovely house but if I went back to Renato there was a chance of losing both.

I had a long chat with Julia and we decided that the best thing to do was to go to St Moritz together to meet Renato and see what he had to offer. Maybe I could work for him just long enough to pay off our debts. If it didn't work out at least we would get a cheap skiing holiday out of it as Renato had agreed to give us food and lodgings as long as we paid our own fare.

The ascent from the Swiss motorway to St Moritz seemed to go on forever but the scenery was spectacular. My first impression on entering St Moritz was not good as it seemed more like a busy town than an intimate skiing village like Gstaad but I soon got used to it. It was great to see Renato after so many years and he hadn't aged a day. What a charmed life that man had. After many years of working at the Palace Hotel Gstaad he was finally replaced by a disco and what happened .... he got a better gig at the Palace Hotel in St Moritz.

As we sat in the luxurious hotel lounge drinking coffee Renato explained that he was unhappy with his guitarist so he wanted to replace him which was why he called me. Neither of us mentioned how badly he had let me down all those years earlier but I did find out why I couldn't contact him during my time on the QE2. Shortly after phoning me his whole band left him without warning plunging him into a very bad period in his life. He lost all his work and was almost destitute when his many friends got together to help him back on his feet.

He took us to the staff canteen to eat and introduced us to his band. I didn't know any of them until a ghost from the past suddenly appeared before me ..... *the dreaded Mario.* Stupid as it may sound we were both pleased to see each other. He had changed considerably having been in a relationship for the last few years with a German woman who I was surprised to see wasn't the trophy girlfriend Mario would have gone for in the past. The next morning we all met in the night club to go through a few songs. As soon as we started playing it struck me what poor musicians they were compared to those I was used to working with and I knew instantly it wasn't going to work out. I told Renato how I felt and he was very understanding although I suspected there was no job anyway and the main reason for calling me was to scare his guitarist into behaving himself.

For the next few days I spent most of the time teaching Julia how to ski and we both loved every minute of it. At the end of the first week we were shocked to discover that Renato was finishing his contract early so we had to move out of our room. We were having such a great time skiing and as I had already cancelled all my gigs it seemed silly to go back a week early so we found ourselves an excellent package deal at a hotel in the centre of town. Of course we couldn't afford it but the good thing about being in serious debt is that a few more pounds here or there doesn't make much difference either way. We had an amazing time with some of the best food and skiing conditions ever. I was expecting to run out of cash by the end of the week but wasn't concerned as I planned to get a cash advance with my credit card. That was when a bank clerk gave me the devastating news:

"I'm sorry sir but you can't use your credit card to get cash advances in Switzerland. It is against our regulations."

"But how can I get some cash?" I asked.

"You'll have to get it transferred from your bank in England."

You won't be surprised to hear that we had no money in our bank in England so there was only one thing I could do. Just a few weeks after shouting at my bank manager "we *can* live within our means" I now had to phone him and say "*Err*, it's me again. I am stranded in St Moritz without any money. Would you mind increasing my overdraft and sending me some cash."

So that's what I did and I have to say he was happy to oblige once I assured him I would clear my overdraft as soon as we returned to England.

We arrived home to find a fresh crop of bills and threatening letters. It was late spring and as there wasn't much work during the summer I knew that by the autumn we would either have to sell our house or face bankruptcy… but there was one last hope.

The previous year I had invented a board game I called *Superstar*. Not only was the game a lot of fun to play but it taught people how to read music at the same time. We tested it with friends and had some great evenings so I submitted it to the games manufacturer Sears who made *Scrabble* and was told I should hear something within a month. After three months I had still not heard anything so I gave them a call.

"We are still looking at it. At the moment it is at the final level where we look at production costs. You should know something within the next couple of weeks," they told me.

I tried not to get excited but it was difficult considering my game had got all the way to the last hurdle. A month later I finally got my answer when it was returned to me with a polite rejection letter. I should have started hawking it around to other companies but didn't have the heart. The constant rejection had finally got to me.

We were celebrating the acquisition of a yet another credit card at our favourite restaurant one night and discussing what to do about our spiralling debt when without thinking I voiced one of my favourite daydreams:

"Wouldn't it be great to sell the house and travel abroad with the profit."

As soon as the words were out of my mouth we looked at each other and smiled.

"Why don't we?" I asked.

Julia's eyes started to sparkle.

"Are you joking?" she said.

Was I joking? I really didn't know. What did we have to lose? The way we were going we would be bankrupt by winter in which case we would lose the house anyway. We both hated our jobs and we couldn't have children. What was the point in struggling to hang onto a life that we didn't like anyway?

"What will we do?" asked Julia.

"That's the beauty of it. With the profit we get from the house we can do anything and go anywhere."

"But the money won't last forever and what about squash? You know I can't live without my game of squash every day."

Although she was asking sensible questions she had no more intention of being sensible than I had.

"We can start by driving to the South of France and looking for a squash club there. We could do some coaching and you could teach aerobics."

Then came the carrot that neither of us could resist.

"We could spend the winter in Gstaad. I read somewhere that there's a squash court at the Palace Hotel so we could coach there and maybe I can find work playing guitar."

For years I had been telling Julia how wonderful Gstaad was and we had always dreamt of going there and now there was a way of making that dream come true. My original idea quickly bore fruit and by the end of the meal our minds were made up. We had walked into that restaurant a couple with no hope and on the edge of bankruptcy and left it with a whole new and exciting life ahead of us. We sat up most of the night making the kind of plans that only people with money can make. I could get *Francesca Suite* onto vinyl which would give me something tangible to sell. For the last year I had been composing and practising classical guitar so I could publish the pieces myself and if I could make enough money from them we could continue to travel indefinitely.

Julia's parents were horrified when we told them our plans but mine had long since stopped being surprised at my actions and as always they offered me their support if it was needed. The next day we put our house on the market and soon found a buyer. The lovely Chrysler 180 I had bought on our return from South Africa was now a complete wreck so as soon we exchanged contracts on the house we splashed out on a beautiful old Jaguar. At £1500 it was a real bargain and if you're going to ride off into the sunset without a care in the world you have to do it in style.

In early June 1978 our house was sold and we were the happiest homeless couple on earth. The previous day I had spent ages writing out cheques to clear all our debts which amounted to a staggering £10,000. We made £28,000 profit from the sale of our house and furniture which still left us with £18,000 in the bank at a time when the average wage was around £70 a week. Of course it was a stupid thing to do but can you imagine how good it felt setting off for Dover in our Jaguar as free as birds with all that adventure ahead of us.

We lent against the ship's rail and watched the white cliffs of Dover disappearing slowly into the distance. No more debt. No more Club Yumi. No more playing party songs. No more driving hundreds of miles to gigs and setting up the band's equipment and no more secretarial work for Julia.

28
Managing Chaos

Our plan was to spend a few days in Gstaad and find a room for the winter season. Obviously the main reason for staying there was the skiing but I also thought it would be a great place to make contacts. Hopefully we would create a little niche for ourselves and return every year. As we drove along Gstaad High Street it was like stepping back in time as it had hardly changed in the eight years since I saw it last. I parked the car and we walked slowly through the village that had haunted me for so long. We found a nice little bedsit at the end of the village in a large chalet called Ludihous. It was opposite the tennis courts which in the winter was an ice rink. The chalet was owned by a formidable woman called Frau Ludi and it consisted of several bedsits and a shop at street level which was crammed full of Swiss bric-a-brac. We agreed to rent the room for four months during the winter and our new life got off to a good start when Frau Ludi offered Julia some work in her shop. Julia was delighted as it would give her the chance to improve her schoolgirl German and meet the many famous people that went to her shop.

We approached the Palace Hotel which had the only squash court in Gstaad and the manager was happy to let us coach there once we told him we didn't expect a wage. We were thrilled that everything was going so smoothly but horrified when we discovered that the court was made of wood so apart from the ball skidding everywhere it sounded like we were playing in a large drum.

With all the arrangements made for the winter we set off for the South of France where we planned to stay for the rest of the summer. We had no idea which town to go to and didn't care just as long as it was near the sea and had squash courts. Squash had never really caught on in France but I remembered seeing an advert for windsurfing and squash holidays in Perpignan so that seemed like a good place to start.

We arrived early evening and as if by magic we looked up to see a large building with SQUASH painted in big white letters on the outside wall. Inside we found a bustling three court club and a young couple from New Zealand who had been coaching and managing it for the past year. We introduced ourselves and I couldn't believe it when the first thing they said to us was:

"You don't want a job do you? We're leaving to coach at a club in Lyon so they need someone here urgently."

What a break. It was exactly what we had hoped for and we had only been in Perpignan for fifteen minutes. After a brief meeting with the club owner we were offered the job. There was no salary but as the club was only open at night it didn't involve much work and in return he would pay for an apartment and we could keep whatever we made from coaching. We found a small apartment in the nearby seaside town of Canet-Plage and sat on the beach all day while I wrote music and Julia brushed up on her French. I planned to produce a series of classical guitar solos and a guitar tutor in the hope that not only would they provide us with an income but they would help to promote *Francesca Suite* when it was released.

It wasn't until Mark and Julie left that we discovered how chaotic the club was. Instead of customers paying for drinks when they bought them we played a little game where we wrote the customer's name on the till receipt and pinned it behind the counter, then as soon as our backs were turned they reached over to grab their till receipts and throw them in the rubbish bin. I approached the owner about this strange system.

"Why don't we take the money when we serve the drink like they do in England?"

"If I did that here people would get upset and stop buying drinks."

"But there's no point in selling drinks if you don't get paid for them."

"Well that's just how we do things here. Most of these people are my friends and I don't want to upset them."

It was the first and last time I tried to reason with him. He was a pleasant enough man who had built the club because of his love for squash but he was a terrible businessman. It soon became obvious that the club was losing money and although he was hoping to sell it our job was safe at least until the end of the summer when we planned to leave anyway.

Managing the club was difficult as people were much more volatile than in England and on several occasions I had to run onto court to stop them from killing each other. They were unsure of the rules and particularly the one that forbids a player deliberately aiming at his opponent's arse. Coaching in French wasn't easy either, particularly as the French for *court, stroke* and *bum* all sounded the same to me so I was always getting them mixed up.

As my writing progressed the whole idea of publishing my own compositions began to flourish. The main item was a guitar tutor backed up by a series of five graded booklets with four classical guitar pieces from beginners to advanced. There were also two concert guitar pieces and cassettes that demonstrated how each piece was played.

The summer flew by quickly and although October was still warm the beaches emptied and the atmosphere disappeared along with the tourists. I had finished writing all my guitar pieces and was keen to get the printing process started so we returned to England. We were only a few hours into our journey when we had to make an unscheduled stop in Montpellier after the fan belt broke. I was becoming disillusioned with my beloved Jaguar when a few weeks earlier I noticed the faultless paint work had started to bubble and it was obvious that the garage I bought it from had simply sprayed over the rust. They had also solved the problem of the engine oil light coming on by removing the light bulb so it took a while for us to realise that there was something wrong with the engine. The next morning we continued our journey with a new fan belt only to grind to a halt just outside Paris when the gearbox packed up. Enough was enough. My brother came out from England to rescue us and we abandoned the Jaguar in France for our breakdown service to sort out.

29
Scaring the SAS

Much as we had enjoyed our time in Perpignan it was great to return to our old squash club and some hard games. I had spent a lot of time training in France and my game had improved so much I was asked to play for the first team in the first division.

I took my compositions to the printers and made arrangements for *Francesca Suite* to be cut and placed an order for five hundred albums. I took Harold Franz to lunch one day and told him about my plans.

"As I can't find a record company to release *Francesca Suite* I am going to do it myself. Would you still like to publish it?" I asked.

"I think you're doing the right thing darling and of course I'd love to publish it. Once it's on vinyl I'm sure I can get it played on the radio. I'll even give you an advance of £100, it's not a lot but it's £100 more than I have ever given to an unknown writer before."

"I am also publishing a guitar tutor and some classical guitar music which I'm sure will help to promote *Francesca Suite*," I said.

Harold seemed enthusiastic and wanted to help.

"I'm going to talk to a friend of mine who is the head of EMI Distribution. They may be interested in distributing your classical guitar music."

We returned to Harold's office where he phoned his friend. He looked pleased with himself as he put the phone down.

"He can't wait to meet you. He's just around the corner from here so go and see him right away."

By the end of that day I had an order for £3000 worth of tutors and sheet music which was enough to pay for the whole project so whatever happened I couldn't lose. If my guitar compositions were a success I thought there might be a chance I would be asked to do some recitals so I bought a beautiful Spanish guitar and intended to devote myself entirely to classical guitar.

We returned to Gstaad in the middle of December 1982 having left the final proofs of my guitar music to be printed while we were away.

It was a good year for celebrities in Gstaad and Julia was constantly pointing out people she recognised. We were trying out ski suits one afternoon when she came out of a cubicle and bumped into Roger Moore. She took one look at him and ran straight back in.

"I know it sounds stupid but when I saw him I got really scared," she said.

I practiced classical guitar every morning for at least four hours while Julia worked in Frau Ludi's shop. In the afternoon we skied and early evening we coached or played squash. Life was great although we were disappointed that we weren't making friends like we had done in France. People we met or coached were friendly but aloof. Despite having plenty of savings left we kept to a strict budget and what with our squash coaching and Julia's wages we were breaking even. Since selling the house everything had gone like clockwork. Julia was becoming fluent in German and she loved working in the shop where her warmth and friendliness had made her a big hit with the customers. I was making great progress with my classical guitar playing and felt I was good enough to do a recital if asked.

One day we were playing at the Palace Hotel squash court when we started talking to a group of men who turned out to be bodyguards for Sheikh Yamani and as they were all keen squash players they asked us for some lessons. There were six of them and each seemed to have unlimited living expenses. They could make as many international calls as they wanted and each had airline cards that gave them free travel to anywhere in the world on their days off. They were also able to invite people to dinner with them so every night after coaching they asked us to join them in the fine dining restaurant before going onto the Greengo night club. They were fantastic guys and although you would never have guessed it by looking at them they had all served in the SAS. The only one who looked the part of an SAS warrior was Mike. He was well over six foot tall, built like a tank and it was impossible to imagine anyone fighting him and coming out alive but despite his appearance he was a very kind and gentle man.

We took Mike skiing with us one day and unwittingly went to a slope that was well beyond his level of ability. When we finally arrived at the bottom after taking an hour to ski a ten minute run Mike took off his skis and ran to the nearest bar which is not easy to do wearing ski boots.

"You know what?" he said after a double whisky put some colour back into his face:

"I have been in some really bad situations in my life. I have killed men, been stabbed three times and shot once but I have never been so scared as I was on that mountain."

A group of Englishmen overhead and joined in our laughter.

"But that was a beginner's run," I said.

"I've never known such adrenaline. Come on. Finish your drink. I want to do it again," he said.

I can’t imagine what it must have cost to permanently employ six bodyguards. One night Julia saw a half lobster on the menu but was concerned that it was £25 a portion and although she loved Lobster she didn’t want to take advantage of their hospitality.

"Do you think it would be alright for me to have the lobster?" she asked.

Mike laughed and to make her feel more comfortable ordered a whole lobster just for himself as a starter. He then ordered three bottles of the most expensive wine and asked if anyone else wanted any.

On the last day of his stay in Gstaad Sheikh Yamani held a dinner party and I was asked to play guitar for it. I was shown to a room where the bodyguards changed and had their breaks. It was an important party with a lot of very rich and powerful people present so the bodyguards were on edge. Mike took a tatty old holdall from the wardrobe and handed out a selection of guns to his colleagues before strapping knives to each of his legs. While he was changing I could see by the scars on his body that he had not been bullshiting about the action he had seen. From that moment he changed from being the kind and gentle Mike to a soldier who wouldn’t hesitate to kill if necessary.

The party was held in a large apartment that was connected to the Palace Hotel but owned by Sheikh Yamani although he rarely used it. There were several bedrooms and a large living room with a beautiful log fire at one end. I played some background music during dinner and later on they asked me to sing for them. Half way through the evening Tony, the leader of the bodyguards pulled me to one side.

"I need to know what your fee is for tonight."

I didn't know what to say.

"Julia and I have had such a fantastic week it doesn't seem right asking for anything," I said.

"Don't be silly. We’ve really enjoyed your company. The Sheikh expects to be charged so tell me what your fee is and he'll be happy to pay it. I know he really likes you."

"I haven't got a clue. I've never done anything like this before."

"Just give me an idea."

What was I to say? In England I would have charged about £45 but that was Switzerland and it was for a very rich man so maybe I should ask for £100. I wanted to say £200 but was afraid Tony would think I was being greedy. Fortunately the problem was taken out of my hands when he was called away urgently.

The rest of the evening went well and when the last of his guests had gone the Sheikh asked me to stay behind to play for him and his family. It was hard to imagine that this kind and softly spoken man sitting in front of me was the leader of OPEC and one of the most powerful men in the world. We talked for a while and he seemed genuinely interested in what I was doing. Finally he showed me to the door and just as I was leaving handed me a 500 franc note (£300). Then he stopped to think for a second, put his hand back in his pocket and handed me another 500 francs. I went into shock. He had paid me £600 for one night's work. The bodyguards laughed when they saw my face and were pleased for me. They also gave me two £70 bottles of Château Lafitte that were left over from dinner. I just couldn't understand how anyone could have so much money to be able to give it away like that.

As the success of the evening sank home to me I began to dream about what could come from it. The bodyguards told me the Sheikh often had dinner parties so he would probably fly me out to play for him in future. Maybe the Sheikh would recommend me to his friends and I would end up with my own jet set band like Renato Sambo. The next day Sheikh Yamani and his entourage left Switzerland so Julia and I were in a serious state of anticlimax. To my great disappointment, I never heard from Sheik Yamani or his bodyguards again.

As much as I enjoyed our remaining time in Gstaad I was ready for a change when the end of the season came. The final proofs of my guitar music had been posted to me and the sight of them in print filled me with excitement. I knew I wasn't going to make my fortune from writing classical guitar music but if I could just make enough to continue travelling and composing I would be more than happy. I had rediscovered my great love for music which had been destroyed by the necessity of earning a living from it. I returned to England a born again musician.

30
The Silly Season

We returned to England at the beginning of May accepting my parents' offer of a place to stay until we decided what to do next. It wasn't an ideal arrangement as we had to sleep on the living room floor but it was only for a few weeks as once money started to roll in from sales of my music we could continue our travels.

EMI were distributing my guitar pieces to music shops throughout the UK and organising reviews in the appropriate magazines backed up by adverts that I was going to place. It was a shock to discover how expensive advertising was but it was worth it as it was not only selling my sheet music but promoting me as an artist at the same time. Harold Franz sent 50 copies of *Francesca Suite* to all the radio stations so everything was set. Harold was concerned about the front cover of *Francesca Suite* which I must admit wasn't one of my best ideas. Being an unknown artist it was essential that the front cover stood out from all the others in a shop. As the album was based on classical music and classical musicians always look so conservative I had a photo taken of me wearing a tee shirt smothered in chocolate sauce and my hair all over the place. I looked horrible but nobody could deny it wasn't an eye catching cover. In my defence, years later Nigel Kennedy did something similar which transformed him from a musician only known within classical circles to a household name.

My only concern was that I had advertised that orders would be dispatched within 48 hours and if there was a big response I might not be able to get them out on time. Every day I went to the local newsagents to see if that month's edition of Classical Guitar Magazine had arrived but it seemed to be later than usual. When it finally arrived I rushed over to the rack and purchased a copy breathless with excitement. My first review and I was sure it was going to be good, heaven knows I deserved it after all the effort I had put into it. I resisted the temptation to read the magazine until I got home and was sitting comfortably. I had no trouble finding the review of my guitar tutor as it filled nearly a whole page. The more I read, the more my world fell apart. It was a hatchet job.

I had made some stupid mistakes in the tutor and should have paid a professional to check it over but I couldn't understand why the reviewer's attack was so personal and included deliberately misleading comments. What had never occurred to me was that whoever reviewed my work would have to be a guitarist themselves which meant they would be in direct competition with me. In writing the tutor I had tried to get away from the way music was taught to me at school and offered a simpler approach but to anyone who had learnt the conventional way it must have been like a red rag to a bull.

I spent two days composing a letter to the magazine to be printed on their Reader's Page but I knew I was just digging a hole for myself so abandoned the idea. I convinced myself that things weren't so bad and that anyone reading the review would see how unfair it was but there is something in human nature that loves to see someone being torn apart.

I tried advertising in the Melody Maker and some other music papers but ended up with six orders in total which covered about 1% of the advertising costs. A few months later I phoned EMI distributors to see how they were doing with my sheet music but they had sold less than me. Harold Franz called to let me know he'd had no response from the radio stations and there was nothing more he could do. The whole project was a disaster. I had made yet another classic mistake: producing something without any idea how to promote it. A few local shops stocked my album on a sale or return basis but when I saw it amongst the hundreds from well known bands I don't know why I ever thought people would choose mine. It was ridiculous to have put all my hope on reviews as even the best reviews are not enough to sell albums without proper promotion.

With no hope of income from my music I was worried about how long our money would last. We had been careful with our spending but it is amazing how quickly savings disappear when there is no money coming in. The thought of going back to our old lives without the consolation of a lovely house was too depressing to consider. We still had the taste of freedom in our mouths and it was terrible to feel it slipping away.

A year later I was reading a copy of another classical guitar magazine and was surprised to see my guitar music being reviewed by a well known female guitarist and teacher. The review was excellent and she recommended it enthusiastically but by then I had lost heart. With no desire to return to freelance gigging and no chance of making a living as a composer it was difficult to escape the conclusion that my career in music was over.

We were gradually sliding downhill and once again our only refuge was on a squash court. We joined an excellent club in Croydon and both played for their first teams. With the standard being so high we were enjoying our squash more than ever but it was having a devastating effect on our bank account. At that point I entered what I call the *silly season* of my life, full of futile attempts at earning a living. I went to bed one night as Derek Newark and woke up the next morning as a cross between Alan Sugar and Mr Bean. It started when I saw an advert in the Exchange and Mart offering stalls to rent at Petticoat Lane Sunday Market. Everyone knew that a stall there was a licence to print money so it looked like the answer to all our prayers. I could sell my music from our stall together with guitars and other musical accessories. To draw a crowd I would play guitar live while Julia did the selling. How could we fail? We found a good supplier so after signing a two month contract with what we thought was the Petticoat Lane Management Company we were in business.

On the first Sunday we left the house at 5 a.m. so we could set up the stall before the market opened. When we arrived the whole area was in chaos as everyone was setting up at the same time and the nearest parking space was a quarter of a mile from our pitch. It took so long to carry our stock from the car that we were panicking in case we weren't ready for the first rush of customers when the market opened but we made it with minutes to spare.

By ten o'clock we hadn't even seen a customer let alone served one. I plugged my guitar into a small amplifier and started playing but the closest I got to an audience was a few people glancing my way in confusion.

"What's he doing?" I heard them think.

"Is he a busker?"

"Should we throw him some money?"

I did gain a few foul weather fans when it started raining but as soon as the shower passed they disappeared.

I had some mild interest in the guitars but no matter how much I lowered the prices I couldn't sell any. One little sod spent half an hour haggling with me to the point where I was offering him the guitar for half what I paid for it and he still wouldn't take it.

"If you're selling it so cheaply there must be something wrong with it." I couldn't win.

Another idea came to me in the changing rooms one day when I saw someone shaking resin from a glass jar onto his hand. Resin is a sticky substance that many squash players put on their hands to improve their grip. There were only two products available, one called Resinpad which no one liked because it was messy and the other an aerosol which no one liked because it was easy to get it mixed up with your underarm deodorant with very unpleasant results. I had a brainwave. Powdered resin in a container that you could shake onto your hand like salt. *Resintube* was born.

We bought a few hundred empty Sweetex containers with special tops that allowed the resin to be shaken out. Unfortunately our Resin supplier wasn't able to grind it fine enough for our purpose so we had to do it ourselves with a little electric coffee grinder which was very tedious and messy. We did an initial batch of 30 boxes and started hawking them around the squash clubs. The response was excellent and within weeks nearly every club in the area was stocking Resintube.

Next we approached a distributor and were thrilled to get an order for 400 boxes from a company in Bournemouth. It was only when we took delivery of our massive order of resin that we realised what we had taken on. There were 16 tubes to a box so it meant filling and labelling 6400 tubes by hand. The filling wasn't so bad, it was grinding the resin in our little coffee grinder that was the problem. Because of all the dust created we had to wear masks and work in the back yard all day. The resin dust got everywhere so at night when I started to sweat during a squash game my whole body became a mass of stickiness.

Although Resintube was selling well it was never going to generate enough income for us to live on so we started supplying squash clubs with other accessories like towelling grips, headbands, wristlets, jogging suits, etc. We managed to find some towelling for headbands which was much lighter than normal so they were very comfortable. It wasn't until the weather got warmer that we discovered that when the headbands became heavy with sweat they stretched and dropped down over people's eyes causing them to crash into the walls in the middle of a rally. It was great fun for people watching but we had to discontinue the product before someone killed themselves. We also did some squash coaching at different clubs but the income was not even enough to pay for our own squash so by the autumn we had ran out of money and were starting to live on credit cards again. I had no choice but to do the unthinkable and look for freelance gigs.

During the depressing drive to my first gig I thought of all the soul destroying songs that were waiting for me without being aware that a new party song had appeared on the scene while I was away. A song that turned sensible adults into raving lunatics. A song more devastating than anything ever inflicted on serious musicians. A song that someone up there commissioned especially to punish me for daring to try and rise above my station in life. It was none other than the dreaded ….. *Birdie Song.*

That was the first time I ever heard *The Birdie Song* and I couldn't believe it when crowds of adults ran onto the dance floor in a frenzy to pretend they were little chickens by shaking their bums and pretending their hands were little beaks. It was an abysmal night and a terrible way to end my months of freedom.

It was common amongst bandleaders to put out more than one band on the same night so although someone paid a lot of money for the famous "Joe Bloggs Orchestra" all they were getting was a bunch of freelance musicians hired for that one night. The real Joe Bloggs would be fronting a band somewhere else assuming he wasn't at home watching television. In general it doesn't really matter if musicians have never played together before as long as everyone reads music. One night I was booked to play for one of these knocked together bands and we were all set up and ready to start when someone pointed out there was no pad. A pad is a pile of music that is handed to each musician at the start of a gig. A bandleader will always have a pad for his main band but for his 2nd division bands he will usually rely on whatever singer he books to provide their own. On that night the singer didn't have his own pad so there we were, a 12 piece danceband with no music to play from. We got through by playing songs that everyone knew but most of the time the brass section did nothing but sway from side to side and pretend to play. It was a complete mess and by the time we had finished our first set both band and audience were relieved to see the disco take over for our break. When it was time for us to go back on stage the organiser came over looking embarrassed and said:

"Would you mind if we leave the disco on. We will pay you but to be honest your first set wasn't very good was it?"

It was said in such an apologetic way that it was impossible to take offence, particularly when it was true. Apart from my time with Cheeserat and Gorilla I don't remember ever being so ashamed to be a musician.

When the bandleader was asked if he was available that night he could have said no and left the gig for another band who would have appreciated the work. The war between discos and musicians was growing fiercer while we were in self destruct mode fuelled by the greed of agents and bandleaders.

31
Undercut

During the decline of our financial affairs I had always taken it for granted that as a last resort I could go back to gigging and at least earn enough money for us to live on but even that was looking doubtful. Discos were replacing live music at an alarming rate and function bands were being priced out of the market due to all the rake offs.

We both liked the idea of managing a squash club and answered an advert in the Squash Player magazine but didn't get the job because of our lack of experience. As most of my success had always come from placing adverts rather than answering them I advertised our services as coaches or squash club managers. We only had one reply:

"Are you still looking for a job in a squash club?" a man asked.

"Yes we are."

"I am the owner of a ten court club in Beckenham and I'm looking for someone to run my bar. Is that the kind of thing you have in mind?"

It wasn't exactly what we had in mind but it sounded interesting so we went along to meet him at the Howdon Squash club in Beckenham.

Don Howell was a wealthy property developer in his early sixties. A year earlier he had bought a large playing field and clubhouse for £25,000 from a cricket club that had gone bankrupt. He built the squash courts next to the club house and with his membership increasing rapidly he needed a professional couple to run the bar for him rather than relying on friends. We got on well together and had a mutual love for squash. Don was a shrewd businessman who never offered a salary to prospective employees but asked them what salary they wanted to do the job. If someone asked for more than he had in mind he just turned them down but if they undervalued themselves he got them for less than he was expecting to pay.

We went home and worked out a deal which included free squash, food and a reasonable salary. Don accepted our terms on a one month trial on condition that we played for his teams which owing to it being a new club were playing in low divisions. It was difficult for new clubs to get promotion in the inter club leagues because they needed good players but good players didn't want to play in low divisions.

A publican friend gave us a crash course on running a bar and within a few days we settled in and were surprised how much we enjoyed it. I put in a good sound system and made up some lively music tapes. I knew nothing about running a bar but I knew a lot about entertaining and my choice of music soon transformed the bar from a quiet and forbidding place to somewhere that people wanted to stay behind and drink after a game of squash. It was also agreed that at the end of our trial period we could move into a flat that was attached to the club so it looked like things were really looking up.

A few days before the end of our trial Don called us into his office for a chat. We were both excited as having doubled the bar takings we took it for granted the job was ours. We were also looking forward to moving into the flat as after seven months with my parents we were desperate for a place of our own. Don started the conversation:

"I'm very happy with what you've done here but I am afraid I won't be offering you a permanent job. I have been interviewing other couples and found one who is prepared to manage the bar for a percentage of the turnover rather than a salary so I have accepted their offer."

We were devastated.

"You mean all the time you've been telling us how well the bar is doing you have been looking for another couple to do the job cheaper?"

"I'm a businessman. I have to take the best deal that is offered to me."

"What percentage is the other couple prepared to take?"

"12%"

"But that's ridiculous. At the present turnover that works out at only £50 a week for the two of them."

"They think they can increase trade enough to make it worthwhile and as they are experienced publicans they must know what they are doing."

"Don't you think there's something strange about that? You know how much fiddling goes on in this business."

"If they start fiddling then it will be picked up by the stocktaker. Anyway they are offering me a £500 security so I will be covered by that."

When the members found out what Don had done they vowed to boycott the club and cause all sorts of trouble but their loyalty was short lived and within a few weeks we were forgotten. Several months later we discovered our replacements had disappeared one day with thousands of pounds in takings and nearly every bottle of spirits in the cellar was filled with water to fool the stocktaker.

In March 1983 after nearly a year of sleeping on the floor at my parent's house we moved to a rented house near Croydon and although the rent was very reasonable it was still more than we could afford. Up until then I had never really worried about anything in my life as something always seemed to turn up. Although we had been in serious debt before there was always plenty of equity in our house to cover that debt. Sitting in our rented house with all the bills to pay and very little money coming in I was seriously worried for the first time as our credit cards moved steadily towards the limit.

One day I heard from a friend that there was a job going as bar steward in a local sports club so I made inquires and managed to get an interview. We applied as a couple and sat with great confidence in front of the club committee.

"Our main concern is that you have been a musician for so long. Do you really think you can settle down to bar work in a small club like this?" one of the committee members asked me. I was ready for that question.

"I can understand your concern but I've had enough of the insecurity of the music business and just want to have a regular wage coming in."

I knew that was what they wanted to hear as people are never so smug as when helping dreamers down from their clouds.

"Thank you very much. We still have some other couples to interview but we'll let you know the outcome as soon as possible."

I knew the interview had gone well but was disheartened that it had ended with the dreaded *don't call us we'll call you* speech that I was all too familiar with. All I could think about as we drove home was how desperately we needed that job.

That night, just as I had resigned myself to days of agonising waiting the phone rang. Julia ran to answer it. She smiled. I felt dizzy. She put the phone down.

"We've got the job!" she screamed.

32
"A camel is a horse designed by a committee"

Sir Alec Issigonis

On our first day at the Tingleton Sports Club we were introduced to our boss and the delights of working for committees. Graham was the chairman of the bar committee and it was his job to show us around despite not having a clue what he was supposed to be showing us. Just as he was leaving I asked him for a key for the squash club as we wanted a game before starting work.

"If you want to play squash here you'll have to join the club," he said.

"But we obviously assumed using the club facilities came with the job?"

"I'm afraid not. Everyone has to pay an annual membership fee. Even Me."

I wasn't concerned as I knew the squash club committee would have something to say about that as they wanted me to play for their first team. After he left I had a good look around the bar and was appalled at the filth and disorganization. On our first night I served a customer with a packet of crisps and just as she went to open it a mouse jumped out from inside and ran across the bar counter. A glass washer that for years club members thought had a black Perspex cover turned out to be clear Perspex with a thick layer of slime on the inside. The club had been around for many years and was staffed by its members who regarded their main duty to be serving their friends with free drinks. The other problem with using volunteers is that nobody wants to do the boring jobs so cleaning or tidying up is always left to the next person on duty. When the club was small it wasn't a problem but with the addition of squash courts membership had grown significantly making it difficult to run with volunteers alone so that's where we came in. The first few nights went well and we enjoyed the job but then I got my first taste of what it would be like working for *The Committee.*

The club comprised of several sports and it was the squash club that had been most instrumental in getting us the job. They were only in the third division but with me playing for them they would be assured of promotion and the same went for Julia and the ladies team. Neither of us wanted to play for them as we were used to playing first division squash but we regarded it as part of our duty. One night the bar treasurer came in for a chat. He was a squash fanatic and played for their first team so had a personal interest in getting promoted next season.

"Are you and Julia going to play for the teams?" he asked.

"We'd be happy to play for you but we're not members."

"What do you mean you're not members? You work here."

"Graham told me we have to pay a membership fee if we want to play squash here. If we have to pay then obviously we're going to play at a club with a higher standard."

He looked bewildered.

"That man is an idiot. Don't worry, I'll sort it out and bring you a fixture list tomorrow."

He returned the next night.

"You are now official members of Tingleton Squash Club. Graham is the only person in the entire club that hadn't taken it for granted you would get free use of all the facilities."

The next day Graham resigned as bar chairman in a storm of protest and bad feeling and that was what life was like for us during our time at Tingleton Sports Club: an endless cycle of bickering between committees none of which seemed to have a clue what they were doing. There were some very capable people on committees but their advice was usually ignored by the other committee members who had only been elected because no one else wanted the job. A large extension to the bar had been built a few years earlier and owing to the committee ignoring the advice of their own architect it had a cheap flat roof which now leaked like a sieve. The club hadn't been decorated for years and although the public health department had given them several warnings nothing was ever done about it. The main bar area was very small and without any ventilation so when it was busy the cigarette smoke was so bad Julia and I had to work in 15 minute shifts so we could stand outside in the cold until our eyes stopped stinging. We were assured that the clubhouse would be renovated and the money was available but it never happened because the committee could never agree on how to spend it.

At the end of our first three months the club had its first stocktake and the excellent results took everyone by surprise. Until then we had been unpopular with some of the members as we had imposed a harsh new rule: everyone had to pay for their drinks. The results showed how much beer had been disappearing every month so people's attitude towards us changed as they knew the only way the club could survive was for the bar to be run efficiently and honestly. Although at first I found it difficult to work for committees I soon discovered that as they had no idea what they were doing I could just smile and agree to whatever they said and then no one knew when I did the opposite.

I enjoyed the summer weekends when there were cricket matches as there was a relaxed atmosphere and we had a good team. I thought about taking up cricket again but after half an hour in the practice nets I was reminded of how hard cricket balls were and was afraid I might damage my hands, or my head for that matter.

In 1984, halfway through our second summer at the club the constant bickering between each section was becoming intolerable as we always seemed to be in the middle of it. One section would complain about us doing what another section had instructed us to do. The cricket committee insisted we served real ale while the other committees said we couldn't because the beer was going off due to there being no cooler in the cellar. The bar committee wanted to charge us £15 a week for a franchise to serve food but all the other committees wanted their members to be able to bring their own food making the franchise worthless.

Autumn brought constant rain which leaked through the clubhouse ceiling making the bar stink of dampness and stale beer when we arrived at 5 p.m. every night to open up. Cricket had finished for the season and was replaced by football. The days grew colder and the thought of spending another winter at that club was depressing. It was the winter Sunday lunchtimes that were the worst when unsupervised children were let loose to wreak havoc leaving a thick carpet of crisps covering the bar floor. When the football match finished there was an hour of frenzied drinking by the players during which time they devastated any area that the children had neglected to trash. It was at the end of one of these dreaded sessions when I was feeling particularly sorry for myself that I had another life changing phone call.

Since the start of that season I had been playing for Don Howell's first team at the Howdon Squash Club. Julia didn't want me to have anything to do with Don after the way he treated us but a part of me liked the old rogue. He was tough but he always kept his word and we shared a common love for squash. Besides, I'd burnt too many bridges in my life and there was no doubt he was very wealthy so maybe one day he would be in a position to help us.

The phone call was from Don and as always he came straight to the point.

"You mentioned some time ago that you would like to have your own squash club one day?"

"Yes we'd love to but I can't see us ever having the money to do that."

"There's a club on the market in Derby which is going very cheap. Why don't you go and look at it and if you are interested maybe we can do a deal together. You could either manage it for me or I could buy it and you could lease it from me."

The next day we went to view the South Derbyshire Squash Club which was built on an industrial estate on the outskirts of Derby. It was a six court club with a large house attached to the side. There was a big car park at the front and acres of open land at the back with the River Derwent flowing at the far end and beyond that were fields complete with matching sheep and cows. It was one of a large chain of squash clubs owned by First Leisure who also owned the North Middlesex Squash Club where we learnt to play. Most of them were built to the same design with the bar on the first floor and large windows where you could watch people playing squash below. I would have killed to own or even manage a club like that.

The freehold asking price was £120,000 which was very low due to bad trading figures but that was obviously down to bad local management so it didn't concern us. We felt like royalty while we were being shown around as prospective buyers. There was nothing in the world we wanted more than to own that squash club but with no savings we knew it was just a pipe dream.

We went straight from there to see Don and ask what kind of deal he had in mind but as always he insisted on leaving it to us to put one together. I lay awake all night trying to figure out what to do but eventually came up with a deal that was so unique that Don's solicitor insisted on getting a QC's opinion before he would let Don sign it.

I proposed we signed a 15 year lease at a rent that gave Don a return of 15% on his investment which I knew was the figure he expected. Under normal circumstances we would also have to pay a lump sum for the lease but as we had no money I offered him six per cent of the turnover meaning the lease would be paid for in a minimum of three years and anything after that would be a bonus for him. Knowing that Don would want a cash payment up front I offering to pay him the first year's rent of £15,000 in advance and to pay for that I borrowed the money from the bank using the lease as collateral despite the fact I didn't actually own it. Everyone was happy and secure so after an agonising wait of six weeks while the solicitors pretended to earn their huge fees we exchanged contracts.

My love of music that had started as a raging inferno had gradually burnt itself out until the day we took over the squash club when it was snuffed out completely ... or so I thought.

33
Apricot and Chips

On December 5th 1984 the club was ours and how wonderful it was walking into *my office* for the first time. I was amazed at the amount of paperwork the previous manager had to do and with great satisfaction I threw the whole lot into the rubbish bin. If we needed something we could go right ahead and buy it without asking anyone's permission.

I soon got the hang of running the club and as it had been neglected for so long it would have been difficult not to improve things. I had always known the club was a great opportunity but I soon discovered we had acquired the perfect business. On the day of completion the seller had to give us a cheque for £3000 being the balance of the annual subscriptions paid by the club members. All our suppliers gave us a month credit which was effectively a large interest free loan. When people played squash or paid their fees the only work we did was put the money in the till. How would you like a machine you put in your living room and once a week you can collect a box full of cash from it? We had one of those, commonly known as a fruit machine. As if all that wasn't enough a brewery rep appeared one day and offered us a £10,000 interest free loan on condition that we served their beer which we already did anyway. With so much cash coming in we paid off our bank overdraft in the first six weeks so for the first time in my life I managed to impress a bank manager.

Having spent so much time in squash clubs I knew exactly what people wanted so I made sure our members had no cause to complain. When people joined the club I introduced them to existing members so they were made to feel welcome. The house attached to the club was much bigger than we needed so we converted the lower half into a gym and saunas doing most of the work myself to save money. On the first day of advertising the new facilities we had a queue of people standing at the bar waiting to join. We gave the members everything they asked for and didn't charge them a penny extra in fees which is why I was astonished to get complaints from a few of the members who said we were taking too much out of the club and not putting enough in. I knew it was impossible to please everyone but it didn't make it any less upsetting. I honestly believe if I had opened a restaurant offering free food some people would have demanded payment for eating there.

One thing that surprised me was how many things were stolen, not members belongings from the changing rooms as I would have expected but general items left around the club. Fire extinguishers were the favourite target and so many went missing that the fire officer advised me to keep them locked in cupboards where at least I knew I could find them in an emergency. Old audio speakers screwed to the changing room walls were taken, fluorescent tubes out of their fittings, rolls of toilet paper and on one occasion even a fuse from a plug socket. This was in a club where most of our members were reasonably well off.

The club went from strength to strength and we were able to employ more staff to ease our workload. We put on lots of special events like cabaret nights, tournaments, friendly matches and discos and they were all well supported so the money was pouring in. Julia held regular aerobics sessions and as it was mainly women that attended classes an influx of men coincidentally appeared in the bar at the same time. After 18 months our turnover more than doubled and our profit was ten times that of our predecessors. We put most of the money back into the club on improvements but still managed to go on exotic summer holidays and skiing twice a year. Some members resented our success despite the fact they could see how hard we worked but most were happy for us.

Success brought with it new problems when the health and fitness section became overcrowded. The ladies changing room was tiny so with 25 women changing after an aerobics class we needed to do something about it before we lost customers. We didn't have enough money for an extension the size we needed so I decided to do most of the work myself. I had done a lot of DIY by then and although it was far bigger than anything I had attempted before if I got into trouble there was a club full of members who were happy to give help or advice when needed. In theory it was a simple job of digging a trench around the perimeter of the new building, filling the trench with concrete and building the walls on top. Easy peasey. I employed a JCB driver to dig the trench which should have taken a day at most but after digging away happily for an hour he got down from his cab and came over to me.

"We've hit the water table," he said.

"Is that bad?"

"Don't know. It means the trenches will fill up with water when I dig past a certain level. Shall I keep digging?"

Talk about the blind leading the blind.

"Go on then. Let's see what happens."

He jumped back into the JCB and resumed digging but every scoop led to soil dropping from the side of the trench into the water. Half an hour later where there should have been a neat little trench 18 inches wide I saw only a small lake. One of our regular members was the very kind and helpful Don Prime who owned the biggest building construction company in Derby. I asked him to take a look and after staring at it in disbelief he said:

"That is the worst building land I have ever seen. You'll have to stop digging and get a structural engineer's report."

I employed a structural engineer who told me the club was built on a land fill site so I needed to go through the huge expense of putting down piles. A cheaper but more complicated option was to construct an elaborate system of steel reinforced concrete to form the foundation. He gave me an idiot proof diagram to follow which resembled a Meccano model so I had no trouble following it. Although technically it was an easy enough job it was very tough physically as I did most of it myself apart from placing 18 huge concrete rings around the perimeter of the site for which I employed a JCB and driver. With all the re-enforcing and shuttering complete I ordered two loads of ready mixed concrete which in theory just had to be poured from the lorry into the trench. It wasn't until the lorries arrived that I discovered they couldn't drive along the side of the trench for fear of the ground collapsing and overturning the lorry.

"Don't worry," said the driver, "it's a dry mix so it won't go solid until the morning."

Like a fool I believed him and watched helplessly as he dropped what looked like enough concrete to build a skyscraper onto my car park. I immediately phoned Don Prime who was horrified at what I'd done and promised to send some labourers as soon as possible. By coincidence my parents were staying with us at the time so my 64 year old father who was always ready to get stuck in insisted on helping me move the concrete with nothing more that a shovel and a wheelbarrow. After two hours of backbreaking work we moved no more than 2% of the rapidly hardening concrete. Just as I was about to collapse (my father was still going strong) Don's labourers arrived with a van full of wheelbarrows and shovels and it was just like the cavalry had arrived. They were amazing. They literally ran around the site with wheelbarrows full of concrete and in forty five minutes they finished just as it was starting to set solid.

What should have taken two days at most took me three months so I accepted my limitations and hired a team of labourers to lay the concrete floor and bricklayers to build the walls. I did most of the rest myself with occasional help from some of the members. The building took eight months to complete with me working twelve hours a day seven days a week. I filled the new gym with equipment and even had an Olympic standard free weight section complete with two giant mirrors for the weightlifters to admire themselves when no one was looking. There was a large changing room and toilets for the ladies with a sauna built into the shower area. It was all fully tiled with top quality fittings and the ladies were delighted with the result. All of this was done without any increase in fees to existing members and yet there were still those who found cause to complain. After another successful advertising campaign our membership rose to 1500 members from the 350 there was when we started. The club was buzzing with activity and everyone was talking about our success story.

It was not only Julia and I who were riding on a cloud at that time but the whole country. It was the middle of the Thatcher boom when it was common knowledge that anyone who was prepared to work hard and invest in business was sure to become rich. Competition in the changing room was no longer about who beat who at squash but who had made the most money on the stock market. Capitalists, Socialists, Communists, we were all buying as many new issue shares as we could and bending every rule in the book to help us get our snouts in the trough. We bought a house as an investment and as our building society manager was one of our members he brought the papers to the club for us to sign so what was normally one of the most traumatic experiences a couple can go through we completed during one lunchtime. We rented the house to four young workers from Rolls Royce who were the perfect tenants.

At that stage I could have just sat back and enjoyed life but I had the taste of success and I wanted more. I needed a new challenge. We had a lot of members from the Rolls Royce factory and it was one of their programmers, Bill Barker who talked me into getting a computer soon after we arrived at the club. He advised me to buy a £1200 Apricot PC with two floppy drives, no hard drive and the latest chips whatever they were. I got it home and switched it on only to be greeted with a black screen showing the characters C:\>. I gave it a gentle tap thinking there was something wrong with it but that didn't help so I asked Bill to come and fix it for me.

"You need a program," he said.

"What's that?"

"It's what makes the computer work."

"You never told me anything about needing programs."

"I'll do a deal with you. I will write a program for you if you help me sell it to other clubs," he said.

Suddenly I was in the software business without any idea what software was. Every evening Bill came to the club to work on a program that would manage our membership as at that time there wasn't anything available for me to buy off the shelf. What he wrote was a great help but there wasn't a day that passed without him having to fix a bug for me. Then out of the blue he announced:

"OK It's ready to sell now. It's your job to write a manual for it."

"What do you mean it's ready to sell? We have to wait until the program is perfect before we can ask people to pay money for it."

"No that's the great thing about software. You sell it and then charge an annual subscription to fix the bugs."

I thought he was off his head but of course he was right. The software business is the only industry where you can sell people faulty products and then charge them extra to fix those faults. I wrote a manual and placed a few adverts in squash magazines but was relieved when nothing came from it.

It was spring 1987 and I still needed a new project to get my teeth into. The club was still doing well but for long term security I thought it would be best to diversify. The obvious choice would have been something in the music business. Maybe start my own band, or form a record company and promote other artists but the fact was I had lost all interest in the music business and resented the way it had treated me.

I always loved listening to afternoon plays on BBC Radio 4 so I thought I would have a go at writing one myself. At first I really struggled but out of the blue I had the extraordinary sensation of characters coming to life in my head and dictating the dialogue to me. I sent it to the BBC but with the countless rejections I'd had over the years I wasn't expecting anything when they sent me an acknowledgement saying they would let me know within a month. Three months later there was still no word from them so I phoned to find out what was happening. The woman spent ages looking for my details and then informed me:

"I've found your play. It has been read and is now with the editor. You should hear within a week or two."

I put the phone down and sat in a trance wondering what to think. The words "it has been read and is now with the editor" kept going round in my head. I looked up the word *editor* in the dictionary to find out exactly what it meant.

Editor: A person who prepares works for publication.

I went into shock. *Prepares works for publication.* If it was going to be rejected why would they be preparing it for publication? Could it really be possible that I was going to have something accepted and hear my play on the radio? Maybe it would be adapted for TV or even a motion picture. I was going to be a writer travelling the world writing best sellers on the veranda of deserted beach houses.

Four weeks later the letter arrived. My heart was pounding as I tore the envelope apart. I quickly scanned the page but only one word caught my attention, the dreaded word .... "unfortunately." It was a rejection letter. I thought I had got used to rejection but that was the worst ever as it felt like a final nail in the coffin of any dream I had that involved the arts.

We were still looking for a new project to get our teeth into when on a family visit to London I made a casual remark to Julia's brother:

"So what have you been up to recently?"

"I've been delivering pizzas for Pizza Hut. It's really catching on in London and we can't get them out fast enough."

A bell rang in my head that reverberated for the rest of my days.

34
Getting Plastered

It was all decided, we were going to open a pizza and pasta restaurant with takeaways and deliveries. Pizza delivery was not yet available in Derby so it was a chance to get in at the beginning. Julia was an amazing cook and had an exceptional talent for catering that she had displayed at the Tingleton Sports Club when she catered for 120 people at the annual dinner and dance. We made a huge profit and the club said how much better it was than the catering company they normally used.

We started looking for premises and there was no shortage of dilapidated buildings to choose from. We settled on a property in a main road one minute's walk from the city centre. It had a double fronted shop window with two rooms at the back and a large apartment upstairs. It was also attached to a warehouse and at the end of that was an old cottage. The rent was very low but the property was in bad condition. Once the restaurant was running smoothly we intended to convert the warehouse into a banqueting room and use the house at the end as the main kitchen with storerooms above. I needed around £60,000 for the development and with such a good reputation at the bank a loan was just a formality.

While we waited for the deal to go through we splashed out on a three week holiday in America. The first few days we spent at the Sheraton Hotel in Los Angeles doing the usual tourist stuff like Disneyland and Universal Studios and I loved every minute of it. We also went to the Grand Canyon, San Francisco and finished up with a week in Hawaii. It was on the beach at the Hawaii Hilton as we watched dolphins swimming around the lagoon that I lay next to Julia and thought to myself: "This is it. I am truly happy." Ever since my affair with Marie I had remained faithful but I had often wondered what I would do if temptation knocked hard enough on my door. Now everything was going so well for us I was content and knew I would never stray again. We had spent the last seven years living in each other's pockets but were closer than ever before. People who saw us thought we were newlyweds as we were always so affectionate towards each other. Now I was going to make Julia's greatest dream come true, to own her own restaurant and I had never seen her so happy.

In early November I started the building work and while I knew it was in a bad state of repair it wasn't until I started working on it that I realised just how bad. I removed some shelves from a wall and all the plaster came with it so all the walls had to be re-plastered. The ceilings had to be replaced due to water damage from a leaky roof and I took away a section of false flooring only to find there was nothing underneath so I had to lay a new concrete floor. It also needed replumbing and rewiring. I knew I couldn't do all the work myself so I hired some contractors and a full time handyman but even then I found it much harder than I had anticipated.

I rewired the entire building and laid acres of floor and wall floor tiles. I gave myself Sundays off from the building work but had to spend most of it doing the squash club accounts. To make matters worse there was an endless procession of council officials employed for the sole purpose of making life difficult for businessmen. A man from the disabled lobby ordered me to change the entire design of my front just so we had a door that opened inwards.

"People in wheelchairs need to be able to enter the premises without assistance," he told me.

"But they will still need assistance to get out."

He shrugged his shoulders.

"But that will add thousands of pounds to my building costs and reduce the number of tables we can have."

"Don't worry. You'll still make a fortune so what's a few thousand pounds to you?" he said in a manner that left no doubt that he hated capitalists.

A few days later I had a visit from the fire officer.

"I'm sorry but your door has to open outwards otherwise if there's a fire and someone falls against it everyone will be stuck inside," he told me.

"Yes that makes perfect sense but the man from the disabled department ordered me to have it opening inwards."

He looked more frustrated than I was.

"I suppose you'll have to leave it as it is then. They have more power than us and until a load of people die in a big fire there is nothing we can do about it."

I could have appealed and definitely won but it would have taken six months and been very expensive. I was trying to turn an eyesore into an attractive restaurant and create jobs and all the council could do was make life as difficult as possible for me.

A few weeks before opening we took on a young couple to manage the restaurant for us and started interviewing staff. We opened on Friday 1st May 1988 and with my job done I handed it all over to Julia. So many times during the five months it took to build the restaurant I had cursed the day I ever started but now it was all over I was delighted with the result and proud to take friends there. It was beautifully decorated and the pizza serving area at the front looked impressive with its oak fittings and large copper extractor fan.

Despite having done most of the work myself the cost of the project had risen to an incredible £120,000. I was concerned at being so much in debt but told myself all property developments went over budget and now we were open the money would start rolling in. It never occurred to me for a minute that the restaurant wouldn't be as successful as the squash club.

The first weekend was much quieter than expected but word soon got around and trade started to pick up. We paid Barbara Windsor £400 to have lunch at the restaurant and although she was great fun I can't say it brought in any more customers. We also used the squash club to promote our restaurant offering a discount to all our members. For once it seemed that everything was going without a hitch. Even if I had considered the possibility of something going wrong I could never have predicted the cataclysmic events that followed.

35
Being Noted

It was one week after the restaurant was launched. You would think when we wake up on a life changing day we would have some kind of premonition of what was going to happen but no, fate sends us bolts of lightening with as much indifference as if ordering a leaf to fall from a tree.

It was a warm spring morning when we woke exhausted but still buzzing with the excitement of a successful weekend at the restaurant. It had been chaos at times and nobody knew what they were doing but in general customers were happy.

"Where shall we eat this Sunday?" I asked. We always ate out for Sunday lunch.

"If you don't mind I'd like to go to the restaurant to prepare things in case it gets busy."

I was surprised as I knew how much Julia loved eating out but I was relieved to see her taking the restaurant so seriously. I went for a long leisurely lunch myself and then to the restaurant where I found Julia in the kitchen making pizza bases. She was covered in flour when she greeted me with a big smile and a hug.

"How was trade then?" I asked.

"Not bad. I'll finish off here and see you at home."

Back at the club I watched some T.V. and wallowed in the luxury of not having anything urgent to do. That afternoon we held a junior squash tournament sponsored by the restaurant and Julia was in her element as she gave out prizes with all the local press cameras clicking away. She loved being under the spotlight and I had never seen her so happy and with so much self confidence. That night she gave me an affectionate hug and went to the restaurant as normal. I gave myself the night off and propped up the bar with some friends. At the end of the night I shut the front door and settled down in my office to do the weekly accounts and wait for Julia to come back from the restaurant. I was happy enough doing office work as long as I had a glass of wine and James Taylor playing on my Walkman. My office was at the front of the building with full length windows looking out onto the car park so I could see when she arrived. I was expecting Julia to return at around 11.30 p.m. so I started to get concerned when at 12.15 a.m. there was still no sign of her. By 1 a.m. just as I was really starting to worry I saw Julia's car pull into the car park. She stormed into my office shouting:

"Why aren't you answering the phone?"

Suddenly I was under attack and had no idea why. I snapped back.

"Because I didn't know it was ringing. I forgot to put it through to the office so it is only ringing in the bar."

"I was calling for ages!"

"Look!" I said, ripping the headphones from my head and waving them at her, "I've got my headphones on. I told you I didn't hear anything."

She stormed out of my office slamming the door behind her in the foulest of tempers. I had no idea what had got into her but I was used to her mood swings which were generally attributed to weight fluctuation. Despite not being the slightest bit overweight she weighed herself twice a day and if she put on even a couple of pounds it put her in a bad mood so I had learnt to make myself scarce around weighing in times. But this was 1 a.m. She couldn't have weighed in at that hour so I must have done something wrong? But that wasn't possible. She was in a good mood when she left for the restaurant that afternoon and I hadn't spoken to her since. I decided to continue working until she had calmed down. A few minutes later I was surprised to see her car drive away. I assumed she must have left something at the restaurant so was irritated that I would have to wait another half an hour for her to go and pick it up. I settled back to work hoping she would return in a better mood. An hour later there was still no sign of her and I was really getting pissed off. I was too tired to continue working so I shut down the computer and went into the bar. I was just about to turn off the lights and make my way to the flat when I noticed a small scrap of paper on the counter. I could easily have missed it.

DEREK. Sorry but I'm moving out. I'll speak to you tomorrow.

That was it. Nothing more, nothing less. After twelve years of marriage I was told it was all over with nothing more than a scrap of paper.

I put the note down and walked over to the full length windows that looked out over the empty car park. The dual carriageway in the distance was deserted and there was a thin layer of mist that amplified the silence. I stood there in a trance feeling sure Julia would return once she had time to think things over. An hour passed and I was still standing there. My body had hardly moved while my mind was in overdrive. She had never given me the slightest indication that she was thinking of leaving and I remembered how warmly she had greeted me at the restaurant that lunchtime. Was it another man? Was she having sex with someone at that very moment? But how could it be another man? She was hopeless at lying. But if it wasn't another man where would she have gone? When I finally accepted that she wasn't going to return I drove to the restaurant to see if her car was there. It wasn't. I returned to the club.

There was nothing more I could do so I went to bed half expecting the phone to ring at any minute. I lay awake staring at the ceiling and tried to imagine life without her. Why was it so cold? I was never cold in bed before. Did anyone else know what was going on? Was she really leaving me or was this just some kind of warning? Why is it that when we are deeply troubled we keep asking ourselves the same questions over and over?

I was awoken by daylight and noises from the room below me. I got dressed quickly and went into the bar trying unsuccessfully to look casual. As soon as I opened the door I heard music and the familiar sound of Julia shouting orders to an aerobics class. I returned to the flat where I was hoping Julia would come straight after her class as I was desperate to find out what was going on. Half an hour after her class finished she had still not shown up so I went into the club where I found her chatting casually with our receptionist. How could she act as if it was just another day?

"Can I have a word with you?" I asked.

I felt angry at the way I was being treated but knew it was important to keep calm. We went to the flat where I locked the door and switched off the phone so for once we wouldn't be disturbed.

"Can you please tell me what the hell is going on? After twelve years of marriage you leave a scrap of paper on the bar telling me you're leaving me like you were leaving a note for the milkman?"

"I'm sorry but you weren't answering the phone," she said.

"I told you why I didn't answer the phone but that's not the point. Ending a marriage by phone isn't much better is it?"

"I just couldn't face you. I've been plucking up the courage to leave for ages and I knew if I said anything you would talk me out of it."

"But I thought you were happy with me?"

"I was until a couple of years ago and then I started to have doubts."

"Have you met someone else?"

"No I swear I haven't but I am attracted to other men. I know if I don't leave now it will only be a matter of time before something does happen."

"So you have known for some time that you were going to leave?"

"Yes I suppose so. I just never had the courage to go through with it."

"You mean you watched me go through the worst five months of my life building the restaurant which was mainly for your benefit and now one week after it's finished you decide it's time to leave. Don't you think you've been using me?"

"It's nothing to do with the restaurant. I would have left anyway."

"Well it's a bit of a coincidence don't you think? Nearly 14 years we've been together and you suddenly decide to leave now?"

She said nothing.

"So where did you stay last night?" I asked.

"In the empty bedroom at our house. Don't you remember? One of our tenants left last month and we haven't replaced him yet."

Of course, I hadn't thought of that. It was a huge weight off my mind knowing she hadn't been unfaithful. We sat down and talked for most of the day but the only conclusion we came to was that she was very confused.

"If you really want to leave then that's OK with me but at least stay for a few days while we talk it through and make sure you're making the right decision. The least we should do is go to Marriage Guidance," I said.

She agreed reluctantly.

"You must understand that if we split up there will be no going back. It may even mean selling the squash club and restaurant," I said.

There was panic in her eyes at the thought of losing everything and I realised her idea of splitting up was that she got her freedom while I kept everything running smoothly.

"You mean you would sell everything just to get your own back on me?" she said angrily.

"Didn't it ever occur to you that if we weren't married I might like to go off and do something else? As long as we have businesses together we are still responsible for each other and that's not my idea of being free and single."

"But I thought you could keep the squash club and I keep the restaurant?"

"You mean I sign the restaurant over to you and you sign the squash club over to me?"

"Yes, I'm sure that would work. I know I can make a go of the restaurant."

So that was her plan all along.

"Great idea. You get the restaurant with its enormous debt and no profit and I get the squash club with no debt and good profit. Where do you think the bank will come for their money if the restaurant goes bust?"

She shrugged her shoulders.

"From the squash club. As long as we are business partners we are responsible for each other. You can go out and buy a Porsche tomorrow and I am equally responsible for that debt," I said.

Julia hated business and was unable to grasp the fragile position we were in having just launched the restaurant entirely on borrowed money.

We talked until our throats hurt but just went around in circles. I needed to clear my head so I took our dog Lena for a long walk. I started to consider what life would be like without Julia and was surprised to find it didn't seem so bad after all. We could sell up and with my share of the money I could start a business of my own or maybe go back to music and work abroad again. But it was all such a mess. Even if Julia agreed to sell the restaurant, who would buy it without trading figures?

That night Julia was at the restaurant while I was sitting alone in our flat. Although I hadn't picked up a guitar in three years I had an irresistible urge to take it out its case and start to tinkle with it. I felt an extraordinary sense of peace while I played nothing in particular with a feeling of floating down a stream. A chord sequence started to develop by itself. Some lyrics came into my head and before I knew it I found I had written the first decent song of my life.

The Gate

The road was long the day was cold
a story that's so often told
a lonely road with no end in sight
no shelter from the night
when there before a gate I stood
that led to nothing but tangled woods
I was wondering what it once had been
when something seemed to call me in

as I walked through the garden
of waste and despair
I was stung by the nettles
chilled by the cold air
I was just about to turn around
when there in the waste ground
was a house as sad as it was old
but still a shelter from the cold

This stately home that had once stood proud
now stood within it's stately shroud
a dark sky laying where the roof had been
such sadness I've never seen
and as I walked from room to room
searching for a way from gloom
I walked into a room so bright
that I was blinded by the light

And there in the corner
over by the far end
a guitar gently weeping
welcome back old friend
we sang and we made rhymes
and talked about old times
sweet music filled the air
such joy was everywhere

As we danced through the garden
of waste and despair
the sun started shining
and pushed aside the cold air
I closed the gate behind me
and continued on my journey
the road reached far into the night
but in the distance there shone a light

All those years I had tried desperately to write a song with lyrics that didn't embarrass me and this came out by itself in twenty minutes. It was so strange.

The next few days were very difficult as Julia changed almost hourly from definitely wanting to leave me to definitely wanting me to stay. I hated the uncertainty and knew something had to be done to stop the situation dragging on forever. One night while Julia was in the middle of a squash match I packed my bags and left the club through the back door so no one would see me. I left a note on our bed.

"*I love you but I can't go on like this. Perhaps it is better if we do separate. I am going away for a while so we can both sort ourselves out. All my love Derek.* "

I drove to London while conflicting emotions played havoc with my brain: the heartache of ending a fourteen year relationship; the relief of getting away from the endless bickering and uncertainty; the excitement of starting a new adventure; the worry of what to do about our businesses; the frustration of working so hard to build up businesses only to lose them to someone else; the joy of being responsible to no one but myself; the sadness of separation.

I checked into a small hotel near Victoria and as I lay on the bed with headlights still flashing in my eyes I knew Julia would have read my note and I wondered what her reaction had been. Was she relieved or upset? I had no idea but she needed to experience life without me.

The next morning I went into the centre of London. It was a glorious spring day and I had an immense feeling of freedom knowing I could do whatever I wanted without asking for anyone's approval. As the day progressed I became more confused than ever. I missed Julia and felt sad when I saw all the places we had been to together like the theatre we saw Jesus Christ Superstar on our first date and the little restaurant next to it where we ate afterwards. There were painful memories everywhere I looked but at the same time I felt exhilarated. I found myself standing outside the Yumi Japanese night club and although the name on the door was different it was still a Japanese club. I felt an overwhelming desire to see Marie again and kept wondering what life would have been like if I had left Julia for her. I had lunch at a tiny Italian restaurant and not once did I have to send food back. Julia said if she only ate 1000 calories a day she wanted those calories to be perfect. It was understandable but frustrating when romantic meals out became an obstacle course of unnecessary calories. I started to notice women smiling at me? Had they always done that and I hadn't noticed? Could I really approach one of those gorgeous women and ask them out? Why did women excite me if I still loved Julia? How is it possible to be so sad and yet so happy at the same time?

It was around 11.00 p.m. when I arrived back at the hotel. I sat in a chair and stared into space as I waited for the right moment to phone Julia. It was so quiet. I visualised her standing behind the squash club bar asking the last customers to leave. I picked up the phone. In a few seconds I would know whether I had to start a whole new life or not. I had enjoyed my day of freedom but sitting in that lonely hotel room I didn't want to lose Julia. I dialled the number. Julia answered immediately.

"Hello," she said.

"Hi, it's me."

"Why did you go off like that? I've been going crazy." There was such desperation in her voice.

"I had no choice. You don't know what you want and I can't go on like that."

"I've made a terrible mistake. You've got to come back. I didn't sleep at all last night. I was even thinking of killing myself."

The threat of suicide might sound melodramatic but it related to a traumatic experience she had during childhood when she saw a woman who had hanged herself and it had always haunted her.

"Are you sure you want me to come back?" I asked.

"I'm certain. I've been so stupid. You have to come back. Everything will be alright."

I was relieved that we were going to stay together but at the same time there was a nagging feeling of disappointment. Was it really possible that now it was me who wanted to separate?

36
Poking Pizzas

Julia threw her arms around me and cried inconsolably. We made up in the time honoured tradition and neither of us doubted that we would spend the rest of our lives together. It was important to put our troubles behind us and concentrate on making a success of the restaurant. Trade had been very slow and the takings were well down.

It was only the next day that I saw the familiar look of doubt on Julia's face.

"Are you having doubts again?" I asked.

"I suppose I am."

"But look how you went to pieces when I left. You even talked about killing yourself."

"That's because you went so suddenly. It was just the shock."

"I have to be honest. I enjoyed my trip to London and even started to think that maybe I also want to separate but we have to be sure we're doing the right thing. Let's go to Marriage Guidance and if you still want to split up I'll go away for a while because there's no way I am staying here if we separate."

Julia phoned a marriage guidance councillor who suggested seeing her alone for the first meeting. The councillor summed up our situation perfectly in one session.

"It sounds to me that you have a father and daughter relationship and now the daughter has grown up and wants to leave home."

It made perfect sense and explained why I also felt the need for freedom. My pain was not of a husband losing his wife but of a father losing his daughter.

Julia still had no idea what she wanted so I went to stay with my brother for a few days to see how she got on by herself. I was only away one night when she insisted I returned. Despite us both accepting that it was best to separate neither of us had the strength to go through with it. It was hard enough separating emotionally but our lives being so tangled up in our businesses made it even more difficult. A mixture of weakness and convenience kept us together and there was no more talk of separating. We had done a good job of keeping our personal problems to ourselves so everyone still thought we were the perfect couple.

With all the turmoil I hadn't been able to update our accounts for several weeks and when I finally got around to it the result came as a terrible shock. The restaurant was losing money and our first stocktake was a disaster. It wasn't just the odd drink or pizza disappearing but whole boxes of supplies. It was hard to believe we had a thief amongst our staff as they all seemed so honest but there was no other explanation. We had to let our managers go and cut down drastically on staff. For the first time since taking over the club we had a problem with cash flow and we still had the quiet summer period in front of us.

As the squash club looked after itself most of the time we did more of the restaurant work ourselves and I even started delivering pizzas. It wasn't until I became more involved that I realised what a difficult business it was. Although everyone loved our pizzas our service ranged from average to terrible. One night I was waiting for the chef to finish a pizza I had to deliver. There must have been 15 customers waiting with me including two elderly couples who had been there for nearly an hour. For the first time I realised nobody in our restaurant knew what they were doing. We used to cover all our pizzas with cheese which was one of the reasons they were so popular but that meant when they were cooked they all looked the same. At one stage we had 10 pizzas on the counter ready to be served but no one knew what pizzas they were so the chef had to poke around under the cheese topping to try and identify them.

While all this was going on there were constant phone calls from people asking what had happened to their pizza delivery and customers waiting not so patiently in the restaurant. Dirty dishes mounted up in the kitchen so even when the pizzas were ready there were no plates to serve them on. It was total chaos and all I wanted was for the ground to swallow me up.

Towards the end of the summer I noticed Julia's mood changing.

"You're thinking about leaving again aren't you?" I asked.

She made no reply so I continued.

"I really think it's time we split up for good." She looked relieved.

"I think you're right."

This time we knew it was for real and both being comfortable with the idea we were able to talk about it rationally.

"So what brought this on again? During the summer you seemed happy enough?" I asked.

"I was but then a couple of weeks ago a man started coming into the restaurant every night for a chat and I suppose we have become attracted to each other."

I should have been eaten up with jealousy but the constant uncertainty over the last few months had worn down my feelings for her.

"You must understand that splitting up means exactly that. There is no way I am going to stay and work with you. One of us has to leave Derby."

There was fear in her face at the prospect of it being her that had to leave.

"If you were to leave what would you do?" I asked.

"I don't know."

"So if you leave you have no idea what to do and I'm sure you don't want to go back to being a secretary but if I leave I have several possibilities. Maybe I could go back to music or open a club of my own. I am happy to go but the trouble is I have tried to leave twice already and both times you dragged me back. I think the best thing is for me to go abroad. We need a clean break and you have to understand that this time I won't be coming back."

"Where will you go?"

"I was thinking of going to the States."

"But how will I run all this by myself? I don't know anything about accounts or the computer?"

"The squash club runs itself most of the time so you can concentrate on the restaurant. I will go away for a few months and return to see how things are going and we can decide then if we need to close the restaurant. But if you want to stay instead of me you'll have to work really hard. If things go well you can get more staff and have some time to yourself but in the beginning it will be very difficult. You won't have much free time or be able to go on foreign holidays for at least a couple of years."

"Don't worry. I know what I'm letting myself in for but it will be worth it. I really think I can make a go of the restaurant," she said.

"You'll have to. It's only the profits from the squash club that keep it going and that can't go on forever. On top of that I am obviously going to need some money to get myself started."

With everything settled we were both relieved the uncertainty was over.

"If only you had told me how you felt before we took on the restaurant I would never have started the project. We could have split everything down the middle so you had the squash club and I had enough money to do whatever I wanted."

I hated the thought of losing everything I had worked so hard for but I couldn't see any alternative. As it stood if we sold everything we would still end up owing money.

Over the next few weeks while I was preparing to leave Julia was elated at the prospect of her freedom but as my departure grew closer she became morose. The last few days she kept throwing her arms around me and crying with heartrending sobs that shook her whole body but then her tears would mix with her laughter as she realised the irony of the situation as it was her that wanted to leave me.

As I walked around the club and locked up for the last time I glanced at the new extension I had built. It seemed to be another of my life's patterns that someone else would always benefit from my hard work. Then the thought occurred to me that it wasn't the squash club and restaurant that I had enjoyed so much as the creation of them. Once they were finished the monotony of running them bored me. I created that extension with the same passion as I created *Francesca Suite* so perhaps I hadn't drifted so far from music after all.

I should have been sad but I wasn't. I would soon be on a plane to America and a new adventure. At 36 I was still young and having made such a success of the squash club I had a good track record in business. I had loved our holiday to the States the previous year and knew it was still a land of opportunity where people didn't have to apologise for their success. I was packed and ready to leave but Julia was in a really bad way. She knew I had to go away and she still wanted us to separate but it didn't stop her sobbing uncontrollably. I tried to comfort her as best I could but I had an overwhelming desire to get away and put it all behind me.

It was a dark and misty September night with the smell of autumn in the air when I got into my hire car. Just me, a suitcase and a guitar driving into the unknown. The stuff dreams are made of. As I pulled away from the car park I looked back to see Julia's silhouette standing behind the full length windows in the same spot as I stood on the night she left me her note.

I drove slowly down the M1 to relish the feeling of freedom. The start of a whole new life. Travel. New people to meet. New love affairs. Where was I going? I had no idea and I was in no rush to decide. I wasn't even sure I would go to the States. Maybe I'd go somewhere in Europe instead, Gstaad or the Mediterranean maybe? What would I do? No idea. Maybe I would go back to music. Maybe I would find a squash club in a holiday resort and coach for a while. Not all life's patterns are negative. I was relying on the pattern that no matter how bad things got for me something always turned up.

37
Bitten by the Apple

It was 5 a.m. when I arrived at Heathrow and looked up at the departure board listing all my possible destinations. I had already made up my mind to go to the States but where in the States? I had a strong urge to go to Los Angeles but reminded myself it wasn't a holiday and that I had to go where there would be the most opportunity. I also had to go somewhere I knew squash was played as it was a great way of making new friends and contacts. The only American city where I was certain they played squash was New York because I had once coached someone who lived there. Where better to start a new life than *The Big Apple.* I bought a single ticket to New York.

I was in the departure lounge when it occurred to me I needed to tell Julia what to say in case my parents rang while I was away as they would know something was wrong if I had gone away without her. I didn't want to tell my family we were splitting up until I was sure it was permanent. It was the last thing I wanted to do but I had to call her.

"Hi it's me. I ...." and before I could say another word she burst out in desperation.

"Derek where are you? I've been trying to contact you."

"I'm at Heathrow."

"I called and asked all the terminals to make an announcement for you to phone me urgently but I couldn't get through."

"What's wrong?" I asked.

"You've got to come back. I'm afraid I'm going to kill myself."

My heart sank. Here we go again.

"What is the point in me coming back? You want this as much as I do."

"I know but I just can't stand it. I feel like I'm going mad. You've got to come back. I've made a terrible mistake." She sounded so desperate.

"I've got no choice now. I'm in the departure lounge and my bag is already on the plane. I'll call you when I get to New York and we'll take it from there."

She agreed reluctantly knowing there was no choice. As the plane took off I could still feel her arms around my neck trying to hold me back. Were we going to spend the rest of our lives breaking up and getting back together again? In the past there was still a part of me that wanted to stay with her but now that part was gone forever.

At the airport in New York I paid a deposit on a hotel room at the tourist desk and took a taxi but after driving around in circles for an hour looking for my hotel the taxi driver dumped me at another hotel where I had no doubt he got commission for introducing mugs like me. I was dreading calling Julia but knew I couldn't relax until I had done so. The phone rang for ages before she answered.

"Hello. South Derbyshire Squash Club."

The bar sounded busy.

"Hi it's me. How are you feeling?"

"I'm fine," she said enthusiastically.

I was taken aback by her extraordinary change of mood since that morning.

"But this morning you were ready to kill yourself?" She laughed.

"Honestly I'm alright now. It was just the shock of you leaving. I know we've done the right thing and I think it's a good idea you start a new life in the States."

"So I don't have to come home?"

"No of course not. You don't have to worry about me any more. I must go now. It's really busy," she said and then hung up.

How could anyone change so dramatically in such a short space of time? That morning she couldn't live without me and now she was talking to me like I was a casual acquaintance. I was relieved at not having to go home but hurt by her indifference. I later discovered the cause of her change of mood was due to her having spent the afternoon with the man she told me about. So that was that. It was all over. I stepped outside the hotel, a single, successful businessman, ready to take New York by storm.

The only thing I was sure of at that stage was that my new life had to include writing so the next morning I went to buy a laptop. I decided on a Toshiba T1000 which had one floppy drive and no hard drive. It would have been a bargain compared to English prices if the salesman hadn't charged me extra for the operating system which I later discovered was already built in. Not being content with that rip off he also talked me into buying extra memory which I later discovered he never installed. Included in the price was a word processing and spreadsheet program but they turned out to be pirated copies. This was at a large respectable looking shop and not some back street dodgy looking place. Computers were always God's gift to the unscrupulous but never more so than in those early days.

As I walked around New York on that sunny day in early September I was taken aback by how rude and impatient everyone was. I saw a woman make a silly but uneventful mistake in her car and heard a policemen scream at her "hey watch what you're doing you asshole." For lunch I tried to order a burger and the waitress was so aggressive I thought she was going to attack me. Everything seemed so tatty and the noise overpowering. My hotel looked alright in the daytime but at night the surrounding streets made me feel like I was in a gangster scene from The Wire. I tried to go out for a pleasant stroll but was pestered so much by men offering me drugs that I had to return to my hotel. The next morning I was determined to give New York a chance but one of the first shops I passed was a travel agent with a big poster of Los Angeles in the front window. I remembered how happy and friendly everyone was there and the next thing I knew I was sitting on a plane waiting to take off.

38
A Bottle of Aspirin

At the car hire desk in Los Angeles airport I was greeted by a woman who looked like she had just stepped out of an episode of Baywatch.

"Good evening sir. Welcome to Los Angeles. How are you tonight? My name is Dawn and I am your Hertz Cars representative. How can I help you today?"

For those who don't speak the lingo that means "hello" in American. I controlled the urge to ask her to marry me and got on with the business of hiring a car. Once the paperwork was done I looked through a copy of the Yellow Pages which was so big I assumed it covered the whole of America but it turned out to be only for Los Angeles. There were thousands of hotels listed and I didn't know where to start but Sunset Boulevard sounded fun and it didn't look too hard to find as I remembered from my holiday that one end of it had an ocean attached. My sense of direction was never very good but even I should be able to find an ocean.

I drove slowly along the coast road listening to relaxing music and enjoying the warm night air through my open car window. Turning into Sunset Boulevard I felt like an actor in a film and half expected to see credits scrolling down the windscreen. Passing through Beverly Hills I had great difficulty deciding which house to buy when I made my fortune.

I was lucky to have chosen a hotel in one of the best areas of Los Angeles, a small stretch of road in West Hollywood known as The Strip, home to a collection of open air restaurants and fashionable boutiques. After checking into my hotel I walked down the road and sat at an outside table at a restaurant called Cravings. I watched in awe as a never ending procession of beautiful people and entertaining characters acted out their roles. The conversation on most tables was about film making and there were several faces I recognised. Everyone was so friendly and there were so many women smiling at me I had to check there was nothing nasty hanging from my nose. One of the waitresses seemed to be giving me special attention and after I paid the bill with my gold card she practically sat on my lap. I knew she was a lot younger than me but I asked her out and was surprised when she accepted. I walked back to my hotel room feeling like a 15 year old who had just been accepted for his first date.

During my flight from New York I had been in a reflective mood and decided there were two things I wanted my new life to include. One was to learn to speak a foreign language fluently and the other to learn Karate so I was amazed to find a karate school right opposite my hotel. I made some enquiries and signed up for an introductory course to start that afternoon. It was a Korean style of Karate called Tang Soo Do and I took to it like a duck to water. My footwork was always pretty good and having spent the last few years trying to hit a tiny ball travelling at hundreds of miles an hour I had no trouble seeing punches and kicks coming towards me so was able to get out of the way at my leisure. Until then I thought I was fit and supple but I had never felt such muscle aches as I did in those first few days of training. It was an excellent purpose built Dojo with three classes a day, six days a week so I was able to train every day. After my first lesson I went to my hotel room to practice and nearly broke my toe when a stray kick connected with the television set.

I was getting ready for my big date when it occurred to me I should go armed with condoms just in case. I hadn't bought any since I was seventeen and you would think that age would reduce the embarrassment of buying the damn things. You would also think that a country so worried about AIDS would make them easy to find. I looked in a big supermarket but couldn't find any and there was no way I was going to ask anyone. Then I went to a small chemist but there were none on display and just as I had summoned the courage to ask the woman behind the counter two beautiful women walked in and smiled at me. I ended up leaving the chemist with the usual bottle of aspirin. I had to forget the condoms otherwise I would be late for my date and there would be no chance of using them anyway. When I saw the gorgeous Lorraine waiting for me in skin tight trousers and long flowing hair I thought I was dreaming. After dinner we were on route to her flat when she sent me into a liquor store to buy some wine. It was right next to the famous night club Whisky a Go Go and as I stood in line wearing a smart casual suit it was me that felt like a freak while the entire cast of The Rocky Horror show bustled around me. When I finally got to the counter there they were .... a whole box full of condoms. Just as I thought I was home and dry I noticed that instead of the conservative brand names I was used to like Durex and Mates they had names like *Stallion's Delight* or *Raging Rod.* Some of them looked so ornate that I wasn't sure whether you were supposed to wear them or have them for dessert. What really worried me was that they were all bright colours so even if they were real condoms I had no idea how Lorraine would react to me approaching her with a fluorescent green chopper. Then there was the certainty that the moment I put my hand into that condom box the Rocky Horror cast would break out into a chorus of "we know what you're doing." I left the store with two bottles of wine, a bottle of aspirin and no condoms.

Lorraine was staying in an apartment owned by the pop star Sting who had lent it to her and her friends. There where gold discs on the walls and pop memorabilia everywhere. We talked for a while and I had the feeling I was being interrogated in some subtle way. We were talking about night clubs when she asked,

"Do you know the Flaming Colossus? That's my favourite club."

"Why don't we go there now?" I asked, trying to impress her with my spontaneity.

"You have to be a member which costs $3000 dollars."

She looked carefully at my reaction.

"What! Are you joking?"

She wasn't joking and I had failed the test. To pass I should have said "that sounds pretty reasonable" without breaking out in a sweat.

It was 14 years since I was last single and I didn't know what was expected of me on a first date so I was relieved when after a couple of drinks Lorraine hinted for me to leave. She saw me to the door where we kissed so passionately I had no doubt she wanted to see me again but when I asked her for another date she told me to call her. I thought it was a brush off but later discovered it was part of the Los Angeles dating game. No matter how much you like someone you never make future arrangements at the end of a date, you have to wait a few days before phoning. I have to say on that occasion it really was a brush off as with just a few questions Lorraine had managed to find out exactly what league I was in and had no hesitation in tossing me back into the sea.

The next day I found a squash club in Santa Monica where I introduced myself and soon had some games booked. Squash was not big in Los Angeles so with the standard being low I was the best player there and soon found myself in demand. I got talking to the receptionist and when I asked her out she accepted enthusiastically. We made arrangements and just before leaving I offered to buy her a drink.

"Thanks but I can't. I'm underage," she said.

I was horrified.

"You mean you are under 18?"

"No I'm 20. You have to be 21 to drink in California."

The extra few years helped to soften the blow but it was confusing as I was seeing her through the same eyes as when I was last single 15 years earlier.

I needed to find a way of making a living and playing music seemed the obvious way to start. The owner of one of the local restaurants agreed to let me play for a week for food only on the understanding that he would employ me if it was a success. The first night was ok but I had forgotten how demoralising it was playing to a restaurant full of people who are ignoring you. A few customers called me over during a break to say how much they enjoyed my music but there were just as many that moved to a table outside to get away from me. By the third night I decided I never wanted to play in another restaurant again as long as I lived.

One day I was surprised to get a phone call from my younger brother David.

"What has happened? We are all worried sick about you," he said.

"Julia and I have spilt up."

"I thought it was something like that."

"Why is everyone so worried?"

"Because mum phoned the squash club and the receptionist told her you had gone to live in America."

I cringed. Why can't people follow the simplest instructions?

Most parents imagine the worst where their children are concerned but mine turned it into an art form. My father, who thought an optimist was someone who discriminated against opticians, always insisted that if he died while I was abroad he didn't want me to return to England for the funeral. It would serve no purpose and the last thing he wanted was to spoil my holiday or jeopardise a good job. With that in mind my father was convinced I was dead and had left instructions not to tell them because it would spoil their impending holiday to Italy. He was so convinced I was dead that he stood beside the garden pond I built them and cried his eyes out.

I settled into a routine of karate, squash and people watching from a pavement table at Cravings at night when I didn't have a date. Life was wonderful. I knew Julia would be working hard but I had spent the last few years stuck in my office or doing building work while she was enjoying herself with the customers so I felt justified.

There was so much to do and it was so easy to meet people. I became good friends with a man named Rob North who started karate training at the same time as me. We were both keen and although he was better than me he had trouble remembering the katas so we often went to his house after training where I helped him. He was a money broker from a rich banking family with an amazing house built in the Hollywood Hills and a spectacular view of Los Angeles. The long wooden balcony had a built in Jacuzzi where we sat with a couple of beers after training most nights. There was no doubt in my mind that Los Angeles was the greatest place on Earth and I was going to be a part of it.

I moved out of my hotel into a little apartment within walking distance to The Strip. Like most apartment buildings it had a swimming pool where I sat every day writing a diary on my lovely new laptop. I enjoyed writing and was determined to write a book but every time I started I found the loneliness too oppressive so I went back onto the streets where everything was so exciting.

One morning while taking my regular breakfast at a local croissant café I started talking to a beautiful Rumanian woman. We were instantly attracted to each other and arranged to have dinner that night. Her name was Gabriella and she had lived in Los Angeles for the previous five years being divorced for the last three of them. She was nothing like the usual bimbos I had been dating since my arrival and it was obvious from the beginning that something was happening between us. On the Sunday we drove in Gabriella's open topped jeep along the Pacific Coast Highway and around the winding coast road that leads to Santa Barbara where we spent a magical day falling in love. That night we went to Universal Studios to see George Benson who for me was the best guitarist I ever heard and it is a travesty he never got the recognition he deserved. His band, the lights, the sound, everything was perfect except for one thing, the physical pain I felt in the knowledge that it would never be me up there on stage playing to such a large ecstatic audience.

As we walked back to the car the air was warm and the moon was full. I turned on the car radio and just like magic the opening bars to my favourite love song *Endless Love* started playing. There was only one way to end a day like that so without speaking we drove to my apartment and made love for the first time. I was in love again and couldn't have been happier.

One night Gabriella and I went to dinner with Rob North and his girlfriend to a restaurant that he was interested in buying. He knew I was looking for a business so he asked if I would be interested in going into partnership with him. I went along with the idea without telling him I would rather cut off my testicles with a blunt knife than have anything more to do with restaurants. His girlfriend, Nina was extremely attractive. She was from Hungary and had moved to Los Angeles ten years earlier. She had obtained a green card by paying an American citizen $1000 to marry her although I never understood why as there couldn’t have been a single man in America that wouldn't have married her for free. Having just celebrated their nine months anniversary of going out together it was the longest relationship Rob had ever had. The next day while relaxing in his Jacuzzi he told me how Nina had played the dating game with mastery and resisted his advances until the day he phoned her from Mexico. He asked her to go to his travel agent and book herself a flight to Mexico where she could stay with him in his luxury villa. She accepted and they had been together ever since.

After one blissful week with Gabriella the unthinkable happened: we split up. We had spent all Saturday together during which time she never stopped analysing our relationship until the evening when she suddenly got angry about something although neither of us was sure exactly what it was. I stormed out of her apartment wondering what on earth had just happened. She called me the following night.

"I'm sorry. I don't know what came over me. Can I come around to see you now?"

She came round and we made up passionately but things were never the same. I was yet to discover that Gabriella suffered from a common American ailment known as *Chronic Analysis.* If I was quiet for a few seconds it meant I was thinking about Julia. When I asked her if she wanted to go out for a drink it meant I was tired of her company and needed to be around other people. If I put my left shoe on before my right it meant I might be a closet axe murderer. In her eyes everything I said or did had a significant other meaning and it got to the point where I was afraid to say or do anything.

Despite bursting the Gabriella bubble, life was great and I looked forward to waking up every morning. Every weekend we went somewhere like Disneyland or Universal Studios and even spent a weekend in Mexico. The only cloud on the horizon was I needed to find a way of making a living. I had been hoping that with my track record I would be able to raise finance for a business of my own but the high commercial property values made it prohibitive. I also hoped I could get a job managing a sports or squash club but I hadn't realised how difficult it was to get a green card.

My interest in music was gradually returning and I practised guitar every day. I put an advert in the local equivalent of the Melody Maker and had very little response although one band did phone and seemed quite interested until I told them I was 36. They responded in disbelief that anyone so ancient could still manage to hold a guitar let alone play one.

Julia phoned me a few times telling me her life had been up and down since I left. She had been out with a few men but they messed her around badly so she was beginning to realise that being single wasn't what she thought it would be. As far as our businesses were concerned everything seemed to be running smoothly.

The weeks went by and I became more and more attached to my new life. My favourite place was Venice Beach, especially on a Sunday when it was full of colourful characters. There was Skateboard Mama, the sixty five old German grandmother who had left her family in Germany just to cruise along Venice Beach on a skateboard every day; Harry Perry the roller skating turbaned guitarist skating from restaurant to restaurant playing guitar so badly that people paid him to go away and the comedians standing on soapboxes many of whom were much better than the famous comedians I had backed in London.

One day in late October I had a long telephone conversation with Julia who told me that she was finding things difficult so I agreed to go back for a while just until we decided what to do with our businesses. Fortunately my brother was working for British Airways so I was able to get cheap flights. It was hard leaving my new home but I had a return ticket in my pocket and told myself it wouldn't be for long.

39
Nail Trauma

I touched down at Heathrow Airport on November 5th and as I drove up the M1 to Derby with Guy Fawkes fireworks exploding everywhere I pretended to myself they were in honour of my homecoming. It was very cold and smoke from thousands of bonfires created a mist that added to a general feeling of eeriness. I was surprised to find myself looking forward to getting back to the club and seeing my old friends again. Julia and I had agreed that I would sleep at the restaurant so I made my way there and arrived at the end of what had apparently been a busy night. I was expecting to see Julia there but all I found was the pizza chef and a waitress both of whom were very young.

"Where is Julia?" I asked.

"She's gone dancing with Sarah," said the waitress.

Sarah was the girl we had employed to manage the squash club so it looked like both businesses were without anyone responsible in charge.

"How often does she go out and leave you like this?"

"Most nights."

I had something to eat and as there were only four customers left in the restaurant I let the staff go home. I looked at the till roll to see how much we had taken that night and was shocked to see that nothing had been rung up for the previous hour despite the fact I had seen at least six people pay their bills and leave. The more I looked into it the more obvious it became that people were stealing from us on a regular basis and even the taxi drivers who delivered the pizzas were in on it. The next morning I saw Julia and told her what had been going on. It didn't take long to work out it was the chef that had been ripping us off and when we showed him the conclusive evidence he admitted everything. We sacked him on the spot.

That night when sitting with friends at our squash club bar I hadn't realised how much I had missed the English sense of humour and our ability to laugh at ourselves. If someone said something stupid we'd all have a good laugh and forget about it. In Los Angeles to laugh at someone's mistake was a capital offence. *Self love* was everything. I knew one woman whose therapist told her to put stickers all over her apartment telling herself how wonderful she was. On the mirror was a sticker saying, "You are a kind and generous person." On the oven door was a note reminded her that "Everyone loves you." I was afraid to go to the toilet for fear of a note being shoved up my arse saying "Your shit smells of roses."

Another big surprise came when I looked across the bar at Julia and instead of seeing a woman I had spent 14 years of my life with I saw a stranger. I felt no jealousy when I saw her with other men and realised I must have fallen out of love with her many years earlier without knowing. We were both very affectionate people and had mistaken our affection for love.

Julia and I got on well together but I realised we had a major problem. Although she loved the restaurant and squash club she didn't like being tied down by them. What was the point of going through the pain of breaking up if she couldn't enjoy the freedom that went with it? She knew the businesses were in trouble but couldn't grasp the fact that there was no longer a father figure around to make everything better. I either had to stay and be solely responsible for the businesses or leave knowing that everything would probably collapse. I also wanted my freedom and was quite prepared to abandon the businesses and walk away with nothing if that's what it took.

The next day I sat in my office and went through the accounts which were far worse than I had expected. The restaurant was losing a lot of money which was exacerbated by the high level of theft. Squash was decreasing in popularity at an alarming rate in clubs all over the country. The members we once relied on to make up the teams and play regularly were getting older and drifting away with no one to take their places. For many years squash courts had been booked solid for seven days in advance but it was now possible to turn up without a booking and play. If I hadn't built the health club section we would have already gone bankrupt and although the club was still making a healthy profit it was not enough to subsidise the loss from the restaurant. We both agreed that the restaurant had to be sold. We had two valuations, one of £90,000 which meant we would break even and the other at £50,000 which would leave us with a debt far greater than we could service let alone pay back. Things were looking bad but at least it was winter so there was a good income from the club.

Over the next few months with the aid of David's cheap flight tickets I went backwards and forwards to Los Angeles where I stayed with Gabriella. It became harder and harder to leave a warm Los Angeles and return to an iced up windscreen and businesses full of problems. My relationship with Gabriella was good but volatile as she was two completely different women. There was the carefree, strong, independent Romanian woman that I loved to be with and the analytical Los Angeles woman who was looking for a man with enough money to take care of her. Gabriella had assumed that anyone with a gold card and a business must be wealthy. I told her from the start what my situation was but she must have thought I was playing the Los Angeles *double bluff* where the player says they are doing badly to discourage others from leeching on them when in fact they are rich.

Gabriella was concerned about her own financial affairs so I offered to run her details through my computer. The result sent her into shock. She had been divorced for three years and had been given a modest settlement that she had used to subsidise her lifestyle but having spent more than she earned her savings had disappeared.

"What does that mean?" she asked.

"It means you'll either have to get a second job or spend a lot less."

"I can't do a second job. I work hard enough as it is."

"In that case you'll have to spend less."

"How can I spend less? Everything listed there are basic essentials."

"There are plenty of things you can cut down on. Take only one holiday a year. Spend less on clothes. Wax your own legs. Do your own nails instead of getting them done in a shop."

"What. Are you crazy!" she cried.

There was sheer horror in her face. To most people nails are the bits at the end of our fingers and toes that God gave us to scratch ourselves with. In Los Angeles, nails are a religion. Every row of shops has a nail parlour where crowds of devoted followers gather every day to worship. There are even *Nail Clubs* where I assume people sit around in a circle and talk about their recent nail traumas. The day I made the unthinkable suggestion that Gabriella should manicure her own fingernails was the day it finally sunk home to her that I had no intention of supporting her even if I could.

"How dare you suggest I live within my means. You're my man and it's up to you to provide these essentials for me."

Those were not the actual words this *independent* woman used but she spent many hours trying to imply them.

Back in England the restaurant was going from bad to worse despite the fact that Julia was working very hard to save it. It is a terrible thing to be running a business that is losing money. You have the choice of selling at a fraction of what it is worth or continue to lose money hoping things will improve but run the risk of going bankrupt in which case it will be worth nothing anyway. Out of desperation we accepted an offer of £50,000 meaning I had broken my back developing a restaurant that was sold for £70,000 less than we paid for it.

Our debts grew bigger by the day while our creditors grew more impatient. The bank insisted we sold our house and although we made £24,000 profit on it due to it being at the top of a housing boom it hardly made a dent in our debt. It broke my heart to think that instead of all the hard work I had put into the restaurant I could have just bought a few houses and rented them out making a fortune for doing practically nothing.

I was sick of my life in England and knew I had to set a date to leave for good. It was time for another long talk with Julia.

"I know you're not interested in the business side of the club but you have to understand it looks like it will go bankrupt," I said.

"Can't we sell it? Then we would both have enough money to start up somewhere else."

"If we were lucky enough to find a buyer for the club all the proceeds from the sale would go into paying off our debts and we would still owe thousands."

She still seemed unconvinced so I continued:

"The simple fact is the squash club won't survive. I don't want anything more to do with it so as far as I am concerned we can close it down tomorrow."

"But what would I do? I can't go back to secretarial work."

"I suggest you stay and keep it going as long as possible putting money aside so when you do get closed down you'll have some stake money to do something else. I will take £2000 to get me started which you can think of as a final settlement but after that I will be on my own."

"So how will you live once you're money has gone?"

"From my personal credit cards at first and then hopefully I'll find a job or some kind of business opportunity. I spoke to Don Howell the other day and he is very interested in opening a squash club in Los Angeles. But make no mistake; it will be tough for both of us."

"It looks pretty grim doesn't it?" she said.

"Yes it does but that's the worst case scenario. As long as you're careful you may be able to keep going for ages. Even when you do get closed down maybe Don will keep you on as manageress."

"I suppose that wouldn't be so bad."

"One important thing to remember is that if you can't pay the rent and he takes the property back he has to compensate us for the improvements we made which amounts to a lot of money."

"Let's hope it won't come to that," she said.

"So that's settled then. You'll stay here and try to keep things going and I'll leave for good?"

"Yes it seems the best idea. I'm happy with that."

When we had returned from South Africa 12 years earlier we bought a German Shepherd we called Lena. In all the years we had her she never once wondered off by herself until three days before I was due to leave Derby for good. I looked everywhere for her and eventually found her sitting by the edge of the river with her paws dangling in the water. I was confused as I had never heard that dogs know when they are going to die so they go off to a quiet place to do it. With great difficulty I struggled with her up the side of the steep river bank and took her to a vet where I left her for the night. A few hours later the vet phoned to say Lena was much better but to leave her there overnight. I had another call a few hours later to say she had died. I always felt bad about taking her away from that idyllic spot on the edge of the river to have her die in the clinical surroundings of a vet although I knew I couldn't have just left her there. It seemed strange enough that she knew exactly when she was going to die but downright spooky that after being with us for so long she should die only three days before Julia and I were going to spilt up for good.

In May 1989 I left the club for the last time. I hugged Julia and drove away feeling a tremendous sense of relief that it was finally all over. I knew it was going to be difficult to make a life in Los Angeles with so little cash and having to live from my credit cards but something would turn up. I would do whatever it took to make a go of it and if that meant working behind a bar to get started then I would be quite happy with that. It was shit or bust and I couldn't return to England until I was a success.

40
Don't Drink the Water

Gabriella picked me up from the airport and we enjoyed a pleasant day together discussing our plans. The next day we had a massive argument and I stormed out for the last time. I never saw her again but I did hear that she had to sell her apartment so it seems that when it came to a choice between her home and her fingernails it was no contest.

Rented accommodation was cheap and plentiful in West Hollywood so I managed to find a nice little apartment within hours. The building manager was an ex-serviceman who had volunteered to serve in Vietnam in order to get away from his wife. I don't know if she was the cause of him changing boats in midstream but John had given up women and was now living happily with a man from Texas and their two poodles. I bought a mattress and a second hand table and chairs so although it wasn't the bachelor pad that dreams are made of it was mine and I was happy. Most important was that it was within walking distance to the karate studio and my favourite cafés. It also had a swimming pool on the roof where I sat each morning to write. As I enjoyed writing so much I thought I'd try a short story and was surprised how effortlessly it came to me. It was called *Lena's Gift* and was about the strange way our dog had died. I showed the story to a few friends who enjoyed it so I submitted it to some magazines. To my great surprise I had phone calls from two of them who said they liked it but it was too long for them to publish although they would be happy to read anything else I wrote. That's when I had the idea that would solve all my problems. It was so obvious I was angry at myself for not having thought of it before. I would be a screenwriter. I feel embarrassed telling you about it now but in my defence it is well known that in Los Angeles they put something in the water that makes everyone think they can write movies.

The next day I took a long pensive walk along Venice Beach and by the time I got home that evening I had a screenplay in my head mapped out from beginning to happy end. It was about a karate teacher who accidentally cripples an up and coming classical guitar recitalist. It had everything: love, martial arts and music. How could I fail?

I set myself a strict routine of writing six hours a day with the occasional break for a swim in the pool or a chat with some of the other friendly pool dwellers. Most nights I spent at Cravings with just a coffee or their cheapest meal. It was a luxury I couldn't afford but I needed to be around people and with any luck I might meet someone there. It was easy to start conversations with strangers as they seemed to love that I was English which of course came naturally to me. Some claimed distant English ancestry as if they wanted to prove themselves to be part of my world when there was I desperately trying to be part of theirs.

I finished the first draft of my screenplay in only two weeks. A week later it was ready to be submitted when I bumped into Nina at Cravings. I knew she had broken up with Rob a month earlier.

"What are you doing now?" I asked.

"Nothing at the moment. My florist shop wasn't doing very well so I closed it down. I heard you're writing a screenplay?"

"Yes that's right."

"Why don't you let me read it? If it's any good I have some contacts in the movie industry I can give it to. If they are interested I could represent you so it could work out well for both of us."

She was such a beautiful woman and we seemed to get on so well. I was desperate to know whether she might be interested in me but she was still getting over her break up with Rob so I kept my feelings to myself. She talked openly about their break up and I had to feel sorry for her. After going out with Rob for a year she had gambled everything by giving him an ultimatum: either they get married or they split up. He went for the second option. She had apparently been engaged to Sylvester Stallone a few years earlier and the same thing happened there. How hard it must have been to be so close to a life of luxury only to have it taken away from her at the last minute. She was now jobless and living in an apartment not much better than mine. I was chatting to Rob one day after karate training when he told me:

"I did love Nina and wouldn't have minded getting married but if we ever divorced I would lose half of everything I own," he said.

I gave Nina my screenplay and we met up a few days later to discuss the verdict.

"I loved it. I have a good friend who reads screenplays for Orion. I'll give it to her and see if she can get us a deal."

With my screenplay in circulation my daydreaming went into overdrive and I started wondering what famous actors could appear in my movie. Maybe I could play the starring role? My English teacher said my rendition of Shylock was so good he refused to believe there was no Jewish blood in me though admittedly whatever part I played I always sounded like a Jewish moneylender. I visualised myself getting out of a big limousine at the Oscars and sitting patiently to find out if the prize for best actor was mine. My daydreaming came to an abrupt halt when the following week Nina called.

"I gave your screenplay to my friend and I'm afraid she didn't like it. She thought it was a bit amateurish."

"Does that mean you're not going to try anyone else? You said you really enjoyed it."

"Yes I loved it but she is an experienced reader so she must know what she's talking about. She said the plot is good and you're definitely on the right track but she suggested you go to screenwriting school and learn properly."

"I'd love to but I don't have the time or the money. If I can't find a way of making a living soon I'll have to go back to England."

I threw in the bit about returning to England in the hope of provoking a reaction from her but there was none. My hopes of a screenwriting career and a relationship with Nina were lost forever.

"Let me know if you write anything else, I'd love to read it," she said.

I was not going to be put off by just one rejection so I looked for other companies to send it to. When I started screenwriting I knew how difficult it would be to get a screenplay accepted but what surprised me was how difficult it was to even get it read. Most companies didn't accept unsolicited scripts and those that did charged a lot of money to read them. For example one company charged $200 dollars to read a screenplay and $500 for a critique. Even if I could have afforded it there was no way of knowing whether the company ever made films from unknown writers or whether they even bothered to read them. I sent a synopsis to 20 film companies and agents who didn't request a payment for reading screenplays and had two replies asking for the full script. On receiving the script the first company said there had been a misunderstanding and that I needed to send them $500 if I wanted it read and the second company rejected it with a standard letter. Out of desperation I paid one of the cheaper film companies to read it and ended up with a $150 rejection letter .... and I thought the music business was tough!

So that was the end of my career as screenwriter. A few months later I read my screenplay again and could see for myself how badly it was written although I still believed it was a good plot. Even if it had been the best script in the world the chances of me getting it accepted were next to nothing. Unless you are incredibly lucky the only way to break into the film industry is to spend your life hanging around in bars and restaurants and pestering everyone in the hope of finding someone who can help you. Several times I was enjoying a quiet drink by myself when a complete stranger sat at my table and introduced themselves to me. The first time it happened I thought how nice that a stranger should be so friendly but then I discovered what he was doing was *working the tables* which is the movie industry equivalent of spamming. It involves going from table to table handing out business cards and chatting to people to see who can be of any use. If only one worthwhile contact comes from the hundreds of people pestered it makes it worthwhile. I was surprised to learn that even if my screenplay had been accepted I would still have been very low in the Hollywood pecking order. I would have received a modest fee and then other writers would have ripped my screenplay apart with me having no choice as to what changes were made. It was also quite common to have a film accepted and paid for but never made.

I continued to go to karate training every day and was improving quickly but had a setback when one of the wilder students broke my finger. I went to the hospital to have it checked out and after an X-ray the doctor came out to the crowded waiting room to give me the news:

"You have a small fracture" he said and proceeded to put a split on my finger. It seemed strange to be treated in a crowded waiting room with everyone knowing my business. I suppose I was lucky I hadn't gone there with prostate trouble.

"Is there going to be any permanent damage?" I asked.

He smiled and replied casually:

"Don't worry it will be fine. You might never play the piano again though."

"But I'm a guitarist."

Unlike me, the people in the waiting room seemed to think this was very amusing.

"I'm sorry. It's a standard joke we make when someone hurts a hand. It will take a while but I can assure you it will heal perfectly."

For the next few weeks I was really worried about my finger as I could hardly move it but it did gradually heal.

The weeks passed quickly while my friends and dates reduced at the same rate as my bank balance and I started to feel very lonely. I still found it easy to meet women but could no longer afford to ask them to dinner. Much as I enjoyed writing it made the loneliness even harder to bear so I could only write in short spells. The one luxury I gave myself was to sit at Cravings restaurant and watch the never ending stream of characters passing by or listen to people talking about the movies. It was easy to see why the film industry was so exciting and why so many lives had been ruined in an effort to become part of it. The frustration of Hollywood is that you can reach out and touch your dream but try and hold onto it and it bursts like a bubble.

Sometimes after Cravings I took a walk down the road to Nicky Blair's bar where for the price of an expensive drink you could sit and watch the Hollywood game being acted out in front of you and even play a bit part at times. There was the Greek woman who sent me a drink and proposed marriage to me ten minutes later. She almost dragged me into a limousine and demanded I went to a night club with her. I might have been tempted even though she bore an uncanny resemblance to one of the goats in Zorba the Greek but I took one look at her evil looking bodyguards and made a run for it. There was also Eleanor who claimed she was once a famous Opera singer whose career was cut short by a road accident. It sounded like bullshit to me but she did seem to know a lot of celebrities. I had wondered if I could go out with someone just for their money and it was Eleanor who provided me with the answer. She took me to an exclusive night club and flashed a gold card that enabled us to walk straight past the dozens of people hoping to get in. She wasn't unattractive but I had absolutely no interest in her romantically. A waiter showed us to a table and when she took my hand and cuddled up close I could feel my skin crawl and the idea of sleeping with her was inconceivable.

A lot of the men I talked to in Nicky Blair's were also very entertaining. There was a very smartly dressed man who spent the whole night introducing himself to strangers.

"Hi, I'm Flip Wilson's son," he repeated like a wind up teddy bear.

He was devastated to learn that I didn't have a clue who Flip Wilson was but instead of leaving it at that he spent the next hour telling me everything his dad had ever done.

"But what about you? What do you do?" I asked.

He looked at me as if to say "Are you crazy? Don't you think being Flip Wilson's son is enough for any man?" and then walked off.

Best of all was the Italian ex boxer who was well known in his time. He was like a dog on heat. Being by himself he needed a partner to add credence to his caveman style of picking up women so he drafted me in. Every woman that walked past us he grabbed hold of and tried to chat up. Apart from the fact that even Wilma Flintstone would have thought twice before going out with him there was also the problem that all the years of being bashed around the head had left him nearly deaf so on the odd occasion when women didn't run away screaming he couldn't hear what they said anyway. Eventually he gave up and shouted:

"Fuck this. I'm going to find a whore."

He paid the bill and left me sitting at the table.

My money was running out and I needed to find work urgently. I would have been happy working behind a bar and there were plenty of jobs around but I needed a green card which I could only get if I married an American citizen which I could have done as my divorce had already come through. Apart from the crazy Greek woman I did have two other offers of marriage from women who wanted a British passport but it was something I was not prepared to consider.

As advertising had always been so successful for me I put an advert in the newspaper offering my services as a personal assistant. I could be a chauffeur, I was good at organising; I could type; I could play guitar and entertain; I was computer literate and most of all I was English; a good thing to be when you're not in England. A woman with a very sexy French accent answered my advert.

"My name iz Rene. I don't ave a job for you but you sound so interesting I wondered if we could meet sometime for a drink?" she said.

"What do you do?" I asked. This was a standard opening L.A. question that I am ashamed to say I adopted.

"I am a chef to a rich man in Beverly Hills."

I had never been on a blind date before and was hesitant but anyone with a voice like that had to be gorgeous and as my social life consisted mainly of watching other people's social lives I thought I'd go for it. We arranged to meet that night at Cravings.

After going to Cravings nearly every day for months I was well known to the waitresses mainly because I had asked most of them out with an awesome lack of success. On the other hand I had taken some very attractive women there so I hoped I wasn't seen as a total loser. It wasn't until I was seated at a table waiting for Rene that I realised it was a mistake to meet her at a place where people knew me as she could have been a 30 stone Sumo wrestler for all I knew. Fortunately it was a busy night so I was able to hide myself away at the back of the restaurant. Every time a lone woman walked in my heart started racing. After several false alarms I noticed people were looking at what I can only describe as a Martian walking up and down the pavement as if it was looking for someone. On closer look I realised it was a tall thin woman with long blond hair and a psychedelic bandanna tied around her forehead. Although she was only in her early thirties her skin was wrinkled enough to belong to a seventy year old. She wore silk baggy psychedelic trousers and a silk blouse made up of hundreds of different brightly coloured patches sewn together. As if all this wasn't conspicuous enough she also wore a huge pair of headphones with two long aerials sticking vertically from each side which was either to receive radio signals or further orders from planet Zorko. It never occurred to me that such a strange creature could be the owner of the sexy French accent so I didn't start worrying until she smiled at me and walked in my direction. I wanted to make a run for it or start speaking in pretend German but my conscience got the better of me.

"Are you Derek?" she said in a voice loud enough to be heard back home on Zorko.

"Yes, please take a seat. I assume you are Rene? Did you find the place alright?"

How could I talk so casually in the middle of such a crisis? I cursed myself for not having made a run for it when I could.
"I am sorry to be late. Is just zat I walk here and iz furzer zan I sought."

"Didn't you say you are living in Beverly Hills?"

"Zat iz right."

"But that is miles away?"

"Iz not so far."

It was just my luck that Jean came to serve us, the only waitress I still had a chance with. She did her best to keep her smirking under control but I could see it wasn't easy.

"Would you like something to eat?" I asked.

"No zank you. I don't eat."

It was a strange answer but I was too relieved to think anything more about it.

"Something to drink then?" I was on a roll.

"I don't drink ezer."

"A coffee or tea then?"

"No zanks. Can I just av a glass of water please."

Jean was loving every minute of it.

"And I'll have a coffee please."

"OK then. That's one coffee and one glass of water," said Jenny loudly.

I was not known for being a big spender but that was ridiculous.

"So you are a chef but you don't eat or drink?" I asked.

Just then I was distracted by Jenny pouring my coffee at the bar and laughing hysterically with the other waitresses.

"I take only zoup and water but I av eaten today zank you."

She talked so slowly I wondered how she managed to remember what came at the end of a sentence considering it was so long after the start of it. After 20 minutes of excruciating boredom I told her I had to go and meet some friends. We said goodbye and I watched as she started walking down Sunset Boulevard towards Beverley Hills with her headphones back on her head. I wasn't sure whether her arms were moving to the music or making signals to the mothership.

It was an unnerving experience but I can't deny that the anticipation of a blind date gave me quite a buzz. It always struck me how ridiculous it is the way we go about looking for love. The most important thing in our lives is who we choose to share it with and yet how do we look for a partner? We just walk around and hope they suddenly appear in front of us. We would never look for a house or car in that way. Even if we do bump into our perfect partner the chances are they will already be in a relationship. Meeting people through dating agencies is a far more sensible way of finding love and while it might not be romantic, neither is loneliness.

I started answering personal ads but with no luck so I placed an advert of my own. I met a few of the women who replied but the meetings ranged from unsuccessful to disastrous. One woman sent me a photograph that showed a very pretty face and unlike some of the women I met she brought the same face with her for our meeting. She had very frizzy shoulder length hair that covered her whole head and face like a blond Brillo Pad. All I could see from the neck up was her nose sticking out through her hair so I spent an hour talking to that nose. Now and again she brushed her hair away to reveal a very pretty face but most of the time I had to make do with the nose.

After giving up on personal ads I thought video dating looked interesting so I called an agency to see if I could afford it.

"I'm afraid we don't give prices over the phone," they told me.

"Why not?"

"Because we have a selection of different offers and we need to talk to you to decide which is the best for you."

"But I want to know what it costs before I come all the way down there."

"I can assure you sir that our service is extremely successful and I am sure we will have no trouble finding you the perfect partner. If you'll just come to see us we can explain everything in detail."

We both repeated ourselves several times until she got the message that I wasn't moving until I knew the cost.

"Our fees range from a basic introductory package which is $500 to our Gold Card service which is $10,000."

"So what do you get for $500?"

"For $500 you get five introductions."

"And what happens if I don't find someone I like in those first five introductions?"

"That is most unlikely sir. We take a lot of trouble making sure the people we match up are compatible."

"OK then what do I get for $10,000?"

"For $10,000 you a get a lifetime membership with unlimited introductions."

"But you've just told me I will find a perfect partner in my first five introductions. Why would I need a lifetime membership?"

From there her sales pitch went rapidly downhill as she obviously wasn't allowed to explain the real purpose of gold card membership which was to separate the financial classes. The reality was that some people spent their life savings to buy gold card membership only to meet others who had done the same. Despite all my efforts, my experience of meeting people through personal ads and dating agencies was a disaster so I went back to the absurd method of hoping I bumped into someone.

By August things were looking very bad. I was almost out of money and bankrupt of ideas for making a living. The loneliness was getting to me so I spent my time going from café to cinema to anywhere else I could be near people rather than go back to my empty apartment. I still met women but the most I could do was ask them for a coffee.

When I first arrived in Los Angeles I still had money and all I could see was a glamorous city full of happy, friendly faces. Now all I could see were people as desperate as me in a city that was vicious in its punishment of weakness and rejection of failure. I met one woman who had been a successful personal agent for six well known actors. Her father died so she had to go and look after her mother for six months. She left her business with a good friend and when she returned her *friend* had taken all her clients. She went from a highly paid glamorous job to nothing.

My circle of friends had reduced to zero and the most disappointing desertion was that of Rob North. We used to get on so well together but the moment he realised I had no money our friendship came to an end. He still called now and again but only to see if my position had changed. But of all the let downs I had at that time the worst was my attempt to find my old friend from Gstaad, Jenny Thaxton. I remembered she came from Bel Air in Los Angeles and that her father was the well known celebrity Lloyd Thaxton. I found his agent's number and asked if he would forward a letter to Jenny through Lloyd Thaxton and he agreed. I was really excited at the thought of seeing her again and sure she would feel the same. A week later I still hadn't heard anything so I phoned the agent who told me:

"I passed on your letter to Lloyd so if you don't hear anything I'm afraid there's nothing more I can do."

I never did hear from Jenny. Did she get the letter? Was she rich and successful and didn't want to be pestered by someone from her past? Was she happily married and her father hadn't passed on the letter for fear of opening a can of worms? I would never know.

By the end of August my credit cards were starting to be declined and I knew I had to return to England but convinced myself it was only a temporary setback and I would return as soon as I had some money. The hardest thing was for me to leave the karate school. In the year since I started I had trained six days a week without fail and I knew I would never find such a good school in England. Taking up karate was one of the best things I ever did and it helped me get through the difficult times to come. Life is often like a street fight with fate jumping out at us from a dark corner and attacking us viciously for no reason. My instructor pounded it into us that if we were attacked there was no point making excuses, we had to put our heads down and overpower whatever it was that threatened us. Whether it is a vicious thug, an illness or a personal tragedy, we all have the means of defending ourselves but just need to train ourselves on how to use them.

I stood utterly dejected in the airport terminal thinking of all the times I had arrived there full of hope. I told myself that failure is just the seed of success but it didn't make me feel any better. Unlike the other times I had returned to England there was no more squash club to go back to so I had to start a whole new life. I always believed that everything happens for a reason but as the plane climbed and the houses slowly disappeared it was difficult to understand what was the purpose of my time spent in Los Angeles. From the day I first turned professional I had had my ups and downs but everything seemed to happen for the best. How could the collapse of everything I had worked for since leaving school be for the best?

41
Ear Fingering

It was quite a culture shock going from Los Angeles to my parents' house in Worthing but as always they were supportive and without a hint of reproach for chasing my reckless dreams. Security like that must be one of the greatest gifts that parents can give their children and one of the easiest for children to take for granted. From my bedroom window I used to watch my mother sitting by the pond staring at the fish and the occasional sparrow that was brave enough to wash in the bird bath that the thrushes ruled over. It occurred to me that despite all the wealth and beauty I had seen during my time in Los Angeles I had not once seen anyone as happy or contented as my mother was by that pond.

One small consolation was that it was a glorious Indian summer so I spent many evenings strolling along Brighton Promenade where there are some spectacular sunsets in the autumn. Although it was a difficult time for me something was happening with my songwriting that filled me with hope and it was during those walks that inspiration came effortlessly. I thought of Marie from the club Yumi and in no time had an entire song complete with lyrics that just needed to be written down.

MARIE (Where are you now)

Many years have now passed by
from the time of which I speak
when the world was such a happy place
and the strong seemed not so weak
she came into my life one day
when all around was dark
we danced around the heavens
and strolled the summer park

When we made love it seemed as if
the sea for us would part
and angels cried with happiness
as they soothed our aching heart
if love comes but once a lifetime
this was surely mine

we'd have been together forever
if fate had not been so unkind

She haunts my days, haunts my nights
the time we spent just seemed so right
I see her face in every star
the memory of her burns so bright
I know the time has passed into eternity
if I could see her one more time
Marie, where are you now

I held her hand, touched her heart
and begged her not to speak
and felt the pain of wasted love
as tears rolled down her cheek
the moment that we parted
will haunt me all my life
but our love was cursed forever
for I already had a wife

And now that time has left me
so lonely and afraid
I have no choice but to walk along
the path my loyalty laid
for Le Grande Amour that I had found
that was from deception born
was blessed by God but scorned by man
and lay on a bed of thorns

The long lost love I had for music reappeared stronger than ever. For the first time I was writing songs that I really believed in so the next step was to record them. Luckily I had kept two guitars and a four track tape recorder so I didn't need much to set up a small studio of my own. I went to a music store in Brighton and was surprised to see that during the six years I had been away from the music business there had been a revolution in electronic equipment. For very little money I bought a keyboard that was not only able to simulate almost any musical instrument but it could also be programmed to build up an entire orchestra. I could now make limitless high quality demos for nothing and without the need for session musicians.

I produced three good demos and sent them out to 10 record companies and publishers. New equipment, new songs and new demos but the same old rejection letters. After feeling sorry for myself for a few days I began for the first time to consider the situation from the record company's point of view. They can't be expected to go through the expense of making a record unless they have a good chance of selling it and even the best song in the world won't sell unless it is promoted. If a company has to go through the expense of promoting a record then why take a gamble on someone unknown when there are hundreds of well known artists also needing promotion? If someone has played in a famous band, acted in a TV soap or even has very big tits then promoters have something to work with but if they are unknown why would anyone buy their records? It was possible to make a person famous by playing their record on the radio but radio stations wouldn't play records unless they were in the shops and you couldn't get them into the shops if they were not being played on the radio. Unless you were lucky or incredibly talented the only chance an unknown artist had to get a record deal was to play live and build up a following. I needed to concentrate on live gigs.

One day I went to Derby to pick up some personal effects and was glad to see that Julia was holding the club together. The debts were as bad as ever but as I predicted the creditors preferred to get something every week rather than close her down and get nothing. I left Derby a little envious of the fact that she still had the club and I had nothing but just because my life in Los Angeles hadn't worked out I had no right to go back on our agreement.

My songwriting went from strength to strength although it was a mystery where my inspiration was coming from. For example I was getting ready to go out one night when I suddenly stopped and picked up my guitar without any conscious decision to do so. The first two lines of a song appeared from nowhere:

Sing for your child, show that you care
there maybe no tomorrow

The next day I went back to the song and twenty minutes later *Sing for Your Child* was born. What on earth possessed me to write about children? I had no children of my own or any experience of them. I had no desire to have children and there was no reason why the subject should have entered my head. The more I wrote the more I felt that someone was dictating to me. I saw creativity as a lake that we all have inside us. Some people never even know it's there, some dip their toes into it and some drink from it. I had fallen in and felt at times that I was drowning.

Another thing that surprised me was that instead of my guitar playing suffering after all those years of neglect I was playing better than ever before. It was a time of great fulfilment and hope for the future but the present was filled with loneliness and uncertainly. Credit card companies were chasing me for money I didn't have and there was a county court judgement against me courtesy of American Express.

I was never so happy as when I was playing with just an acoustic guitar so a friend suggested I should try getting onto the folk circuit where there was a modest living to be made and some artists like Suzanne Vega and Billy Bragg had been discovered there. As I had never been to a folk club I wanted to see one in action so I started with a small club held every Saturday in a tiny room above The Lewes Arms public house. Ten of us sat on chairs in a circle. Everyone seemed to know each other and was chatting quietly when without warning an elderly man started singing *It's a Long Way to Tipperary* without any musical accompaniment. I thought it was some kind of joke at first but soon realised he was serious and the evening's entertainment had begun.

When he finished he introduced a woman sitting opposite holding a teddy bear and she also started to sing unaccompanied. Her voice was not good and the song collapsed three times when she forgot the words. I had stumbled into what was known in the folk club scene as a *singaround* where everyone takes turns to sing a song or recite poetry. Most of the people in the circle sang something and although the standard was very low everyone enjoyed themselves. Then came the Guest Artist. This varies from a local member who accepts donations to an established artist who charges a fee. On this occasion the guest artist was a middle aged female singer accompanied by her boyfriend on guitar. They were a reasonable act though I found it off putting that she spent most of the time singing with her finger in her ear, a strange habit adopted by some folk singers. When a band is playing loudly a singer may put his finger in his ear to help him to pitch the occasional note when he can't hear himself sing but I never understood the need to do this in a quiet folk club although there were times I could understand the audience doing it.

I declined the invitation to sing myself and left the club at the end of the night feeling depressed. If that was an example of what folk clubs were like they were not going to be much use to me although I have to say I found the people very warm and friendly. Fortunately a few days later I went with a friend to The Willows folk club at Arundel and that was everything I hoped it would be. It was run once a week by an amusing and efficient elderly couple. After hearing my demo tape they gave me a booking but the next slot wasn't for another seven months so any hopes of being an overnight success went straight out the window. I started putting a program together and wrote some flashy ragtime guitar solos to give my act variety. I put my best songs and instrumentals onto a sixty minute cassette that I could sell at gigs and sent copies to the main folk magazines that reviewed cassettes by unknown artists.

If all the clubs were like The Willows I would have been happy but I soon discovered that most were just social gatherings where people got together for a good old singsong. In clubs that booked guest artists there seemed to be a conflict between the main artist who people paid to see and singers from the audience some of whom people would have paid extra not to see. On one occasion I went to see the well known folk singer Judy Collins but was disappointed when she was only able to perform for 15 minutes due to the number of floor singers who insisted on singing.

I contacted all the main folk clubs in the country but then came up against a major hurdle. Most clubs wouldn't book unknown acts unless they went along and appeared as floor singers a few times which is like taking part in an amateur talent competition. If you appear with amateurs you will appear amateur and the irony is the very quality that makes a good artist stand out in concert is the very thing that makes them appear pretentious as a floor singer.

It was disheartening but I refused to give up on the folk club scene although I knew it would be a long time before I would be able to make a living from it. I had no choice but to do the one thing I had been dreading since leaving Derby. I had to put together a program of cover versions to try and find work in pubs and clubs. I was finally writing songs I was proud of and now I had to stop writing them to relearn the same old songs I had been playing for years and which bored me to tears.

42
A Recipe for Shoestrings

I approached several agents in the area and was given my first gig which was at the Lancing British Legion, a typical social club where people drink cheap beer and listen to different acts singing the same songs over and over again. Despite all my experience it was the first time I'd ever worked alone and I was surprised how hard it was despite having a good little drum machine to help fill out the sound. I played all the wrong songs with no confidence and when I tried to talk to the audience I succeeded only in mumbling to my shoes. I thought I went down really badly so I was so surprised to be asked back there the following month. I learnt a lot more songs that were suitable for that kind of venue so on my return visit I felt much more confident and had a much better night.

Shortly after Christmas I drove to Derby to collect the last of my belongings. I was surprised to find that Julia had gone on her third foreign holiday in six months and left Jim, one of the club's least trustworthy members in charge. He was playing squash when I arrived and as there was no one on duty behind the bar customers were serving themselves. After his game Jim joined me for a drink and gave me all the latest news.

"Julia went on a last minute package holiday with her boyfriend and left me in charge. It wouldn't have been so bad but we had a booking for 100 people on New Year's Eve and I was the only person on duty."

It was obvious from what Jim told me that Julia had given up on the club which was understandable but if she didn't want it any more I was annoyed that she hadn't given me the option of taking over.

"Can you give me the keys to the flat. I want to get my things," I said.

He looked up at me sheepishly.

"Julia said I had to be with you if you go into the flat."

I was so angry. In all the years Julia and I had been together she had never known me cheat anyone. Legally I was entitled to empty the till and the safe and take anything I wanted from the club but wouldn't have dreamt of doing so whatever the situation. Jim saw how angry I was and handed me the key. I went into the flat and took everything that belonged to me and things that were jointly owned I left so there would be no argument. Up until that day Julia and I had remained good friends but as far as I was concerned that was the end.

A few months later I heard that Julia went to live with her new boyfriend and employed a manager for the squash club. What with the extra wage for the manager and her not being around to keep an eye on things the club quickly collapsed and after not paying the rent or talking to Don about it he was forced to take the club back. She was given two hours to collect her personal belongings and vacate the premises. A few months later she split up with her boyfriend so she had no club, no job, no home and no boyfriend. If she had given me the option of taking over from her I would have jumped at the chance. I knew I could have worked something out with Don and at least made a living while I pursued my songwriting career.

In February 1990 some friends of mine went to work in Oman and asked me to house sit for them. Although I got on well with my parents and they enjoyed having me there it was with great joy I moved into my new home in Arundel and with a few gigs in my diary I felt things were finally going my way. The tiny little detached cottage was the perfect environment for a writer. It was set back from the main road and tucked into a peaceful corner so it was easy to look out the large window into the garden and imagine that I was in the middle of nowhere. The peace and solitude of that cottage bore a never ending supply of new songs and my whole existence seemed to be in tune with music and the creative process. As for my quality of life it was abysmal. I had very little work which hadn't been so bad while I was living with my parents but now I had bills to pay. I set myself a budget of £1 a day for food and while some cooks may be able to do wonders with that I was most definitely not one of them. Not only were my meals done on a shoestring budget but they actually tasted like shoestrings. When the loneliness got too much for me I went to the local pub just to be around people but I soon felt the need to return to my writing as every minute I wasn't working was an extra minute before my life was back on track.

I had a good little folk act put together and was keen to play the clubs regardless of how low the fee was but I was finding it impossible to get bookings. My only hope was to get good reviews for my cassettes in the folk magazines. It took months before they were published but when they were the reviews were as follows:

Frankly, Derek's acoustic work is the best thing I've heard since I lived with David Qualey in Germany and he's got a platinum album. Derek has great skill and imagination. It's obvious he could be very big in the folk scene if that's the direction he wants to take. - FOLK ON

A magnificent collection of songs combined with some extraordinary guitar playing. - FOLK ON TAP

With such good reviews I was sure it would be easy to get bookings so I sent out a fresh batch of cassettes with copies of the reviews to every club in the country but didn't get a single reply. I tried phoning the clubs to ask what they thought of my music but was told that it didn't matter how good the reviews or cassettes were, they wouldn't give me a booking unless I first appeared as a floor singer even if it meant travelling 200 miles to do it. I was beginning to give up hope when one night I went to one of the best folk clubs in the country, The Railway Club in Portsmouth. It was a special evening with Rik Sanders from Fairport Convention as the guest artist. The organiser had agreed to let me play three songs during Rik's break and it was exactly the kind of venue I was hoping to play at. It had a proper lighting and sound system and at least 200 people in the audience as opposed to the usual 20 or 30 in most busy folk clubs. When I stepped up to the microphone I was bursting with excitement and confidence as I played the intro to *A Chair by the Window.* The stage, the sound, the lighting, everything was perfect. Being blinded by the spotlights I was unable to see how the audience were reacting but as I gently strummed the finishing chord the audience erupted and continued clapping for at least a minute. I was so overcome with emotion that I was hardly able to announce the next song. I finished my short set and left the stage to a thunderous round of applause. The organiser took the microphone and said the words that reverberated in my head for days afterwards.

"I thought he was brilliant. Don't worry we'll be booking him for a gig later."

At the end of the evening, four other clubs asked for my phone number and said they would contact me soon about a booking.

I hardly slept that night I was so excited at the thought of word getting around about my floor spot. I was sure to get bookings from it and hopefully it would snowball. It was weeks before The Railway Club organiser finally gave me a booking and that was for six month ahead so by the time I played it everyone had forgotten me and I never did get calls from the other four clubs. With great regret I had to give up on the folk music scene. It was a shame because it had the possibility of being the perfect platform for unknown songwriters playing acoustic music.

That winter seemed to go on forever and my little cottage was permanently cold. I sent out demo tapes of my new songs to dozens of different companies and although the feedback was far more encouraging than in the past there was still no sign of a record deal. One day when I was at my lowest ebb I had a call from a woman who was directing a street play for the Brighton Festival.

"We need a guitarist to play some background music during our performance and someone has recommended you. I am afraid it is an amateur production so we can't afford to pay you anything."

"I'm sorry but I do this for a living. I don't work for nothing,"

"How much do you charge?"

"It depends on the situation but usually about £85 a gig."

She was disappointed but I told her there must be plenty of keen amateurs who would love to be a part of her production. The next day she phoned again to say she had been unable to find anyone and would I reconsider. She was so persistent I took her number and told her I'd think about it just to get rid of her although I had no intention of calling her back. The next morning I sat down to my usual breakfast of coffee and burnt toast when I noticed the woman's phone number. It occurred to me that if I agreed to play for £10 expenses I would come out with a profit of £5 after paying for petrol. It was a pathetic fee and by coincidence was exactly what I got paid for my first ever gig 20 years earlier but it still meant five days food for me. I phoned the woman back with my proposal which she gratefully accepted but the minute I put the phone down I regretted it. I even considered not turning up but she sounded so relieved I would have felt terrible letting her down. The reason I mention this boring episode is to emphasise that it was nothing more than sheer desperation that led me to the best thing that ever happened to me in my life.

43
Welcome to Croatia

I went along to the first rehearsal held at The Friends Centre in Brighton and as I walked round in circles trying to find the side entrance I was angry with myself for accepting such a low paid gig. Inside there were a few people standing around and while I was introducing myself I noticed a beautiful woman sitting in the corner giving me a lovely warm smile. We couldn't take our eyes off each other. Her name was Federika Glavich. The story of the Glavich family of Croatia is fascinating and requires a book of its own but to sum up, it was a very wealthy family who had everything taken away from them when the communists seized power in Yugoslavia in 1945. With life being so hard under the communists Federika's family emigrated to Peru when she was one year old. She loved her life in Peru but was keen to travel and so at 18 went to England to study at the Chelsea College of Art where she was regarded by everyone as being an exceptionally gifted student. She won several prizes and her future looked very bright. Whilst still at college she fell in love with a fellow student, they got married and a year later had a daughter, Siobhan. They moved to Brighton and despite being heavily pregnant Federika commuted to London to finish her degree. After their second child Danny was born their marriage deteriorated although they stayed together for five years before separating for good.

After the rehearsal Federika and I went for a coffee and got to know each other. From there our relationship developed quickly but it was very volatile as we had both been the dominant partner in our marriages. Every time we argued I felt an overwhelming urge to walk away but something always made me stay.

In June my friends returned from the Middle East and wanted their house back. It was a relief not having to worry about the bills any more but going back to my parents was a giant step backwards. My financial situation was so bad I forced myself to stop writing songs and phone every agent in the country until I found work. I always hated phoning agents as so many of them treat entertainers like pests rather than their means of making a living. Fortunately I was only on my third call when I was offered a job.

"Would you be interested in a holiday centre near Great Yarmouth? One of their bars has a solo keyboard player and they need someone like you to liven things up. You can start straight away if you want."

I had no idea what a holiday centre was but it sounded fun and as the money wasn't bad I accepted the job. It was only when he gave me the address that he mentioned the dreaded word...... *Pontins.*

"Pontins? Is this a holiday camp?" I asked.

"Yes but don't worry. These holiday companies have invested millions to improve their facilities and get away from the old Hi-Di-Hi image."

When I first turned professional I would have loved to have done a holiday camp season but I seemed to bypass that rung of the ladder. The musicians I worked with later in my career always made fun of holiday camp gigs and regarded them as only slightly more prestigious than street busking. Of course I had no choice but to accept the job and it was a great relief to know I would have a regular wage coming in but it was with a heavy heart I said goodbye to Federika and made my way to Hemsby near Great Yarmouth.

44
The Epidemic

I arrived at Pontins in the middle of a cold, wet day in mid June. Mike, the depressingly young entertainments manager showed me around the camp and we sat down to talk in the bar where I would be performing. Despite being the middle of the day the room was dark and gloomy with the smell of dampness, stale smoke and beer. At one end of the bar was a big screen TV showing tennis from Wimbledon and in the middle sat two solitary old ladies fast asleep. There was rubbish everywhere and a general feeling of decay that oozed from every corner. I just couldn't understand why anyone would want to spend their holidays there but who knows; maybe those two old ladies thought they were having the time of their lives.

"Until now we've had Dennis on keyboards by himself. He's very good but he doesn't sing so the customers have been complaining there's no atmosphere in this bar. We need you to get things going," said Mike.

I only half listened to him as my mind was on how I could best make my escape.

"I have to be honest; this isn't what I was expecting. My agent told me that Pontins had spent a fortune doing up their camps?"

"That's right. They spent over a £1000 painting the ballroom this year."

I thought he was being sarcastic but no, he genuinely believed £1000 was a lot of money for a multi million pound organisation to spend on renovation. We walked in the rain across the putting green and after showing me to my chalet we arranged to meet later when he would introduce me to Dennis. My chalet was the same kind as those given to the holidaymakers and about the size of a large beach hut with a small bathroom. There was a bed which took up the entire length of one wall and it was only inches away from the front door so campers who used to leave their doors open could be seen laying half naked on their beds.

As soon as I was left alone I took a walk around the camp just to make sure it wasn't a bad dream. I phoned the agent to complain about his misrepresentation and begged him to find me work elsewhere but he was obviously relieved to have found someone to do the job that no one else wanted. As I walked back to my chalet the drizzle turned to heavy rain and I was drenched in no time. I decided that no matter how badly I needed the money I had to escape but I needed a bath to warm myself up first. By the time I was dressed and feeling human again it was time to meet Mike. I still wanted to escape but it would have meant walking past him to get to my car so I had no choice but to meet him as arranged.

Mike was waiting with Dennis who was obviously relieved that I had arrived to take some of the pressure from him. A couple of friendly Bluecoats joined us and they also seemed pleased to see me. We started chatting and had a few beers and suddenly things didn't seem so bad after all. Maybe I would stay and do one night just to see how it went. That night, the inmates (referred to as campers by the management) gave me a good reception and to my amazement I found myself settling in and even enjoying the gig.

I got on well with Dennis though he was hard work at times. He was a Welshman whose only interest in life was reading about UFOs. The problem I had with him was that he spent the whole day eating raw garlic which when mingled with his cheap aftershave meant there was a ten metre no go area where even the camp cats refused to enter. Working with him was difficult as he had only ever worked as a solo organist so I would sometimes be in the middle of a song when his mind wandered and he would start playing something else. It wasn't until the last week that he mentioned in passing that he was almost deaf in one ear.

"But why didn't you tell me before? I've been standing by your deaf ear. We could have easily changed sides," I said.

"Oh yeah, I never thought of that," he replied and returned to his UFO magazine.

The campers in my bar were great fun and very appreciative. It was the first time I had so much contact with an audience and as I grew accustomed to talking and joking with them my confidence grew. I did feel embarrassed at the way campers were treated although it didn’t seem to bother them. Wherever I worked in the past staff (except for musicians) were never allowed to mix or go into areas set aside for customers. I assumed that due to low pay the staff at Pontins were able to do whatever they wanted. There were times when the swimming pool and sun loungers were entirely taken over by staff and campers seemed to be almost apologetic about using the facilities they had paid for. There was a large staff accommodation block at the bottom of the camp where every night came the sounds of parties and drunkenness. This was a small camp that catered for older people so it was as if Saga Holidays and Club 18 to 30 had merged.

At one point management became concerned when the entire dining room staff were hit by an epidemic of love bites. It started one day when a waitress came in with a couple of bites on her neck and went to great lengths to display them to everyone she passed. The next day another girl had some and soon all the staff were competing against each other to see who had the most. It got so bad that the manager insisted all love bites had to be covered by sticking plasters but as plasters in food areas had to be bright blue they were more conspicuous than what they were supposed to cover. No one wanted to admit to being without a love life so even staff without love bites wore plasters and before long there was an ocean of blue plasters floating around the dining hall with the only skin visible being that which was covered by tattoos. One girl had an entire strip of plaster covering her throat from ear to ear so it looked liked she was wearing a blue surgical collar.

The food was terrible and on one occasion Dennis was served with a shepherds pie which was so runny he ran to the toilet to be sick. I have to say I quite enjoyed it as the good thing about being such a bad cook is you can eat any old shit.

In July Federika went to stay with her parents in Dubrovnik for the school summer holidays as she did every year. She wrote to me regularly and one line in particular stuck in my head. "The Chetnicks have armed themselves and it looks like there's going to be a war."

I had to laugh. In my reply I wrote:

"A war in Europe? Don't be silly."

I set up a small recording studio in my chalet and spent all day recording before working all night in the bar. With all the songs I had written in Arundel I had enough material to fill five cassettes which I intended to sell at gigs. By the end of the season I had paid off all my debts and even had a little saved so my time at Pontins had been invaluable although it was an experience I did not intend to repeat.

I returned to my parents' house and the task of promoting my songs. Before going any further I decided I needed a stage name that was more snappy than Derek Newark. I had a lot of trouble coming up with anything and so mentioned it to my father. I wasn't expecting much help as he was not the most creative of men but he took me by surprise as parents often do.

"How about Nemo? That was your grandfather's nickname," he said.

It sounded good to me. My grandfather died long before I was born and I knew very little about him so I asked for more information and how he got the nickname.

Grandfather Nemo was a well known and much loved character in Lambeth. Although he lived a happy and carefree life he spent most of it avoiding work of any kind so my father was brought up in a slum. Nemo was one of eight children from wealthy parents who owned a bookbinder's shop in South London. When Nemo's father died he inherited the shop and was apparently a very good bookbinder himself. He was not the most romantic of men and the reason he gave for marrying my grandmother was because she was very good at ironing collars. He did just enough work to fuel his addiction to cigarettes and whist drives so his bookbinding business gradually went down the pan and he spent the rest of his days waiting for small legacies. He never paid a penny in property tax so occasionally he was sent to prison which he regarded as a health farm as he had to abstain from cigarettes and had much better food than at home. At whist drives he preferred to remain anonymous so always signed his name as Nemo which is Latin for "no one."

I really liked the name and so decided to adopt it but I was still stuck for a surname when from out of nowhere the name *James* came into my head.

"How about Nemo James?" I asked.

"That sounds good."

"It's official then. My new name is Nemo James."

"How spooky" said my father after a few minutes silence, "your grandfather had a brother called James and he was a poet."

That was the first I ever heard of James as my father had no interest in family history and never talked about his uncles. It was a few months later that someone pointed out to me that Nemo was *omen* spelt backwards.

That winter I moved in with Federika and for the first time experienced the pleasure of Christmas with children and despite having no money Federika was always able to make Christmas very special. On Christmas Eve Federika's father phoned from what was now the Independent Republic of Croatia.

"They are playing Christmas carols on the radio," he said with great emotion.

To you and I that might not be the most earth shattering news but under communist rule Christmas was forbidden so that was the first year it could be openly celebrated.

Gigs were still few and far between and I was starting to get into debt again so I decided to jump on the bandwagon and put together backing tracks for me to play along with; a kind of glorified karaoke. My parents had a small loft which I converted into a studio and I sat there every day during the freezing winter months making up backing tracks wearing fingerless gloves and a woolly hat. After two months I had enough tracks to get through a gig so I put together a promotional tape and sent it to several agents. A few days later I had a call from an agent called Eva Clarence who turned out to be the best agent I ever knew.

"I sent your publicity to the Hilton hotel in Dubai and they have just confirmed a three months contract for you starting next week. It pays £320 a week with free food and accommodation and obviously your fare paid."

Oh what joy. I only had a week to prepare myself which included making flight cases for all my equipment so when the day came for my departure I was shattered. I hated leaving Federika for so long but she was very understanding and accepted I had no choice. As the complimentary drinks took effect a tremendous sense of relief swept over me and an excitement for the new adventure to come. Things were definitely looking up.

45
Me and Humphrey Bogart

I hate cold weather, so stepping from the plane into the hot Middle Eastern sun was exactly what I needed after three months of working in a freezing cold loft. There was a car waiting for me at the airport that took me to a nice little studio apartment in an accommodation block used for managers and entertainers of the Hilton Hotel.

It was March 1991, just after the Gulf War so I was still a little apprehensive about the situation which was why I was alarmed on my first night when I was awoken at 5 a.m. by a lot of commotion in the distance. In my sleepy state it sounded like someone was issuing orders through a PA system and for a moment I was afraid we were being invaded. It turned out to be morning prayers delivered through the million watt PA system of a distant Mosque.

The next night I started working at the Humphrey's Bar which was named after the actor Humphrey Bogart. I was contracted to play five hours a night, six nights a week with only ten minutes break each hour. It was a shock to my system having to play such long hours but I was just happy to be earning a good salary and working in such a pleasant environment. All the managers and staff were very friendly and for once there were no problems. It took a while to get used to my new stage name and half the time I didn't realise when people were calling me. I knew I'd done the right thing in changing my name as apart from being more snappy, Nemo was easy to pronounce and remember for people of all nationalities. On occasions when I really got the audience going they would chant, NEMO! NEMO! NEMO! It wouldn't have had quite the same effect if they had been chanting DEREK! DEREK! DEREK!

Apart from the long hours it was an excellent gig with full use of all the amenities including the Hilton Beach Club. I loved Dubai and used to spend most of my nights off walking around the souks taking in the exciting atmosphere. There was Indian and Arabic music playing everywhere and having a stomach like an ox I was able to eat anything the street vendors had to offer. I enjoyed the boat ride across the creek so much I would go back and forth several times just for the fun of it. The shops were full of designer clothes that were fake but of excellent quality and bootleg music cassettes were so cheap that all the stores offered 11 albums for the price of 10. The hotel manager was very pleased with me and I was assured there would be as much work in the Middle East as I wanted.

Because of the Gulf War Dubai was full of American servicemen. When a big aircraft carrier like the Nimitz or The Abraham Lincoln was in port my bar was packed with the best audiences I ever had. They loved everything I played and it was the first time for many years I was able to play rock music. I had a display of my five original cassettes and there were times when servicemen were queuing up to buy them. As the ships came back to port frequently people who had bought my tapes and listened to them at sea were coming in just to hear me play them live. In particular they took to heart my song *A Chair by the Window* and insisted I played it two or three times a night.

The hotel extended my three month contract and although I missed Federika I was in no position to turn work down. Fortunately she managed to find someone to look after her children so she was able to come out for a short visit. It was during that stay that we were walking past the hotel gift shop when we noticed the newspaper headlines:

"YUGOSLAV ARMY SHELLS DUBROVNIK."

It was unbelievable. One of the most wonderful and unique cities in the world was being bombarded by plane and sea while its defenceless civilians were under siege. Federika phoned her parents who had returned from Peru a few years earlier ironically because they felt it was becoming too dangerous due to high levels of crime. There was no answer at their house so she tried their house on the nearby island of Šipan and was relieved to find they were safe and sound having left Mlini before it was invaded. All the properties along the coast leading to Dubrovnik were broken into by the invading army and everything of any value was stolen. Mlini was lucky not to suffer too much destruction but in the adjoining villages of Srebeno and Kupari nearly everything was destroyed.

By September I was more than ready to go home but I was offered a four months contract in Bahrain. Accepting it meant I could return to England with enough money to record and release my own CD so I agreed to do it. I was missing Federika a lot and was worried she might get fed up waiting for me but as always she was very understanding and assured me she would wait as long as it took.

There were two bars in my hotel in Bahrain. One was Country and Western and being the most popular bar in Bahrain was always packed. I was playing in the other bar which was always empty and the reason for employing me was to see if I could improve trade. It was a stupid idea because the two bars were only yards apart so it meant they were competing with each other. People came to the hotel and stood at the entrance to both bars. One was bustling with life and the other was empty so even people who didn't like Country and Western chose that bar because of the atmosphere. On Christmas Eve I played to three people before returning to my lonely hotel room. I told the hotel manager I wanted to leave before the end of my contract and he agreed as my performances hadn’t made any difference to the turnover.

46
War on Television

It was two years since I left Los Angeles with my tail between my legs but I still felt my music would have a much better chance in the States. In England there was only one music chart that mattered and nearly all record company interest was directed towards that. In the States there were charts and radio programs for most styles of music so it was possible to be successful without ever being in the mainstream charts. If I went back to Los Angeles with some good demos I felt sure I could get a record deal. I bought some new recording equipment and made demos of *The Workhouse Child, Rosemary and Time* and *Stargazer* which had been a big success with the American servicemen. The result was far better than anything I had previously produced so with great excitement I set out for a week to the city of my dreams.

It was the end of January when I arrived in Los Angeles on what felt like a lovely summer's day. I hired a car and made my way to the Park Sunset Hotel where I had stayed during those first few magical weeks after separating from Julia for the first time. The first thing I did was pay a visit to my old karate school. In England I had eventually managed to find an excellent school doing Tang Soo Do and was now only two grades away from black belt.

I made up ten promotional packages and sat by the phone to make some appointments. I had read a book on how to get a record deal and it said the most important thing was to make appointments rather than send tapes and it went into great detail on how to get those appointments. I phoned the first record company on my list and managed to get through to the A&R department.

"Hi. My name is Nemo James. I'm a singer songwriter and I've come out from England to look for a deal. I wonder if you could spare me a few minutes of your time to listen to some of my songs?"

"I'm afraid we're very busy at the moment but we'd love to hear them. If you put them in the post I promise we'll listen to them as soon as possible."

"But I've come all the way from England and I'll only be here a few days. I would really like to meet with you. I am sure you'll be interested in my music."

"Sorry Nemo but it's impossible at the moment. Drop them off and I'll try and listen to them during the week." He hung up abruptly.

I had the same response from every company I phoned. I had travelled 6000 miles to take Los Angeles by storm but couldn't even get an appointment let alone a record deal. I sat on the edge of the bed wanting to scream with frustration. The next day I delivered my demos to several companies with a note saying I would be at the Park Sunset Hotel for another six days. I knew it was highly unlikely anyone would listen to my demos while I was there so I could just as well have sent them from England and saved myself a journey.

The days passed slowly and I found that Los Angeles had lost all of its magic for me. Unlike the last time I was there I wasn't interested in meeting anyone as I was very much in love with Federika so I just watched the silly dating game being played all around me and shuddered to think I was once a part of it. After four days I hadn't heard anything and knew I wasn't going to so I returned to England earlier than planned.

The only good thing that came from my trip to Los Angeles was that I found an excellent book called *How to Make it in the New Music Business* by James Riordan. It said that the music business had changed in recent years and record companies were no longer prepared to take chances on promoting unknown artists or bands. The only solution was to produce my own CD and do all the promotion myself. If the CD started to sell then there was a chance that record companies would approach me and if they didn't I would at least have a proper CD to sell on gigs.

It broke my heart having to spend all my savings on yet more equipment but it meant I could then make as many professional quality CDs as I wanted. The Dubai Hilton had asked me back in April so as least I knew there would be some money coming in soon. I recorded more demos and with the better recording equipment and my increased ability in programming the quality was better than ever. I sent them to a few record companies but this time didn't care when they were rejected as I was going to release my own CD anyway.

The day before I was due to leave for Dubai I had a phone call.

"This is John Dye from Blenheim Music Publishing. You sent me some demos a few weeks ago?" I had forgotten all about it.

"Yes that's right."

"I'm very impressed with them. Can you send me some more?"

With all the false alarms I'd had in the past it was difficult to get excited so I sent him a cassette full of my songs and thought nothing more about it.

In Dubai there were far fewer servicemen than the year before so my bar was very quiet and time dragged slowly. It is bad enough playing the same old songs every night to a large appreciative audience but playing them to a handful of people who don't even realise you are there is soul destroying.

Discos had long since waged war on live musicians but now other enemies had joined in the fight. Drummers had already been replaced by drum machines in many studio sessions and now they were being used by live bands. Backing tapes reduced bands from five or six members to one or two and keyboards had become so sophisticated that mediocre keyboard players could program difficult solos so all that was needed was to push a button and pretend to be playing it themselves. Some entertainers couldn't play at all so mimed in front of a keyboard all night long. Karaoke was replacing bands at many venues and as if all that wasn't enough now there was a new enemy on the block......televisions.

Six weeks before the end of my contract two large televisions were installed in my bar. Before starting work each night I asked for them to be turned off but some customers insisted they were left on. It wasn't that they didn't like my music or that they were actually watching the television, it was just that they liked to have it on in the background. I can only assume it is some kind of adult equivalent of a baby's dummy. One night there was nearly a fight between some customers who wanted them left on and those who had come to see me and wanted them turned off. I refused to play unless the televisions were switched off which resulted in me not playing at all for two nights while I sat in the bar for five hours. We came to a compromise with televisions being left on but with the sound turned off which meant I had to entertain people while their eyes were continually drawn to the television. Imagine making a speech with a large television above you showing a football match. Even people who hate football will find themselves distracted and look at the screen at regular intervals. After that I hated going to work and couldn't wait to return to England but what was I going to do there? It all seemed hopeless when after 23 years of rejection I finally received the letter that I had always dreamed of.

47
The Cliff Hanger

Dear Nemo

Thank you for the demos you sent me which I liked very much and I think this is your best way forward. Firstly I do think that the compositions you sent me are very good material, the arrangements and production are simple and very effective and would perhaps be overdone if altered.

The lyrics in my opinion are brilliant but in order to appreciate the quality of the songs they must be heard a few times, hence your big problem, you need as much air-play as possible. If your songs were to be distributed on a C.D. with full promotion then I think good coverage of airplay would follow, to this end I would be prepared to finance the whole operation as long as you supply the finished master and allow Blen-heim Music to publish the songs on the C.D.

I've enclosed copies of the publishing contract and a very simple record contract, I hope we can do some business soon, if not I'm sure you'll have success in the future, your songs are the best I've heard in ten years of listening to demos and I wish you every bit of luck with the majors. John Dye. Rosie Records.

I was stunned. Was this really it? Was I really being offered a record deal? I went straight to the phone and called him.

"Hi John. I've just received your letter."

"Hi Nemo. I loved your songs. Are you interested in my proposition?"

"Yes of course. I finish this contract at the end of June so we can meet then to discuss it."

"Excellent. I played your tape to a few of my colleagues and they were so impressed that they also want to get involved."

On my returned to England I met John Dye in a pub near Marble Arch to discuss the contract. He was an antiques dealer who had started a publishing company ten years earlier but without much success. He did have a near miss when he got one of his artists played on BBC Radio 2 as record of the week but was unable to capitalise on it due to a problem getting the records into the shops on time, a mistake he was not going to repeat.

"I have never had anyone I really believed in before but I like your songs so much I'm prepared to put everything I've got behind you," he said.

John wasn't quite what I had hoped for as a record company executive but we got on well and he was full of confidence which I found encouraging. He did seem to have some good contacts and as he was the only person in 23 years that was prepared to invest in me I was hardly in a position to pick and choose. We agreed on the basic terms of the contract and then went to see his colleague who had heard my demos and was keen to meet me. We were shown into an office and I was introduced to Tony Peters, the head of A&R for the major music publisher Acuff-Rose.

"Hi Nemo. I expect John has told you I love *The Workhouse Child* and feel sure I can do something with it if you are prepared to sign over the publishing rights to us."

Although I had agreed to give the publishing rights to John he was happy to sign some of them over to Acuff-Rose who were in a much better position to launch a song and that would help promote the album. Everything was agreed so the next step was for me to record the album. Over the next few weeks I worked harder than ever to make sure I had the best recording possible. I had to produce, engineer, program, sing and play all the instruments in my parents' tiny badly ventilated loft in the middle of a hot summer. I took the finished recordings to John and Tony Peters and they were happy with them so my job was done and I just had to wait for the CDs to be pressed. A few days later I had a call from an excited John:

"Get down to the Acuff-Rose now. Tony Peters has been speaking to Cliff Richard's manager and there's a good chance he will release *The Workhouse Child* as his Christmas song this year. You have to sign over the publishing rights before he goes any further."

The Dickensian theme of *The Workhouse Child* together with Cliff's Christian beliefs made it the perfect Christmas song for him.

We all met at the Acuff-Rose office where a press photo was taken of Tony and I signing the contract. Everything was happening so fast it was difficult to take it all in. An agonising week later I got a call from John.

"Sorry but Cliff has turned down *The Workhouse Child.* He thinks it's too risky to sing a serious song at Christmas so he's going to release another love song."

"That's a blow. Tony sounded so sure."

"It's not all bad news. He has had such good feedback for *The Workhouse Child* from BBC producers he says there will be no trouble getting it playlisted."

I took it with a pinch of salt but the next day John called again.

"Get down to Acuff-Rose by lunchtime. Five of the top BBC radio producers have agreed to play *The Workhouse Child* so not only will it be playlisted but they think it will be record of the week on Radio 2."

I was speechless. Was I really on the brink of fame?

"The only thing is in order to get radio plays we have to release a CD single with three tracks from the album and Tony wants the publishing rights to those tracks."

"Is that alright with you?"

"Yeah, no problem. I still own the recording rights so I will get money from sales of the single and I'll still own the rights to the other songs on the album. With a big company like Acuff-Rose behind us we can't fail. Tony Peters is one of the most respected men in the music business."

I rushed up to London to sign another publishing deal with Acuff-Rose and spent the rest of the afternoon strolling around with a knot in my stomach. This was really it! At last it was going to happen for me. My music was going to be played on national radio and heard by millions of people. I would be able to walk into shops and see *my* CD sitting in the rack. I would be listening to the radio and suddenly *my* song would start playing.

The next night I was driving past the Brighton Conference Centre and noticed a long queue of people waiting to get into a Chris Rea concert. It was inconceivable to think that one day people would queue up to see me perform my own songs. For 24 years I had been a glorified juke box playing other people's songs many of which I hated but now all that was in the past. People would actually listen to what I was singing instead of talking to their friends or eating their meal. I didn't even care about the money. All I wanted was to make enough to continue writing and to perform in concerts rather than pubs. The road had been terribly long and hard but now I was so close to my dream that it actually hurt.

48
A Bright Future

There was a catch 22 that most unknown artists needed to overcome.

- You couldn't get played on national radio unless your CD was in the record shops.
- You couldn't get a CD in the record shops unless it was getting played on national radio.

John's master plan was to get *The Workhouse Child* on the Radio 2 playlist. That in itself was not enough to insure good sales but it would at least help persuade a distributor to get my single into the shops. John could then start promoting me and once the single started to sell he would release the album and everything would hopefully fall into place. *Everything* depended on the song being played regularly on national radio. The CD single was pressed and Tony Peters was kind enough to write the following sleeve notes.

When I first heard "THE WORKHOUSE CHILD" I knew this was a future standard and that Nemo James has a rare talent. When you hear this CD single, which contains just some of the great songs from the pen of Nemo James, we hope you agree.

"You're very lucky. It's not like Tony to put his name to sleeve notes," said John.

The BBC producers met every Monday morning to discuss the playlist for that week and it was that little committee that could make or break me. With five of the top BBC producers on our side Tony told us getting *The Workhouse Child* on the list was just a formality. Even if it wasn't playlisted the producers were still going to push it on their own programs so I couldn't lose. The suspense was terrible. Monday morning came and I was sitting by the telephone desperate to hear the news that could finally launch my career. The phone rang. It was John.

"Bad news. They turned it down. Most of the producers wanted to play it but the head of light music thought it was too "folky".

"But how can it be down to one man to decide?"

"In theory it's not but there's been a big shake up at the BBC. Everyone is afraid of losing their jobs so no one wants to rock the boat."

"But the producers can still play my song can't they?"

"Apparently not. There was a new rule imposed last week. There are 2000 songs on the computer at any one time and producers can only play songs that are on that computer. The producers are livid about it and say the system won't last long as it is so unfair but it's ruined our chances. Once a song has been turned down it is almost impossible to get it considered again."

So that was that. Yet again the ladder was pulled out from underneath me. There was still hope as Tony was confident he could get other artists to record *The Workhouse Child* and maybe the album would be playlisted even if the single wasn't. Everyone told me not to worry and that my future was bright. That was all very well but the present was shit as I had to start looking for gigs in pubs and clubs again.

Christmas came and went and I was without money, gigs and my long awaited album. Just as I was doubting that it would ever be pressed John called to say my debut album, *Touch The Moon* was finally ready. The CD looked very professional with a little booklet containing the lyrics. On the front cover was a painting Federika had done of a child looking at the moon through the window of a workhouse. John sent 200 copies to every radio station and DJ in the country and whilst I was happy that things were at last starting to move I was concerned that he hadn't hired a promotion company as promised. I knew only too well what a waste of time it was sending music through the post without anything to back it up.

Feedback from local radio stations was non existent until I had a surprise phone call from BBC Radio Derby. One of the members of my squash club was a producer there so I had sent him my album in the hope he could get it played.

"Hi. My name is Dave Wright. Ashley Franklin gave me a copy of your CD."

"What do you think of it?" I asked.

"I love it. Would you like to come along and do a live interview with me? I have a prime time program on Saturday mornings."

We arranged a date and after phoning John to tell him the good news we agreed that I should organise a concert to coincide with the radio program. I booked a small concert hall in the centre of Derby and arranged for posters to be printed. Everything was in place when I had a phone call from Radio Derby. The woman's voice was cold.

"I understand you are booked to appear on the Dave Wright show on Saturday?" she said.

"Yes, that's right."

"I'm afraid we have to cancel the interview. Dave's program has been dropped."

"But surely you are going to honour his commitments? My record company is putting on a concert on the strength of that interview."

"I'm sorry but the decision has been made," she said before hanging up abruptly.

Everything had been paid for so there was no point in cancelling the concert. The night before the big event I went to Derby and met my old friend Nellie at the squash club. I had such happy memories of a thriving happy club so it was a shock to see the place so deserted and run down. It was a Tuesday night in the middle of the season and it should have been packed but there were only six people in the bar and two courts in use.

"What are you drinking Nellie," I asked.

"A pint of lager thanks. Only the manager is on duty and he's probably in the flat watching television. You have to press that buzzer and he'll come out and serve you."

I thought he was joking but it turned out to be true. I pushed the magic buzzer and a few minutes later the manager came out to serve me making it obvious he wasn't happy about the interruption to his television viewing. We took a walk around the premises and it was heartbreaking to see what had become of it. Most of the health and fitness area I had worked so hard to develop had been torn down as Don must have had other plans for it which he abandoned. The expensive Hydro Spa had been ripped out and was laying in what used to be the crèche. The beautiful relaxation area was full of builder's rubbish and the fountain was dry and lifeless. Nothing had been repaired or painted since the day I left and the club notice board that used to be full of forthcoming events and league tables was empty.

The next afternoon I walked onto the stage of the beautiful concert hall for a sound check. It was the perfect venue for me and the kind of place I had dreamt of playing. There was seating for 250 people with proper lighting and an excellent P.A. system with the luxury of an engineer to operate it for me. I even had my own dressing room and wondered how many successful artists appreciated the luxury of not having to change in the men's toilets taking care to keep their stage clothes from trailing on a piss soaked floor. Everything was perfect except for one tiny detail .... I hadn't sold a single ticket!

That night when the curtain was drawn and I started my performance there was a grand total of seven people in the audience which included my brother and his wife, Nellie and a couple of other loyal friends from the squash club. There were only two people in the audience I didn't know. I sang my heart out and finished to the kind of rapturous applause that only an audience of seven can give.

I met John a few days later to discuss his latest plan to promote my album.

"I want to hire a promotional company who say they can get us concerts all over the country. I pay them £1000 in advance and we get to keep all the income from ticket sales until the £1000 is paid off. After that we pay them 20% commission. What do you think?" he said.

"What kind of guarantee do they give that they will get us concerts?" I asked.

"We didn't discuss that. It's best if you speak to them about the finer details."

The next day I called the promotional company who confirmed my suspicion that it was one of the most blatant scams I had ever seen. They gave no guarantee of any concerts or promotion so they were basically just agents who took £1000 commission up front for gigs they may or may not get. The fact that John was prepared to sign with them made me realise what little he knew about the music business and I told him not to waste any more money. It was the end of the road for us and I needed to concentrate on finding work quickly as I was once again getting into debt.

After another round of agent calling I was offered a job on a new ship that P&O were launching called The Pride of Bilbao sailing from Portsmouth to Santander in Spain. It was a long way from my dream of playing my own songs in concert but at least I would be earning money again.

49
Playing for Nothing

Grosvenor Productions was an agency that booked acts for big companies like P&O. By calling themselves a *Production Company* rather than an agency they managed to get away with charging an overall figure for entertainment and take whatever commission they wanted from the acts rather than the conventional 15%. The beauty of it was they didn't actually do anything for their scandalously high commission as they got other agents to find the acts for them.

I boarded the Pride of Bilbao at Portsmouth and it wasn't until an hour before sailing that the terms of my contract were made clear to me. I was supposed to work five hours a day which was bad enough but the cruise director split those hours so I was doing nights, lunchtimes and departures. My cabin consisted of a six foot bunk bed which took the entire length of one wall and a tiny shower-toilet cubicle. There were no cupboards so the only place I had to put clothes was a four inch clothes rail. The ship had been bought from a Swedish ferry company so the cabins were only ever designed for overnight accommodation. The good news was that the bar I was playing in was fantastic. It was small and intimate and with people actually listening to me I had the feeling I was playing in concert every day. I sang a lot of my own songs and as the return trip took three days people started to become familiar with my songs and even requested them. I ended up making more money from selling my albums than from my salary.

Although I enjoyed performing, my quality of life aboard ship was abysmal. I lived for my one night off a week when I ran to the station to catch the train back to Brighton to be with Federika for a few hours only to return to the ship at 5 a.m. the next morning. One night bad weather made us so late getting back to Portsmouth that all the entertainers had to give up their precious night off to entertain the passengers. It turned out to be the busiest night ever in all the bars as bored passengers ate and drank far more than usual. In return for us giving up our night off and our commitment to the passengers P&O gave us absolutely nothing extra.

Despite the awful way entertainers were treated by P&O I enjoyed my time on the ship although I was happy to leave at the end of my three month contract. All my debts were cleared, I had money in the bank and my confidence was at an all time high. I had sold over 700 albums so how could anyone say there was no market for my music?

The winter of 1994 passed and by March I was once again getting into debt when I had another call from Eva Clarance.

"I think I might have a gig for you in Madeira. Are you interested?"

The way it usually works for overseas contracts is the agent contacts the act first to see if they are available and then sends their details to the venue for approval. The period between being asked if I was available and having the gig confirmed was agony. I put the phone down and searched frantically for an atlas to find out where the hell Madeira was. Since the Pride of Bilbao I had been studying Spanish and so was disappointed to learn they spoke Portuguese in Madeira. It was another one of my life's patterns to learn languages that I would never use and so forget them. Ten days later, to my great relief the gig was confirmed.

50
Sex on the Dance Floor

As I looked across the bay at the lovely view of Funchal all the disappointment of the last year disappeared and I felt a contentment I hadn't known in years. The air was warm and sweet and the sea gently caressed the rocks below. After dinner I took an evening stroll and everywhere I walked there was the strong scent of flowers. I could sense there was something special about Madeira.

The Carlton Palms was one of a chain of hotels on the island. It had originally been a Quinta (farmhouse) built on a banana plantation before a four star hotel and a timeshare apartment block was added. The Quinta itself had been converted into a bar downstairs and offices upstairs and I was booked to play in the bar. It was a magnificent building and I often stood at the front door looking out to sea imagining how wonderful life must have been for the farm owners. I was given a room in the nearby Carlton Hotel which belonged to the same hotel chain. I had never been to a place that was so universally loved by all that visited it. There was virtually no crime and it was common to see young girls walking along deserted streets late at night without any fear of harm. A few days after my arrival Madeira held its annual Flower Festival. I liked flowers as much as the next man but I couldn't see how you could make a big deal out of a few bunches of daffodils but I went along out of curiosity. There was a long procession of floats covered with flowers and in between each float were children dancing and singing. At one point the procession stopped and a large group of beautifully dressed children started swaying gently with flowers held high while the hypnotic music of Satie's *Gymnopédies* came floating through the air. I was moved to tears. Some groups of children danced while others sang. It was amazing.

I started learning Portuguese and with my knowledge of Spanish and Italian I picked it up fairly quickly though I was still far from fluent in any language.

I had a 15 minute break every hour when I visited as many tables as possible to socialise. One night I was speaking to a German woman who didn't speak English but did speak a little Italian. Her husband was sitting next to her and feeling safe in the knowledge that he wouldn't understand she started making improper suggestions to me in Italian. I did my best to play it down and went back on stage but it turned out her husband understood more than she thought. He meekly complained about her behaviour but instead of apologising she got on her feet and started punching and kicking him, providing far more entertainment to the hotel guests than I ever could.

As always there was a fly in the ointment which on this occasion came in the form of a Gestapo trained food and beverage Manager called Klaus. Coming from a wealthy family he intended to own his own hotel one day but for now was content to learn the trade at the Carlton Palms. Since he started working there profits had increased dramatically and it was his idea to get an entertainer from England to liven up the bar. He was only 27 and hadn't yet learnt that success doesn't always lead to reward; it can also lead to envy and resentment from colleagues. He was very highly strung and at times would shake with frustration when he felt his skills were not being recognised by his superiors. I got on very well with Klaus most of the time but I found his ruthless quest for better results difficult to cope with. Guests were always offering me drinks and I was under strict instructions to order the most expensive to boost the takings although I never did.

It was one of the most enjoyable gigs I ever did. Unlike one night stands when I met people and usually never saw them again, at the Carlton Palms people were on holiday for a week or two so I had the chance to get to know them. In return they got to know my music and most of the regulars bought a CD from me so I was making a lot of money on CD sales.

It was around that time that I started to notice a disturbing trend in live music. When entertainers first started using backing tracks they were created themselves so some degree of musical ability was needed but now I was beginning to see acts that had bought backing tracks off the shelf. Singers with no experience other than the occasional Karaoke night were working as professional entertainers without a musical instrument in sight. Some venues insisted on acts that had instruments but didn't know the acts were miming. A friend of mine in Dubai told me there was a band with four pretty young Russian girls who spent five hours a night pretending to play instruments and miming to a backing track. I even heard of one guitarist playing on a French ship who didn't sing at all but played guitar along with a tape of someone else singing. So now it wasn't only discos replacing musicians but people who were pretending to be musicians.

My love for Madeira grew stronger each day and although I missed Federika I dreaded the thought of going back to England. She came out to see me a couple of times and we had a wonderful time exploring the island. Even the dogs seemed to have their own place in Madeira heaven. The attitude of the locals was that you can do whatever you want as long as you don't cause trouble and the same rule applied to dogs. They strolled around in packs of ten or more not bothering anyone and not once did I see dog poo on the pavement. I counted 15 dogs one day lying in the middle of a busy side road like something out of 101 Dalmatians and the cars just made their way calmly around them. There was one little black mongrel that used to come into the bar every night and sit on its hind legs begging for food with irresistible charm. Most of the guests loved her and brought food from the restaurant to feed her but that incensed Klaus as it meant the dog was eating for nothing. He got so worked up about it that one night he presented a woman with a bill for what the dog had eaten. When she complained to the manager Klaus got into trouble so he decided something had to be done. He phoned the authorities.

"Vi ave dangerous dog at ze hotel. You must take avay immediately."

"You will have to phone the fire service. There is only one dog catcher's van on the island and they have it."

So Klaus phoned the fire service.

"Vi ave stray dog zat is upsets my costomers. Please kom und take avay."

"I can't," said the fireman.

"But are you not responsible for catching ze strays?"

"Yes we are."

"Then vhy you no can do it?"

"Because we are firemen. We are not going to waste our time with dogs."

"Zen vhy you ave van to catch dogs?"

"I don't know. You must ask the authorities."

This was all too much for the super efficient Klaus who would have loved to have drowned the dog but was afraid someone would see him. In desperation he threw the dog in the boot of his car, drove 35 miles to the other side of the island and left it there. Life was bliss for Klaus until four days later when the dog returned to the bar showing everyone its little worn out paws making it more irresistible than ever. I have to say there was one night when I could have drowned the bitch myself. The bar was packed and I had everyone in a party mood when I noticed the dance floor starting to clear. The black dog was right in the middle of the dance floor being shagged by one of its many doggy admirers. I tried to keep on playing but the whole place erupted with laughter making my job impossible. They were locked together for twenty minutes before I could carry on playing.

My contract was extended for another nine months which was longer than I would have liked but it would finally give me enough savings to settle down with Federika for good. She had been very patient with me but I couldn't expect her to wait forever and I knew I didn't want to lose her. I used to phone Federika on my day off and it was one week when she was on holiday in Croatia that she gave me some extraordinary news. Although the war was still going on in some parts of Croatia the coastline leading to Dubrovnik had been liberated and people had returned to their homes. Federika always went to stay with her parents for the six week summer holiday and having missed the previous two summers due to the war she was desperate to go that year even if things were still unsettled. I called her parents' home but there was no answer. I called their home in Šipan and was relieved to hear her answer the phone.

"Have you heard the news?" she said.

I hadn't heard any news since landing in Madeira as it's the kind of place you can easily forget the world's troubles.

"We were bombed and had to escape to Šipan."

She went on to explain.

It was a beautiful Sunday afternoon in the tiny coastal village of Mlini where Federika's parents lived and as usual the beach was filled with happy families. Tiny children were building sandcastles and paddling in the sea and parents were relieved that life was back to normal after the terrible war had ended. Tourists hadn't yet returned to the region but it was customary for families that lived inland to visit the many seaside villages along the coast. It is perfectly safe to let children run free in Mlini as everyone knows each other and the whole village acts like one family so if there is ever a problem someone will always be there to help. Federika's children were on the beach with their friends while she was at home preparing the dinner. The village is built on a steep hill and Federika's family lives half way up that hill. Without warning she heard whistling overhead and an explosion below her. In a blind panic she ran down the hill to find her children while shells were exploding all around her. It was irrational but what mother wouldn't behave like that when they believe their children's lives are in danger. Fortunately she found them safe and sound in the basement of the Hotel Mlini. The next day they drove along the main coastal road with fires burning everywhere and still the occasional shell falling. At Slano they were met by a friend of the family who took them by boat to the island of Šipan and although there was only women, children and Federika's elderly parents, shells were landing all around them as if someone was aiming at them. For the rest of the summer they remained on Šipan where they had no further troubles.

I loved Madeira but after nine months away I'd had enough and as I wanted to spent Christmas with Federika I finished my contract early. With money in the bank and my confidence at an all time high having sold over a thousand albums I felt it was time to stop messing around and make one big effort to establish myself as a singer-songwriter.

51
You Can Go Back

The contrast between the warm sunny day in Madeira when I left and the English winter was a shock to my system but it was great to be home and enjoy a Christmas together for once not having to worry about money. I had no idea how to proceed with my career but knew I had to produce better promotional material so my first job was to buy a new computer as I was still using the laptop I bought in New York which was well past its dump by date. I had only ever used DOS so as Microsoft Windows and Microsoft Office meant nothing to me I had to learn how to use them before starting on my publicity.

By April I had managed to get to grips with my new computer and produced some impressive publicity. I couldn't face going back to working in pubs and clubs so I thought I'd try and find work in Switzerland. The money would be very good and as the contracts would be short I wouldn't have to be away from home for too long. I bought a cheap flight ticket through my brother and had some friends in Bern so the only serious expense would be a hire car. At Geneva airport I had my first taste of how expensive Switzerland was when the cost of hiring a car was so outrageous I had to forget the idea. I enquired about a train ticket to Bern but even that cost twice the price of my plane ticket. I sat on a bench for an hour deciding whether to abandon the trip and take the next flight back to England or not but I eventually decided to stay.

The next morning I rose early for my journey to the past. It is only a 45 minute drive from Bern to Gstaad but by train it involves three changes and takes three hours. The last part of the journey was made in what looked like a small novelty train. It was a beautiful day and as we started our ascent the scenery was breathtaking. The whole journey was filled with nostalgia but during our stop in Schönreid some young students got in and as they started chatting about their exploits it was like listening to my past. They were saying all the same things with the same confidence that my friends and I had said on the same train all those years ago. I was taken aback at one point when I was sure Jenny Thaxton had boarded the train and sat opposite me. I wondered if I should say something but then realised she was not much older than Jenny was when I last saw her 23 years earlier.

The train pulled into the tiny station in Gstaad and I stepped out into the dazzling sunshine. It came as a shock to see how little the village had changed. Being between seasons it was very quiet but it was still a wonderful place to sit in an open air café and watch the world go by. Before starting my quest for work I took a slow walk to the apartment building where Jenny had rented a room and we had spent so many exhausting nights together. There was the kind of peace that you only find in the mountains and as I stood staring at her ground floor window how clearly I could visualise a young girl washing her long golden hair over the wash basin. I forced myself out of my nostalgic trance and made my way back along the high street to the task in hand.... to find work.

My first stop was The Palace Hotel. I summoned up courage and went through the revolving doors at the entrance, the same revolving doors that Peter Sellers struggled through with his suitcase in one of my favourite films *The Return of the Pink Panther.*

"Is it possible to speak to the manager?" I asked.

"Of course. If you would just wait a minute." The receptionist made a short phone call and a man appeared.

"Hello, I'm Mr Ferrari, the manager. How can I help you?"

Mr Ferrari? Was he serious? I decided he was too charming to be taking the piss.

"I am a solo entertainer from England and I am looking for work in the area. I was hoping you would consider using me at the Palace."

I handed him my publicity package.

"Mr Schertz the owner will need to look at this and he is away until next week. I will give it to him as soon as he returns," he said.

It was disappointing as I knew what little chance I had depended on me seeing Mr Schertz personally and there was no way I could afford to stay in Switzerland for another week. Outside the hotel I looked across the car park to a row of old dark wooden garages and could almost see Bill and I changing the clutch on my Ford Cortina just before our long drive to Athens.

I left my publicity packages at a couple of other places but didn't hold out much hope. Working in Gstaad again was a pipe dream and I never really expected anything to come from the trip. If nothing else I'd had an exquisite stroll down memory lane. As I was walking back to the station I noticed a poster advertising live music at a pub in Saanen, a small village two kilometres from Gstaad. I took the next train to Saanen and walked into the Hotel Boo where I found the owner standing behind the bar. He took a quick look through my brochure and called to the barman.

"Can you hand me my diary please," he said. Was I dreaming?

"How about next weekend? Friday, Saturday and Sunday. It's Easter weekend so I've had trouble finding someone. I pay 200 Francs a night plus food and accommodation."

That was only five days away and although it would be a struggle to return to England and be back for the weekend I accepted the job and resisted the temptation to kiss him. I couldn't believe my luck. I would only break even on the first trip but if all went well the owner promised me two weeks during the summer and winter seasons. Many bands had worked in Gstaad for decades so if I could just get my foot in the door I would be set up for life. My songwriting career would always come first but if I could just get a well paid job in Gstaad for the winter season it would get me through the rest of the year.

While I was in England preparing for the trip I sent a fax to Mr Schertz to say I had left a package with him and would be in Gstaad the following week and how much I would like to meet him. It was while I was packing my gear to leave that the phone rang and a fax started appearing. The first thing I saw was the magical letterhead of the Palace Hotel.

Dear Nemo
Thanks for your fax. I will be happy to meet you to discuss a possible engagement.
Regards - Ernst Schertz.

I finished packing my car and sat motionless behind the wheel for a few minutes, relishing every minute of my departure. How vividly I could see a young ambitious musician pulling away in an old Austin A40 towards a village he had never heard of without the slightest idea of the impact that village would have on the rest his life. Who says you can't go back in time.

52
Me and Julie Andrews

For most of my life I have suffered from obstacle dreams which have led to many a bad night's sleep. I would turn up at an airport to find I had forgotten my suitcase. I would hurry home to get my suitcase only to find myself on the wrong train having left my guitar at the airport. My drive to Gstaad was an obstacle dream come true.

It was a pleasant drive filled with daydreams of flying all over the world as a jet setting entertainer but then my twelve year old Ford Sierra brought me back down to earth. I was just north of Baden Baden in Germany, about 200 miles from Gstaad when I found myself in a bad traffic jam on the autobahn. I noticed steam coming from the bonnet and the temperature gauge started to move slowly towards that little red area that tells you when you are in deep shit. I pulled over and called my breakdown service and waited two hours in the cold for them to arrive.

"I no kan fix here. Must take to garage to fix."

"Do you think you can fix it straight away?" I asked pleadingly.

"No way. Iz too late. Everybody go home."

"What about in the morning?"

If he fixed it quickly I could still make the gig the following night.

"No way. Everybody on holidays till Tuesday. You come back Tuesday."

I was devastated. Was I really going to miss one of the most important gigs of my life just because it was Easter? I had to find a way of completing my journey.

"Please take me to a hotel to unload my gear. In the morning I will hire a car," I said.

"No way. No can hire car. Everybody closed till Tuesday," he said. I was desperate.

"Where is the nearest airport then? I can hire a car from there."

"Frankfurt. 100 kilometres distanz," he said.

"I'll have to go there in the morning. Please take me to a hotel."

I was upsetting his routine. All he wanted to do was take my car to his garage but he eventually got the message that I was determined to continue my journey even if it meant pushing the car all the way.

"I ave friend mit car hire bizness. I call him."

When we arrived at his garage he called his friend.

"Is OK. He come in half hour mit car."

My relief was short lived when he told me it would cost £145 a day. When the hire car arrived I transferred all my equipment to it and continued on my journey. I was on the winding ascent to Gstaad having been on the road for 24 hours when I hit a curb really hard and it wasn't until I arrived at the Hotel Boo at 4 a.m. that I realised I had ruined two tyres and lost a wheel trim. I was mentally and physically wrecked but I still had to carry all my equipment up two flights of stairs as even in Switzerland I couldn't bring myself to leave it in the car in case it was stolen. It wasn't until I woke the next morning that the full cost of my breakdown really hit me. I knew how expensive Germany was and apart from the repairs to my car I was afraid to think what the damage to the hire car would cost.

My first night playing at the Hotel Boo was excellent. The owner was so pleased he asked me to stay for the following weekend which would not only help pay for my car repairs but also meant I had somewhere to stay until my meeting at the Palace Hotel. Tuesday came and I phoned for the verdict on my car.

"I no can fix car. I ave taken to Ford garage."

I phoned the Ford main dealer who thankfully spoke much better English.

"I'm afraid we need to take the engine apart to find out what the problem is and we need your permission before we can start."

I had no choice but to agree knowing I was handing him a blank cheque.

"When will it be ready?"

"We will start on it now. Maybe we can tell you something tomorrow."

"I have to drive there tomorrow to return my hire car so *please* have it finished by then, otherwise I'll have to make the journey twice."

"Ok. We will try."

To avoid having to pay an extra day's car hire I had to leave at 3 a.m. but as I arrived 20 minutes past the deadline they charged me extra anyway which took my total car hire bill to over £700. As I had to pay for the extra day I kept the car and drove to the Ford Garage.

"We have good news for you. It is the head gasket. We can fix it today," said the garage manager.

"That's such a relief. How much will it cost?"

"About 1400 Deutch Marks."

"What! That's £400," I said in disbelief, "the car only cost me £500."

I had no choice but to accept the quote and spend the day in Baden Baden where I phoned my bank manager who begrudgingly agreed to extend my overdraft for two weeks. On the way back from Baden Baden I got completely lost and was panicking that if I didn't get the hire car back by 5 p.m. I would have to pay for yet another extra day as well as a hotel for the night so I could take the car back in the morning. I made it with minutes to spare and parked down an alley where I hoped they wouldn't notice the ruined tyres. Everything was going well until the manager offered to drive me back to the Ford garage in his own car which unfortunately was parked down the alley. Just as he was doing a three point turn he stopped opposite my hire car and it felt like the whole world was pointing to those damn tyres with the bits of rubber hanging off. I don't know whether he didn't notice them or felt he had already ripped me off enough but he didn't say anything and drove me to the garage as planned. In the garage they greeted me with yet more bad news.

"I am afraid we found other faults with your car. As I couldn't contact you and knew you needed to take the car today we went ahead."

"So what is the final bill?" I asked.

"It comes to 2700 Deutsch Marks."

That was nearly £800 for a job that would cost no more than £150 in England. I knew I had been robbed blind but what could I do? I just wanted the whole nightmare to end. The next problem was they didn't accept the "universally accepted" payment coupons that my breakdown insurance gave me. He drove me to a cash machine in town but a message appeared on the screen implying it was out of order. We tried three other cash machines before I realised they were giving the wrong message and the problem was my overdraft hadn't gone through yet. After an hour of negotiating with the garage owner and handing him over nearly every penny I had he let me take the car and trusted me to take him what I still owed on the way back to England.

Finally I was on my way back to Gstaad although the nightmare was not over. After 10 p.m. in Switzerland most petrol stations were unmanned and only accepted payment by credit card at the pump but of course my card still wasn't working. I put my last £10 in an exchange machine which after taking the minimum commission gave me £6 worth of German Marks. After a nerve racking journey without money for food or even a cup of coffee I made it back to Gstaad at 3 a.m. with a few drops of petrol to spare. The total bill for my breakdown including car hire and recovery came to around £2000 although half of that was covered by insurance.

A few days later I went to meet Mr. Schertz, one of the owners of the Palace Hotel. The receptionist showed me to his office where he sat behind an expensive looking desk. I remembered him well from my days with Renato.

"So, how can I help you?" he said with a big friendly smile.

"I am a solo entertainer from England. I left a package with Mister Ferrari last week. Have you had a chance to look at it?"

"I don't remember seeing anything like that."

I was annoyed the package hadn't been passed on and wondered if the charming Mr Ferrari had thrown it in the bin.

"No problem. I have another one here."

I handed him my publicity package and he put the cassette into his tape player.

"Where do you think we might be able to use you?" he asked.

"In the Greengo?"

"But you know it's been a disco for years?"

I gave him a long persuasive speech and knew I had him on my side when he said:

"I'd love to see live music back in the Greengo. I hate the music they play now but that's what my staff tell me people want these days."

"Why not give it a try during the summer season? I am sure it will work out," I said.

"What is your fee?"

"300 francs a day."

"OK. We'll try it for five days during the tennis tournament which is the only time we're full during the summer. If it's successful I'll book you back for the winter season."

He then wrote a quick contract and even offered to pay my fare from England. It was a real pleasure to deal with such a gentleman. He ordered coffee and we started chatting.

"So what brought you to Gstaad then?" he asked.

"I used to work here over twenty years ago with Renato Sambo."

He looked surprised.

"You used to play with Renato in the Greengo?"

"Yes. It was the best time of my life. I always dreamt of returning one day. Have you any idea what Renato is doing now?" I asked.

"Yes I do. He is working here at the Palace."

I couldn't believe it. It seemed that his charmed life had continued when after several years at the Palace Hotel in St Moritz they finally replaced him with a disco and what happened? he found a job in the fine dining restaurant at the Palace Hotel in Gstaad. Mr Schertz and I talked about old times for a while and just before leaving I said:

"Don't tell Renato about me. I want to surprise him. I haven't seen him for 16 years."

When I stepped outside the hotel and saw the mountains all around me I had an overwhelming urge to run around the car park like Julie Andrews singing *The Sound of Music* but I was afraid Mr Schertz might see me and change his mind for fear of employing a madman. If I was offered a winter season at the Palace I would earn enough in three months to keep me going through the whole year.

I strolled along to the side entrance of the Greengo and through the white tunnel that leads into a small reception area. It was pitch black and there was total silence as I opened the smoked glass door and entered the deserted night club. I found a light switch and when I turned it on it was like turning on a time machine. Not a single thing had changed since the first time I saw it all those years earlier. It must have been renovated many times but they had always kept the decor exactly the same. I looked at the small stage where I used to stand next to Mario and the wall that Renato told me off for leaning against on the night my legs hurt so much from my first day's skiing.

The Hotel Boo booked me back for three week in the summer which fitted in perfectly with my gig at the Palace. The next five weeks I spent adding more songs to my act which took me to around 500 backing tracks covering almost any kind of gig. Having such a large repertoire meant I could play every night in the same place without having to repeat the same song too often. The stage was set for me to take Gstaad by storm.

53
Spaghetti Western

My summer booking at the Hotel Boo was erratic. One Monday night the bar was packed with people singing and dancing from start to finish and they had a record bar take for a summer's night. On other nights there were no more than six people in the bar none of whom seemed to be aware that I was there. Like so many hotels in the area it was doing badly due to the high value of the Swiss Franc keeping the tourists away. There was only one couple staying in the hotel and they spent most of the time moaning about how outrageously expensive everything was. The chances of being booked back there in the winter were fading fast when one night a hotel owner from Zweisimmen (about 25 kilometres from Gstaad) saw me playing and offered me a job at his hotel bar for two weeks during the next winter season at 50 Francs more than I would have asked for. It was a relief to know that whatever happened at the Palace I at least had one job in the area for the winter.

One night I went to the Palace Hotel to surprise Renato and as I walked down the long corridor that led to the restaurant I recognised his unmistakable voice. I stood at the entrance to the restaurant and looked at the immaculately dressed Renato. He looked up at me quickly and then back to his song lyrics. He hadn't aged a day. I looked at the rest of the band and was surprised to see Gianni on piano playing as beautifully as ever. I sat at the bar and when the song finished Renato glanced up at me again only this time with a puzzled expression on his face. He instructed the musicians to play something by themselves and walked over to me. Just as he came within hugging distance the big friendly smile I remembered so well lit up his face and he threw his arms around me.

"Derek! What are you doing here?" he asked.

"I'm playing at the Hotel Boo in Saanen."

"Excuse me a minute," said Renato as be left me abruptly to go and welcome two elegantly dressed old ladies that had just walked into the restaurant and were obviously friends of his. Judging by the way they were falling all over him he had not lost any of his charm. Once they were seated he told his musicians to take a break and led me to an unused function room where they sat when they weren't playing. After more hugging he ordered some drinks and introduced me to his band. I gave him a brief account of my life since we last met but I was conscious of the fact I was talking to a man who had spent most of his life bumping into old friends so I cut my story short.

"So tell me what you have been doing," I said.

"Things are getting difficult. I only have a four piece band now and it's hard finding work even for that. Up until this last winter we were going to Japan every year but even they have changed to a disco."

"Do you ever hear from Mario?" I asked.

"Yes he came to Gstaad last year to spend a week skiing with me. He left the band years ago to open a shoe shop in Naples. He's always asking if he can come back to me but I'm happy with the bass player I've got."

"Is he still with that German woman?"

"Yes, he married her and they run the shop together. Did you hear about Paolo?"

Paolo was the trumpet player and Mario's vagina hunting partner.

"No?"

"He died of a brain tumour."

I liked Paolo and was shocked to hear of his death. Memories of our first day's skiing together came flooding back.

"Look," I said to Renato as I rolled up my trouser leg and pointed to a scar on my knee:

"Paulo gave me that on our first day's skiing."

Everyone laughed while I told them about me and the excitable Paolo in a horrible tangle of skis while he screamed "Boja Dio. Cazzone. Merda" as we lay on the snow in hysterics.

I was delighted to hear that Gianni had been happily married for many years as I had always remembered him as a very kind but lonely man.

"Did you ever marry again?" I asked Renato.

"No but I've been living with someone for the last few years."

I had no doubt she would be a very rich woman, not that he would be with someone just for their money but because he was lucky. I enjoyed our reunion but whilst meeting Renato all those years earlier had changed the course of my life I was under no illusion that I held any importance in his.

At last, the day came to move my gear to the Palace Hotel. I was shown my room and the staff canteen both of which were a stark contrast to the conditions I enjoyed when I was working with Renato. After lunch I went to the Greengo and set up my equipment. The stage which once held seven musicians comfortably now had just a giant disco unit so I had to set up to one side making it clear there was only one star of the show and it wasn't me.

When I started playing at 10 p.m. the club was empty but it gradually filled and I got people dancing which was unheard of at that time of night. Mark Turner (the DJ) and I agreed to share the night with each of us doing one hour sets. During my first break the club continued to fill up and was about half full when I returned to start my second set. For the first time since I could remember I was nervous as I knew how difficult it would be to compete against a disco. I had spent a lot of time arranging my backing tracks so there was only a small gap of one or two seconds between songs. That gap might not sound long but it's a lifetime when people have to stop dancing to wait for the next song.

I was ready to start my set and was expecting an introduction from Mark but never having spoken to an audience before he froze leaving a gaping silence followed by a mass exodus from the dance floor. I felt like the baddy in a Spaghetti Western who walks into a crowded bar and everything goes quiet. I gritted my teeth and started playing. To my relief a couple I had spoken to during my break started dancing and as so often happens they were followed by others until the dance floor was full again. I did some old Rock 'n Roll standards and disco favourites and the whole atmosphere changed from serious dancing to fun dancing. Just as I thought everything was going well a group of people walked out giving me a really dirty look as if to say "what the hell do you think you're doing? This is a disco. You've got no right to be here!"

I finished my set and sat down in the changing room until I stopped shaking with adrenaline. I had enjoyed it and was relieved it had been a success but the pressure had been terrible. There was not a concert hall in the world I would have been afraid to play in but playing in a disco was far more nerve-wracking and I realised I had made a big mistake.

I looked around the changing room and noticed a sticker advertising the latest Mark Turner "Mix". In a studio, mixing was always done by a producer who decides what volume to put each instrument at so every song ever recorded is a mix. What I couldn't understand was how this could be done by a DJ so I asked Mark exactly what he meant by his "mix."

"It's a tape I've put together of some of my favourite tracks," he said.

"So they are just a compilation of other people's recordings that you copy onto cassette and sell them as your own album?"

"That's right. I had one customer ask me to put all the songs I played that night onto a tape and he gave me £200 for the two cassettes. I told him it was too much but he insisted."

In DJ terms mixing can also involve taking someone else's recording and adding to it, a bit like a musical collage. I knew one brilliant trumpet player who was employed by a DJ to play short solos over the top of some well known recordings. To me it seemed like taking a famous painting and hiring artists to paint a door here and a moustache there over the top of it. Then I started noticing DJ's being referred to as musicians and publicity announcing them giving a live "Performance" somewhere. Discos were the best thing that ever happened to people who love dancing but the elevation of DJ's to superstardom and the charging of huge ticket prices to watch "Live Performances" which consist of someone standing motionless behind some decks playing music must be one of the most successful hypes in history. Even if a DJ creates the music he plays, paying to see his "Performance" is like paying to see a Lady Gaga concert where she does nothing all night but play her records.

I stood at the back of the stage with Mark and watched the dance floor filling up while the music blasted into every inch of the club. I was dreading going back on stage and was just at the point where I was praying to be abducted by aliens when Mr Ferrari came to my rescue.

"Maybe it will be better if you wait until the club gets quieter before going back on. The bar manager will let you know when the time is right," he said.

That was the final degradation of the night. Bar managers always resented the special treatment given to musicians so this bar manager took great delight in making me wait around until 4.30 a.m. without playing before telling me to pack up for the night.

The next night I was relieved to be asked to play in the main banqueting hall for a press dinner, an event I was well suited to and which went very well. The rest of the week was a farce as I started the evening off until a few guests came in and the bar manager took me off to make way for the real music. I just sat around most of the night talking to people and quite enjoyed myself once I had accepted defeat. What surprised me was to find that nearly everyone I spoke to regardless of age said they didn't like the music that was being played. They loved the atmosphere but not the music that created it.

I was disappointed that things hadn't worked out at the Palace but at least I had the job in Zweisimmen during the winter season which ironically had better pay and conditions than the Palace.

54
It Will Never Catch On

On my return to England I had planned to join Federika on holiday in Croatia but although she was safe in Šipan trouble had started to flare up in other regions while towns were being liberated from Serbian occupation. There were no flights to Dubrovnik so after resigning myself to yet another year without seeing Croatia I decided to put all my effort into seeing if I could make a decent living in England. In Gstaad I had been very lonely and was finding it harder and harder to be apart from Federika. I was also enjoying my karate training which I had kept up regularly. I was only one grade away from black belt but because of all my travelling was never at home when the tests were held.

I approached every live music pub within a 30 mile radius and sent letters to 70 agents. I sent a mail shot to 170 golf clubs knowing they all had two or three dances a year but I didn't get a single reply. I sent letters to 200 social clubs knowing that most of them have entertainment at least once or twice a week and had four replies only one of which led to a gig. Considering the effort I had made the response was poor but I did get some gigs so at least it was a start.

I thought I'd also have one last try to promote my songs and subscribed to the very expensive songwriter's magazine *Songlink International* which published the names of famous artists who were looking for songs. I created my own publishing company and over the next six months sent out 120 cassettes but the only replies I had were from people trying to sell me something. I still refused to give up. I bought a modem for my computer so I could send faxes. The modem came with a one month's free internet access and although I had no idea what the internet was it sounded fun so I thought I'd give it a try. To connect I had to dial a number in a different city meaning I had to pay the national call rate. Most of the time the number was engaged and on the rare occasion I connected to the internet I had no idea what to do. On the even rarer occasion when I stumbled on something interesting I would lose the connection. The "free" trial was costing me a fortune in phone calls which most of the time led to nothing but frustration. As far as I was concerned the internet was a stupid idea which would never catch on.

In February I went back to Switzerland for my ten day contract in Zweisimmen and I was lucky to be offered another week's work at the excellent Hotel Gstaaderhof at the edge of Gstaad. I hadn't skied for years so was really looking forward to it. Despite being tired from the long drive I woke early the first morning to take a short walk to the Wispile ski slope where I had narrowly survived my first afternoon's skiing. When I reached the slope my heart sank: all I could see was grass. How was that possible in the middle of the winter season? Where I remembered hundreds of happy people skiing and laughing in the glorious sunshine now there was only grass and silence. The whole village was deserted and I found it heartbreaking.

I played in the Gstaaderhof bar that night and whilst there were not many customers it was a good night and the owner booked me for the Rado Tennis Open in the summer. The next day I started at the Hotel Krone in Zweisimmen where the atmosphere was even bleaker. Zweisimmen is much lower than Gstaad and with no snow the village had nothing to offer. Skiing was one of the great loves of my life so I was determined to ski regardless of the conditions but after a couple of days alternating between grass and ice I had to stop before I killed myself.

I spent most days hanging around Gstaad as it was too depressing to stay in the ghost town that was Zweisimmen. By the end of my two week stay I was more than ready to return to England. Physically Gstaad hadn't changed but the heart of the village had been torn out and it was not the place I had spent half a lifetime dreaming about. No longer were there celebrities, playboys and colourful characters sitting in every café. They used to joke that you could illegally park your car up against a policeman's trouser leg but now every inch of road was strictly governed and fines enforced. An abundance of new bars and hotels had opened spreading the tourists too thinly to create an atmosphere in any of them.

I returned to England where I continued to work hard to find more gigs but it was an uphill struggle. I returned to the Gstaaderhof Hotel in the summer but it wasn't a success. In common with the rest of the village my bar was quiet at the beginning of the week and packed at the weekend but there was not enough trade to warrant my fee. The thin thread that tied me to Gstaad was getting thinner.

With the war in Croatia finally at an end I set out with Federika and her two kids for a six week summer holiday. I was finally going to see the place that she never stopped talking about. We drove the 1000 miles to the port of Rijeka where we caught a boat for the 20 hour voyage along the beautiful Dalmatian coastline to Dubrovnik. During the 15 minute drive from Dubrovnik to Mlini it was a shock to see the destruction caused by the Yugoslav army.

Mlini was the most beautiful place I had ever seen. It is a small village where everyone knows each other so it was daunting at first being constantly surrounded by Federika's countless friends and family all speaking in Croatian but I was made to feel welcome and soon settled in. We stayed in an apartment at the bottom of Federika's parents' house with a small garden where the kitchen and eating area was. There was a lovely view of the sea which was only 50 metres from our terrace and we were surrounded by bougainvillea and fruit trees. It was paradise.

As I relaxed and began to enjoy the important things in life it was good to be liberated from my ambitions for a while but it forced me to face a few unpleasant home truths. I was 44 with no regular income and no pension. Even if I was prepared to work abroad again the Filipino bands who had once undercut English bands were now being undercut by Russian bands so it was hardly worthwhile going anyway. On the plus side my relationship with Federika was stronger than ever and for the first time in years I felt secure.

England was a terrible anticlimax after having had such a long and enjoyable holiday in Croatia. I found it very difficult going back to the same old gigs playing the same old music and constantly getting in and out of debt. I had done everything I possibly could to establish myself as a singer-songwriter and believed no one had ever worked harder and with more conviction to achieve their dreams. I was at another crossroads in my life and had to change direction but before deciding what to do I felt the need to write down everything that had happened to me. It was a mixture of wanting closure from the past and putting off the future.

55
A Shocking Time

It was January 1997 and although I was pleased with the progress of my book it was taking a lot longer than expected. What had started out as a bit of fun had turned into a major project on which I was pinning all my hopes.

Owing to increasing debt I accepted a three month job in a pub in Beirut which I forever referred to as *the land of broken promises*. Everyone was very friendly but it took me a while to learn that "you must come round to our house one day to try some real Lebanese cooking" is Lebanese for "we like you" and has nothing to do with actually going to people's houses.

On my first meeting with the pub owner he couldn't do enough for me.

"If you want anything just call me any time of day or night and I will make sure you get it," he said.

"Well actually my hotel room is very cold. I would be grateful if you could do something about that," I said.

I was expecting to see a nice warm heater in my room the next day but all I got was two vests handed to me like they were the crown jewels. My hotel room was on a main road where drivers honked their car horns for no reason all day and night. It was also directly beneath the main flight path where planes flew in and out 24 hours a day making the whole room shake. As if that wasn't enough on my first night there was a small earthquake.

The traffic was total chaos with no traffic lights or pedestrian crossings. When I needed to cross the road I had to use the local system which involved running as fast as you can whilst saying your prayers. Even the pavements weren't safe as motorcycles used them when the roads were blocked and I am not talking about riding tentatively but the same speed as on the road. In the pub there was no earthing so I was continuously getting electric shocks from the microphone. It would have been a simple job for an electrician to rig up an earth but although the owner was happy to pay $10,000 for a new sound system he was not prepared to pay a few dollars for something that couldn't be heard or seen with the only benefit being it might save someone's life.

"Don't worry. No one ever gets electrocuted in the Lebanon" was the assurance he gave me whenever I asked for something to be done. Eventually he put a small piece of carpet on the floor and assured me that would keep me safe. As you may have guessed I didn't enjoy my stay in Lebanon and it made me more determined than ever to stay in England.

That summer we went back to Croatia for the summer holidays and Federika had her own exhibition during the Dubrovnik Festival. It was a great success with Federika selling nearly all her paintings and getting excellent reviews from the local press. I was very happy for her but it struck me that her business was even harder than mine. It is possible for an unknown songwriter to earn millions in royalties from a song that takes only fifteen minutes to write but an unknown artist gets only a small fee from a painting regardless of how successful it becomes. The art gallery was known mainly for its exhibitions of modern art and while the paintings they exhibited might well have been very clever they rarely sold any of them. Federika put several noses out of joint by selling nearly all her paintings and it seemed to me that some art experts only regard a painting as having any merit when no one wants to buy it.

By the time we returned to England I had finished the 12th draft of my book so gave it to a few friends to read and waited anxiously for their reaction. I had every confidence in my music but no idea whether my book was any good. One of the people I sent it to was Barrie Tracey, a well established journalist and author of several books. He had bought a CD from me on the Pride of Bilbao.

"I love your music and I love your book" he called especially to tell me. I waited for the inevitable *but,*

"But I have to tell you it's almost impossible to get anything published even for established authors and an autobiography from someone unknown will be even harder."

I knew all along it would be very unlikely I would get my book published but I wrote it mainly for my own benefit and found the process very enjoyable. As I went slowly through my life I was surprised at how everything seemed to fit together like a jigsaw puzzle. 30 years earlier I had been sitting in an office bored stiff when I decided to teach myself to touch type. I only did it because I hoped it would improve my guitar playing but with the advent of personal computers that skill became invaluable. Events I thought were disastrous at the time turned out to be a natural progression to something far better. I remembered reading Voltaire's *Candide* many years earlier and thinking what a stupid book it was with the main character going through countless disasters but always remaining happy as he believed it all happened for the best. Now 30 years after reading that simple little story I began to see the wisdom in it.

It was the end of the road for me and the music business as there was really nothing else I could try. I sent a synopsis of my book to 20 publishers and although I was hopeful, the Ghost of Rejections Past kept my dreaming to a minimum. Rejections of my synopsis came back fast and furious and it seemed I wasn't even going to be able get my book read let alone published. Eventually I did get a request to read the book from a company called Minerva Press. I sent the manuscript and they replied saying how brilliant it was and for only £7000 they would be happy to publish it. I had seen enough scams in my time to know this was one so even if I had the money I wouldn't have been tempted.

I would never give up on my dreams but for now I had to find a way of making a decent living. But what could I do? Even if I did sacrifice my freedom for a normal job who was going to employ a 45 year old musician without any qualifications? I started looking in the situations vacant columns and was shocked to see how low wages were even for graduate jobs. I was only getting one or two gigs a week but even that was more than many jobs were offering for five days a week. It was a bleak time in my life.

56
Chaos in Zimbabwe

How much easier resolving to start a new life is than actually doing it. I wracked my brains daily trying to think of what would suit me but I no longer had the luxury of youth where I could try out different careers until I found the right one. My brother David came to stay with us for a few days and I was telling him about my predicament. He was an I.T. project manager for British Airways at the time.

"You spend so much time on the computer why don't you do that for a living?" he asked. I laughed.

"You're joking. I would never be able to do anything like that."

"I have people working for me on £500 a week who know less than you do."

It was kind of him to say so but there was no way I was going to believe that. Whenever I took my computer to be fixed I stood in awe as I watched technicians work on it and wondered how could anyone be so clever? Much as I enjoyed working on my computer it terrified me and I had been bitten by it several times.

On July 2nd 1998 after being together for 8 years Federika and I were married. I had been wanting to ask her for years but was waiting until we were more secure but as that was never going to happen I popped the question and she accepted once she had recovered from the shock. We had no money so we hired a beachside café in Ferring near Worthing for £100 and Federika did the catering with the help of a good friend while I was at a gig. I made up a tape of salsa music and everyone danced outside the café next to beach. Despite being on a shoestring budget everyone said it was one of the best weddings they had ever been to.

I continued doing gigs once or twice a week with reaction to my performance varying from people who thought I was the best thing since sliced bread to those who asked me how could I call myself a musician if I didn't know *The Birdie Song*. There were also those who made it clear to me they preferred the pub when it was quiet and I was just an intrusion. On one occasion I was playing in an upmarket Chinese restaurant for the very appreciative Chinese owner. It was a good night and I had everyone dancing around the tables having a brilliant time. Everyone loved me except for the owner's English girlfriend who spent the entire evening telling people how awful I was. She was one of the most obnoxious women I ever played to which is why I was so happy when she became the victim of the best put down I ever heard. While I was packing up she was boasting to the remaining customers how great the Chinese were.

"Once you have had sex with a Chinese man you never want any other," she said for the tenth time.

"Yeah but half an hour later you feel like you want another one," came the reply from a customer who was even more fed up with her than I was.

I no longer got any pleasure from doing gigs and dreaded the week-ends coming around. Most Saturdays the lottery draw was being shown on television while I was setting up my equipment and I always said if my numbers came up I would leave all my gear where it was and go home. The gig that finally broke the camel's back was a nursing home in Hove. The money wasn't bad and as it was only for one hour in the middle of the afternoon I could hardly turn it down. I was led to a large living room where about twenty old people were waiting for me to entertain them. I started singing some old singalongs and counted six people who were actually awake. One man asked me while I was in the middle of a song:

"Can you sing *Distant Drums*?"

It is astonishing the number of people I came across who think it is possible to sing and talk to them at the same time. I stopped playing to answer.

"I'm sorry but I don't know that one," I said and started singing again.

He then got up, walked slowly out of the room, turned around and returned to his chair. He stopped me singing again to ask:

"Can you sing *Distant Drums*?"

This went on for the entire hour that I performed although he moved so slowly I was at least able to get through one song during his travels.

The following September after returning from another six week holiday in Croatia I was still no closer to finding a new career so I gave myself a deadline of one month. If I couldn't find anything by then I would resort to the traditional musician's safety net of driving a taxi. One day I was browsing around Borders bookshop in Brighton when in the computer section I noticed a pack of books claiming to contain everything needed to pass the six exams required to become a Microsoft Certified Systems Engineer (MCSE). I always thought that people who worked in computers had been to university so it was exciting to think that such a qualification was within reach. I opened the first book and tried to make sense of it but it was like reading a foreign language. I put the book back and went to the music section where I felt more at home. A few days later I was discussing my future with Federika.

"The only think I can think of doing is taxi driving," I said. Federika hated the idea.

"There must be something else you can do. How about computers?"

"I did look at a computer course in Borders but it was way beyond me."

"That's a great idea. You're really good with computers. Look how you sorted out that problem the man in the shop couldn't fix."

"Yeah, after three weeks and 100 phone calls. That was the most frustrating thing I've ever done. Don't you remember I actually cried at one point?"

"Which just goes to show how persistent you are. I am sure you can do it. Just give it a try."

The next day I returned to Borders and took another look at the Microsoft course. It cost an incredible £320 and considering I earned £80 a night from gigs it was way more than I could afford. I picked the books up and put them back again at least ten times. Then I did nothing but stare at them for half an hour. Taxi driving was something I could do standing on my head whereas computers meant more debt for something I would probably fail at anyway. I was leaning towards taxi driving but anyone who has a Croatian wife will know the fear of incurring her wrath and it was probably that which made me walk out of the store with the books in my hand. I told my parents what I was doing and they were so happy they insisted on paying for the course for me. It was very touching but put even more pressure on me to succeed.

I picked up the first book "Networking Essentials" and took it to my favourite coffee shop in Hove. I ploughed through the first chapter laughing and shaking my head wondering how on earth anyone could understand any of it. If the books hadn't been so expensive I think I would have given up there and then but I put my head down and read it slowly line by line with my lips moving for added support. A few days later I had a big breakthrough when I discovered I could ignore a lot of the things I didn't understand as they weren't important anyway. Six weeks later I was ready to take my first exam but had a shock when I discovered that including the train fare to London it would cost nearly £100 an exam so I couldn't afford to fail.

When I pulled into Victoria station I was more nervous than I had ever been on stage. The exams were on computer and were mainly multiple choice questions with a time limit and the result shown at the end. I went quickly through the questions answering those I knew for certain but there were plenty I had to return to and think more carefully about. I was struggling with the last couple of questions when a message appeared on the screen telling me my time was up and to wait while my results were calculated. It was the first time in my life I really cared whether I passed an exam or not so my heart was racing. The screen changed and the first thing I noticed was the word "Congratulations." I couldn't believe my eyes when I discovered I had passed. During my journey home I felt more elated than I had done for years as it dawned on me that becoming a computer engineer was a real possibility.

The more I studied, the easier I found the whole process which seemed to be built on learning only what was needed to pass exams rather than understanding the subject. I asked David to see if there were any jobs going at British Airways and although he was now stationed in Johannesburg he was still good friends with the I.T. manager at Heathrow so he got me an interview. I bought my first suit since I was fifteen years old and attended the interview with every confidence. It didn't hurt being David's brother.

"David was very highly thought of here. If you are half as good as him I will be more than happy. You'll be next in line for a job when one becomes available which shouldn't be too long," said my prospective boss.

I was a little disappointed I couldn't start straight away but it was just as well as it would have been difficult finishing my studies and working full time. Two months went by and I only had one more exam to pass when I had an email from British Airways saying a job was available and it was mine if I wanted it. The basic salary was three times more than I was making on a good week as a musician and with overtime I would double that.

My new job was based at Heathrow and for the first few weeks I went by train so I could study during the journey. It was hard work fitting it all in and getting up at 6 a.m. every morning but I loved the work. I was getting sick of studying and found the last exam particularly tedious but I passed it easily and so became a fully qualified Microsoft Systems engineer despite the fact I had never even seen half the equipment I was expected to fix.

I was put in a team which covered Eastern Europe and Africa. A few of my work colleagues resented me getting the job with no experience but their attitudes soon changed when they saw how willing I was and how quickly I learnt. I was the only MSCE in the office and although I lacked practical experience what I had learnt during my studies proved invaluable and I was soon fixing faults that had some of my more experienced colleagues beaten. There were a few brilliant engineers who everything depended on but most had been given responsibilities in particular areas of I.T. so their general knowledge was limited. Despite earning high salaries some were actually hopeless and one in particular had been banned from some sites because he caused more problems than he solved.

After three weeks training at a British Airways office near Heathrow I was sent on my first trip which was to Romania with a colleague who was showing me the ropes. We flew Club Class and stayed at a five star hotel with all expenses paid. I was in heaven and with no one in the Romanian office knowing the first thing about fixing computers we were treated like knights in shining armour. After Romania there was a steady stream of overseas jobs which included Johannesburg so I was able to visit David. Being the new kid I was on the lowest wage of anyone in the office but it was still a fortune compared to what I was used to. I was even paid time and a half while I was travelling so for a ten hour trip to Africa I was paid £120 to watch movies and sleep in club class. If only life had been like that in the music business.

I loved the work and found it interesting how different the repercussions of making mistakes can be in different jobs. In most professions mistakes can be easily rectified without any serious problems. As a musician if I made a mistake on stage most people didn't even know and even if they did it was instantly forgotten. If a carpenter cuts a bit of wood the wrong size or a secretary makes the worst of spelling mistakes it can be easily corrected. If a network engineer types a dot in the wrong place or pushes the wrong button it can bring chaos to an entire organisation. On one occasion I was with my boss in Harare airport when I removed the wrong plug and it was half an hour before we discovered the entire check in area had ground to a halt. But the good thing about working in I.T. was that there was never a profession where it was so easy to pass the buck. As customers never understood a word you were saying you could tell them any old bollocks so we told the airport manager the problem was down to a faulty didgeridoo in Timbuktu and he was happy.

I loved everything about my new career and my only regret about leaving the music business was that I hadn't done it earlier. It was so strange not having to worry about money any more and even stranger deciding where to put my savings. I would have stayed with British Airways for years had that not been against my life's patterns. At the end of my first year they started outsourcing some of their I.T. requirements so I was advised to start looking for another job.

A few days later I saw an advert in the local paper for a network manager in a large college in Sussex and although it meant a drop in salary it was still well paid for a local job. I was not really experienced enough to be a network manager so I half heartedly filled in the application form making several mistakes and crossings out. The form had to be completed by hand and having spent so much time over the previous few years using a computer my hand was no longer able to control a pen. Thirty five people applied for the job and I was one of the six chosen for an interview. The process lasted the whole day and started with my five opponents and I sitting in the staff room feeling like animals in a zoo.

We were given a tour of the college which was very large and spread out having been extended many times over the years. It was two separate sites one mile apart with around 1300 students ranging from 11 to 18 years old.

Five different people interviewed me during the morning with a final interview at the end of the day attended by all the big knobs. I realised they needed to find the right person for the job but it all seemed a bit over the top to me. It meant that the last candidate to be interviewed had to wait in the staff room for four hours until it was his turn whereas I was lucky as I only had to wait for two hours. During the final interview I was given a detailed report of the state of the college network. As no one understood the report I was asked to explain it to them in simple terms which was easy for me because they were the only terms I knew. The report had been carried out by the local council and despite costing £600 it had several factual errors in it which I was happy to point out. My contract with British Airways could have lasted for another five or six months so I wasn't bothered whether I was offered the job or not and I suppose it was that attitude that made me appear more confident than I had a right to be. Soon after I arrived home the college called and offered me the job subject to references. I never could understand the sense in offering someone the job first and then applying for references later but that was the way they did things. I had an excellent reference from British Airways so I knew that wouldn't be a problem.

One of the reasons I wanted to change my life was in the hope of finding security. Being employed by the local council with the sick pay, holiday pay and excellent pension plan I couldn't have found a more secure job. I was very sad to hand in my notice at British Airways as I had found them to be excellent employers and working there was one of the best times of my life. If I had known then what I was letting myself in for at the college I would never have accepted that job and would have been happy to sacrifice security for sanity.

57
Learning Chaos

I turned up for work on my first day full of enthusiasm for the enormous task that lay ahead. My office was about the size of a large toilet cubicle and was shared with the I.T. teachers and my only technician. It was in the middle of the computer suite which comprised of four classrooms with around 90 computers in total so it was like a general having to control a military campaign from the middle of a battle field. Their network was such a disaster that the parents had formed an action group to get something done about it. In the past they had employed network managers on the cheap and bought computers that were knocked together by a local company using whatever bits and pieces they could lay their hands on. After they were installed the company went bust so the college was left with 90 new computers that were ready for the scrap heap. Students were spending weeks doing course work only to find it disappearing from the server. Out of desperation the management agreed to pay the proper going rate for a network manager which is where I came in.

The government had rightly decided to promote the use of computers in education and allocated countless millions of pounds for that purpose but gave it directly to schools to let them decide how to spend it. The result was management purchasing equipment and services they didn't understand and there was no shortage of sharks ready to relieve them of that money. Imagine you wake up tomorrow to find you are on the finance committee of a space shuttle and you have to decide how to allocate resources and you will get an idea of the situation.

It is impossible to exaggerate the state of chaos that existed around the computer network when I started. While I.T. teachers had only basic network security rights some of the students were administrators meaning they could bring the network to its knees whenever they wanted which they frequently did. The cabling system was completely wrong for the size of their network so if a single computer was disconnected the whole system went down. Students frequently ripped out cables from the computers which meant I had to spend hours searching around the building to find which computer it was.

The lack of control that some teachers had on students resulted in my already impossible workload being increased by constant vandalism. Mouse balls continually disappeared making half the computers in a suite unusable until I replaced them. Brightness would be turned down on monitors until it looked like they weren't working. Voltage switches on the backs of PC's were changed so they caught fire when switched on. Coins were put in the CD drawers so they wouldn't open. On/off switches were removed. Bubble gum was put in printers to make them jam. Keyboard characters were switched around and countless other ingenious ways of making my job much harder than it already was.

I only had one part time technician whose behaviour was so bad that he was suspended leaving me to develop the network and support 150 decrepit computers with no help. It was three months before I was given another junior technician and as the salary was so low we could only afford a school leaver so a lot of my time was spent training him. The demands and expectations of the school were far higher than those in private industry yet their resources were far lower.

Most frustrating of all was the lack of any I.T. training given to teachers which meant I spent a lot of my time showing individuals the simplest tasks. I pleaded with the management to let me give the teachers group training but they always refused. Things got so bad I put my foot down and said I couldn't continue unless I had an office in a quiet location. I also insisted on taking most of the network down for a few weeks until I had sorted it all out properly. After that things became more bearable although for the first four years I still only had one part time technician on such a low salary we could only attract school leavers that I had to train. If I was off sick for even a day the whole college was at risk of severe disruption. My father in law died and I wanted to go to his funeral in Croatia with Federika. With only one inexperienced technician to cover for me it was tactfully explained to me that I was entitled to go but doing so would mean the students' education would probably suffer and it was this emotional blackmail I was constantly threatened with.

Working very long unpaid hours I gradually built the network up thinking that once I had a grip on it things would get easier but they never did. The more reliable the network became the more staff wanted to use it and the more demanding they became. Demands bore no relation to the fact there was only me and one inexperienced technician who was frequently on sick leave. After four years my staffing budget was finally increased to allow for two technicians but still on very low wages so the best we could find was a van driver and a pizza delivery boy who both wanted to learn the trade. By then the network had increased to around 450 computers spread throughout the entire college and the whole organisation was totally dependant on the network working efficiently but the more I got it under control the more management demanded further development. The biggest problem was that despite holding such an important position in the smooth running of the college I was not allowed to sit on the senior leadership committee. The result was a committee who didn't know the first thing about computers committing large sums of money to I.T. projects without anyone at the meeting to advise them. My line manager would be given the task of explaining to me what was wanted but as she didn't really understand what was wanted I was often given the wrong instructions which wasted a lot of money and dramatically increased my workload.

There seemed to be a complete indifference to the spending of public money. Each department was given their own I.T. budget to spend however they wanted so sometimes one department bought software not knowing it had already been bought by another department. Sometimes the software was so badly written it was unusable on a network so it had to be scrapped. Some software required a lot more support than others so the true cost was much more than the purchase price. There was no control on printing so the cost of ink was astronomical. We paid £8000 a year for internet access that the local council insisted we use when we could have got perfectly acceptable internet access for £500. Every year we spent thousands of pounds on equipment that didn't work or was impractical. Around £10,000 was spent on video conferencing equipment which was hardly ever used, another unnecessary extravagance sold to the college by slick businessmen saying it was the latest *must have.* I could write pages of examples where public money was spent recklessly on I.T. and yet one art teacher told me she had been refused an extra £50 for paintbrushes she needed desperately.

On the positive side I had at long last found the security I thought would forever escape me and for the first time in my life I had long term savings and a pension plan. It was inconceivable that I would ever lose my job as the college would always need a network manager and even if I was the worst network manager in the world the procedure for sacking someone was so long and complicated I would have reached retirement age before they could have got rid of me.

We were still going to Croatia every year and as I was unable to find a program to help me learn Croatian I taught myself programming and wrote *WordBanker* which concentrated on building a vocabulary rather than getting bogged down with complicated grammar. I was so pleased with it I started selling it on the internet and although it was never going to make me rich it did give me a little pin money and I found the process a relaxing refuge from work.

I kept up with my karate training and after thirteen years I finally got my black belt. In many styles you can get a black belt in three years but the master at our club was so strict it took a minimum of 7 years but what with injuries and work pressure most students took as long as me. The test took a day and a half which not only included every technique I ever learnt but also a written test as Tang Soo Do is a very traditional style of karate involving a lot of discipline and protocol. It was a great achievement but short lived. I was only able to train for another year as I was struggling to get up the two flights of stairs to our flat let alone fight with someone twenty years younger than me.

By the end of my fourth year at the college I was really beginning to feel the strain when as soon as I completed one impossible deadline another one was set. When the college failed its Ofsted inspection we were put under special measures with poor management being cited as the main reason. The head teacher resigned and was replaced by a *superhead* who some of us suspected had just been released from a mental asylum. On his first day he called a meeting of all the staff to introduce himself and put across his most important points being that he was a self employed tax dodger and an amateur opera singer. He also told us he didn't believe in meetings and repeated it during the countless meetings he called. Most of the students walked out of his first assembly after he called some of them "a disgrace to the town" and made every pupil stand up and sit down several times. He was only there a few weeks when he was replaced and after calling yet another meeting of all the staff so he could say goodbye he broke out into song with a student accompanying him on piano. A new temporary head teacher took over until a permanent one was employed several months later. The general opinion of the new permanent head teacher was not good so I was not looking forward to my first meeting with him.

"I am shocked to find the college website hasn't been updated for three years. Why is that?" he asked aggressively.

"I created the site in my own time three years ago on the strict understanding that someone else would update it as I don't have the time."

"Well you'll just have to find the time. That is now your top priority."

"You do realise I have to support 500 computers and 1500 users with just myself and two inexperienced technicians?"

"You'll just have to do the best you can. The website comes first."

"So what happens if a teacher contacts me to say they can't teach a class because the computers aren't working?"

"Obviously get them working but then get back to the website," he said becoming irritated.

"But that happens several times a day not to mention all the other jobs that are essential to keeping the network going."

"I am sending a letter to all the parents tomorrow announcing the launch of our new website three weeks from now. I expect it to be ready by then."

Talk about holding a gun to my head.

"I will do the site but once it is launched you'll have to find someone else to maintain it. It is a full time job in itself," I said reluctantly.

"If anything we will be reducing I.T. staff not increasing it. If you feel you can't maintain the web site I will have to take another look at how I.T. support is organised at the college."

His meaning was clear: do as you're told or you'll be sacked. All over the college were notices telling students that bullying would not be tolerated and yet the biggest bully in the college was the head teacher. On more than one occasion female members of staff were seen running from his office in tears.

I set to work on the website but although I had a basic knowledge of web design I was far from being competent as the skills required are very different to networking. The more time I spent on the website the more complaints I had from staff waiting for support some of whom were unable to do their jobs until their computers were fixed. Completing the website with such a tight deadline was hard enough but the new head had no idea what he wanted and was constantly changing his mind. As the deadline grew nearer I became more anxious and had trouble sleeping. I had to work late into the night and weekends while all the time there were the never ending demands for support. At least 50% of the site content was not given to me until the day before the deadline so I was up until 2 a.m. finishing the website. I felt terrible but despite being exhausted I woke at 5 a.m. and as I couldn't get back to sleep I went into work. I was only there for an hour when I felt so bad I had to go home. It was a Friday so I thought if I took it easy over the weekend I would be fully recovered by Monday. Monday came and I felt worse than ever so went to see the doctor who not surprisingly diagnosed stress and gave me three weeks off work.

At the end of the three weeks I felt much better but was dreading going back to work to face further confrontations with the head teacher. The day before my return I had a call from my boss.

"The head has resigned. The whole college is in shock," she said.

"Why?"

"The only thing we've been told is that it's for personal reasons."

"So who is taking over?"

"The council have already found someone and promised us she will only be a figurehead until they appoint another permanent head. She won't be making any drastic changes."

I returned to work and for a while things seemed better but despite the council's promise the new temporary head teacher put in process more changes and long term spending commitments than anyone had done in years. She pushed for a £100,000 expenditure on I.T. equipment which created a lot of extra work for everyone on deciding how to spend it. She was the complete opposite to the previous head teacher and by gentle persuasion and encouragement got far more work from the staff than bullying ever did. She instilled a spirit of "let's all pull together to get this college out of special measures" and we all followed her like sheep. Instead of my workload being reduced after my stress related illness it was increased with a major new I.T. project put into place without any planning or consultation with me. As if that wasn't bad enough the only member of staff who knew how to implement the new system was made redundant so for the first three weeks of the new school year the college was in chaos. Classes of 32 students were turning up for I.T. lessons but couldn't get on the computers because they didn't have accounts. Everyone was screaming at me to create accounts for them but I couldn't because no one knew who the new students were or whose job it was to process them. After two weeks of everyone running around like headless chickens management employed an administrator from the council at great expense to sort out the mess. After giving the administrator the wrong information it turned out to be another disaster so they had to go back to the woman who was made redundant and pay her thousands to get them out of trouble. All of this put me under more pressure than ever and having returned from Croatia rested I was once again reduced to a nervous wreck.

In October 2005 a new permanent head was appointed. I looked up her name on the internet and discovered she had left her last college following accusations of "staff bullying, harassment and victimisation" that was just what we needed.

The following spring the network had settled down and I was feeling pleased with myself as with the recent system upgrade I had taken the college network from total chaos to one of the most efficient and up to date in the country. My two technicians were working well together so for the first time in six years I began to feel I was on top of things. I made a big effort to try and relax more at work but strangely enough that's when it all started: the more I relaxed, the worse I felt.

One day there was a meeting called to inform us of a staff reorganisation. I sat in the hall with my head in my hands feeling terrible and resenting having to waste my time at yet another meeting which didn't concern me. We were handed a few sheets of paper and the first thing I saw was a flowchart so I immediately put the pile face down on the chair next to me. I had developed an allergy to flowcharts as management had become addicted to them and the only thing I ever saw flowing from them was a never ending supply of buzzwords. The head teacher started talking and from what I could gather there were going to be some staff redundancies. As the college would always need a network manager it didn't concern me and once again I was wasting my time being there. It wasn't until a few of us returned to my office that someone asked me:

"Where is your job on the flowchart?"

I had a thousand things to do and felt like shit so didn't want to be bothered with it but thought I should take a look even though it had to be a mistake. But she was right. There was no network manager anywhere on the flowchart, just a senior technician. I called my boss.

"That's correct," she told me, "there will no longer be a network manager. You have the choice of accepting a demotion to senior technician or being made redundant."

I took another look at the flowchart. The proposal was to demote me with a big drop in pay whilst doing the same job with extra responsibilities. I looked further and discovered that every member of support staff was being asked to work much harder for less money. A week later I was called to a meeting with the head teacher and my line manager.

"Have you decided whether you want to apply for the senior technician's job?" asked my line manager.

"There's no decision to make. I already have a job as network manager so why would I apply for a lower paid job?"

"I'm afraid the position of network manager will no longer be available."

"I'm not stupid. The job is still there, it's just that you've given it a different title. There's no way I am going to accept demotion."

"In that case I am afraid you will be made redundant. Here is a list of the packages which depend on whether you take voluntary redundancy or not."

I went straight to the package for compulsory redundancy which involved a much bigger payout and when I saw the figures three little bells appeared in front of my eyes.

"That's fine with me but I won't be volunteering for redundancy. You will have to make it compulsory," I said.

They looked surprised. Being 54 they thought I would be terrified of unemployment and could be bullied into accepting whatever shit was thrown at me. They didn't know that being in and out of work was a natural way of life for me. I went back to my office and took a closer look at the package. As I was over 50 I would get access to my pension and with compulsory redundancy I would get an extra six years added to my entitlement. It meant a small pension and a lump sum which relative to my past put me in the same league as Bill Gates. It meant Federika and I could achieve our dream of living in Croatia as long as we returned to England for a few months each year and I did some contract work. I felt resentful having worked so hard and achieved so much for the college that I was now being dumped for someone cheaper but accepted it was just the kind of thing that happened in the workplace. Once I had resigned myself to the situation it was a tremendous relief and I started working only the hours I was paid for. Three weeks later I was called to another meeting. My line manager looked uncomfortable as the head teacher started talking.

"I am afraid redundancy is no longer on the table. We feel you are too valuable to the college to lose," she said. My heart sank.

"You mean I will be keeping my job under the same conditions?"

"No your old job will no longer exist. We are offering you the job of senior technician and you have three weeks to decide if you want to apply for it."

"Let me get this right. You want to scrap my contract and have me apply for the same job with a different title and a big cut in salary and pension entitlement?"

"That's right" she said without any hint of embarrassment.

"I can inform you right now that I won't be applying for anything. You can either make me redundant or honour the terms of my contract as you can't make any significant change to it unless I agree."

"Yes we can. I have checked with the council's legal department and they said that as it is a staff reorganisation we are entitled to end your contract without paying redundancy."

"Then they are wrong."

They looked down on me from a great height as if only a moron would question the council's legal department.

I returned to my office trembling with anger at the way they were trying to cheat me. Having had a business of my own I was familiar with employment law and well aware of my rights. It was also common sense. What would be the point of having contracts if employers could just tear them up whenever it suited them? The next day I contacted a solicitor who confirmed what I had said. I sent an official letter to the head teacher saying I was not prepared under any circumstance to accept any change to my contract.

From that point on my health took a nose dive. The anger I felt at the way I was being treated combined with the general feeling of anxiety that had been building up over the previous couple of years. I knew I was in the right but had lost all trust in my employers and wondered if they had a trick up their sleeve. The uncertainty made me feel worse and I began to go whole nights without sleep. At the college I did as little work as possibly but that only seemed to make me feel worse.

You may well ask if I was no longer able to handle the pressure why didn't I just leave? If I was working in a factory and was forced to use a machine without a safety guard no one would expect me to leave my job rather than risk losing my arm in an accident. By law an employer has to make sure their machinery is safe but unfortunately the same consideration is not shown to an employee's mental safety. Of course it is not reasonable to expect each employee to be treated according to what they are capable of handling but there is a level of pressure which everyone would agree is excessive. In my case the pressure I was put under was clearly against government guidelines for I.T. support which was already far lower than guidelines for private industry. The local council recognising the danger of pushing employees too hard produced a document entitled "Dignity at Work" and yet those guidelines were ignored by the college.

Why should I have lost my job because the college was not fulfilling its legal obligations particularly when their irresponsible behaviour had damaged my health to the point where it would be difficult for me to hold down another job?

I was left in this state of limbo for three weeks when I had a call from my boss.

"I have some good news. The council have decided that considering your feelings about staying they will be making you redundant after all."

It was a great relief but I was irritated at how it was made to sound like they were doing me a favour instead of simply complying with employment regulations. In all my years in the music business I came across plenty of sharp practices but never had I known such bad behaviour as from the management of that college which is the one place you would expect fairness and honesty. On paper their wage bill was reduced but in reality taxpayers paid my pension unnecessarily for the next eleven years and got a less experienced network manager in return. During the last few weeks of that school year most of the support staff handed in their notice rather than accept a pay cut and none of them claimed redundancy as they were told they were not entitled to it.

On the last day of term as happened every year all the staff gathered together in the assembly hall and those who were leaving gave a farewell speech. It was always a very special occasion with everyone relieved to have survived another year and looking forward to a six week well earned break. As much as I was looking forward to that day I was beginning to feel uncomfortable around crowds of people which surprised me as that's where I had spent most of my working life. I sat at the entrance to the doorway so I had an escape route if I felt bad. I had a fantastic speech worked out but the minute I stood up I felt dizzy and totally drained of energy. With cotton wool where my brain was supposed to be I just mumbled a few words and accepted my leaving present. I went back to my office to collect my personal effects and as I drove away for the last time I felt ecstatic that the nightmare was finally over. I had no idea that the nightmare was just beginning.

60
Don't Panic

I arrived in Croatia during the first week of August. Federika met me at the airport having gone a few weeks earlier like she always did and we planned to stay until the end of September. I would have liked to stay longer but we had some family commitments that included a 60th wedding anniversary dinner in Milan for my parents. After that I planned to do some contract work until the next spring when we would go to live in Croatia permanently.

After Croatia became independent in 1991 the government began a program of returning property confiscated by the communist government in 1945. Federika's father benefited from that program and although he was only given 22% of the value of the assets it was still a lot of money. One of the properties returned to them was the five star Hotel Argentina and with the proceeds of that sale he bought Federika a house so that each of his three daughters had their own property in Mlini. It is a beautiful three story house set behind an old aqueduct with the two top stories overlooking the sea only 50 metres away. As houses in Mlini are always passed down to family members it is rare for one to be on the market so we were very lucky. Our house was left to an elderly couple who lived opposite and as quality of life is everything in Mlini they would only sell to someone they knew. Federika's father was the most respected man in the village and as they also knew Federika and I they were happy to welcome us as neighbours.

For the first couple of weeks I was determined to be as lazy as humanly possibly and achieved that goal admirably. I knew I was a physical and mental wreck but naturally assumed that after a couple of months relaxing in the sun I would be fully recovered. There are two places to swim from in Mlini, a pebbly beach or a large terrace in front of the hotel Mlini but because of the tables and chairs we always sat on the terrace with countless family and friends. There is a low wall that separates the terrace from the sea and that was where you would find me in a horizontal position most of the day. I alternated between reading and swimming or to be more precise, diving in the sea to cool off and getting out.

Although I felt relaxed I was troubled by a strange ache at the back of my ear and feeling constantly tired and dizzy. By the fourth week the pain was getting worse and I was surprised to find myself feeling anxious for no reason. One day we were at a jewellery shop in Dubrovnik choosing some ear rings for Federika's 50th birthday when I was overcome with an extraordinary sense of fatigue and could barely stand up. We went to the Gradska Kavana and I barely made it to a chair when I started to feel like I was in the most terrible danger. During my years as a musician working in dodgy pubs and clubs I had been threatened and attacked several times including once with a broken bottle but I always kept my head and reacted calmly. Sitting at that café with nothing more dangerous than a custard tart in front of me I found myself completely panic stricken. The feeling grew worse until I really thought I was going to die. It took half an hour for the feeling to pass and to regain enough strength in my legs to walk to a taxi and return to Mlini. I didn't know it at the time but I had suffered a panic attack.

By the time we got home I felt normal again and wondered what on earth had come over me. Over the next few days I gradually felt worse and spent most of my time indoors as I felt very anxious outside the house. One day I forced myself to go and lay on the beach for a while thinking it would do me good but after a few minutes another panic attack came over me so I hurried back to the house. I lay on the bed in a state of terror and suddenly burst into tears at which point Federika insisted I went to the hospital. At the hospital they gave me lots of tests and said there was nothing wrong with me but gave me some diazepam which helped. Just to reassure myself they suggested I went for an ultrasound scan and as private health care is so cheap in Croatia we were able to get an appointment straight away despite being a Saturday. I am not normally prone to hypochondria but with the pain at the back of my ear and the dizziness I was worried it might be a tumour so it was a relief when the ultrasound and other tests confirmed that I was physically in the best of health. The next day I felt bad again so Federika took me to a neurologist who diagnosed depression and gave me a course of anti depressants and tranquilisers. At first I laughed at him. I had never felt so bad in my whole life but I didn't feel in the least bit depressed. It was the best time of my life and I didn't have a single thing to worry about so how could I be depressed?

A week later we flew back to England. I was so tired I had to stop half way up the steps to the aeroplane to rest. During the flight when I would have expected to panic I felt perfectly relaxed. It was all so confusing.

The first thing I did in England was to see my doctor who I was half expecting to wave a magic wand and make me better. I told him what had happened and showed him the pills I had been described.

"Both those have been banned in this country as they are highly addictive," he said.

I explained everything and he seemed to be in no doubt I did have depression.

"I don't really want to start taking drugs," I said.

"You could try Cognitive Behaviour Therapy. Studies have shown it is just as effective as drugs. Unfortunately you will have to go private as it is not generally available on the national health. If you look on the internet you will see plenty of people offering CBT."

"But what I don't understand is if my illness is caused by stress why was it when I left my job and all the stress was gone I started feeling worse?"

"That is very common. When you are under a lot of pressure you repress it in order to get on with your job. When the pressure is removed all that stress gets released and comes to the surface. It is very common in soldiers who function perfectly on the battlefield but go to pieces when they get home."

At home I didn't feel too bad most of the time but as soon as I got any distance from our flat I started to panic and had to return. I was determined not to let it beat me so two or three times a day I went for a walk and tried to go just a few yards further each time. After three weeks I felt a great triumph in getting all the way around the block. What was on the back of my mind constantly was that I still had to go to Italy for my parents' anniversary dinner and there was no way I could miss it. When the day arrived Federika queued up to check-in while I sat on a chair cursing myself for not staying at home. The doctor had given me some diazepam to help me with my anxiety but although it did help it also made me very tired so I found myself lagging behind my 86 year old father. The trip was such an ordeal but I had no doubt it did me a lot of good.

I tried CBT and several other therapies but none of them helped. Most of them seemed to be based on improving self esteem or dealing with personal problems and tragedies. I must have been unique in having so few reasons to be depressed. I had no money worries, had plenty of self confidence and a happy home life. As far as I could make out my condition was brought about purely from overwork and the only cure was to stop working. I was shocked at what little help there was available from the national health. I was allowed one session with the surgery counsellor and after waiting five months for the first available appointment came away with a relaxation tape. I knew if I needed help I would have to get it myself.

There was plenty of advice on the internet but much of it was conflicting and didn't apply to me. The only thing that everyone seemed to agree on was that exercise was very good for those suffering from depression so I booked myself a one week skiing holiday in Italy. On the first day the sun was shining without a cloud in the sky. I skied all day and felt the best I had done in years. As I sat down for lunch in the warm sunshine I was convinced after a week of skiing therapy I would return to

England fully cured. The next morning I woke full of enthusiasm but was half way through breakfast when I felt so bad I barely made it to my room where I slept for the rest of the morning. I skied for a few hours in the afternoon but it was very hard going. On the third day I felt so bad I made enquiries about going home but it was so complicated with flights and transfers that I had to stay.

Back in England I started the slow path to recovery which constantly changed from improvement to regression which in itself was depressing. I couldn't go to the cinema or theatre and the idea of finding work as a contractor was unthinkable. One thing I did find very helpful was fly fishing which combined the exercise of walking around a lake all day with the relaxation of fishing. It was the only place I knew I would feel good all day but even there I had a setback when I started to feel depressed while fishing at my favourite trout lake. That's when I finally accepted it was depression and went to the doctor for medication.

61
The Middle

In the middle of May 2007 we were ready to leave England and begin our lives in Croatia. My stepson Danny was still living in our flat which suited us as it gave us somewhere to stay when we returned to England for visits. The days leading up to our departure were traumatic for me as anxiety drained every ounce of strength I had but Federika was a tower of strength and took everything in hand. I read somewhere deep in the British Airways website that although 23 kilos was the baggage allowance they would take 32 kilos without extra charge so in an effort to pack an entire household into four suitcases two of our bags weighed over 32 kilos which prevented the conveyor belt from working. We frantically moved stuff from suitcase to suitcase to hand luggage and eventually got through with ounces to spare. During all this there was a long queue of people watching us so I was surprised I wasn't anxious. It was only when we got to the long queue at security that my mind started to wander and I began to consider the possibility of dying at any minute. Federika saw how much I was suffering and was afraid we might have to abandon our departure but I was going to get on that flight if it killed me. I felt a tightness in my chest and intense heat as my head started spinning. I crouched down for a few minutes almost sitting on the floor and as the queue moved slowly the feeling started to pass. At the other side of security we entered the duty free area and suddenly I didn't have a care in the world. Anxiety disorder is such a strange affliction. I spent hours trying to discover patterns that might trigger anxiety attacks but could find nothing constant. I could be happily watching a light television program when out of the blue it took hold of me and there was nothing I could do but take a tranquiliser. As the plane thrust forward for take off I felt perfectly relaxed whilst ironically a woman in the next row was shaking with the fear of flying.

At Dubrovnik airport we were met by both Federika's sisters. It was a glorious sunny day with a strong smell of orange blossom as we went through the metal gates at the entrance to our house. Although we had been away for six months our cat Jutko was waiting patiently seeming to know in that way cats do that we were coming. I had spent every summer holiday for the previous ten years in Croatia and every year it had been harder to return to England. Living in a sleepy Mediterranean seaside village had always been my greatest dream and now it was really coming true. We had dinner sitting on our balcony overlooking the sea. The air was warm and perfumed and blackbirds entertained us with their priceless songs. How long we would last before running out of money I had no idea but in Mlini things like that don't seem to matter, people live each day as it comes and accept it for what it is rather than what it isn't.

That night as I sat back in my chair looking up at the stars I started thinking of all the things I would to do in my new life. Top of my list was to build a little recording studio and start writing songs again with the luxury of not having to worry about getting a record deal. I would write what I wanted to write instead of what I thought I should write in the vain attempt of making a living from it.

I once read that even the longest dream lasts just a few seconds. I never really believed that but I have just realised that the bell is still tolling despite the fact I am only halfway through my story.

Maybe it is true after all.
When I look back at my life it did seem to pass in seconds.
Maybe that was the dream and this is reality.

www.ingramcontent.com/pod-product-compliance
Lightning Source LLC
Chambersburg PA
CBHW030913120626
46554CB00001B/129

* 9 7 8 0 9 5 6 7 9 8 6 0 2 *